The yellowbacks... classics of popular fiction

The yellowjackets or yellowbacks were a great series of bestselling adventure and crime thrillers that had its origins in the mid to late 19th century following on from the 'penny dreadfuls'. They virtually began the mass market revolution of the early 20th century with a clear standard format and imprint/series livery (what would today be called branding). Hodder & Stoughton published the yellowjackets in two main series with series run dates of: 1923-1939 and later 1949-1957.

As the tagline ('where thrillers really began') on the back cover implies, the imprint and series focused on thrillers that were the bestsellers of their time. This current reissue or retro revival if you will, brings back many of these masterpieces, now classics in their own way and extends it further by including key titles from that period that were either great crime or thriller or even general commercial fiction (including sub-genres of noir, horror, gothic, romance, westerns, etc.) influences of their time. There are some perennial favourites and many rarities either lost or not easily available being revived in the current series. Writers and characters ranged from adventure heroes like Bulldog Drummond, Allan Quatermain, Richard Hannay or the Saint through thriller grandmasters Edgar Wallace and E. Phillips Oppenheim, crime and mystery maestros like Patricia Wentworth, GK Chesterton, Agatha Christie and the Detection club, to western and swashbucklers like Zane Grey, Max Brand, Captain Blood and even romance or general fiction classics like Hermina Black, Denise Robins, Marie Corelli or Stella Morton. These were books that had storytelling at their heart and always entertained.

The yellowbacks had both hardback (with varying design elements) and paperback (which built the series look) versions with the latter still carrying the imprint 'yellowjacket'. The current reissues pay tribute to both and use an amalgam of elements from both editions while retaining the complete yellow (or 'mustard-plaster') livery with the author's name in blue beveled type with a 'simulated emboss' effect and a white outer 'outline', and the book title in black. These reissues retain the distinctive size of the original mass market paperback and follow the three main category variations—the thrillers (crime, westerns, mystery, adventure) had blue lettering for the author's name, while Romance and softer general fiction had red; and other categories like humour had green.

For more detail and a full list of titles visit https://www.hachetteindia.com/home/yellowbacks

THE RECOLLECTIONS OF A DETECTIVE POLICE OFFICER

THE RECOLLECTIONS OF A DETECTIVE POLICE OFFICER

Thomas Waters aka William Russell (1806–1876) was an English writer considered among the first and most prolific authors to write 'police memoirs' or detective stories (some published under the pseudonym 'Waters' or 'Thomas Waters'). He also wrote nautical adventures (under the pseudonym 'Lieutenant Warneford, R.N.'), and legal stories.

Russell is thought to have been born in Southampton in 1806, and in the late 1840s started contributing an irregular series of stories to *Chambers's Edinburgh Journal* between 1849 and 1852. He also contributed to *The London Journal, St. James's Magazine*, and *The Sixpenny Magazine.*

Ten of Russell's Chambers detective stories were subsequently published in unauthorized editions in New York in 1852 and 1853, entitled *The Recollections of a Policeman.* The same ten, plus two additional stories, were then collated into a volume entitled *Recollections of a Detective Police-Officer*, published in London in 1856 (also reprinted with slightly different titles). A collection of his sea stories appeared in Tales of the Coast Guard (also 1856), and *Leaves from the Diary of a Law Clerk* was published in 1857. Among other works, *Autobiography of an English Detective was* published in two volumes in 1863.

THE RECOLLECTIONS
OF A DETECTIVE POLICE OFFICER

Thomas Waters

HODDER AND STOUGHTON YELLOW JACKET
hachette

The Recollections of a Detective Police Officer
First Published by Covent Garden Press in 1856.

This Hodder Yellowback edition © Hachette India 2023
(Registered Name: Hachette Book Publishing India Pvt. Ltd.)
An Hachette UK Company www.hachetteindia.com

1

The texts in these editions in most cases have been reprinted as is, with minimal editorial changes and by and large no bowdlerizing for political correctness; though in some editions, a few words and phrases considered archaic, or those considered offensive now, along with archaic punctuation may have been modified in places to make the text more accessible to today's readers. The narratives, language, beliefs, social mores and/or cultural depictions, in these volumes are a reflection of their times and must be viewed as such. They may also contain certain cultural, racial and gender prejudices and stereotypes that may be outdated or clearly wrong then and wrong today; but their removal would be tantamount to claiming these prejudices never existed. The Publisher does not endorse or support those depictions or stereotypes; and these books have been made available for a discerning audience that will read it for entertainment value and a chronicle/record of popular fiction of past times.

Cover design by Priya Singh adapted from the original classic yellowjacket by Hodder & Stoughton.

Cover illustration by Ishan Trivedi.

Series note: Some of the books in the series (unless otherwise credited) may have cover or inside illustrations from the original yellowbacks or early editions, and while full restoration has been attempted, some images may be grainy or faded due to the condition of the original material. The end notes or bonus material or blurb details may have been sourced from the public domain or free use publications such as Wikipedia and attribution is hereby made also allowing similar free use reproduction from here. Sources requiring further specific attribution may write in and further detailing and/or corrections shall be made in subsequent printings/editions.

Reprint specifications may be subject to change including but not limited to finishes, paper, colour sections.

ISBN: 978-93-5731-179-3

Hachette Book Publishing India Pvt. Ltd.
4th & 5th Floors, Corporate Centre,
Plot No. 94, Sector 44, Gurugram - 122 003, India

Typeset in Electra LT STD 10/12.5 pt by Manipal Technologies Limited, Manipal

Printed and bound in India by Manipal Technologies Limited, Manipal

MIX
Paper from responsible sources
FSC™ C043100

CONTENTS

I

THE GAMBLER

A little more than a year after the period when adverse circumstances—chiefly the result of my own reckless follies—compelled me to enter the ranks of the metropolitan police, as the sole means left me of procuring food and raiment, the attention of one of the principal chiefs of the force was attracted towards me by the ingenuity and boldness which I was supposed to have manifested in hitting upon and unraveling a clue which ultimately led to the detection and punishment of the perpetrators of an artistically-contrived fraud upon an eminent tradesman of the west end of London. The chief sent for me; and after a somewhat lengthened conversation, not only expressed approbation of my conduct in the particular matter under discussion, but hinted that he might shortly need my services in other affairs requiring intelligence and resolution.

"I think I have met you before," he remarked with a meaning smile on dismissing me, "when you occupied a different position from your present one? Do not alarm yourself: I have no wish to pry unnecessarily into other men's secrets. Waters is a name common enough in *all* ranks of society, and I may, you know"—here the cold smile deepened in ironical expression—"be mistaken. At all events, the testimony of the gentleman whose recommendation obtained you admission to the force—I have looked into the matter since I heard of your behavior in the late business—is a sufficient guarantee that nothing more serious than imprudence and folly can be laid to your charge. I have neither right nor inclination to inquire further. Tomorrow, in all probability, I shall send for you."

I came to the conclusion, as I walked homewards, that the chief's intimation of having previously met me in a another sphere of life was a random and unfounded one, as I had seldom visited London in my prosperous days, and still more rarely mingled in its society. My wife, however, to whom I of course related the substance of the conversation, reminded me that he had once been at Doncaster during the races; and suggested that he might possibly have seen and noticed me there. This was a sufficiently probable explanation of the hint; but whether the correct one or not, I cannot decide, as he never afterwards alluded to the subject, and I had not the slightest wish to renew it.

Three days elapsed before I received the expected summons. On waiting on him, I was agreeably startled to find that I was to be at once employed on a mission which the most sagacious and experienced of detective-officers would have felt honored to undertake.

"Here is a written description of the persons of this gang of blacklegs, swindlers, and forgers," concluded the commissioner, summing up his instructions. "It will be your object to discover their private haunts, and secure legal evidence of their nefarious practices. We have been hitherto baffled, principally, I think, through the too hasty zeal of the officers employed: you must especially avoid that error. They are practised scoundrels; and it will require considerable patience, as well as acumen, to unkennel and bring them to justice. One of their more recent victims is young Mr. Merton, son, by a former marriage, of the Dowager Lady Everton. Her ladyship has applied to us for assistance in extricating him from the toils in which he is meshed. You will call on her at five o'clock this afternoon—in plain clothes of course—and obtain whatever information on the subject she may be able to afford. Remember to communicate *directly* with me; and any assistance you may require shall be promptly rendered." With these, and a few other minor directions, needless to recapitulate, I was dismissed to a task which, difficult and possibly perilous as it might prove, I hailed as a delightful relief from the wearing monotony and dull routine of ordinary duty.

I hastened home; and after dressing with great care—the best part of my wardrobe had been fortunately saved by Emily from the wreck of my fortunes—I proceeded to Lady Everton's mansion. I was immediately marshalled to the drawing-room, where I found her ladyship and her daughter—a beautiful, fairy-looking girl—awaiting my arrival. Lady Everton appeared greatly surprised at my appearance, differing, as I daresay it altogether did, from her abstract idea of a policeman, however attired or disguised; and it was not till she had perused the note of which I was the bearer, that her haughty and incredulous stare became mitigated to a glance of lofty condescendent civility.

"Be seated, Mr. Waters," said her ladyship, waving me to a chair. "This note informs me that you have been selected for the duty of endeavoring to extricate my son from the perilous entanglements in which he has unhappily involved himself."

I was about to reply—for I was silly enough to feel somewhat nettled at the noble lady's haughtiness of manner—that I was engaged in the public service of extirpating a gang of swindlers with whom her son had involved himself, and was there to procure from her ladyship any information she might be possessed of likely to forward so desirable a result; but fortunately the remembrance of my actual position, spite of my gentleman's attire, flashed vividly upon my mind; and instead of permitting my glib tongue to wag irreverently in the presence of a right honorable, I bowed with deferential acquiescence.

Her ladyship proceeded, and I in substance obtained the following information:

Mr. Charles Merton, during the few months which had elapsed since the attainment of his majority, had very literally "fallen amongst thieves." A passion for gambling seemed to have taken entire possession of his being; and almost every day, as well as night, of his haggard and feverish life was passed at play. A run of ill-luck, according to his own belief—but in very truth a run of downright robbery—had set in against him, and he had not only dissipated all the ready money which he had inherited, and the large sums which the foolish indulgence of his lady-mother had supplied him with, but had involved himself in bonds, bills, and other obligations to a frightful amount. The principal agent in effecting this ruin was one Sandford—a man of fashionable and dashing exterior, and the presiding spirit of the knot of desperadoes whom I was commissioned to hunt out. Strange to say, Mr. Merton had the blindest reliance upon this man's honor; and even now—tricked, despoiled as he had been by him and his gang—relied upon his counsel and assistance for escape from the desperate position in which he was involved. The Everton estates had passed, in default of male issue, to a distant relative of the late lord; so that ruin, absolute and irremediable, stared both the wretched dupe and his relatives in the face. Lady Everton's jointure was not a very large one, and her son had been permitted to squander sums which should have been devoted to the discharge of claims which were now pressed harshly against her.

I listened with the deepest interest to Lady Everton's narrative. Repeatedly during the course of it, as she incidentally alluded to the manners and appearance of Sandford, who had been introduced by Mr. Merton to his mother and sister, a suspicion, which the police papers had first awakened, that the gentleman in question was an old acquaintance of my own, and one, moreover, whose favors I was extremely desirous to return in kind, flashed with increased conviction across my mind. This surmise I of course kept to myself; and after emphatically cautioning the ladies to keep our proceedings a profound secret from Mr. Merton, I took my leave, amply provided with the resources requisite for carrying into effect the scheme which I had resolved upon. I also arranged that, instead of waiting personally on her ladyship, which might excite observation and suspicion, I should report progress by letter through the post.

"If it *should* be he!" thought I, as I emerged into the street. The bare suspicion had sent the blood through my veins with furious violence. "If this Sandford be, as I suspect, that villain Cardon, success will indeed be triumph—victory! Lady Everton need not in that case seek to animate my zeal by promises of money recompense. A blighted existence, a young and gentle wife by his means cast down from opulence to sordid penury, would stimulate the dullest craven that ever crawled the earth to energy and action. Pray Heaven my suspicion prove correct; and then, oh mine enemy, look well to yourself, for the avenger is at your heels!"

Sandford, I had been instructed was usually present at the Italian Opera during the ballet: the box he generally occupied was designated in the memoranda of the police: and as I saw by the bills that a very successful piece was to be performed that evening, I determined on being present.

I entered the house a few minutes past ten o'clock, just after the commencement of the ballet, and looked eagerly round. The box in which I was instructed to seek my man was empty. The momentary disappointment was soon repaid. Five minutes had not elapsed when Cardon, looking more insolently-triumphant than ever, entered arm-in-arm with a pale aristocratic-looking young man, whom I had no difficulty, from his striking resemblance to a portrait in Lady Everton's drawing-room, in deciding to be Mr. Merton. My course of action was at once determined on. Pausing only to master the emotion which the sight of the glittering reptile in whose poisonous folds I had been involved and crushed inspired, I passed to the opposite side of the house, and boldly entered the box. Cardon's back was towards me, and I tapped him lightly on the shoulder. He turned quickly round; and if a basilisk had confronted him, he could scarcely have exhibited greater terror and surprise. My aspect, nevertheless, was studiously bland and conciliating, and my outstretched hand seemed to invite a renewal of our old friendship.

"Waters!" he at last stammered, feebly accepting my proffered grasp—"Who would have thought of meeting you here?"

"Not you, certainly, since you stare at an old friend as if he were some frightful goblin about to swallow you. Really—"

"Hush! Let us speak together in the lobby. An old friend," he added in answer to Mr. Merton's surprised stare. "We will return in an instant."

"Why, what is all this, Waters?" said Cardon, recovering his wonted *sangfroid* the instant we were alone. "I understood you had retired from amongst us; were in fact—what shall I say?"—

"Ruined—done up! Nobody should know that better than you."

"My good fellow, you do not imagine—"

"I imagine nothing, my dear Cardon. I was very thoroughly done—done *brown*, as it is written in the vulgar tongue. But fortunately my kind old uncle—"

"Passgrove is dead!" interrupted my old acquaintance, eagerly jumping to a conclusion, "And you are his heir! I congratulate you, my dear fellow. This is indeed a charming 'reverse of circumstances.' "

"Yes; but mind I have given up the old game. No more dice-devilry for me. I have promised Emily never even to touch a card again."

The cold, hard eye of the incarnate fiend—he was little else—gleamed mockingly as these "good intentions" of a practised gamester fell upon his ear; but he only replied, "Very good; quite right, my dear boy. But come, let me introduce you to Mr. Merton, a highly connected personage I assure you. By the by, Waters," he added in a caressing, confidential tone, "my name, for family and other reasons, which I will hereafter explain to you, is for the present Sandford."

"Sandford!"

"Yes: do not forget. But *allons*, or the ballet will be over."

I was introduced in due form to Mr. Merton as an old and esteemed friend, whom he—Sandford—had not seen for many months. At the conclusion of the ballet, Sandford proposed that we should adjourn to the European Coffee-house, nearly opposite. This was agreed to, and out we sallied. At the top of the staircase we jostled against the commissioner, who, like us, was leaving the house. He bowed slightly to Mr. Merton's apology, and his eye wandered briefly and coldly over our persons; but not the faintest sign of interest or recognition escaped him. I thought it possible he did not know me in my changed apparel; but looking back after descending a few steps, I was quickly undeceived. A sharp, swift glance, expressive both of encouragement and surprise, shot out from under his penthouse brows, and as swiftly vanished. He did not know how little I needed spurring to the goal we had both in view!

We discussed two or three bottles of wine with much gaiety and relish. Sandford especially was in exuberant spirits; brimming over with brilliant anecdote and sparkling badinage. He saw in me a fresh, rich prey, and his eager spirit revelled by anticipation in the victory which he nothing doubted to obtain over my "excellent intentions and wife-pledged virtue." About half-past twelve o'clock he proposed to adjourn. This was eagerly assented to by Mr. Merton, who had for some time exhibited unmistakeable symptoms of impatience and unrest.

"You will accompany us, Waters?" said Sandford, as we rose to depart. "There is, I suppose, no vow registered in the matrimonial archives against *looking on* at a game played by others?"

"Oh no; but don't ask me to play."

"Certainly not;" and a devilish sneer curled his lip. "Your virtue shall suffer no temptation be assured."

We soon arrived before the door of a quiet, respectable looking house in one of the streets leading from the Strand: a low peculiar knock, given by Sandford, was promptly answered; then a password, which I did not catch, was whispered by him through the key-hole, and we passed in.

We proceeded upstairs to the first floor, the shutters of which were carefully closed, so that no intimation of what was going on could possibly reach the street. The apartment was brilliantly lighted: a roulette table and dice and cards were in full activity: wine and liquors of all varieties were profusely paraded. There were about half-a-dozen persons present, I soon discovered, besides the gang, and that comprised eleven or twelve well-dressed desperadoes, whose sinister aspects induced a momentary qualm lest one or more of the pleasant party might suspect or recognise my vocation. This, however, I reflected, was scarcely possible. My beat during the short period I had been in the force was far distant from the usual haunts of such gentry, and I was otherwise unknown in London. Still, questioning glances were eagerly directed towards my introducer; and one big burly fellow, a foreigner—the rascals were the scum of various countries—was very unpleasantly inquisitorial. "*Y'en réponds!*" I heard Sandford say in answer to his iterated queries; and he added something in a whisper which brought a sardonic smile to the fellow's lips, and induced a total change in his demeanor towards myself. This was reassuring; for though provided with pistols, I should, I felt, have little chance with such utterly reckless ruffians as those by whom I was surrounded. Play was proposed; and though at first stoutly refusing, I feigned to be gradually overcome by irresistible temptation, and sat down to blind hazard with my foreign friend for moderate stakes. I was graciously allowed to win; and in the end found myself richer in devil's money by about ten pounds. Mr. Merton was soon absorbed in the chances of the dice, and lost large sums, for which, when the money he had brought with him was exhausted, he gave written acknowledgements. The cheating practised upon him was really audacious; and anyone but a tyro must have repeatedly detected it. He, however, appeared not to entertain the slightest suspicion of the "fair-play" of his opponents, guiding himself entirely by the advice of his friend and counsellor, Sandford, who did not himself play. The amiable assemblage broke up about six in the morning, each person retiring singly by the back way, receiving, as he departed, a new password for the next evening.

A few hours afterwards, I waited on the commissioner to report the state of affairs. He was delighted with the fortunate *début* I had made, but still strictly enjoined patience and caution. It would have been easy, as I was in possession of the password, to have surprised the confederacy in the act of gaming that very evening; but this would only have accomplished a part of the object aimed at. Several of the fraternity—Sandford amongst the number—were suspected of uttering forged foreign banknotes, and it was essential to watch narrowly for legal evidence to insure their conviction. It was also desirable to restore, if possible, the property and securities of which Mr. Merton had been pillaged.

Nothing of especial importance occurred for seven or eight days. Gaming went on as usual every evening, and Mr. Merton became of course more and more involved: even his sister's jewels—which he had surreptitiously obtained, to such a depth of degredation will this frightful vice plunge men otherwise honorable—had been staked and lost; and he was, by the advice of Sandford, about to conclude a heavy mortgage on his estate, in order not only to clear off his enormous 'debts of honor,' but to acquire fresh means of 'winning back'—that *ignus-fatuus* of all gamblers—his tremendous losses! A new preliminary 'dodge' was, I observed, now brought into action. Mr. Merton esteemed himself a knowing hand at *ecarté*: it was introduced; and he was permitted to win every game he played, much to the apparent annoyance and discomfiture of the losers. As this was precisely the snare into which I had myself fallen, I of course the more readily detected it, and felt quite satisfied that a *grand coup* was meditated. In the meantime I had not been idle. Sandford was *confidentially* informed that I was only waiting in London to receive between four and five thousand pounds—part of Uncle Passgrove's legacy—and then intended to immediately hasten back to canny Yorkshire. To have seen the villain's eyes as I incidentally, as it were, announced my errand and intention! They fairly flashed with infernal glee! Ah, Sandford, Sandford! you were, with all your cunning, but a sand-blind idiot to believe the man you had wronged and ruined could so easily forget the debt he owed you!

The crisis came swiftly on. Mr. Merton's mortgage-money was to be paid on the morrow; and on that day, too, I announced the fabulous thousands receivable by me were to be handed over. Mr. Merton, elated by his repeated triumphs at ecarté, and prompted by his friend Sandford, resolved, instead of cancelling the bonds and obligations held by the conspirators, to redeem his losses by staking on that game his ready money against those liabilities. This was at first demurred to with much apparent earnestness by the winners; but Mr. Merton, warmly seconded by Sandford, insisting upon the concession, as he deemed it, it was finally agreed that ecarté should be the game by which he might hope to regain the fortune and the peace of mind he had so rashly squandered: the last time, should he be successful—and was he not sure of success?—he assured Sandford, that he would ever handle cards or dice. He should have heard the mocking merriment with which the gang heard Sandford repeat this resolution to amend his ways—*when* he had recovered back his wealth!

The day so eagerly longed for by Merton and the confederates—by the spoilers and their prey—arrived; and I awaited with feverish anxiety the coming on of night. Only the chief conspirators—eight in number—were to be present; and no stranger except myself—a privilege I owed to the moonshine legacy I had just received—was to be admitted to this crowning triumph of successful fraud. One only hint I had ventured to give Mr. Merton, and that under a promise, 'on his honor as a gentleman,' of inviolable secrecy. It was this: "Be sure, before commencing play tomorrow night, that the bonds and obligations you have signed, the jewels you have lost, with a sum in notes or gold to make up an equal amount to that which you mean to risk, is actually deposited on the table." He promised to insist on this condition. It involved much more than he dreamt of.

My arrangements were at length thoroughly complete; and a few minutes past twelve o'clock the whispered password admitted me into the house. An angry altercation was going on. Mr. Merton was insisting, as I had advised, upon the exhibition of a sum equal to that which he had brought with him—for, confident of winning, he was determined to recover his losses to the last farthing; and although his bonds, bills, obligations, his sister's jewels, and a large amount in gold and genuine notes, were produced, there was still a heavy sum deficient. "Ah, by the by," exclaimed Sandford as I entered, "Waters can lend you the sum for an hour or two—for a *consideration*," he added in a whisper. "It will soon be returned."

"No, thank you," I answered coldly. "I never part with my money till I have lost it."

A malignant scowl passed over the scoundrel's features; but he made no reply. Ultimately it was decided that one of the fraternity should be despatched in search of the required amount. He was gone about half an hour, and returned with a bundle of notes. They were, as I hoped and expected, forgeries on foreign banks. Mr. Merton looked at and counted them; and play commenced.

As it went on, so vividly did the scene recall the evening that had sealed my own ruin, that I grew dizzy with excitement, and drained tumbler after tumbler of water to allay the fevered throbbing of my veins. The gamblers were fortunately too much absorbed to heed my agitation. Merton lost continuously—without pause or intermission. The stakes were doubled—trebled—quadrupled! His brain was on fire; and he played, or rather lost, with the recklessness of a madman.

"Hark! what's that?" suddenly exclaimed Sandford, from whose Satanic features the mask he had so long worn before Merton had been gradually slipping. "Did you not hear a noise below?"

My ear had caught the sound; and I could better interpret it than he. It ceased.

"Touch the signal-bell, Adolphe," added Sandford.

Not only the play, but the very breathing of the villains, was suspended as they listened for the reply.

It came. The answering tinkle sounded once—twice—thrice. "All right!" shouted Sandford. "Proceed! The farce is nearly played out."

I had instructed the officers that two of them in plain clothes should present themselves at the front door, obtain admission by means of the password I had given them, and immediately seize and gag the door-keeper. I had also acquainted them with the proper answer to the signal-wring—three distinct pulls at the bell-handle communicating with the first floor. Their comrades were then to be admitted, and they were all to silently ascend the stairs, and wait on the landing till summoned by me to enter and seize the gamesters. The back entrance to the house was also securely but unobtrusively watched.

One only fear disturbed me: it was lest the scoundrels should take alarm in sufficient time to extinguish the lights, destroy the forged papers, and possibly escape by some private passage which might, unknown to me, exist.

Rousing myself, as soon as the play was resumed, from the trance of memory by which I had been in some sort absorbed, and first ascertaining that the handles of my pistols were within easy reach—for I knew I was playing a desperate game with desperate men—I rose, stepped carelessly to the door, partially opened it, and bent forward, as if listening for a repetition of the sound which had so alarmed the company. To my great delight the landing and stairs were filled with police-officers—silent and stern as death. I drew back, and walked towards the table at which Mr. Merton was seated. The last stake—an enormous one—was being played for. Merton lost. He sprang upon his feet, death-pale, despairing, overwhelmed, and a hoarse execration surged through his clenched teeth. Sandford and his associates coolly raked the plunder together, their features lighted up with fiendish glee.

"Villain!—traitor!—miscreant!" shrieked Mr. Merton, as if smitten with sudden frenzy, and darting at Sandford's throat: "You, devil that you are, have undone, destroyed me!"

"No doubt of it," calmly replied Sandford, shaking off his victim's grasp; "and I think it has been very artistically and effectually done too. Snivelling, my fine fellow, will scarcely help you much."

Mr. Merton glared upon the taunting villain in speechless agony and rage.

"Not quite so fast, *Cardon*, if you please," I exclaimed, at the same time taking up a bundle of forged notes. "It does not appear to me that Mr. Merton has played against equal stakes, for unquestionably this paper is not genuine."

"Dog!" roared Sandford, "Do you hold your life so cheap?" and he rushed towards me, as if to seize the forged notes.

I was as quick as he, and the levelled tube of a pistol sharply arrested his eager onslaught. The entire gang gathered near us, flaming with excitement. Mr. Merton looked bewilderedly from one to another, apparently scarcely conscious of what was passing around him.

"Wrench the papers from him!" screamed Sandford, recovering his energy. "Seize him—stab, strangle him!"

"Look to yourself, scoundrel!" I shouted with equal vehemence. "Your hour is come! Officers, enter and do your duty!"

In an instant the room was filled with police; and surprised, panic-stricken, paralysed by the suddenness of the catastrophe, the gang were all secured without the slightest resistance, though most of them were armed, and marched off in custody.

Three—Sandford, or Cardon; but he had half-a-dozen *aliases*, one of them—were transported for life: the rest were sentenced to various terms of imprisonment. My task was effectually accomplished. My superiors were pleased to express very warm commendation of the manner in which I had acquitted myself; and the first step in the promotion which ultimately led to my present position in another branch of the public service was soon afterwards conferred upon me. Mr. Merton had his bonds, obligations, jewels, and money, restored to him; and, taught wisdom by terrible experience, never again entered a gaming-house. Neither he nor his lady-mother was ungrateful for the service I had been fortunate enough to render them.

II

GUILTY OR NOT GUILTY?

A few weeks after the lucky termination of the Sandford affair I was engaged in the investigation of a remarkable case of burglary, accompanied by homicide, which had just occurred at the residence of Mr. Bagshawe, a gentleman of competent fortune, situated within a few miles of Kendal in Westmoreland. The particulars forwarded to the London police authorities by the local magistracy were chiefly these:

Mr. Bagshawe, who had been some time absent at Leamington, Warkwickshire, with his entire establishment, wrote to Sarah King—a young woman left in charge of the house and property—to announce his own speedy return, and at the same time directing her to have a particular bedroom aired, and other household matters arranged for the reception of his nephew, Mr. Robert Bristowe, who, having just arrived from abroad, would, he expected, leave London immediately for Five Oaks' House. The positive arrival of this nephew had been declared to several tradesmen of Kendal by King early in the day preceding the night of the murder and robbery; and by her directions butcher-meat, poultry, fish, and so on, had been sent by them to Five Oaks for his table. The lad who carried the fish home stated that he had seen a strange young gentleman in one of the sitting-rooms on the ground-floor through the half-opened door of the apartment. On the following morning it was discovered that Five Oaks' House had been, not indeed broken *into*, but broken *out of*. This was evident from the state of the door fastenings and the servant-woman barbarously murdered. The neighbors found her lying quite dead and cold at the foot of the principal staircase, clothed only in her nightgown and stockings, and with a flat chamber candlestick tightly grasped in her right hand. It was conjectured that she had been roused from sleep by some noise below, and having descended to ascertain the cause, had been mercilessly slain by the disturbed burglars. Mr. Bagshawe arrived on the following day, and it was then found that not only a large amount of plate, but between three and four thousand pounds in gold and notes—the produce of government stock sold out about two months previously—had been carried off. The only person, except his niece, who lived with him, that knew there was this sum in the house, was his nephew Robert Bristowe, to whom he had written, directing his letter to the Hummums Hotel, London, stating that the sum for the long-contemplated purchase of Ryland's had been some time lying idle at Five Oaks, as he had wished to consult him upon his bargain before finally concluding it. This Mr. Robert Bristowe was now nowhere to be seen or heard of; and what seemed to confirm beyond a doubt the—to Mr. Bagshawe and his niece—torturing, horrifying suspicion that this nephew was the burglar and assassin, a portion of the identical letter written to him by his uncle was found in one of the offices! As he was nowhere to be met with or heard of in the neighborhood of Kendal, it was surmised that he must have returned to London with his booty; and a full description of his person, and the dress he wore, as given by the fishmonger's boy, was sent to London by the authorities. They also forwarded for our use and assistance one Josiah Barnes, a sly, sharp, vagabond-sort of fellow, who had been apprehended on suspicion, chiefly, or rather wholly, because of his former intimacy with the unfortunate Sarah King, who had discarded him, it seemed, on account of his incorrigibly idle, and in other respects disreputable habits. The *alibi* he set up was, however, so clear and decisive, that he was but a few hours in custody; and he now exhibited great zeal for the discovery of the murderer of the woman to whom he had, to the extent of his perverted instincts, been sincerely attached. He fiddled at the festivals of the humbler Kendalese; sang, tumbled, ventriloquized at their tavern orgies; and had he not been so very highly-gifted, might, there was little doubt, have earned a decent living as a carpenter, to which profession his father, by dint of much exertion, had about half-bred him. His principal use to us was, that he was acquainted with the features of Mr. Robert Bristowe; and accordingly, as soon as I had received my commission and instructions, I started off with him to the Hummums Hotel, Covent Garden. In answer to my inquiries, it was stated that Mr. Robert Bristowe had left the hotel a week previously without settling his bill—which was, however, of very small amount, as he usually paid every evening—and had not since been heard of; neither had he taken his luggage with him. This was odd, though the period stated would have given him ample time to reach Westmoreland on the day it was stated he *had* arrived there.

"What dress did he wear when he left?"

"That which he usually wore: a foraging-cap with a gold band, a blue military surtout coat, light trousers, and Wellington boots."

The precise dress described by the fishmonger's errand-boy! We next proceeded to the Bank of England, to ascertain if any of the stolen notes had been presented for payment. I handed in a list of the numbers furnished by Mr. Bagshawe, and was politely informed that they had all been cashed early the day before by a gentleman in a sort of undress uniform, and wearing a foraging cap. Lieutenant James was the name indorsed upon them; and the address Harley Street, Cavendish Square, was of course a fictitious one. The cashier doubted if he should be able to swear to the person of the gentleman who changed the notes, but he had particularly noticed his dress. I returned to Scotland Yard to report *no* progress; and it was then determined to issue bills descriptive of Bristowe's person, and offering a considerable reward for his apprehension, or such information as might lead to it; but the order had scarcely been issued, when who should we see walking deliberately down the yard towards the police-office but Mr. Robert Bristowe himself, dressed precisely as before described! I had just time to caution the inspector not to betray any suspicion, but to hear his story, and let him quietly depart, and to slip with Josiah Barnes out of sight, when he entered, and made a formal but most confused complaint of having been robbed something more than a week previously—where or by whom he knew not—and afterwards deceived, bamboozled, and led astray in his pursuit of the robbers, by a person whom he now suspected to be a confederate with them. Even of this latter personage he could afford no tangible information; and the inspector, having quietly listened to his statement—intended, doubtless, as a mystification—told him the police should make inquiries, and wished him good-morning. As soon as he had turned out of Scotland Yard by the street leading to the Strand, I was upon his track. He walked slowly on, but without pausing, till he reached the Saracen's Head, Snow-Hill, where, to my great astonishment, he booked himself for Westmoreland by the night-coach. He then walked into the inn, and seating himself in the coffee-room, called for a pint of sherry wine and some biscuits. He was now safe for a short period at any rate; and I was about to take a turn in the street, just to meditate upon the most advisable course of action, when I espied three buckishly-attired, bold-faced looking fellows—one of whom I thought I recognised, spite of his fine dress—enter the booking-office.

Naturally anxious in my vocation, I approached as closely to the door as I could without being observed, and heard one of them—my acquaintance sure enough; I could not be deceived in that voice—ask the clerk if there were any vacant places in the night-coach to Westmoreland. To Westmoreland! Why, what in the name of Mercury could a detachment of the swell-mob be wanting in that country of furze and frieze-coats? The next sentence uttered by my friend, as he placed the money for booking three insides to Kendal on the counter was equally, or perhaps more puzzling: "Is the gentleman who entered the office just now—him with a foraging cap I mean—to be our fellow-passenger?"

"Yes, he has booked himself; and has, I think, since gone into the house."

"Thank you: good-morning."

I had barely time to slip aside into one of the passages, when the three gentlemen came out of the office, passed me, and swaggered out of the yard. Vague, undefined suspicions at once beset me relative to the connection of these worthies with the "foraging-cap" and the doings at Kendal. There was evidently something in all this more than natural, if police philosophy could but find it out. I resolved at all events to try; and in order to have a chance of doing so, I determined to be of the party, nothing doubting that I should be able, in some way or other, to make one in whatever game they intended playing. I in my turn entered the booking-office, and finding there were still two places vacant, secured them both for James Jenkins and Josiah Barnes, countrymen and friends of mine returning to the "north countrie."

I returned to the coffee-room, where Mr. Bristowe was still seated, apparently in deep and anxious meditation, and wrote a note, with which I despatched the inn porter. I had now ample leisure for observing the suspected burglar and assassin. He was a pale, intellectual-looking, and withal handsome young man, of about six-and-twenty years of age, of slight but well-knit frame, and with the decided air—travel-stained and jaded as he appeared—of a gentleman. His look was troubled and careworn, but I sought in vain for any indication of the starting, nervous tremor always in my experience exhibited by even old practitioners in crime when suddenly accosted. Several persons had entered the room hastily, without causing him even to look up. I determined to try an experiment on his nerves, which I was quite satisfied no man who had recently committed a murder, and but the day before changed part of the produce of that crime into gold at the Bank of England, could endure without wincing. My object was, not to procure evidence producible in a court of law by such means, but to satisfy my own mind. I felt a growing conviction that, spite of appearances, the young man was guiltless of the deed imputed to him, and might be the victim, I could not help thinking, either of some strange combination of circumstances, or, more likely, of a diabolical plot for his destruction, essential, possibly, to the safety of the real perpetrators of the crime; very probably—so ran my suspicions—friends and acquaintances of the three gentlemen who were to be our fellow-travelers. My duty, I knew, was quite as much the vindication of innocence as the detection of guilt; and if I could satisfy myself that he was not the guilty party, no effort of mine should be wanting, I determined, to extricate him from the perilous position in which he stood. I went out of the room, and remained absent for some time; then suddenly entered with a sort of bounce, walked swiftly, and with a determined air, straight up to the box where he was seated, grasped him tightly by the arm, and exclaimed roughly, "So I have found you at last!" There was no start, no indication of fear whatever—not the slightest; the expression of his countenance, as he peevishly replied, "What the devil do you mean?" was simply one of surprise and annoyance.

"I beg your pardon," I replied; "the waiter told me a friend of mine, one *Bagshawe*, who has given me the slip, was here, and I mistook you for him."

He courteously accepted my apology, quietly remarking at the same time that though his own name was Bristowe, he had, oddly enough, an uncle in the country of the same name as the person I had mistaken him for. Surely, thought I, this man is guiltless of the crime imputed to him; and yet—At this moment the porter entered to announce the arrival of the gentleman I had sent for. I went out; and after giving the newcomer instructions not to lose sight of Mr. Bristowe, hastened home to make arrangements for the journey.

Transformed, by the aid of a flaxen wig, broad-brimmed hat, green spectacles, and a multiplicity of waistcoats and shawls, into a heavy and elderly, well-to-do personage, I took my way with Josiah Barnes—whom I had previously thoroughly drilled as to speech and behavior towards our companions—to the Saracen's Head a few minutes previous to the time for starting. We found Mr. Bristowe already seated; but the "three friends," I observed, were curiously looking on, desirous no doubt of ascertaining *who* were to be their fellow-travelers before venturing to coop themselves up in a space so narrow, and, under certain circumstances, so difficult of egress. My appearance and that of Barnes—who, sooth to say, looked much more of a simpleton than he really was—quite reassured them, and in they jumped with confident alacrity. A few minutes afterwards the "all right" of the attending ostlers gave the signal for departure, and away we started.

A more silent, less social party I never assisted at. Whatever amount of "feast of reason" each or either of us might have silently enjoyed, not a drop of "flow of soul" welled up from one of the six insides. Every passenger seemed to have his own peculiar reasons for declining to display himself in either mental or physical prominence. Only one or two incidents—

apparently unimportant, but which I carefully noted down in the tablet of my memory—occurred during the long, wearisome journey, till we stopped to dine at about thirty miles from Kendal; when I ascertained, from an overheard conversation of one of the three with the coachman, that they intended to get down at a roadside tavern more than six miles on this side of that place.

"Do you know this house they intend to stop at?" I inquired of my assistant as soon as I got him out of sight and hearing at the back of the premises.

"Quite well: it is within about two miles of Five Oaks' House."

"Indeed! Then you must stop there too. It is necessary I should go on to Kendal with Mr. Bristowe; but you can remain and watch their proceedings."

"With all my heart."

"But what excuse can you make for remaining there, when they know you are booked for Kendal? Fellows of that stamp are keenly suspicious; and in order to be useful, you must be entirely unsuspected."

"Oh, leave that to me. I'll throw dust enough in their eyes to blind a hundred such as they, I warrant ye."

"Well, we shall see. And now to dinner."

Soon after, the coach had once more started. Mr. Josiah Barnes began drinking from a stone bottle which he drew from his pocket; and so potent must have been the spirit it contained, that he became rapidly intoxicated. Not only speech, but eyes, body, arms, legs, the entire animal, by the time we reached the inn where we had agreed he should stop, was thoroughly, hopelessly drunk; and so savagely quarrelsome, too, did he become, that I expected every instant to hear my real vocation pointed out for the edification of the company. Strange to say, utterly stupid and savage as he seemed, all dangerous topics were carefully avoided. When the coach stopped, he got out—

how, I know not—and reeled and tumbled into the tap-room, from which he declared he would not budge an inch till next day. Vainly did the coachman remonstrate with him upon his foolish obstinacy; he might as well have argued with a bear; and he at length determined to leave him to his drunken humor. I was out of patience with the fellow; and snatching an opportunity when the room was clear, began to upbraid him for his vexatious folly. He looked sharply round, and then, his body as evenly balanced, his eye as clear, his speech as free as my own, crowed out in a low exulting voice, "Didn't I tell you I'd manage it nicely?" The door opened, and, in a twinkling, extremity of drunkenness, of both brain and limb, was again assumed with a perfection of acting I have never seen equalled. He had studied from nature, that was perfectly clear. I was quite satisfied, and with renewed confidence obeyed the coachman's call to take my seat. Mr. Bristowe and I were now the only inside passengers; and as farther disguise was useless, I began stripping myself of my superabundant clothing, wig, spectacles, &c., and in a few minutes, with the help of a bundle I had with me, presented to the astonished gaze of my fellow-traveler the identical person that had so rudely accosted him in the coffee-room of the Saracen's Head inn.

"Why, what, in the name of all that's comical, is the meaning of this?" demanded Mr. Bristowe, laughing immoderately at my changed appearance.

I briefly and coolly informed him; and he was for some minutes overwhelmed with consternation and astonishment. He had not, he said, even heard of the catastrophe at his uncle's. Still, amazed and bewildered as he was, no sign which I could interpret into an indication of guilt escaped him.

"I do not wish to obtrude upon your confidence, Mr. Bristowe," I remarked, after a long pause; "but you must perceive that unless the circumstances I have related to you are in some way explained, you stand in a perilous predicament."

"You are right," he replied, after some hesitation. "*It is* a tangled web; still, I doubt not that some mode of vindicating my perfect innocence will present itself."

He then relapsed into silence; and neither of us spoke again till the coach stopped, in accordance with a previous intimation I had given the coachman, opposite the gate of the Kendal prison. Mr. Bristowe started, and changed color, but instantly mastering his emotion, he calmly said, "You of course but perform your duty; mine is not to distrust a just and all-seeing Providence."

We entered the jail, and the necessary search of his clothes and luggage was effected as forbearingly as possible. To my great dismay we found amongst the money in his purse a Spanish gold piece of a peculiar coinage, and in the lining of his portmanteau, very dexterously hidden, a cross set with brilliants, both of which I knew, by the list forwarded to the London police, formed part of the plunder carried off from Five Oaks' House. The prisoner's vehement protestations that he could not conceive how such articles came into his possession, excited a derisive smile on the face of the veteran turnkey; whilst I was thoroughly dumbfounded by the seemingly complete demolition of the theory of innocence I had woven out of his candid open manner and unshakeable hardihood of nerve.

"I dare say the articles came to you in your sleep!" sneered the turnkey as we turned to leave the cell.

"Oh," I mechanically exclaimed, "in his sleep! I had not thought of that!" The man stared; but I had passed out of the prison before he could express his surprise or contempt in words.

The next morning the justice-room was densely crowded, to hear the examination of the prisoner. There was also a very numerous attendance of magistrates; the case, from the position in life of the prisoner, and the strange and mysterious circumstances of the affair altogether, having excited an extraordinary and extremely painful interest amongst all classes in the town and neighborhood. The demeanor of the accused gentleman was anxious certainly, but withal calm and collected; and there was, I thought, a light of fortitude and conscious probity in his clear, bold eyes, which guilt never yet successfully stimulated.

After the hearing of some minor evidence, the fishmonger's boy was called, and asked if he could point out the person he had seen at Five Oaks on the day preceding the burglary? The lad looked fixedly at the prisoner for something more than a minute without speaking, and then said, "The gentleman was standing before the fire when I saw him, with his cap on; I should like to see this person with his cap on before I say anything." Mr. Bristowe dashed on his foraging-cap, and the boy immediately exclaimed, "That is the man!" Mr. Cowan, a solicitor, retained by Mr. Bagshawe for his nephew, objected that this was, after all, only swearing to a cap, or at best to the *ensemble* of a dress, and ought not to be received. The chairman, however, decided that it must be taken *quantum valeat*, and in corroboration of other evidence. It was next deposed by several persons that the deceased Sarah King had told them that her master's nephew had positively arrived at Five Oaks. An objection to the reception of this evidence, as partaking of the nature of "heresay," was also made, and similarly overruled. Mr. Bristowe begged to observe "that Sarah King was not one of his uncle's old servants, and was entirely unknown to him: it was quite possible, therefore, that he was personally unknown to her." The bench observed that all these observations might be fitly urged before a jury, but, in the present stage of the proceedings, were uselessly addressed to them, whose sole duty it was to ascertain if a sufficiently strong case of suspicion had been made out against the prisoner to justify his committal for trial. A constable next proved finding a portion of a letter, which he produced, in one of the offices of Five Oaks; and then Mr. Bagshawe was directed to be called in. The prisoner, upon hearing this order given, exhibited great emotion, and earnestly intreated that his uncle and himself might be spared the necessity of meeting each other for the first time after a separation of several years under such circumstances.

"We can receive no evidence against you, Mr. Bristowe, in your absence," replied the chairman in a compassionate tone of voice; "but your uncle's deposition will occupy but a few minutes. It is, however, indispensable."

"At least, then, Mr. Cowan," said the agitated young man, "prevent my sister from accompanying her uncle: I could not bear *that*."

He was assured she would not be present; in fact she had become seriously ill through anxiety and terror; and the crowded assemblage awaited in painful silence the approach of the reluctant prosecutor. He presently appeared—a venerable, white-haired man; seventy years old at least he seemed, his form bowed by age and grief, his eyes fixed upon the ground, and his whole manner indicative of sorrow and dejection. "Uncle!" cried the prisoner, springing towards him. The aged man looked up, seemed to read in the clear countenance of his nephew a full refutation of the suspicions entertained against him, tottered forwards with out-spread arms, and, in the words of the Sacred text, "fell upon his neck, and wept," exclaiming in choking accents, "Forgive me—forgive me, Robert, that I ever for a moment doubted you. Mary never did—never, Robert; not for an instant."

A profound silence prevailed during this outburst of feeling, and a considerable pause ensued before the usher of the court, at a gesture from the chairman, touched Mr. Bagshawe's arm, and begged his attention to the bench. "Certainly, certainly," said he, hastily wiping his eyes, and turning towards the court.

"My sister's child, gentlemen," he added appealingly, "who has lived with me from childhood: you will excuse me, I am sure."

"There needs no excuse, Mr. Bagshawe," said the chairman kindly; "but it is necessary this unhappy business should be proceeded with. Hand the witness the portion of the letter found at Five Oaks. Now, is that your handwriting; and is it a portion of the letter you sent to your nephew, informing him of the large sum of money kept for a particular purpose at Five Oaks?"

"It is."

"Now," said the clerk to the magistrates, addressing me "please to produce the articles in your possession."

I laid the Spanish coin and the cross upon the table.

"Please to look at those two articles, Mr. Bagshawe," said the chairman. "Now, sir, on your oath, are they a portion of the property of which you have been robbed?"

The aged gentleman stooped forward and examined them earnestly; then turned and looked with quivering eyes, if I may be allowed the expression, in his nephew's face; but returned no answer to the question.

"It is necessary you should reply, Yes or No, Mr. Bagshawe," said the clerk.

"Answer, uncle," said the prisoner soothingly: "fear not for me. God and my innocence to aid, I shall yet break through the web of villany in which I at present seem hopelessly involved."

"Bless you, Robert—bless you! I am sure you will. Yes, gentlemen, the cross and coin on the table are part of the property carried off."

A smothered groan, indicative of the sorrowing sympathy felt for the venerable gentleman, arose from the crowded court on hearing this declaration. I then deposed to finding them as previously stated. As soon as I concluded, the magistrates consulted together for a few minutes; and then the chairman, addressing the prisoner, said, "I have to inform you that the bench are agreed that sufficient evidence has been adduced against you to warrant them in fully committing you for trial. We are of course bound to hear anything you have to say; but such being our intention, your professional adviser will perhaps recommend you to reserve whatever defence you have to make for another tribunal: here it could not avail you."

Mr. Cowan expressed his concurrence in the intimation of the magistrate; but the prisoner vehemently protested against sanctioning by his silence the accusation preferred against him.

"I have nothing to reserve," he exclaimed with passionate energy; "nothing to conceal. I will not owe my acquittal of this foul charge to any trick of lawyer-craft. If I may not come out of this investigation with an untainted name, I desire not to escape at all. The defence, or rather the suggestive facts I have to offer for the consideration of the bench are these:— On the evening of the day I received my uncle's letter I went to Drury Lane theatre, remaining out very late. On my return to the hotel, I found I had been robbed of my pocket-book, which contained not only that letter, and a considerable sum in bank-notes, but papers of great professional importance to me. It was too late to adopt any measures for its recovery that night; and the next morning, as I was dressing myself to go out, in order to apprise the police authorities of my loss, I was informed that a gentleman desired to see me instantly on important business. He was shown up, and announced himself to be a detective police-officer: the robbery I had sustained had been revealed by an accomplice, and it was necessary I should immediately accompany him. We left the hotel together; and after consuming the entire day in perambulating all sorts of by-streets, and calling at several suspicious-looking places, my officious friend all at once discovered that the thieves had left town for the west of England, hoping, doubtless, to reach a large town and get gold for the notes before the news of their having been stopped should have reached it. He insisted upon immediate pursuit. I wished to return to the hotel for a change of clothes, as I was but lightly clad, and night-traveling required warmer apparel. This he would not hear of, as the night-coach was on the point of starting. He, however, contrived to supply me from his own resources with a greatcoat—a sort of policeman's cape—and a rough traveling-cap, which tied under the chin. In due time we arrived at Bristol, where I was kept for several days loitering about; till, finally, my guide decamped, and I returned to London. An hour after arriving there, I gave information at Scotland Yard of what had happened, and afterwards booked myself by the night-coach for Kendal. This is all I have to say."

This strange story did not produce the slightest effect upon the bench, and very little upon the auditory, and yet I felt satisfied it was strictly true. It was not half ingenious enough for a made-up story. Mr. Bagshawe, I should have stated, had been led out of the justice-hall immediately after he had finished his deposition.

"Then, Mr. Bristowe," said the magistrate's clerk, "assuming this curious narrative to be correct, you will be easily able to prove an *alibi*?"

"I have thought over that, Mr. Clerk," returned the prisoner mildly, "and must confess that, remembering how I was dressed and wrapped up—that I saw but few persons, and those casually and briefly, I have strong misgivings of my power to do so."

"That is perhaps the less to be lamented," replied the county clerk in a sneering tone, "inasmuch as the possession of those articles," pointing to the cross and coin on the table, "would necessitate another equally probable, though quite different story."

"That is a circumstance," replied the prisoner in the same calm tone as before, "which I cannot in the slightest manner account for."

No more was said, and the order for his committal to the county jail at Appleby on the charge of "wilful murder" was given to the clerk. At this moment a hastily-scrawled note from Barnes was placed in my hands. I had no sooner glanced over it, than I applied to the magistrates for an adjournment till the morrow, on the ground that I could then produce an important witness, whose evidence at the trial it was necessary to assure. The application was, as a matter of course, complied with; the prisoner was remanded till the next day, and the court adjourned.

As I accompanied Mr. Bristowe to the vehicle in waiting to convey him to jail, I could not forbear whispering, "Be of good heart, sir, we shall unravel this mystery yet, depend upon it." He looked keenly at me; and then, without other reply than a warm pressure of the hand, jumped into the carriage.

"Well, Barnes," I exclaimed as soon as we were in a room by ourselves, and the door closed, "what is it you have discovered?"

"That the murderers of Sarah King are yonder at the Talbot where you left me."

"Yes: so I gather from your note. But what evidence have you to support your assertion?"

"This! Trusting to my apparent drunken imbecility, they occasionally dropped words in my presence which convinced me not only that they were the guilty parties, but that they had come down here to carry off the plate, somewhere concealed in the neighborhood. This they mean to do tonight."

"Anything more?"

"Yes. You know I am a ventriloquist in a small way, as well as a bit of a mimic: well, I took occasion when that youngest of the rascals—the one that sat beside Mr. Bristowe, and got out on the top of the coach the second evening, because, freezing cold as it was, he said the inside was too hot and close—"

"Oh, I remember. Dolt that I was, not to recall it before. But go on."

"Well, he and I were alone together in the parlor about three hours ago—I dead tipsy as ever—when he suddenly heard the voice of Sarah King at his elbow exclaiming, 'Who is that in the plate closet?' If you had seen the start of horror which he gave, the terror which shook his failing limbs as he glanced round the apartment, you would no longer have entertained a doubt on the matter."

"This is scarcely judicial proof, Barnes; but I dare say we shall be able to make something of it. You return immediately; about nightfall I will rejoin you in my former disguise."

It was early in the evening when I entered the Talbot, and seated myself in the parlor. Our three friends were present, and so was Barnes.

"Is not that fellow sober yet?" I demanded of one of them.

"No; he has been lying about drinking and snoring ever since. He went to bed, I hear, this afternoon; but he appears to be little the better for it."

I had an opportunity soon afterwards of speaking to Barnes privately, and found that one of the fellows had brought a chaise-cart and horse from Kendal, and that all three were to depart in about an hour, under pretence of reaching a town about fourteen miles distant, where they intended to sleep. My plan was immediately taken: I returned to the parlor, and watching my opportunity, whispered into the ear of the young gentleman whose nerves had been so shaken by Barnes' ventriloquism, and who, by the way, was *my* old acquaintance—"Dick Staples, I want a word with you in the next room." I spoke in my natural voice, and lifted, for his especial study and edification, the wig from my forehead. He was thunderstruck; and his teeth chattered with terror. His two companions were absorbed over a low game at cards, and did not observe us. "Come," I continued in the same whisper, "there is not a moment to lose; *if you would save yourself*, follow me!" He did so, and I led him into an adjoining apartment, closed the door, and drawing a pistol from my coat-pocket, said—"You perceive, Staples, that the game is up: you personated Mr. Bristowe at his uncle's house at Five Oaks, dressed in a precisely similar suit of clothes to that which he wears. You murdered the servant—"

"No—no—no, not I," gasped the wretch; "not I: I did not strike her—"

"At all events you were present, and that, as far as the gallows is concerned, is the same thing. You also picked that gentleman's pocket during our journey from London, and placed one of the stolen Spanish pieces in his purse; you then went on the roof of the coach, and by some ingenious means or other contrived to secrete a cross set with brilliants in his portmanteau."

"What shall I do—what shall I do?" screamed the fellow, half dead with fear, and slipping down on a chair; "what shall I do to save my life—my life?"

"First get up and listen. If you are not the actual murderer—"

"I am not—upon my soul I am not!"

"If you are not, you will probably be admitted king's evidence; though, mind, I make no promises. Now, what is the plan of operations for carrying off the booty?"

"They are going in the chaise-cart almost immediately to take it up: it is hidden in the copse yonder. I am to remain here, in order to give an alarm should any suspicion be excited, by showing two candles at our bedroom window; and if all keeps right, I am to join them at the crossroads, about a quarter of a mile from hence."

"All right. Now return to the parlor: I will follow you; and remember that on the slightest hint of treachery I will shoot you as I would a dog."

About a quarter of an hour afterwards his two confederates set off in the chaise-cart: I, Barnes, and Staples, cautiously followed, the latter handcuffed, and superintended by the ostler of the inn, whom I for the nonce pressed into the king's service. The night was pitch dark, fortunately, and the noise of the cart-wheels effectually drowned the sound of our footsteps. At length the cart stopped; the men got out, and were soon busily engaged in transferring the buried plate to the cart. We cautiously approached, and were soon within a yard or two of them, still unperceived.

"Get into the cart," said one of them to the other, "and I will hand the things up to you." His companion obeyed.

"Hollo!" cried the fellow, "I thought I told you—"

"That you are nabbed at last!" I exclaimed, tripping him suddenly up. "Barnes, hold the horse's head. Now, sir, attempt to budge an inch out of that cart, and I'll send a bullet through your brains." The surprise was complete; and so terror-stricken were they, that neither resistance nor escape was attempted. They were soon handcuffed and otherwise secured; the remainder of the plate was placed in the cart; and we made the best of our way to Kendal jail, where I had the honor of lodging them at about nine o'clock in the evening. The news, late as it was, spread like wildfire, and innumerable were the congratulations which awaited me when I reached the inn where I lodged. But that which recompensed me a thousandfold for what I had done, was the fervent embrace in which the white-haired uncle, risen from his bed to assure himself of the truth of the news, locked me, as he called down blessings from Heaven upon my head! There are blessed moments even in the life of a police-officer.

Mr. Bristowe was of course liberated on the following morning; Staples was admitted king's evidence; and one of his accomplices—the actual murderer—was hanged, the other transported. A considerable portion of the property was also recovered. The gentleman who—to give time and opportunity for the perpetration of the burglary, suggested by the perusal of Mr. Bagshawe's letter—induced Mr. Bristowe to accompany him to Bristol, was soon afterwards transported for another offence.

III

X. Y. Z.

The following advertisement appeared in several of the London journals in the year 1832:—"If Owen Lloyd, a native of Wales, and who, it is believed, resided for many years in London as clerk in a large mercantile establishment, will forward his present address to X. Y. Z., Post-Office, St. Martin's-le-Grand, to be left till called for, he will hear of something greatly to his advantage."

My attention had been attracted to this notice by its very frequent appearance in the journal which I was chiefly in the habit of reading, and, from professional habits of thinking, I had set it down in my own mind as a *trap* for some offender against the principles of *meum* and *tuum*, whose presence in a criminal court was very earnestly desired. I was confirmed in this conjecture by observing that, in despair of Owen Lloyd's voluntary disclosure of his retreat, a reward of fifty guineas, payable by a respectable solicitor of Lothbury, was ultimately offered to any person who would furnish X. Y. Z. with the missing man's address. "An old bird," I mentally exclaimed on perusing this paragraph, "and not to be caught with chaff; that is evident." Still more to excite my curiosity, and at the same time bring the matter within the scope of my own particular functions, I found, on taking up the "Police Gazette," a reward of thirty guineas offered for the *apprehension* of Owen Lloyd, whose person and manners were minutely described. "The pursuit grows hot," thought I, throwing down the paper, and hastening to attend a summons just brought me from the superintendent; "and if Owen Lloyd is still within the four seas, his chance of escape seems but a poor one."

On waiting on the superintendent, I was directed to put myself in immediate personal communication with a Mr. Smith, the head of an eminent wholesale house in the City.

"In the City!"

"Yes; but your business with Mr. Smith is relative to the extensive robbery at his West-end residence a week or two ago. The necessary warrants for the apprehension of the suspected parties have been, I understand, obtained, and on your return will, together with some necessary memoranda, be placed in your hands."

I at once proceeded to my destination, and on my arrival, was immediately ushered into a dingy back-room, where I was desired to wait till Mr. Smith, who was just then busily engaged, could speak to me. Casting my eyes over a table, near which the clerk had placed me a chair, I perceived a newspaper and the "Police Gazette," in both of which the advertisements for the discovery of Owen Lloyd were strongly underlined. "Oh, ho," thought I; "Mr. Smith, then, is the X. Y. Z. who is so extremely anxious to renew his acquaintance with Mr. Owen Lloyd; and I am the honored individual selected to bring about the desired interview. Well, it is in my new vocation—one which can scarcely be dispensed with, it seems, in this busy scheming life of ours."

Mr. Smith did not keep me waiting long. He seemed a hard, shrewd, businessman, whose still wiry frame, brisk, active gait and manner, and clear, decisive eye, indicated—though the snows of more than sixty winters had passed over his head—a yet vigorous life, of which the morning and the noon had been spent in the successful pursuit of wealth and its accompaniment—social consideration and influence.

"You have, I suppose, read the advertisements marked on these papers?"

"I have, and of course conclude that you, sir, are X. Y. Z."

"Of course, conclusions," rejoined Mr. Smith with a quite perceptible sneer, "are usually very silly ones: in this instance especially so. My name, you ought to be aware, is Smith: X. Y. Z., whoever he may be, I expect in a few minutes. In just seventeen minutes," added the exact man of business; "for I, by letter, appointed him to meet me here at one o'clock precisely. My motive in seeking an interview with him, it is proper I should tell you, is the probability that he, like myself, is a sufferer by Owen Lloyd, and may not therefore object to defray a fair share of the cost likely to be incurred in unkenneling the delinquent, and prosecuting him to conviction; or, which would be far better, he may be in possession of information that will enable us to obtain completely the clue I already almost grasp. But we must be cautious: X. Y. Z. *may* be a relative or friend of Lloyd's, and in that case, to possess him of our plans would answer no purpose but to afford him an opportunity of baffling them. Thus much premised, I had better at once proceed to read over to you a few particulars I have jotted down, which, you will perceive, throw light and color over the suspicions I have been within these few days compelled to entertain. You are doubtless acquainted with the full particulars of the robbery at my residence, Brook Street, last Thursday fortnight?"

"Yes; especially the report of the officers, that the crime must have been committed by persons familiar with the premises and the general habits of the family."

"Precisely. Now, have you your memorandum-book ready?"

"Quite so."

"You had better write with ink," said Mr. Smith, pushing an inkstand and pens towards me. "Important memoranda should never, where there is a possibility of avoiding it, be written in pencil. Friction, thumbing, use of any kind, often partially obliterates them, creating endless confusion and mistakes. Are you ready?"

"Perfectly."

"Owen Lloyd, a native of Wales, and, it was understood, descended from a highly-respectable family there. About five feet eight; but I need not describe his person over again. Many years with us, first as junior, then as head clerk; during which his conduct, as regards the firm, was exemplary. A man of yielding, irresolute mind—if indeed a person can be said to really possess a mind at all who is always changing it for some other person's—incapable of saying "No" to embarrassing, impoverishing requests—one, in short, Mr. Waters, of that numerous class of individuals whom fools say are nobody's enemies but their own, as if that were possible—"

"I understand; but I really do not see how this bears upon—"

"The mission you are directed to undertake? I think it does, as you will presently see. Three years ago, Owen Lloyd having involved himself, in consequence of the serious defect of character I have indicated, in large liabilities for pretended friends, left our employment; and to avoid a jail, fled, no one could discover whither. Edward Jones, also a native of the principality, whose description, as well as that of his wife, you will receive from the superintendent, was discharged about seven years since from our service for misconduct, and went, we understood, to America. He always appeared to possess great influence over the mind of his considerably younger countryman Lloyd. Jones and his wife were seen three evenings since by one of our clerks near Temple Bar. I am of opinion, Mr. Waters," continued Mr. Smith, removing his spectacles, and closing the note-book, from which he had been reading, "that it is only the first step in crime, or criminal imprudence, which feeble-minded men especially long hesitate or boggle at;

and I now more than suspect that, pressed by poverty, and very possibly yielding to the persuasions and example of Jones—who, by the way, was as well acquainted with the premises in Brook Street as his fellow-clerk—the once honest, ductile Owen Lloyd, is now a common thief and burglar."

"Indeed!"

"Yes. A more minute search led to the discovery, the day before yesterday, of a pocket-book behind some book-shelves in the library. As no property had been taken from that room—though the lock of a large iron chest, containing coins and medals, had been evidently tampered with—the search there was not at first very rigorous. That pocket-book—here it is—belonged, I know, to Owen Lloyd when in our service. See, here are his initials stamped on the cover."

"Might he not have inadvertently left it there when with you?"

"You will scarcely think so after reading the date of the five-pound note of the Hampshire County Bank, which you will find within the inner lining."

"The date is 1831."

"Exactly. I have also strong reason for believing that Owen Lloyd is now, or has been lately, residing in some part of Hampshire."

"That is important."

"This letter," continued Mr. Smith; and then pausing for a brief space in some embarrassment, he added—"The commissioner informed me, Mr. Waters, that you were a person upon whose good sense and *discretion*, as well as sagacity and courage, every confidence might be placed. I therefore feel less difficulty than I otherwise should in admitting you a little behind the family screen, and entering with you upon matters one would not willingly have bruited in the public ear."

I bowed, and he presently proceeded.

"Owen Lloyd, I should tell you, is married to a very amiable, superior sort of woman, and has one child, a daughter named Caroline, an elegant, gentle-mannered, beautiful girl I admit, to whom my wife was much attached, and she was consequently a frequent visitor in Brook Street. This I always felt was very imprudent; and the result was, that my son Arthur Smith—only about two years her senior; she was just turned of seventeen when her father was compelled to fly from his creditors—formed a silly, boyish attachment for her. They have since, I gather from this letter, which I found yesterday in Arthur's dressing-room, carried on, at long intervals, a clandestine correspondence, waiting for the advent of more propitious times—which, being interpreted," added Mr. Smith with a sardonic sneer, "means of course my death and burial."

"You are in possession, then, if Miss Caroline Lloyd is living with her father, of his precise place of abode?"

"Not exactly. The correspondence is, it seems, carried on without the knowledge of Owen Lloyd; and the girl states in answer, it should seem, to Arthur's inquiries, that her father would never forgive her if, under present circumstances, she disclosed his place of residence—*we* can now very well understand that—and she intreats Arthur not to persist, at least for the present, in his attempts to discover her. My son, you must understand, is now of age, and so far as fortune is concerned, is, thanks to a legacy from an aunt on his mother's side, independent of me."

"What post-mark does the letter bear?"

"Charing-Cross. Miss Lloyd states that it will be posted in London by a friend; that friend being, I nothing doubt, her father's confederate, Jones. But to us the most important part of the epistle is the following line:—'My father met with a sad accident in the forest some time ago, but is now quite recovered.' The words *in the forest* have, you see, been written over, but not so entirely as to prevent their being, with a little trouble, traced.

Now, coupling this expression with the Hampshire bank-note, I am of opinion that Lloyd is concealed somewhere in the New Forest."

"A shrewd guess, at all events."

"You now perceive what weighty motives I have to bring this man to justice. The property carried off I care little comparatively about; but the intercourse between the girl and my son must at any cost be terminated—"

He was interrupted by a clerk, who entered to say that Mr. William Lloyd, the gentleman who had advertised as "X. Y. Z." desired to speak to him. Mr. Smith directed Mr. Lloyd to be shewn in; and then, snatching up the "Police Gazette," and thrusting it into one of the table-drawers, said in a low voice, but marked emphasis, "A relative, no doubt, by the name: be silent, and be watchful."

A minute afterwards Mr. Lloyd was ushered into the room. He was a thin, emaciated, and apparently sorrow-stricken man, on the wintry side of middle age, but of mild, courteous, gentlemanly speech and manners. He was evidently nervous and agitated, and after a word or two of customary salutation, said hastily, "I gather from this note, sir, that you can afford me tidings of my long-lost brother Owen: where is he?" He looked eagerly round the apartment, gazed with curious earnestness in my face, and then again turned with tremulous anxiety to Mr. Smith. "Is he dead? Pray do not keep me in suspense."

"Sit down, sir," said Mr. Smith, pointing to a chair. "Your brother, Owen Lloyd, was for many years a clerk in this establishment—"

"*Was—was!*" interrupted Mr. Lloyd with greatly-increased agitation: "Not now, then—he has left you?"

"For upwards of three years. A few days ago—pray do not interrupt me—I obtained intelligence of him, which, with such assistance as you may possibly be able to afford, will perhaps suffice to enable this gentleman"—pointing to me—"to discover his present residence."

I could not stand the look which Mr. Lloyd fixed upon me, and turned hastily away to gaze out of the window, as if attracted by the noise of a squabble between two draymen, which fortunately broke out at the moment in the narrow, choked-up street.

"For what purpose, sir, are you instituting this eager search after my brother? It cannot be that—No, no—he has left you, you say, more than three years: besides, the bare supposition is as wicked as absurd."

"The truth is, Mr. Lloyd," rejoined Mr. Smith after a few moments' reflection, "there is great danger that my son may disadvantageously connect himself with your—with your brother's family—may, in fact, marry his daughter Caroline. Now I could easily convince Owen—"

"Caroline!" interjected Mr. Lloyd with a tremulous accent, and his dim eyes suffused with tears—"Caroline!—ay, truly *her* daughter would be named Caroline." An instant after, he added, drawing himself up with an air of pride and some sternness: "Caroline Lloyd, sir, is a person who, by birth, and, I doubt not, character and attainments, is a fitting match for the son of the proudest merchant of this proud city."

"Very likely," rejoined Mr. Smith dryly; "but you must excuse me for saying that, as regards *my* son, it is one which I will at any cost prevent."

"How am I to know," observed Mr. Lloyd, whose glance of pride had quickly passed away, "that you are dealing fairly and candidly with me in the matter?"

In reply to this home-thrust, Mr. Smith placed the letter addressed by Miss Lloyd to his son in the hands of the questioner, at the same time explaining how he had obtained it.

Mr. Lloyd's hands trembled, and his tears fell fast over the letter as he hurriedly perused it. It seemed by his broken, involuntary ejaculations, that old thoughts and memories were deeply stirred within him. "Poor girl!—so young, so gentle and so sorely tried! Her mother's very turn of thought and phrase. Owen, too, artless, honorable, just as he was ever, except when the dupe of knaves and villains."

He seemed buried in thought for some time after the perusal of the letter; and Mr. Smith, whose cue it was to avoid exciting suspicion by too great eagerness of speech, was growing fidgetty. At length, suddenly looking up, he said in a dejected tone, "If this is all you have ascertained, we seem as far off as ever. I can afford you no help."

"I am not sure of that," replied Mr. Smith. "Let us look calmly at the matter. Your brother is evidently not living in London, and that accounts for your advertisements not being answered."

"Truly."

"If you look at the letter attentively, you will perceive that three important words, 'in the forest,' have been partially erased."

"Yes, it is indeed so; but what—"

"Now, is there no particular locality in the country to which your brother would be likely to betake himself in preference to another? Gentlemen of fancy and sentiment," added Mr. Smith, "usually fall back, I have heard, upon some favorite haunt of early days when pressed by adversity."

"It is natural they should," replied Mr. Lloyd, heedless of the sneer. "I have felt that longing for old haunts and old faces in intensest force, even when I was what the world calls prospering in strange lands; and how much more—But no; he would not return to Wales—to Caermarthen—to be looked down upon by those amongst whom our family for so many generations stood equal with the highest. Besides, I have personally sought him there—in vain."

"But his wife—*she* is not a native of the principality?"

"No. Ah! I remember. The forest! It must be so! Caroline Heyworth, whom we first met in the Isle of Wight, is a native of Beaulieu, a village in the New Forest, Hampshire. A small, very small property there, bequeathed by an uncle, belonged to her, and perhaps has not been disposed of. How came I not to think of this before? I will set out at once—and yet pressing business requires my stay here for a day or two."

"This gentleman, Mr. Waters, can proceed to Beaulieu immediately."

"That must do then. You will call on me, Mr. Waters—here is my address—before you leave town. Thank you. And God bless you, sir," he added, suddenly seizing Mr. Smith's hand, "for the light you have thrown upon this wearying, and, I feared, hopeless search. You need not be so anxious, sir, to send a special messenger to release your son from his promise of marriage to my niece. None of us, be assured, will be desirous of forcing her upon a reluctant family." He then bowed, and withdrew.

"Mr. Waters," said Mr. Smith with a good deal of sternness, as soon as we were alone, "I expect that no sentimental crotchet will prevent your doing your duty in this matter?"

"What right," I answered with some heat, "have you, sir, to make such an insinuation?"

"Because I perceived, by your manner, that you disapproved my questioning Mr. Lloyd as to the likeliest mode of securing his brother."

"My manner but interpreted my thoughts: still, sir, I know what belongs to my duty, and shall perform it."

"Enough: I have nothing more to say."

I drew on my gloves, took up my hat, and was leaving the room, when Mr. Smith exclaimed, "Stay one moment, Mr. Waters: you see that my great object is to break off the connection between my son and Miss Lloyd?"

"I do."

"I am not anxious, you will remember, to press the prosecution *if, by a frank written confession of his guilt*, Owen Lloyd places an insuperable bar between his child and mine. You understand?"

"Perfectly. But permit me to observe, that the *duty* you just now hinted I might hesitate to perform, will not permit me to be a party to any such transaction. Good-day."

I waited on Mr. William Lloyd soon afterwards, and listened with painful interest to the brief history which he, with childlike simplicity, narrated of his own and brother's fortunes. It was a sad, oft-told tale. They had been early left orphans; and deprived of judicious guidance, had run—William more especially—a wild career of dissipation, till *all* was gone. Just before the crash came, they had both fallen in love with the same woman, Caroline Heyworth, who had preferred the meeker, more gentle-hearted Owen, to his elder brother. They parted in anger. William obtained a situation as bailiff and overseer of an estate in Jamaica, where, by many years of toil, good fortune, and economy, he at length ruined his health and restored his fortunes; and was now returned to die rich in his native country; and, as he had till an hour before feared, unlamented and untended save by hirelings. I promised to write immediately I had seen his brother; and with a sorrowful heart took leave of the vainly-rejoicing, prematurely-aged man.

I arrived at Southampton by the night-coach—the railway was but just begun, I remember—and was informed that the best mode of reaching Beaulieu—Bewley, they pronounced it—was by crossing the Southampton river to the village of Hythe, which was but a few miles distance from Beaulieu. As soon as I had breakfasted, I hastened to the quay, and was soon speeding across the tranquil waters in one of the sharp-stemmed wherries which plied constantly between the shores. My attention was soon arrested by two figures in the stern of the boat, a man and woman. A slight examination of their features sufficed to convince me that they were Jones and his wife. They evidently entertained no suspicion of pursuit; and as I heard them tell the boatmen they were going on to *Bewley*, I determined for the present not to disturb their fancied security. It was fortunate I did so. As soon as we had landed, they passed into a mean-looking dwelling, which, from some nets, and a boat under repair, in a small yard in front of it, I concluded to be a fisherman's. As no vehicle could be readily procured, I determined on walking on, and easily reached Beaulieu, which is charmingly situated just within the skirts of the New Forest, about twelve o'clock. After partaking of a slight repast at the principal inn of the place—I forget its name; but it was, I remember, within a stone's-throw of the celebrated Beaulieu Abbey ruins—I easily contrived, by a few careless, indirect questions, to elicit all the information I required of the loquacious waiting-maid. Mr. Lloyd, who seemed to bear an excellent character, lived, I was informed, at a cottage about half a mile distant from the inn, and chiefly supported himself as a measurer of timber—beech and ash: a small stock—the oak was reserved for government purposes—he usually kept on hand. Miss Caroline, the girl said, did beautiful fancy-work; and a group of flowers painted by her, as natural as life, was framed and glazed in the bar, if I would like to see it. Upon the right track sure enough! Mr. Lloyd, there could be no longer a doubt, had unconsciously betrayed his unfortunate, guilty brother into the hands of justice, and I, an agent of the iron law, was already upon the threshold of his hiding-place! I felt no pleasure at the success of the scheme. To have bravely and honestly stood up against an adverse fate for so many years, only to fall into crime just as fortune had grown weary of persecuting him, and a long-estranged brother had returned to raise him and his to their former position in society, was melancholy indeed! And the young woman too, whose letter breathed so pure, so gentle, so patient a spirit!—it would not bear thinking about—and I resolutely strove to look upon the affair as one of everyday routine. It would not do, however; and I was about to quit the room in no very enviable frame of mind, when my boat companions, Mr. and Mrs. Jones, entered, and seated themselves at one of the tables. The apartment was rather a large one, and as I was seated in the corner of a box at some distance from the entrance, they did not at first observe me; and several words caught my ear which awakened a strong desire to hear more. That I might do so, I instantly adopted a very common, but not the less often very successful device. As soon as the newcomers perceived me, their whispered colloquy stopped abruptly; and after a minute or so, the man said, looking hard at me, "Good-day, sir; you have had rather a long walk?" and he glanced at my dusty boots.

"Sir," I replied, enclosing my left ear with my hand in the manner of a natural ear-trumpet, "did you speak?"

"A dusty walk," he rejoined in a voice that might have been heard in a hurricane or across Fleet Street.

"One o'clock!" I replied, pulling out my watch. "No: it wants a quarter yet."

"Deaf as the Monument," said Jones to his companion. "All right."

The suspended dialogue was but partially resumed.

"Do you think," said the woman, after the lapse of about five minutes—"do you think Owen and his family will go with us? I hope not."

"Not he: I only asked him just for the say-so of the thing. He is too chicken-hearted for that, or for anything else that requires pluck."

Finishing the spirits and water they had ordered, they soon afterwards went out. I followed.

As soon as we had gone about a hundred paces from the house, I said, "Pray can you tell me which is Mr. Lloyd the beech-merchant's house?"

"Yes," replied the man, taking hold of my arm, and hallooing into my ear with a power sufficient to really deafen one for life: "we are going there to dine."

I nodded comprehension, and on we journeyed. We were met at the door by Owen Lloyd himself—a man in whose countenance guilelessness, even to simplicity, seemed stamped by nature's own true hand. So much, thought I, for the reliance to be placed on physiognomy! "I have brought you a customer," said Mr. Jones; "but he is as deaf as a stone." I was courteously invited in by signs; and with much hallooing and shouting, it was finally settled that, after dinner, I should look over Mr. Lloyd's stock of wood. Dinner had just been placed on the table by Mrs. Lloyd and her daughter. A still very comely, interesting woman was Mrs. Lloyd, though time and sorrow had long since set their unmistakeable seals upon her. Her daughter was, I thought, one of the most charming, graceful young women I had ever seen, spite of the tinge of sadness which dwelt upon her sweet face, deepening its interest if it somewhat diminished its beauty. My heart ached to think of the misery the announcement of my errand must presently bring on such gentle beings—innocent, I felt confident, even of the knowledge of the crime that had been committed. I dreaded to begin—not, Heaven knows, from any fear of the men, who, compared with me, were poor, feeble creatures, and I could easily have mastered half-a-dozen such; but the females—that young girl especially—how encounter *their* despair? I mutely declined dinner, but accepted a glass of ale, and sat down till I could muster sufficient resolution for the performance of my task; for I felt this was an opportunity of quietly effecting the capture of both the suspected criminals which *must* not be neglected.

Dinner was just over when Mrs. Lloyd said, "Oh, Mr Jones, have you seen anything of my husband's pocket-book? It was on a shelf in the room where you slept—not the last time, but when you were here about three weeks ago. We can find it nowhere; and I thought you might possibly have taken it by mistake."

"A black, common-looking thing?" said Jones.

"Yes."

"I *did* take it by mistake. I found it in one of my parcels, and put it in my pocket, intending of course to return it when I came back; but I remember, when wanting to open a lock of which I had lost the key, taking it out to see if it contained a pencil-case which I thought might answer the purpose; and finding none, tossing it away in a pet, I could not afterwards find it."

"Then it is lost?"

"Yes; but what of that? There was nothing in it."

"You are mistaken," rejoined Owen; "there was a five-pound country note in it, and the loss will—What is the matter, friend?"

I had sprung upon my feet with uncontrollable emotion: Mr. Lloyd's observation recalled me to myself, and I sat down again, muttering something about a sudden pain in the side.

"Oh, if that's the case," said Jones, "I'll make it up willingly. I am pretty rich, you know, just now."

"We shall be much obliged to you," said Mrs. Lloyd; "its loss would be a sad blow to us."

"How came you to send those heavy boxes here, Jones?" said Owen Lloyd. "Would it not have been better to have sent them direct to Portsmouth, where the vessel calls?"

"I had not quite made up my mind to return to America then; and I knew they would be safer here than anywhere else."

"When do you mean to take them away? We are so badly off for room, that they terribly hamper us."

"This evening, about nine o'clock. I have hired a smack at Hythe to take us, bag and baggage, down the river to meet the liner which calls off Portsmouth tomorrow. I wish we could persuade you to go with us."

"Thank you, Jones," replied Owen in a dejected tone. "I have very little to hope for here; still my heart clings to the old country."

I had heard enough; and hastily rising, intimated a wish to look at the timber at once. Mr. Lloyd immediately rose, and Jones and his wife left the cottage to return to Hythe at the same time that we did. I marked a few pieces of timber, and promising to send for them in the morning, hastened away.

A mountain seemed removed from off my breast: I felt as if I had achieved a great personal deliverance. Truly a wonderful interposition of Providence, I thought, that has so signally averted the fatal consequences likely to have resulted from the thoughtless imprudence of Owen Lloyd, in allowing his house to be made, however innocently, a receptacle for stolen goods, at the solicitations, too, of a man whose character he knew to be none of the purest. He had had a narrow escape, and might with perfect truth exclaim—

"There's a Divinity that shapes our ends,
Rough-hew them how we will."

The warrants of which I was the bearer, the London police authorities had taken care to get indorsed by a magistrate of the county of Hampshire, who happened to be in London, so that I found no difficulty in arranging effectually for the capture and safe custody of Jones and his assistants when he came to fetch his booty.

I had just returned to the Beaulieu inn, after completing my arrangements, when a carriage drove furiously up to the door, and who should, to my utter astonishment, alight, but Mr. William Lloyd, and Messrs. Smith, father and son. I hastened out, and briefly enjoining caution and silence, begged them to step with me into a private room. The agitation of Mr. Lloyd and of Mr. Arthur Smith was extreme, but Mr. Smith appeared cold and impassive as ever. I soon ascertained that Arthur Smith, by his mother's assistance, I suspect, had early penetrated his father's schemes and secrets, and had, in consequence, caused Mr. William Lloyd to be watched home, with whom, immediately after I had left, he had a long conference. Later in the evening an *éclaircissement* with the father took place; and after a long and stormy discussion, it was resolved that all three should the next morning post down to Beaulieu, and act as circumstances might suggest. My story was soon told. It was received of course with unbounded joy by the brother and the lover; and even through the father's apparent indifference I could perceive that his refusal to participate in the general joy would not be of long duration. The large fortune which Mr. William Lloyd intimated his intention to bestow upon his niece was a new and softening element in the affair.

Mr. Smith, senior, ordered his dinner; and Mr. Lloyd and Arthur Smith—but why need I attempt to relate what *they* did? I only know that when, a long time afterwards, I ventured to look in at Mr. Owen Lloyd's cottage, all the five inmates—brother, uncle, lover, niece, and wife—were talking, laughing, weeping, smiling, like distracted creatures, and seemed utterly incapable of reasonable discourse. An hour after that, as I stood screened by a belt of forest-trees in wait for Mr. Jones and company, I noticed, as they all strolled past me in the clear moonlight, that the tears, the agitation had passed away, leaving only smiles and grateful joy on the glad faces so lately clouded by anxiety and sorrow. A mighty change in so brief a space!

Mr. Jones arrived with his cart and helpers in due time. A man who sometimes assisted in the timber-yard was deputed, with an apology for the absence of Mr. Lloyd, to deliver the goods. The boxes, full of plate and other valuables, were soon hoisted in, and the cart moved off. I let it proceed about a mile, and then, with the help I had placed in readiness, easily secured the astounded burglar and his assistants; and early the next morning Jones was on his road to London. He was tried at the ensuing Old-Bailey sessions, convicted, and transported for life; and the discretion I had exercised in not executing the warrant against Owen Lloyd was decidedly approved of by the authorities.

It was about two months after my first interview with Mr. Smith that, on returning home one evening, my wife placed before me a piece of bride-cake, and two beautifully-engraved cards united with white satin ribbon, bearing the names of Mr. and Mrs. Arthur Smith. I was more gratified by this little act of courtesy for Emily's sake, as those who have temporarily fallen from a certain position in society will easily understand, than I should have been by the costliest present. The service I had rendered was purely accidental: it has nevertheless been always kindly remembered by all parties whom it so critically served.

IV

THE WIDOW

In the winter of 1833 I was hurriedly, and, as I at the time could not help thinking, precipitately despatched to Guernsey, one of the largest of the islands which dot the British Channel, in quest of a gentleman of, till then, high character on the Stock Exchange, who, it was alleged, had absconded with a very large sum of money intrusted to him for investment by a baronet of considerable influence in official quarters. From certain circumstances, it was surmised that Guernsey would be his first hiding-place, and I was obliged to post all the way to Weymouth in order to save the mail packet, which left that place on the Saturday evening, or night rather, with the Channel-Island mails. Mr.—had gone, it was conjectured, by way of Southampton. My search, promptly and zealously as I was aided by the Guernsey authorities, proving vain, I determined on going on to Jersey, when a letter arrived by post informing me that the person of whom I was in pursuit had either not intended to defraud his client, or that his heart had failed him at the threshold of crime. A few hours after I had left London he had reappeared, it seems, in his counting-house, after having a few minutes previously effected the investment of the money in accordance with his client's instructions, and was now, through his attorney, threatening the accuser and all his aiders and abettors with the agreeable processes that in England usually follow sharply at the heels of such rash and hasty proceedings.

My mission over, I proposed to retrace my steps immediately, but unfortunately found myself detained in the island for nearly a week by the hurricane-weather which suddenly set in, rendering it impossible for the mail or other steam-packets to cross the Channel during its continuance. Time limped slowly and heavily away; and frequently, in my impatience to be gone, I walked down to the bleak pier, and strained my eyes in the direction in which the steamer from Jersey *should* appear. Almost every time I did so I encountered two persons, who, I could see, were even more impatient to be gone than myself, and probably, I thought, with much more reason. They were a widow lady, not certainly more than thirty years of age, and her son, a fine curly-haired boy, about eight or nine years old, whose natural light-heartedness appeared to be checked, subdued, by the deep grief and sadness which trembled in his mother's fine expressive eyes, and shrouded her pale but handsome face. He held her by the hand; often clasping it with both his tiny ones, and looking up to her as she turned despondingly away from the vacant roadstead and raging waters, with a half-frightened, half-wondering expression of anxious love, which would frequently cause his mother to bend down, and hurriedly strive to kiss away the sorrowful alarm depicted in the child's face. These two beings strangely interested me; chiefly perhaps because, in my compelled idleness, I had little else except the obstinate and angry weather to engage my attention or occupy my thoughts. There was an unmistakable air of 'better days' about the widow—a grace of manner which her somewhat faded and unseasonable raiment rendered but the more striking and apparent. Her countenance, one perceived at the first glance, was of remarkable comeliness; and upon one occasion that I had an opportunity of observing it, I was satisfied that, under happier influences than now appeared to overshadow her, those pale interesting features would light up into beauty as brilliant as it was refined and intellectual.

This introduces another walking mystery, which, for want of something better to do, I was conjuring out of my fellow-watchers on the pier. He was a stoutish, strongly-set man of forty years of age, perhaps scarcely so much, showily dressed in new glossy clothes; French-varnished boots, thin-soled enough, winter as it was, for a drawing-room; hat of the latest *gent* fashion; a variegated satin cravat, fastened by two enormous-headed gold pins, connected with a chain; and a heavy gold chain fastened from his watch waistcoat-pocket over his neck. The complexion of his face was a cadaverous white, liberally sprinkled and relieved with gin and brandy blossoms, whilst the coarseness of his not overly-clean hands was with singular taste set off and displayed by some half-dozen glittering rings. I felt a growing conviction, especially on noticing a sudden change in the usual cunning, impudent, leering expression of his eyes, as he caught me looking at him with some earnestness, that I had somewhere had the honor of a previous introduction to him. That he had not been, lately at all events, used to such resplendent habiliments as he now sported, was abundantly evident from his numerous smirking self-surveys as he strutted jauntily along, and frequently stopping before shops that, having mirrors in their windows, afforded a more complete view of his charming person. This creature I was convinced was in some way or other connected, or at any rate acquainted, with the young and graceful widow. He was constantly dogging her steps; and I noticed with surprise, and some little irritation, that his vulgar bow was faintly returned by the lady as they passed each other; and that her recognition of him, slight and distant as it was, was not unfrequently accompanied by a blush, whether arising from a pleasurable emotion or the reverse, I could not for some time determine. There is a mystery about blushes, I was, and am quite aware, not easily penetrable, more especially about those of widows. I was soon enlightened upon that point. One day, when she happened to be standing alone on the pier—her little boy was gazing through a telescope I had borrowed of the landlord of the hotel where I lodged—he approached, and before she was well aware of his intention, took her hand, uttering at the same time, it seemed, some words of compliment. It was then I observed her features literally flash with a vividness of expression which revealed a beauty I had not before imagined she possessed. The fellow absolutely recoiled before the concentrated scorn which flushed her pale features, and the indignant gesture with which she withdrew her hand from the contamination of his touch. As he turned confusedly and hastily away, his eyes encountered mine, and he muttered some unintelligible sentences, during which the widow and her son left the spot.

"The lady," said I, as soon as she was out of hearing, "seems in a cold, bitter humor this morning; not unlike the weather."

"Yes, Mr. Wat—I beg pardon, Mr. What's-your name, I would say?"

"Waters, as I perceive you know quite well. My recollection of you is not so distinct. I have no remembrance of the fashionable clothes and brilliant jewellery, none whatever; but the remarkable countenance I *have* seen."

"I dare say you have, Waters," he replied, reassuming his insolent, swaggering air. "I practice at the Old Bailey; and I have several times seen you there, not, as now, in the masquerade of a gentleman, but with a number on your collar."

I was silly enough to feel annoyed for a moment at the fellow's stupid sarcasm, and turned angrily away.

"There, don't fly into a passion," continued he with an exulting chuckle. "I have no wish to be ill friends with so smart a hand as you are. What do you say to a glass or two of wine, if only to keep this confounded wind out of our stomachs? It's cheap enough here."

I hesitated a few seconds, and then said, "I have no great objection; but first, whom have I the honor of addressing?"

"Mr. Gates. William Gates, *Esquire*, attorney-at-law."

"Gates! Not the Gates, I hope, in the late Bryant affair?"

"Well—yes; but allow me to say, Waters, that the observations of the judge on that matter, and the consequent proceedings, were quite unjustifiable; and I was strongly advised to petition the House on the subject; but I forbore, perhaps unwisely."

"From consideration chiefly, I dare say, for the age and infirmities of his lordship, and his numerous family?"

"Come, come," rejoined Gates with a laugh; "don't poke fun in that way. The truth is, I get on quite as well without as with the certificate. I transact business now for Mr. Everard Preston: you understand?"

"Perfectly. I now remember where I have seen you. But how is it your dress has become so suddenly changed? A few weeks ago, it was nothing like so magnificent?"

"True, my dear boy, true: quite right. I saw you observed that. First-rate, isn't it? Every article genuine. Bond and Regent Street, I assure you," he added, scanning himself complacently over. I nodded approval, and he went on—"You see I have had a windfall; a piece of remarkable luck; and so I thought I would escape out of the dingy, smoky village, and air myself for a few days in the Channel."

"A delightful time of the year for such a purpose truly. Rather say you came to improve your acquaintance with the lady yonder, who, I dare say, will not prove ultimately inflexible?"

"Perhaps you are right—a little at least you may be, about the edges. But here we are; what do you take—port?"

"That as soon as anything else."

Mr. Gates was, as he said, constitutionally thirsty, and although it was still early in the day, drank with great relish and industry. As he grew flushed and rosy, and I therefore imagined communicative, I said, "Well, now, tell me who and what is that lady?"

The reply was a significant compound gesture, comprising a wink of his left eye and the tap of a forefinger upon the right side of his nose. I waited, but the pantomimic action remained uninterpreted by words.

"Not rich apparently?"

"Poor as Job."

"An imprudent marriage probably?"

"Guess again, and I'll take odds you'll guess wrong; but suppose, as variety is charming, we change the subject. What is your opinion now of the prospects of the ministry?"

I saw it was useless attempting to extract any information from so cunning a rascal; and hastily excusing myself, I rose, and abruptly took my leave, more and more puzzled to account for the evident connection, in some way or other, of so fair and elegant a woman with a low attorney, struck off the rolls for fraudulent misconduct, and now acting in the name of a person scarcely less disreputable than himself. On emerging from the tavern, I found that the wind had not only sensibly abated, but had become more favorable to the packet's leaving Jersey, and that early the next morning we might reasonably hope to embark for Weymouth. It turned out as we anticipated. The same boat which took me off to the roads conveyed also the widow—Mrs. Grey, I saw by the cards on her modest luggage—and her son. Gates followed a few minutes afterwards, and we were soon on our stormy voyage homewards.

The passage was a very rough, unpleasant one, and I saw little of the passengers in whom, in spite of myself, as it were, I continued to feel so strong an interest, till the steamer was moored alongside the Weymouth quay, and we stood together for a brief space, awaiting the scrutiny and questionings of the officers of the customs. I bowed adieu as I stepped from the paddle-box to the shore, and thought, with something of a feeling of regret, that in all probability I should never see either of them again. I was mistaken, for on arriving early the next morning to take possession of the outside place booked for me by the coach to London through Southampton, I found Mrs. Grey and her son already seated on the roof. Gates came hurriedly a few minutes afterwards, and ensconced himself snugly inside. The day was bitterly cold, and the widow and her somewhat delicate-looking boy were but poorly clad for such inclement weather. The coachman and myself, however, contrived to force some rough, stout cloaks upon their acceptance, which sufficed pretty well during the day; but as night came on rainy and tempestuous, as well as dark and bleak, I felt that they must be in some way or other got inside, where Gates was the only passenger. Yet so distant, so frigidly courteous was Mrs. Grey, that I was at a loss how to manage it. Gates, I saw, was enjoying himself hugely to his own satisfaction. At every stage he swallowed a large glass of brandy and water, and I observed that he cast more and more audaciously-triumphant glances towards Mrs. Grey. Once her eye, though studiously I thought averted from him, caught his, and a deep blush, in which fear, timidity, and aversion seemed strangely mingled, swept over her face. What *could* it mean? It was, however, useless to worry myself further with profitless conjectures, and I descended from the roof to hold a private parley with the coachman. A reasonable bargain was soon struck: he went to Mrs. Grey and proposed to her, as there was plenty of room to spare, that she and her son should ride inside.

"It will make no difference in the fare," he added, "and it's bitter cold out here for a lady."

"Thank you," replied the widow after a few moments' hesitation; "we shall do very well here."

I guessed the cause of her refusal, and hastened to add, "You had better, I think, accept the coachman's proposal: the night-weather will be dreadful, and even I, a man, must take refuge inside." She looked at me with a sort of grateful curiosity, and then accepted, with many thanks, the coachman's offer.

When we alighted at the Regent Circus, London, I looked anxiously but vainly round for someone in attendance to receive and greet the widow and her son. She did not seem to expect anyone, but stood gazing vacantly, yet sadly, at the noisy, glaring, hurrying scene around her, her child's hand clasped in hers with an unconsciously tightening grasp, whilst her luggage was removed from the roof of the coach. Gates stood near, as if in expectation that his services must now, however unwillingly, be accepted by Mrs. Grey. I approached her, and said somewhat hurriedly, "If, as I apprehend, madam, you are a stranger in London, and consequently in need of temporary lodgings, you will, I think, do well to apply to the person whose address I have written on this card. It is close by. He knows me, and on your mentioning my name, will treat you with every consideration. I am a police-officer; here is my address; and any assistance in my power, shall, in any case," and I glanced at Gates, "be freely rendered to you." I then hastened off, and my wife an hour afterwards was even more anxious and interested for the mysterious widow and her son than myself.

About six weeks had glided away, and the remembrance of my fellow-passengers from Guernsey was rapidly fading into indistinctness, when a visit from Roberts, to whose lodgings I had recommended Mrs. Grey, brought them once more painfully before me. That the widow was poor I was not surprised to hear; but that a person so utterly destitute of resources and friends, as she appeared from Roberts' account to be, should have sought the huge wilderness of London, seemed marvelous. Her few trinkets, and nearly all her scanty wardrobe, Roberts more than suspected were at the pawnbroker's. The rent of the lodgings had not been paid for the last month, and he believed that for some time past they had not had a sufficiency of food, and were *now* in a state of literal starvation! Still, she was cold and distant as ever, complained not, though daily becoming paler, thinner, weaker.

"Does Gates the attorney visit her?" I asked.

"No—she would not see him, but letters from him are almost daily received."

Roberts, who was a widower, wished my wife to see her: he was seriously apprehensive of some tragical result; and this, apart from considerations of humanity, could not be permitted for his own sake to occur in his house. I acquiesced; and Emily hurriedly equipped herself, and set off with Roberts to Sherrard Street, Haymarket.

On arriving at home, Roberts, to his own and my wife's astonishment, found Gates there in a state of exuberant satisfaction. He was waiting to pay any claim Roberts had upon Mrs. Grey, to whom, the ex-attorney exultingly announced, he was to be married on the following Thursday! Roberts, scarcely believing his ears, hastened up to the first floor, to ascertain if Mrs. Grey had really given authority to Gates to act for her. He tapped at the door, and a faint voice bidding him enter, he saw at once what had happened. Mrs. Grey, pale as marble, her eyes flashing with almost insane excitement, was standing by a table, upon which a large tray had been placed covered with soups, jellies, and other delicacies, evidently just brought in from a tavern, eagerly watching her son partake of the first food he had tasted for two whole days! Roberts saw clearly how it was, and stammering a foolish excuse of having tapped at the wrong door, hastened away. She had at last determined to sacrifice herself to save her child's life! Emily, as she related what she had seen and heard, wept with passionate grief, and I was scarcely less excited: the union of Mrs. Grey with such a man seemed like the profanation of a pure and holy shrine. Then Gates was, spite of his windfall, as he called it, essentially a needy man! Besides—and this was the impenetrable mystery of the affair—what inducement, what motive could induce a mercenary wretch like Gates to unite himself in marriage with poverty—with destitution? The notion of his being influenced by sentiment of any kind was, I felt, absurd. The more I reflected on the matter, the more convinced I became that there was some villainous scheme in process of accomplishment by Gates, and I determined to make at least one resolute effort to arrive at a solution of the perplexing riddle. The next day, having a few hours to spare, the thought struck me that I would call on Mrs. Grey myself. I accordingly proceeded towards her residence, and in Coventry Street happened to meet Jackson, a brother officer, who, I was aware, from a few inquiries I had previously made, knew something of Gates's past history and present position. After circumstantially relating the whole matter, I asked him if he could possibly guess what the fellow's object could be in contracting such a marriage?

"Object!" replied Jackson; "Why, money of course: what else? He has by some means become aware that the lady is entitled to property, and he is scheming to get possession of it as her husband."

"My own conviction! Yet the difficulty of getting at any proof seems insurmountable."

"Just so. And, by the way, Gates is certainly in high feather just now, however acquired. Not only himself, but Rivers his cad, clerk he calls himself, has cast his old greasy skin, and appears quite spruce and shining. And—now I remember—what did you say was the lady's name?"

"Grey."

"Grey! Ah, then I suppose it can have nothing to do with it! It was a person of the name of Welton or Skelton that called on us a month or two ago about Gates."

"What was the nature of the communication?"

"I can hardly tell you: the charge was so loosely made, and hurriedly withdrawn. Skelton—yes, it *was* Skelton—he resides in pretty good style at Knightsbridge—called and said that Gates had stolen a cheque or draft for five hundred pounds, and other articles sent through him to some house in the city, of which I think he said the principal was dead. He was advised to apply through a solicitor to a magistrate, and went away, we supposed, for that purpose; but about three hours afterwards he returned, and in a hurried, flurried sort of way said he had been mistaken, and that he withdrew every charge he had made against Mr. Gates."

"Very odd."

"Yes; but I don't see how it can be in any way connected with this Mrs. Grey's affairs. Still, do you think it would be of any use to sound Rivers? I know the fellow well, and where I should be pretty sure to find him this evening."

It was arranged he should do so, and I proceeded on to Sherrard Street. Mrs. Grey was alone in the front apartment of the ground-floor, and received me with much politeness. She had, I saw, been weeping; her eyes were swollen and bloodshot; and she was deadly pale; but I looked in vain for any indication of that utter desolation which a woman like her, condemned to such a sacrifice, might naturally be supposed to feel. I felt greatly embarrassed as to how to begin; but at length I plunged boldly into the matter; assured her she was cruelly deceived by Gates, who was in no condition to provide for her and her son in even tolerable comfort; and that I was convinced he had no other than a mercenary and detestable motive in seeking marriage with her. Mrs. Grey heard me in so totally unmoved a manner, and the feeling that I was really meddling with things that did not at all concern me, grew upon me so rapidly, as I spoke to that unanswering countenance, that by the time I had finished my eloquent harangue, I was in a perfect fever of embarrassment and confusion, and very heartily wished myself out of the place. To my further bewilderment, Mrs. Grey, when I had quite concluded, informed me—in consideration, she said, of the courtesies I had shewn her when we were fellow-travelers—that she was perfectly aware Mr. Gates' motive in marrying her was purely a mercenary one; and her own in consenting to the union, except as regarded her son, was, she admitted, scarcely better. She added—riddle upon riddles!—that she knew also that Mr. Gates was very poor—insolvent, she understood. I rose mechanically to my feet, with a confused notion swimming in my head that both of us at all events could not be in our right senses. This feeling must have been visible upon my face; for Mrs. Grey added with a half-smile, "You cannot reconcile these apparent contradictions; be patient; you will perfectly comprehend them before long. But as I wish not to stand too low in your estimation, I must tell you that Mr. Gates is to subscribe a written agreement that we separate the instant the ceremony has been performed. But for that undertaking, I would have suffered any extremity, death itself, rather than have consented to marry him!"

Still confused, stunned, as it were, by what I had heard, my hand was on the handle of the door to let myself out, when a thought arose in my mind. "Is it possible, Mrs. Grey," I said, "that you can have been deceived into a belief that such a promise, however formally set down, is of the slightest legal value?—that the law recognises, or would enforce, an instrument to render nugatory the solemn obligation you will, after signing it, make, 'to love, honor, obey, and cherish your husband?' " I had found the right chord at last. Mrs. Grey, as I spoke, became deadly pale; and had she not caught at one of the heavy chairs, she would have been unable to support herself.

"Do I understand you to say," she faintly and brokenly gasped, "that such an agreement as I have indicated, duly sealed and witnessed, could not be summarily enforced by a magistrate?"

"Certainly it could not, my dear madam, and well Gates knows it to be so; and I am greatly mistaken in the man, if, once the irrevocable ceremony over, he would not be the first to deride your credulity."

"If that be so," exclaimed the unfortunate lady with passionate despair, "I am indeed ruined—lost! Oh my darling boy, would that you and I were sleeping in your father's quiet grave!"

"Say not so," I exclaimed with emotion, for I was afflicted by her distress. "Honor me with your confidence, and all may yet be well."

After much entreaty, she despairingly complied. The substance of her story, which was broken by frequent outbursts of grief and lamentation, was as follows:—She was the only child of a London merchant—Mr. Walton we will call him—who had lived beyond his means, and failed ruinously to an immense amount. His spirits and health were broken by this event, which he survived only a few months. It happened that about the time of the bankruptcy she had become acquainted with Mr. John Grey, the only son of an eminent East India merchant, but a man of penurious disposition and habits.

"Mr. Ezekiel Grey?"

The same. They became attached to each other, deeply so; and knowing that to solicit the elder Grey's consent to their union would be tantamount to a sentence of immediate separation and estrangement, they unwisely, thoughtlessly, married, about ten months after Mr. Walton's death, without the elder Grey's knowledge. Gates, an attorney, then in apparently fair circumstances, with whom young Mr. Grey had become acquainted, and Anne Crawford, Maria Walton's servant, were the witnesses of the ceremony, which, after due publication of banns, was celebrated in St. Giles's Church. The young couple, after the marriage, lived in the strictest privacy, the wife meagrely supported by the pocket-money allowance of Mr. Ezekiel Grey to his son. Thus painfully elapsed nine years of life, when, about twelve months previous to the present time, Mr. Grey determined to send his son to Bombay, in order to the arrangement of some complicated claims on a house of agency there. It was decided that, during her husband's absence, Mrs. John Grey should reside in Guernsey, partly with a view to economy, and partly for the change of air, which it was said their son required—Mr. Gates to be the medium through which money and letters were to reach the wife Mr. Ezekiel Grey died somewhat suddenly about four months after his son's departure from England, and Mrs. Grey had been in momentary expectation of the arrival of her husband, when Gates came to Guernsey, and announced his death at Bombay, just as he was preparing for the voyage to England! The manner of Gates was strange and insolent; and he plainly intimated that without his assistance both herself and child would be beggars; and that assistance he audaciously declared he would only afford at the price of marriage! Mrs. Grey, overwhelmed with grief for the loss of a husband by whom she had been as constantly as tenderly beloved, and dizzy with ill-defined apprehension, started at once for London. A copy of the will of Mr. Ezekiel Grey had been procured, by which in effect he devised all his estate, real and personal, to his son; but in the event of Mr. John Grey dying unmarried, or without lawful issue, it went to his wife's nephew Mr. Skelton—

"Skelton of Knightsbridge?"

Yes: in case of Mr. John Grey marrying, Skelton was to be paid an immediate legacy of five thousand pounds. So far, then, us fortune went, the widow and her son seemed amply provided for. So Mrs. Grey thought till she had another interview with Gates, who unblushingly told her that unless she consented to marry him, he would not prove, though he had abundant means of doing so, that the person she had married at St. Giles's Church was the son of Ezekiel Grey, the eminent merchant! "The name," said the scoundrel, "will not help you; there are plenty of John Greys on that register; and as for Anne Crawford, she has been long since dead." Mrs. Grey next called on Mr. Skelton, and was turned out of the house as an impostor; and finally, having parted with everything upon which she could raise money, and Gates reiterating his offer, or demand rather, accompanied by the proposal of an immediate separation, she had consented.

"Courage, madam!" I exclaimed at the end of her narrative, of which the above is the substance, and I spoke in a tone of joyous confidence, which, more than my words, reassured her: "I already see glimpses of daylight through this maze of villainy. Gates has played a desperate game certainly, but one which we shall, you may rely on it, easily baffle." A knock at the door interrupted me. I peered through the blind, and saw that it was Gates: "Silence—secrecy!" I emphatically urged in a low voice, and with my finger on my lip, and left the room before the street-door could be answered; and by my friend Roberts' contrivance, I was in a few minutes afterwards in the street, all the time unobserved by the intruder.

The next day early Jackson called on me. He had seen Rivers, but he seemed to know nothing, except, indeed, that it was quite true Gates had received a five-hundred pound draft from a house in India, which he, Rivers, had got notes for at the Bank of England. There were also in the same parcel a gold watch, he knew, and some jewelry, but from whom it all came, he, Rivers, was ignorant. Nothing but that had Jackson been able to discover.

"Call you that nothing?" said I, starting up, and hastily swallowing my last cup of coffee. "It is enough, at all events, to transport William Gates, Esquire!"

I had to wait that morning on especial business on the commissioner; and after the business upon which I had been summoned had been despatched, I related the case of Grey *versus* Gates as clearly and succinctly as I could. He listened with great attention, and in about a quarter of an hour I left him with as clear and unmistakable a path before me as it was possible to desire. I was passing down the stairs when I was resummoned.

"You quite understand, Waters, that Skelton is not for a moment to be lost sight of till his deposition has been taken?"

"Certainly, sir."

"That will do then."

Arrived at home, I despatched my wife in a cab for Mrs. Grey. She soon arrived, and as much as was necessary of our plan I confided to her. Mr. Gates had pressed her earnestly that the ceremony should take place on the following morning. By my directions she now wrote, although her trembling fingers made an almost unintelligible scrawl of it, that as it *was* to be, she agreed to his proposition, and should expect him at nine o'clock.

Two hours afterwards, Jackson and I, having previously watched the gentleman home, knocked at Mr. Skelton's house, Knightsbridge, and requested to see him. At the very moment, he came out of a side-room, and was proceeding upstairs.

"Mr. Skelton," said I, stepping forward, "I must have a private interview with you!" He was in an instant as pale as a corpse, and shaking like an aspen—such miserable cowards does an evil conscience make men—and totteringly led the way, without speaking, to a small library.

"You know me, Mr. Skelton, and doubtless guess the meaning of my errand?"

He stammered out a denial, which his trembling accents and ashy countenance emphatically denied.

"You and Gates of the Minories are engaged in a felonious conspiracy to deprive Mrs. Grey and her infant son of their property and inheritance!"

Had he been struck by a cannon-shot, he could not have fallen more suddenly and helplessly upon the couch close to which he was standing.

"My God!" he exclaimed, "What is this?"

Perceiving he was quite sufficiently frightened, I said, "There is no wish on Mrs. Grey's part to treat you harshly, so that you aid us in convicting Gates. For this purpose, you must at once give the numbers of the notes Gates obtained for the cheque, and also the letter in which the agent at Bombay announced its transmission through Gates."

"Yes—yes!" he stammered, rising, and going to a secrétaire. "There is the letter."

I glanced over it. "I am glad to find," I said, "that you did not know by this letter that the money and other articles here enumerated had been sent by the dying husband to his wife through Gates."

"I most solemnly assure you I did not!" he eagerly replied, "until—until—"

"Mr. Gates informed you of it, and seduced you to conspire with him. He has been playing a double game. Whilst amusing you, he purposes marrying Mrs. Grey tomorrow morning!"

"Is it possible? But I suspected—"

"No doubt. In the meantime, you will, if you please, accompany us. There is every desire to spare you," I added, perceiving him hesitate; "but our orders are peremptory." With a very ill grace Mr. Skelton complied, and we were rapidly driven off.

The next morning Jackson, Skelton, and myself, were in Sherrard Street before daybreak. Mrs. Grey was already up and at eight o'clock we sat down with her and her son to an excellent breakfast. She was charmingly dressed in the wedding garments which Gates had purchased with her stolen money, and I almost felt it in my heart to pity the unfortunate bridegroom, rascal as he was, about to be suddenly disappointed of such a bride and such a fortune! It was very necessary that she should be so arrayed, for, as we had thought quite probable, Rivers called a few minutes past eight with a present of jewelry, and the bride's appearance must have completely disarmed any suspicion which his master might have entertained.

Breakfast was over: Mrs. Grey, with her son, was seated on a couch in the front room, and we were lying *perdu* in the next apartment, separated only by folding-doors, when a coach drew up before the house; a bridegroom's impatient summons thundered at the door; and presently forth stepped Mr. Gates, resplendently attired, followed by his man Rivers, who was, it appeared, to give the bride away. Mr. Gates entered the presence of beautiful Mrs. Grey in immense triumph. He approached her with the profoundest gallantry; and was about to speak, when Jackson and I, who had been sedulously watching through the chink of the slightly-opened doors, advanced into the room, followed by Mr. Skelton. His attitude of terror and surprise was one of the most natural performances I ever witnessed. He turned instinctively as if to flee. My grasp was in an instant on his collar.

"The game is up, my good Mr. Gates: I arrest you for felony!"

"Felony!"

"Ay, truly. For stealing a gold watch, diamond pin, and a cheque for five hundred pounds, sent through you to this lady."

All his insolent swagger vanished in an instant, and the abject scoundrel threw himself at Mrs. Grey's feet, and absolutely howled for mercy.

"I will do anything," he gaspingly protested; "anything you require, so that you will save me from these men!"

"Where is Crawford?" I asked, desirous of taking immediate, but not, I hope, unfair advantage of the rascal's terror; "She who witnessed this lady's marriage?"

"At Leamington, Warwickshire," he replied.

"Very good. Now, Mrs. Grey, if you will leave us, I shall be obliged. We must search this gentleman, and perhaps—". She vanished in an instant: her gentleness of disposition was, I saw, rapidly mastering all resentment. I carried the watch we took out of Gates's pocket to her, and she instantly recognised it to be her husband's. A fifty and a twenty-pound bank-note, corresponding to the numbers on our list, we extricated from the disappointed bridegroom's pocket-book. "And now, sir, if you please," said I, "we will adjourn to your lodgings." A savage scowl was his only reply, not at all discomposing to me, and we were soon busy ransacking his hidden hoards. We found several other articles sent by Mr. John Grey to his wife, and three letters to her, which, as corroborative evidence, would leave no doubt as to *who* her husband was. Our next visit was to a police court, where Mr. William Gates was fully committed for trial. He was in due time convicted of stealing the watch, and sentenced to transportation for seven years.

Mrs. Grey's marriage, and her son's consequent succession to the deceased merchant's wealth, were not disputed. She has never remarried, and lives now in beneficent affluence in one of the new squares beyond the Edgeware Road with her son, who though now six-and-twenty years of age, or thereabouts, is still unappropriated; but "the good time is coming," so at least hinted a few days ago the fashionable "Morning Post."

V

THE TWINS

The records of police courts afford but imperfect evidence of the business really effected by the officers attached to them. The machinery of English criminal law is, in practice, so subservient to the caprice of individual prosecutors, that instances are constantly occurring in which flagrant violations of natural justice are, from various motives, corrupt and otherwise, withdrawn not only from the cognizance of judicial authority, but from the reprobation of public opinion. Compromises are usually effected between the apprehension of the inculpated parties and the public examination before a magistrate. The object of prosecution has been perhaps obtained by the preliminary step of arrest, or a criminal understanding has been arrived at in the interval; and it is then found utterly hopeless to proceed, however manifest may have appeared the guilt of the prisoner. If you adopt the expedient of compelling the attendance of the accused, it is, in nine cases out of ten, mere time and trouble thrown away. The utter forgetfulness of memory, the loose recollection of facts so vividly remembered but a few hours before, the delicately-scrupulous hesitation to depose confidently to the clearest verities evinced by the reluctant prosecutor, render a conviction almost impossible; so that, except in cases of flagrant and startling crimes, which are of course earnestly prosecuted by the crown lawyers, offences against "our sovereign lady the Queen, her crown, and dignity," as criminal indictments run, if no aggrieved subject voluntarily appears to challenge justice in behalf of his liege lady, remain unchastised, and not unfrequently unexposed. From several examples of this prevalent abuse which have come within my own knowledge, I select the following instance, merely changing the names of the parties:

My services, the superintendent late one afternoon informed me, were required in a perplexed and entangled affair, which would probably occupy me for some time, as orders had been given to investigate the matter thoroughly. "There," he added, "is a Mr. Repton, a highly-respectable country solicitor's card. He is from Lancashire, and is staying at Webb's Hotel, Piccadilly. You are to see him at once. He will put you in possession of all the facts—surmises rather, I should say, for the facts, to my apprehension, are scant enough—connected with the case, and you will then use all possible diligence to ascertain first if the alleged crime has been really committed, and if so, of course to bring the criminal or criminals to justice."

I found Mr. Repton, a stout, bald-headed, gentlemanly person, apparently about sixty years of age, just in the act of going out. "I have a pressing engagement for this evening, Mr. Waters," said he, after glancing at the introductory note I had brought, "and cannot possibly go into the business with the attention and minuteness it requires till the morning. But I'll tell you what: one of the parties concerned, and the one, too, with whom you will have especially to deal, is, I know, to be at Covent Garden Theatre this evening. It is of course necessary that you should be thoroughly acquainted with his person; and if you will go with me in the cab that is waiting outside, I will step with you into the theatre, and point him out." I assented; and on entering Covent Garden pit, Mr. Repton, who kept behind me, to avoid observation, directed my attention to a group of persons occupying the front seats of the third box in the lower tier from the stage, on the right-hand side of the house. They were—a gentleman of about thirty years of age; his wife, a very elegant person, a year or two younger; and three children, the eldest of whom, a boy, could not have been more than six or seven years old. This done, Mr. Repton left the theatre, and about two hours afterwards I did the same.

The next morning I breakfasted with the Lancashire solicitor by appointment. As soon as it was concluded, business was at once entered upon.

"You closely observed Sir Charles Malvern yesterday evening, I presume?" said Mr. Repton.

"I paid great attention to the gentleman you pointed out to me," I answered, "if he be Sir Charles Malvern."

"He is, or at least—But of that presently. First let me inform you that Malvern, a few months ago, was a beggard gamester, or nearly so, to speak with precision. He is now in good bodily health, has a charming wife, and a family to whom he is much attached, an unencumbered estate of about twelve thousand a year, and has not gambled since he came into possession of the property. This premised, is there, think you, anything remarkable in Sir Charles's demeanor?"

"Singularly so. My impression was, that he was laboring under a terrible depression of spirits, caused, I imagined, by pecuniary difficulties. His manner was restless, abstracted. He paid no attention whatever to anything going on on the stage, except when his wife or one of the children especially challenged his attention; and then, a brief answer returned, he relapsed into the same restless unobservance as before. He is very nervous too. The box door was suddenly opened once or twice, and I noticed his sudden start each time."

"You have exactly described him. Well, that perturbed, unquiet feverishness of manner has constantly distinguished him since his accession to the Redwood estates, and only since then. It strengthens me and one or two others in possibly an unfounded suspicion, which—But I had better, if I wish to render myself intelligible, relate matters in due sequence.

"Sir Thomas Redwood, whose property in Lancashire is chiefly in the neighborhood of Liverpool, met his death, as did his only son Mr. Archibald Redwood, about six months ago, in a very sudden and shocking manner. They were out trying a splendid mare for the first time in harness, which Sir Thomas had lately purchased at a very high price. Two grooms on horseback were in attendance, to render assistance if required, for the animal was a very powerful, high-spirited one. All went very well till they arrived in front of Mr. Meredith's place, Oak Villa. This gentleman has a passion for firing off a number of brass cannon on the anniversary of such events as he deems worthy of the honor. This happened, unfortunately, to be one of Mr. Meredith's gunpowder days; and as Sir Thomas and his son were passing, a stream of light flashed directly in the eyes of the mare, followed by the roar of artillery, at no more than about ten paces off. The terrified animal became instantly unmanageable, got the bit between her teeth, and darted off at the wildest speed. The road is a curved and rugged one; and after tearing along for about half a mile, the off-wheel of the gig came, at an abrupt turn, full against a milestone. The tremendous shock hurled the two unfortunate gentlemen upon the road with frightful violence, tore the vehicle almost completely assunder, and so injured the mare, that she died the next day. The alarmed grooms, who had not only been unable to render assistance, but even to keep up with the terrified mare, found Mr. Archibald Redwood quite dead. The spine had been broken close to the nape of the neck: his head, in fact, was doubled up, so to speak, under the body. Sir Thomas still breathed, and was conveyed to Redwood Manor House. Surgical assistance was promptly obtained; but the internal injuries were so great, that the excellent old gentleman expired in a few hours after he had reached his home. I was hastily sent for; and when I arrived, Sir Thomas was still fully conscious. He imparted to me matters of great moment, to which he requested I would direct, after his decease, my best care and attention. His son, I was aware, had but just returned from a tour on the continent, where he had been absent for nearly a twelvemonth; but I was not aware, neither was his father till the day before his death, that Mr. Archibald Redwood had not only secretly espoused a Miss Ashton—of a reduced family, but belonging to our best gentry—but had returned home, not solely for the purpose of soliciting Sir Thomas's forgiveness of his unauthorized espousals, but that the probable heir of Redwood might be born within the walls of the ancient manor house. After the first burst of passion and surprise, Sir Thomas, one of the best-hearted men in the universe, cordially forgave his son's disobedience—partly, and quite rightly, imputing it to his own foolish urgency in pressing a union with one of the Lacy family, with which the baronet was very intimate, and whose estate adjoined his.

"Well, this lady, now a widow, had been left by her husband at Chester, whilst he came on to seek an explanation with his father. Mr. Archibald Redwood was to have set out the next morning in one of Sir Thomas's carriages to bring home his wife; and the baronet, with his dying breath, bade me assure her of his entire forgiveness, and his earnest hope and trust that through her offspring the race of the Redwoods might be continued in a direct line. The family estates, I should tell you, being strictly entailed on heirs-male, devolved, if no son of Mr. Archibald Redwood should bar his claim, upon Charles Malvern, the son of a cousin of the late Sir Thomas Redwood. The baronet had always felt partially towards Malvern, and had assisted him pecuniarily a hundred times. Sir Thomas also directed me to draw as quickly as I could a short will, bequeathing Mr. Charles Malvern twenty thousand pounds out of the personals. I wrote as expeditiously as I could, but by the time the paper was ready for his signature, Sir Thomas was no longer conscious. I placed the pen in his hand, and I fancied he understood the purpose, for his fingers closed faintly upon it; but the power to guide was utterly gone, and only a slight, scrambling stroke marked the paper as the pen slid across it in the direction of the falling arm.

"Mr. Malvern arrived at the manor-house about an hour after Sir Thomas breathed his last. It was clearly apparent through all his sorrow, partly real, I have no doubt, as well as partly assumed, that joy, the joy of riches, splendor, station, was dancing at his heart, and, spite of all his efforts to subdue or conceal it, sparkling in his eye. I briefly, but gently as I could, acquainted him with the true position of affairs. The revulsion of feeling which ensued entirely unmanned him; and it was not till an hour afterwards that he recovered his self-possession sufficiently to converse reasonably and coolly upon his position. At last he became apparently reconciled to the sudden overclouding of his imaginatively-brilliant prospects, and it was agreed that as he was a relative of the widow, he should at once set off to break the sad news to her. Well, a few days after his departure, I received a letter from him, stating that Lady Redwood—I don't think, by the way, that, as her husband died before succeeding to the baronetcy, she is entitled to that appellation of honor; we, however, call her so out of courtesy—that Lady Redwood, though prematurely confined in consequence of the intelligence of her husband's untimely death, had given birth to a female child, and that both mother and daughter were as well as could be expected. This, you will agree, seemed perfectly satisfactory?"

"Entirely so."

"So I thought. Mr. Malvern was now unquestionably, whether Sir Charles Malvern or not, the proprietor of the Redwood estates, burthened as with a charge, in accordance with the conditions of the entails, of a thousand pounds life annuity to the late Mr. Redwood's infant daughter.

"Sir Charles returned to Redwood manor-house, where his wife and family soon afterwards arrived. Lady Redwood had been joined, I understood, by her mother, Mrs. Ashton, and would, when able to undertake the journey, return to her maternal home. It was about two months after Sir Thomas Redwood's death that I determined to pay Lady Redwood a visit, in order to the winding up of the personal estate, which it was desirable to accomplish as speedily as possible; and then a new and terrible light flashed upon me."

"What, in heaven's name!" I exclaimed, for the first time breaking silence—"What could there be to reveal?"

"Only," rejoined Mr. Repton, "that, ill, delirious, as Lady Redwood admitted herself to have been, it was her intimate, unconquerable conviction *that she had given birth to twins*!"

"Good God! And you suspect—"

"We don't know what to suspect. Should the lady's confident belief be correct, the missing child might have been a boy. You understand?"

"I do. But is there any tangible evidence to justify this horrible suspicion?"

"Yes; the surgeon-apothecary and his wife, a Mr. and Mrs. Williams, who attended lady Redwood, have suddenly disappeared from Chester, and, from no explainable motive, having left or abandoned a fair business there."

"That has certainly an ugly look."

"True; and a few days ago I received information that Williams has been seen in Birmingham. He was well dressed, and not apparently in any business."

"There certainly appears some ground for suspicion. What plan of operations do you propose?"

"That," replied Mr. Repton, "I must leave to your more practised sagacity. I can only undertake that no means shall be lacking that may be required."

"It will be better, perhaps," I suggested, after an interval of reflection, "that I should proceed to Birmingham at once. You have of course an accurate description of the persons of Williams and his wife ready?"

"I have; and very accurate pen-and-ink sketches I am told they are. Besides these, I have also here," continued Mr. Repton, taking from his pocket-book a sheet of carefully-folded satin paper, "A full description of the female baby, drawn up by its mother, under the impression that twins always—I believe they generally do—closely resemble each other. 'Light hair, blue eyes, dimpled chin'—and so on. The lady—a very charming person, I assure you, and meek and gentle as a fawn—is chiefly anxious to recover her child. You and I, should our suspicions be confirmed, have other duties to perform."

This was pretty nearly all that passed, and the next day I was in Birmingham.

The search, as I was compelled to be very cautious in my inquiries, was tedious, but finally successful. Mr. and Mrs. Williams I discovered living in a pretty house, with neat grounds attached, about two miles out of Birmingham, on the coach road to Wolverhampton. Their assumed name was Burridge, and I ascertained from the servant-girl, who fetched their dinner and supper, beer, and occasionally wine and spirits, from a neighboring tavern, that they had one child, a boy, a few months old, of whom neither father nor mother seemed very fond. By dint of much perseverance, I at length got upon pretty familiar terms with Mr. Burridge, *alias* Williams. He spent his evenings regularly in a tavern; but with all the painstaking, indefatigable ingenuity I employed, the chief knowledge I acquired, during three weeks of assiduous endeavor, was, that my friend Burridge intended, immediately after a visit which he expected shortly to receive from a rich and influential relative in London, to emigrate to America, at all events to go abroad. This was, however, very significant and precious information; and very rarely, indeed, was he, after I had obtained it, out of my sight or observation. At length perseverance obtained its reward. One morning I discerned my friend, much more sprucely attired than ordinarily, make his way to the railway station, and there question with eager looks every passenger that alighted from the first-class carriages. At last a gentleman, whom I instantly recognized, spite of his shawl and other wrappings, arrived by the express train from London. Williams instantly accosted him, a cab was called, and away they drove. I followed in another, and saw them both alight at a hotel in New Street. I also alighted, and was mentally debating how to proceed, when Williams came out of the tavern, and proceeded in the direction of his home. I followed, overtook him, and soon contrived to ascertain that he and his wife had important business to transact in Birmingham the next morning, which would render it impossible he should meet me, as I proposed, till two or three o'clock in the afternoon at the earliest; and the next morning, my esteemed friend informed me, he would leave the place, probably forever. An hour after this interesting conversation, I, accompanied by the chief of the Birmingham police, was closeted with the landlord of the hotel in New Street, a highly-respectable person, who promised us every assistance in his power. Sir Charles Malvern had, we found, engaged a private room for the transaction of important business with some persons he expected in the morning, and our plans were soon fully matured and agreed upon.

I slept little that night, and immediately after breakfast hastened with my Birmingham colleague to the hotel. The apartment assigned for Sir Charles Malvern's use had been a bedroom, and a large wardrobe, with a high wing at each end, still remained in it. We tried if it would hold us, and with very little stooping and squeezing, found it would do very well. The landlord soon gave us the signal to be on the alert, and in we jammed ourselves, locking the wing-doors on the inside. A minute or two afterwards, Sir Charles, and Mr. and Mrs. Williams entered, and, paper, pens, and ink having been brought, business commenced in right earnest. Their conversation it is needless to detail. It will suffice to observe that it was manifest Sir Charles, by a heavy bribe, had induced the accoucheur and his wife to conceal the birth of the male child, which, as I suspected, was that which Williams and his spouse were bringing up as their own. I must do the fictitious baronet the justice to say that he had from the first the utmost anxiety that no harm should befall the infant. Mr. Malvern's nervous dread lest his confederates should be questioned, had induced their hurried departure from Chester, and it now appeared that he had become aware of the suspicions entertained by Mr. Repton, and could not rest till the Williams's and the child were safe out of the country. It was now insisted, by the woman more especially, that the agreement for the large annual payment to be made by Sir Charles should be fairly written out and signed in plain "black and white," to use Mrs. Williams' expression, in order that no future misunderstandings might arise. This, Mr. Malvern strongly objected to; but finding the woman would accept of no other terms, he sullenly complied, and at the same time reiterated, that if any harm should befall the boy—to whom he intended, he said, to leave a handsome fortune—he would cease, regardless of consequences to himself, to pay the Williams's a single shilling.

A silence of several minutes followed, broken only by the scratching of the pen on the paper. The time to me seemed an age, squeezed, crooked, stifled as I was in that narrow box, and so I afterwards learned it did to my fellow-sufferer. At length Mr. Malvern said, in the same cautious whisper in which they had all hitherto spoken, "This will do, I think;" and read what he had written. Mr. and Mrs. Williams signified their approval; and as matters were now fully ripe, I gently turned the key, and very softly pushed open the door. The backs of the amiable trio were towards me, and as my boots were off, and the apartment was thickly carpeted, I approached unperceived, and to the inexpressible horror and astonishment of the parties concerned, whose heads were bent eagerly over the important document, a hand, which belonged to neither of them, was thrust silently but swiftly forward, and grasped the precious instrument. A fierce exclamation from Mr. Malvern as he started from his seat, and a convulsive scream from Mrs. Williams as she fell back in hers, followed; and to add to the animation of the tableau, my friend in the opposite wing emerged at the same moment from his hiding-place.

Mr. Malvern comprehended at a glance the situation of affairs, and made a furious dash at the paper. I was quicker as well as stronger than he, and he failed in his object. Resistance was of course out of the question; and in less than two hours we were speeding on the rail towards London, accompanied by the child, whom we entrusted to Williams' servant-maid.

Mrs. Repton was still in town, and Mrs. Ashton, Lady Redwood, and her unmarried sister, in their impatience of intelligence, had arrived several days before. I had the pleasure of accompanying Mrs. Repton with the child and his temporary nurse to Osborne's Hotel in the Adelphi; and I really at first feared for the excited mother's reason, or that she would do the infant a mischief, so tumultuous, so frenzied, was her rapturous joy at the recovery of her lost treasure. When placed in the cot beside the female infant, the resemblance of the one to the other was certainly almost perfect. I never saw before nor since so complete a likeness. This was enough for the mother; but, fortunately, we had much more satisfactory evidence, legally viewed, to establish the identity of the child in a court of law, should the necessity arise for doing so.

Here, as far as I am concerned, all positive knowledge of this curious piece of family history ends. Of subsequent transactions between the parties I had no personal cognizance. I only know there was a failure of justice, and I can pretty well guess from what motives. The parties I arrested in Birmingham were kept in strict custody for several days; but no inducement, no threats, could induce the institutors of the inquiry to appear against the detected criminals.

Mrs. and Miss Ashton, Lady Redwood and her children, left town the next day but one, for Redwood Manor; and Mr. Repton coolly told the angry superintendent that "he had no instructions to prosecute." He, too, was speedily off, and the prisoners were necessarily discharged out of custody.

I saw about three weeks afterwards in a morning paper that Mr. Malvern, "whom the birth of a posthumous heir in a direct line had necessarily deprived of all chance of succession to the Redwood estates, and the baronetcy, which the newspapers had so absurdly conferred on him, was, with his amiable lady and family, about to leave England for Italy, where they intended to remain some time." The expressed, but uncompleted will of the deceased baronet, Sir Thomas Redwood, had been, it was further stated, carried into effect, and the legacy intended for Mr. Malvern paid over to him. The Williams's never, to my knowledge, attained to the dignity of a notice in the newspapers; but I believe they pursued their original intention of passing over to America.

Thus not only "Offence's gilded hand," but some of the best feelings of our nature, not unfrequently, "shove by Justice," and place a concealing gloss over deeds which, in other circumstances, would have infallibly consigned the perpetrators to a prison, or perhaps the hulks. Whether, however, any enactment could effectually grapple with an abuse which springs from motives so natural and amiable, is a question which I must leave to wiser heads than mine to discuss and determine.

VI

THE PURSUIT

The reader need scarcely be told that albeit police-officers like other men, chiefly delight to recount their *successful* exploits, they do, nevertheless, experience numerous and vexatious failures and disappointments. One especially I remember, of which the irritating recollection did not pass away for many weeks. I had been for some time in pursuit of a rather eminent rascal, though one young in years, and by marriage respectably connected, who, by an infamous abuse of the trust reposed in him by the highly-respectable firm who employed him, had contrived to possess himself of a large sum of money, with which, or at least with the portion of it falling to his share—for we discovered that he had been for some time connected with a gang of first-rate swindlers—he hoped to escape to America. The chase was hot after him; and spite of all his doublings and turnings, and the false scents adroitly thrown out by his confederates with the view to favor his escape, I at last fairly ran him to earth at Plymouth, though in what precise spot of it he burrowed I could not for the moment ascertain. Neither was I well acquainted with his features; but in the description of his person furnished me there were certain indelible marks enumerated which, upon strict examination, could not fail to determine his identity. He purposed, I ascertained, to attempt leaving England in a barque bound for New York, which was to sail from Plymouth on the day after I arrived there. Of this I was fully satisfied, and I determined to capture him on board. Accordingly, about half an hour before the ship was to sail, and after all the passengers had embarked, two of the local officers and I got into a boat which I had some time previously engaged to be in readiness, and put off to the vessel. The wind was decidedly fair for the emigrant ship; and so stiffly did it blow from the north-east, that four hands, I was informed, were required, not indeed to convey us swiftly out, but to pull the boat back against the wind, and the strong tide which would be running outside the breakwater. The sea dashed smartly at times over the boat, and the men pulled their sou'-wester caps well over their eyes, to shield themselves from the blinding spray. We were speedily on board; and the captain, although much annoyed at the delay, paraded his motley passengers as well as crew before us; but to my extreme surprise our bird was not amongst them! Every possible and impossible hiding-place was thoroughly but vainly searched; and we were at length compelled to a reluctant admission that the gentleman we were in quest of, had not yet honored the captain of the *Columbia* with his patronage.

We sullenly returned into the boat; and the instant we did so, the anchor, already atrip, was brought home; the ship's bows fell rapidly off; her crowded canvass dilated and swelled in the spanking breeze, and she sprang swiftly off upon her course. It was a pretty and somewhat exciting spectacle; and I and my companions continued to watch the smartly-handled vessel with much interest till a point of land hid her from our view. We then turned our faces towards Plymouth, from which, I was surprised to find, we were apparently as distant as ever. "The tide, let alone the wind, is dead against us!" growled the master of the boat, who was now pulling the near oar, in reply to a remark from one of the Plymouth officers. This man had steered on going out. A quick suspicion flashed across me. "Where is the other boatman who came out with us?" I sharply demanded. The old seaman, instead of replying, turned himself half round towards the weather-bow oar, exclaiming, "Easy, Billy—easy; let her nose lay a little closer to the wind!" This, I readily saw, was done to conceal a momentary confusion, arising from the suddenness of my question—a very slight one by the by, for the fellow was an old man-of-war's man, with a face hardened and bronzed by service, weather, grog, and tobacco smoke. I repeated the question in a more peremptory tone. The veteran first deliberately squirted a mouthful of tobacco juice over the side, and then with an expression of his cast-iron phiz, which it is impossible by words to convey a distinct idea of, so compounded was it of diabolical squint, lamb-like simplicity, and impudent cunning, replied, "That wor a passenger to Yankee Land—a goin' there, I'm purty suspicious, for the benefit of his health." I looked at the Plymouth officers, and they at me. The impudent ingenuity of the trick that had been played us seemed scarcely credible. "He—he—ho—ho!" rumbled out of the tobacco-stifled throat of the old rogue, "If he wor somebody you wanted, it wor uncommon well done. Didn't you obsarve him jump into the main chains of the barkey jist as you wor leavin' on her, and cast us off a minute afterwards? He perfarred stoppin' with us whilst you wor rummagin' the hooker—he—he—ho—ho!"

It was useless bandying words with the fellow; and though I felt desperately savage, I had sense enough to hold my tongue. "Pull smartly," said one of the Plymouth officers; "a shot will bring her too yet."

"Why, ay," rejoined the imperturbable seaman; "it mout, if you could get speech of the admiral in time; but I'm thinkin' we shall be a good while yet pullin' in against this choppin' wind and head sea."

And sure enough they were! More than another hour, by some boatman-craft unexplainable by me, for the sailors apparently rowed with all their might, were we in reaching the landing-place; and by that time all chance of compelling the return of the *Columbia* was long past.

It would be, I knew, impossible to *prove* complicity on the part of the owner of the boat with the escaped felon, and I preferred to digest the venom of my spleen in silence, rather than by a useless display of it to add to the chuckling delight of the old rascal of a boatman.

We had passed some distance along the quay when one of the local officers, addressing a youngish sailor, who, with folded arms and a short pipe in his mouth was standing in philosophical contemplation of the sea and weather, said, "I suppose there is no chance of the emigrant ship that sailed a while ago putting in at any other port along the coast?"

The man took the pipe from his mouth, regarded the questioner for a few moments with an expression of contemptuous curiosity anything but flattering to its object, and bawled out, addressing himself to a weather-beaten seaman a few yards off, "I say, Tom Davis, here's a Blue Bottle as wants to know the name and bearins of the port off the Land's End which the barkey that sailed awhile agone for Ameriker with a north-easter kicking her endways is likely to bring up in: I'm not acquainted with it myself or else I'd tell the gentleman."

The laugh from two or three bystanders which followed this sally greatly irritated the officer, and he would have indulged in an angry reply had not his more prudent comrade taken him by the arm and urged him away.

"Ay, ay," said the veteran addressed as Tom Davis, as we were passing him, "Jim there has always got plenty of jawing tackle aboard; but, Lord love ye, he's a poor dumb cretur at understanding the signs of the weather! He's talkin' about north-easters, and don't see that the wind's beginning to chop about like a bumbo at woman with a dozen customers round her. It's my opinion, and Tom Davis ought by this time to be summut of a judge, that, instead of a north-easter, it's a precious sight more likely to be blowing a sou'-wester before two hours are past, and a sneezer too; and then the *Columby*, if she ha'nt made a good offin', which she is not likely to have done, will be back again in a brace of shakes."

"Do you think it probable," I eagerly asked, "that the *Columbia* will be obliged to put back into Plymouth?"

"I don't know about *probable*. It's not so sure as death or quarter-day, but it's upon the cards for all that."

"Will it be early in the night, think you, that she will run in, if at all?"

"Ah! there now you wants to know too much;" said the old seaman turning on his heel. "All I can say is, that if you find in an hour or so's time that the wind has chopped round to the sou'-west, or within a p'int or two, and that it's blowin' the buttons off your coat one after another, the *Columby*, if she's lucky, wont be far off."

The half-bantering prediction of the old seaman was confirmed by others whom we consulted, and measures for preventing our quarry from landing, and again giving us the slip, were at once discussed and resolved upon. We then separated, and I proceeded to the tavern at which I had put up to get some dinner. I had not gone far when my eye fell upon two persons whose presence there surprised as well as somewhat grieved me. One was the young wife of the criminal on board the *Columbia*. I had seen her once in London, and I knew, as before intimated, that she was of respectable parentage. There was no exultation in her countenance. She had no doubt followed or accompanied her husband to Plymouth for the purpose of furthering his escape, and now feared that the capricious elements would render all the ingenuity and boldness that had been brought into play vain and profitless.

She was a mild-looking, pretty woman—very much so, I doubt not, till trouble fell upon her, and wonderfully resembled the female in the "Momentous Question;" so remarkably indeed, that when, years afterwards, I first saw that print, I felt an instantaneous conviction that I had somewhere met with the original of the portrait; and after much puzzlement of brain remembered when and where. The resemblance was doubtless purely accidental; but it was not the less extraordinary and complete. She was accompanied by a gray-haired man of grave, respectable exterior, whom I at once concluded to be her father. As I passed close by them, he appeared about to address me, and I half-paused to hear what he had to say; but his partly-formed purpose was not persisted in, and I proceeded on my way.

After dining, I returned to the quay. The wind, as foretold, was blowing directly from the south-west; and during the short pace of time I had been absent, had increased to a tempest. The wild sea was dashing with terrific violence against the breakwater, discernible only in the fast-darkening night by a line of white tumultuous foam and spray, which leaped and hissed against and over it.

"A dirty night coming on," said a subaltern officer of the port whom I had previously spoken with; "the *Columbia* will, I think, be pretty sure to run in with the tide."

"When do you say is the very earliest time she may be expected?"

"Well, in my opinion, judging from where she was when I was on the look-out a quarter of an hour agone, not under three hours. Let me see. It's now just upon the stroke of five about eight o'clock, I should say, she will be here; certainly not before, perhaps much later; and if the captain is very obstinate, and prefers incurring a rather serious risk to returning, it may be of course not at all."

I thanked him, and as remaining on the bleak quay till eight o'clock or thereabout was as useless as unpleasant, I retraced my steps towards the Royal George Tavern; calling in my way on the Plymouth officers, and arranging that one of them should relieve me at ten o'clock; it having been previously agreed that we should keep an alternate watch during the night of two hours each. I afterwards remembered that this arrangement was repeated, in a tone of voice incautiously loud, at the bar of a public-house, where they insisted upon my taking a glass of porter. There were, I should say, more than a dozen persons present at the time.

The fire was blazing brightly in the parlor of the Royal George when I entered, and I had not been seated near it many minutes before I became exceedingly drowsy; and no wonder, for I had not been in bed the previous night, and the blowing of the wind in my eyes for a couple of hours had of course added greatly to their heavy weariness. Habit had long enabled me to awake at any moment I had previously determined on, so that I felt no anxiety as to oversleeping myself; and having pulled out my watch, noticed that it was barely half-past five, wound it up, and placed it before me on the table, I settled myself comfortably in an arm-chair, and was soon sound asleep.

I awoke with a confused impression, not only that I had quite slept the time I had allotted myself, but that strangers were in the room and standing about me. I was mistaken in both particulars. There was no one in the parlor but myself, and on glancing at the watch I saw that it was but a quarter-past six. I rose from the chair, stirred the fire, took two or three turns about the room, listened for a few minutes to the howling wind and driving rain which shook and beat against the casement, sat down again, and took up a newspaper which was lying on the table.

I had read for some time when the parlor door opened, and who should walk in but the young wife and elderly gentleman whom I had seen in the street. I at once concluded that they had sought me with reference to the fugitive on board the *Columbia*; and the venerable old man's rather elaborate apologies for intrusion over, and both of them seated on the side of the fireplace opposite to me, I waited with grave curiosity to hear what they might have to say.

An awkward silence ensued. The young woman's eyes, swollen with weeping, were bent upon the floor, and her entire aspect and demeanor exhibited extreme sorrow and dejection. I pitied her, so sad and gentle did she look, from my very soul. The old man appeared anxious and careworn, and for some time remained abstractedly gazing at the fire without speaking. I had a mind to avoid a painful, and, I was satisfied, profitless interview, by abruptly retiring; and was just rising for the purpose when a fiercer tempest-blast than before, accompanied by the pattering of heavy rain-drops against the window-panes, caused me to hesitate at exposing myself unnecessarily to the rigor of such a night; and at the same moment the gray-haired man suddenly raised his eyes and regarded me with a fixed and grave scrutiny.

"This war of the elements," he at last said; "this wild uproar of physical nature, is but a type, Mr. Waters, and a faint one, of the convulsions, the antagonisms, the hurtful conflicts ever raging in the moral world."

I bowed dubious assent to a proposition not apparently very pertinent to the subject, which I supposed chiefly occupied his mind, and he proceeded.

"It is difficult for dim-eyed beings such as we are always to trace the guiding hand of the ever-watchful Power which conducts the complex events of this changing, many-colored life to wise and foreseen issues. The conflicts of faith with actual experience are hard for poor humanity to bear, and still keep unimpaired the jewel beyond price of unwavering trust in Him to whom the secrets of all hearts are known. Ah, sir! guilt, flaunting its vanities in high places—innocence in danger of fetters—are perplexing subjects to dwell upon!"

I was somewhat puzzled by this strange talk, but, hopeful that a meaning would presently appear, I again silently intimated partial concurrence in his general views.

"There is no longer much doubt, Mr. Waters, I believe," he after a few moments added in a much more business-like and sensible tone, "that the *Columbia* will be forced back again, and that the husband of this unhappy girl will consequently fall into the hands of the blind, unreasoning law.... You appear surprised.... My name, I should have mentioned, is Thompson; and be assured, Mr. Waters, that when the real facts of this most unfortunate affair are brought to your knowledge, no one will more bitterly regret than yourself that this tempest and sudden change of wind should have flung back the prey both you and I believed had escaped upon these fatal shores."

"From your name I presume you to be the father of this young woman, and—"

"Yes," he interrupted; "and the father-in-law of the innocent man you have hunted down with such untiring activity and zeal. But I blame you not," he added, checking himself—"I blame you not. You have only done what you held to be your duty. But the ways of Providence are indeed inscrutable!"

A passionate burst of grief from the pale, weeping wife testified that, whatever might be the fugitive husband's offences or crimes against society, he at least retained *her* affection and esteem.

"It is very unpleasant," I observed, "to discuss such a subject in the presence of relatives of the inculpated person, especially as I as yet perceive no useful result likely to arise from it; still, since you as it were force me to speak, you must permit me to say, that it appears to me you are either grossly deceived yourself, or attempting for some purpose or other to impose upon my credulity."

"Neither, sir—neither," replied Mr. Thompson with warmth. "I certainly am not deceived myself, and I should hope that my character, which I doubt not is well known to you, will shield me from any suspicion of a desire to deceive others."

"I am quite aware, Mr. Thompson, of your personal respectability; still you may be unwittingly led astray. I very much regret to say, that the evidence against your daughter's husband is overwhelming, and I fear unanswerable."

"The best, kindest of husbands!" broke in the sobbing wife; "The most injured, the most persecuted of men!"

"It is useless," said I, rising and seizing my hat, "to prolong this conversation. If he be innocent, he will no doubt be acquitted; but as it is now close upon half-past seven o'clock, I must beg to take my leave."

"One moment, sir," said Mr. Thompson hastily. "To be frank with you, it was entirely for the purpose of asking your advice as an experienced person that we are here. You have heard of this young man's father?"

"Joel Masters?—Yes. A gambler, and otherwise disreputable person, and one of the most specious rascals, I am told, under the sun."

"You have correctly described him. You are not perhaps acquainted with his handwriting?"

"Yes, I am; partially so at least. I have a note in my pocket—here it is—addressed to me by the artful old scoundrel for the purpose of luring me from the right track after his son."

"Then, Mr. Waters, please to read this letter from him, dated Liverpool, where it appears he was yesterday to embark for America."

The letter Mr. Thompson placed in my hands startled me not a little. It was a circumstantial confession addressed by Joel Masters to his son, setting forth that he, the father, was alone guilty of the offence with which his unfortunate son was charged, and authorizing him to make a full disclosure should he fail in making his escape from the country. This was, I thought, an exceedingly cheap kind of generosity on the part of honest Joel, now that he had secured himself by flight from the penalties of justice. The letter went on to state where a large amount of bank-notes and acceptances, which the writer had been unable to change or discount, would be found.

"This letter," said I, "is a very important one; but where is the envelop?"

Mr. Thompson searched his pocket-book: it was not there. "I must have dropped it," he exclaimed, "at my lodgings. Pray wait till I return. I am extremely anxious to convince you of this unfortunate young man's innocence. I will not be more than a few minutes absent." He then hurried out.

I looked at my watch: it wanted five-and-twenty minutes to eight. "I have but a very few minutes to spare," I observed to the still passionately grieving wife; "and as to the letter, you had better place it in the hands of the attorney for the defence."

"Ah, sir," sobbed the wife, raising her timid eyes towards me, "you do not believe us or you would not be so eager to seize my husband."

"Pardon me," I replied, "I have no right to doubt the truth of what you have told me; but my duty is a plain one, and must be performed."

"Tell me frankly, honestly," cried the half-frantic woman with a renewed burst of tears, "if, in your opinion, this evidence will save my unhappy, deeply-injured husband? My father, I fear, deceives me—deceives himself with a vain hope."

I hesitated to express a very favorable opinion of the effect of a statement, obnoxious, as a few moments' reflection suggested, to so much suspicion. The wife quickly interpreted the meaning of my silence, and broke at once into a flood of hysterical lamentation. It was with the greatest difficulty I kept life in her by copious showers of water from the decanter that stood on the table. This endured some time. At last I said abruptly, for my watch admonished me that full ten minutes had been passed in this way, that I must summon the waiter and leave her.

"Go—go," said she, suddenly rallying, "since it must be so. I—I will follow."

I immediately left the house, hastened to the quay, and, on arriving there, strained my eyes seaward in search of the expected ship. A large bark, which very much resembled her, was, to my dismay, riding at anchor within the breakwater, her sails furled, and everything made snug for the night. I ran to the landing-steps, near which two or three sailors were standing.

"What vessel is that?" I asked, pointing to the one which had excited my alarm.

"*The Columbia*," replied the man.

"*The Columbia!* Why, when did she arrive?"

"Some time ago. The clock chimed a quarter-past eight as the captain and a few of the passengers came on shore."

"A quarter-past eight! Why, it wants nearly half an hour to that now!"

"Does it though? Before you are ten minutes older you'll hear the clock strike nine!"

The man's words were followed by a merry mocking laugh close to my elbow: I turned sharply round, and for the first and last time in my life felt an almost irresistible temptation to strike a woman. There stood the meek, dove-eyed, grief-stricken wife I had parted from but a few minutes before, gazing with brazen impudence in my face.

"Perhaps, Mr. Waters," said she with another taunting laugh, "perhaps yours is London time; or, which is probably more likely, watches sometimes sleep for an hour or so as well as their owners." She then skipped gaily off.

"Are you a Mr. Waters?" said a custom-house official who was parading the quay.

"Yes—and what then?"

"Only that a Mr. Joel Masters desired me to say that he was very much grieved he could not return to finish the evening with you, as he and his son were unfortunately obliged to leave Plymouth immediately."

It would have been a real pleasure to have flung the speaker over the quay. By a great effort I denied myself the tempting luxury, and walked away in a fever of rage. Neither Joel Masters nor his son could afterwards be found, spite of the unremitting efforts of myself and others, continued through several weeks. They both ultimately escaped to America; and some years afterwards I learned through an unexpected channel that the canting, specious old rascal was at length getting his deserts in the establishment of Sing-Sing. The son, the same informant assured me, had, through the persuasions and influence of his wife, who probably thought justice might not be so pleasantly eluded another time, turned over a new leaf, and was leading an honest and prosperous life at Cincinnati.

VII

LEGAL METAMORPHOSES

The respectable agent of a rather eminent French house arrived one morning in great apparent distress at Scotland Yard, and informed the superintendent that he had just sustained a great, almost ruinous loss, in notes of the Bank of England and commercial bills of Exchange, besides a considerable sum in gold. He had, it appeared, been absent in Paris about ten days, and on his return but a few hours previously, discovered that his iron chest had been completely rifled during his absence. False keys must have been used, as the empty chest was found locked, and no sign of violence could be observed. He handed in full written details of the property carried off, the numbers of the notes, and every other essential particular. The first step taken was to ascertain if any of the notes had been tendered at the bank. Not one had been presented; payment was of course stopped, and advertisements descriptive of the bills of exchange, as well as of the notes, were inserted in the evening and following morning papers. A day or two afterwards, a considerable reward was offered for such information as might lead to the apprehension of the offenders. No result followed; and spite of the active exertions of the officers employed, not the slightest clue could be obtained to the perpetrators of the robbery. The junior partner in the firm, M. Bellebon, in the meantime arrived in England, to assist in the investigation, and was naturally extremely urgent in his inquiries; but the mystery which enveloped the affair remained impenetrable. At last a letter, bearing the St. Martin le Grand post-mark, was received by the agent, M. Alexandre le Breton, which contained an offer to surrender the whole of the plunder, with the exception of the gold, for the sum of one thousand pounds. The property which had been abstracted was more than ten times that sum, and had been destined by the French house to meet some heavy liabilities falling due in London very shortly. Le Breton had been ordered to pay the whole amount into Hoare's to the account of the firm, and had indeed been severely blamed for not having done so as he received the different notes and bills; and it was on going to the chest immediately on his return from Paris, for the purpose of fulfilling the peremptory instructions he had received, that M. le Breton discovered the robbery.

The letter went on to state that should the offer be acceded to, a mystically worded advertisement—of which a copy was enclosed—was to be inserted in the "Times," and then a mode would be suggested for safety—in the interest of the thieves of course—carrying the agreement into effect. M. Bellebon was half-inclined to close with this proposal, in order to save the credit of the house, which would be destroyed unless its acceptances, now due in about fourteen days, could be met; and without the stolen moneys and bills of exchange, this was, he feared, impossible. The superintendent, to whom M. Bellebon showed the letter, would not hear of compliance with such a demand, and threatened a prosecution for composition of felony if M. Bellebon persisted in doing so. The advertisement was, however, inserted, and an immediate reply directed that Le Breton, the agent, should present himself at the old Manor-house, Green Lanes, Newington, unattended, at four o'clock on the following afternoon, bringing with him of course the stipulated sum *in gold*. It was added, that to prevent any possible treason (*trahison*, the letter was written in French,) Le Breton would find a note for him at the tavern, informing him of the spot—a solitary one, and far away from any place where an ambush could be concealed—where the business would be concluded, and to which he must proceed unaccompanied, and on foot! This proposal was certainly quite as ingenious as it was cool, and the chance of outwitting such cunning rascals seemed exceedingly doubtful. A very tolerable scheme was, however, hit upon, and M. le Breton proceeded at the appointed hour to the Old Manor-House. No letter or message had been left for him, and nobody obnoxious to the slightest suspicion could be seen near or about the tavern. On the following day another missive arrived, which stated that the writer was quite aware of the trick which the police had intended playing him, and he assured M. Bellebon that such a line of conduct was as unwise as it would be fruitless, inasmuch as if "good faith" was not observed, the securities and notes would be inexorably destroyed or otherwise disposed of, and the house of Bellebon and Company be consequently exposed to the shame and ruin of bankruptcy.

Just at this crises of the affair I arrived in town from my unsuccessful hunt after the fugitives who had slipped through my fingers at Plymouth. The superintendent laughed heartily, not so much at the trick by which I had been duped, as at the angry mortification I did not affect to conceal. He presently added, "I have been wishing for your return, in order to intrust you with a tangled affair, in which success will amply compensate for such a disappointment. You know French too, which is fortunate; for the gentleman who has been plundered understands little or no English." He then related the foregoing particulars, with other apparently slight circumstances; and after a long conversation with him, I retired to think the matter over, and decide upon the likeliest mode of action. After much cogitation, I determined to see M. Bellebon *alone*, and for this purpose I despatched the waiter of a tavern adjacent to his lodgings, with a note expressive of my wish to see him instantly on pressing business. He was at home, and immediately acceded to my request. I easily introduced myself; and after about a quarter of an hour's conference, said carelessly—for I saw he was too heedless of speech, too quick and frank, to be intrusted with the dim suspicions which certain trifling indices had suggested to me—"Is Monsieur le Breton at the office where the robbery was committed?"

"No: he is gone to Greenwich on business, and will not return till late in the evening. But if you wish to re-examine the place, I can of course enable you to do so."

"It will, I think, be advisable; and you will, if you please," I added, as we emerged into the street, "permit me to take you by the arm, in order that the *official* character of my visit may not be suspected by any one there."

He laughingly complied, and we arrived at the house arm in arm. We were admitted by an elderly woman; and there was a young man—a moustached clerk—seated at a desk in an inner room writing. He eyed me for a moment, somewhat askance I thought, but I gave him no opportunity for a distinct view of my features; and I presently handed M. Bellebon a card, on which I had contrived to write, unobserved, "send away the clerk." This was more naturally done than I anticipated; and in answer to M. Bellebon's glance of inquiry, I merely said, "That as I did not wish to be known there as a police-officer, it was essential that the minute search I was about to make should be without witnesses." He agreed; and the woman was also sent away upon a distant errand. Every conceivable place did I ransack; every scrap of paper that had writing on it I eagerly perused. At length the search was over, apparently without result.

"You are quite sure, Monsieur Bellebon, as you informed the superintendent, that Monsieur le Breton has no female relations or acquaintances in this country?"

"Positive," he replied. "I have made the most explicit inquiries on the subject both of the clerk Dubarle and of the woman-servant."

Just then the clerk returned, out of breath with haste I noticed, and I took my leave without even now affording the young gentleman so clear a view of my face as he was evidently anxious to obtain.

"No female acquaintance!" thought I, as I re-entered the private room of the tavern I had left an hour before. "From whom came, then, these scraps of perfumed note-paper I have found in his desk I wonder?" I sat down and endeavored to piece them out, but after considerable trouble, satisfied myself that they were parts of different notes, and so small, unfortunately, as to contain nothing which separately afforded any information except that they were all written by one hand, and that a female one.

About two hours after this I was sauntering along in the direction of Stoke-Newington, where I was desirous of making some inquiries as to another matter, and had passed the Kingslaw Gate a few hundred yards, when a small discolored printed handbill, lying in a haberdasher's shop window, arrested my attention. It ran thus:—"Two guineas reward.—Lost, an Italian greyhound. The tip of its tail has been chopped off, and it answers to the name of Fidèle." Underneath, the reader was told in writing to "inquire within."

"Fidèle!" I mentally exclaimed. "Any relation to M. le Breton's fair correspondent's Fidèle, I wonder?" In a twinkling my pocket-book was out, and I reperused by the gas-light on one of the perfumed scraps of paper the following portion of a sentence, "*ma pauvre Fidèle est per*"—. The bill, I observed, was dated nearly three weeks previously. I forthwith entered the shop, and pointing to the bill, said I knew a person who had found such a dog as was there advertised for. The woman at the counter said she was glad to hear it, as the lady, formerly a customer of theirs, was much grieved at the animal's loss.

"What is the lady's name?" I asked.

"I can't rightly pronounce the name," was the reply. "It is French, I believe; but here it is, with the address, in the day-book, written by herself."

I eagerly read—"Madame Levasseur, Oak Cottage; about one mile on the road from Edmonton to Southgate." The hand-writing greatly resembled that on the scraps I had taken from M. le Breton's desk; and the writer was French too! Here were indications of a trail which might lead to unhoped-for success, and I determined to follow it up vigorously. After one or two other questions, I left the shop, promising to send the dog to the lady the next day. My business at Stoke-Newington was soon accomplished. I then hastened westward to the establishment of a well-known dog-fancier, and procured the loan, at a reasonable price, of an ugly Italian hound: the requisite loss of the tip of its tail was very speedily accomplished, and so quickly healed, that the newness of the excision could not be suspected. I arrived at the lady's residence about twelve o'clock on the following day, so thoroughly disguised as a vagabond Cockney dog-stealer, that my own wife, when I entered the breakfast parlor just previous to starting, screamed with alarm and surprise. The mistress of Oak Cottage was at home, but indisposed, and the servant said she would take the dog to her, though, if I would take it out of the basket, she herself could tell me if it was Fidèle or not. I replied that I would only show the dog to the lady, and would not trust it out of my hands. This message was carried upstairs, and after waiting some time outside—for the woman, with natural precaution, considering my appearance, for the safety of the portable articles lying about, had closed the street-door in my face—I was readmitted, desired to wipe my shoes carefully, and walk up. Madame Levasseur, a showy looking woman, though not over-refined in speech or manners, was seated on a sofa, in vehement expectation of embracing her dear Fidèle; but my vagabond appearance so startled her, that she screamed loudly for her husband, M. Levasseur. This gentleman, a fine, tall, whiskered, moustached person, hastened into the apartment half-shaved, and with his razor in his hand.

"Qu'est ce qu'il y a donc?" he demanded.

"Mais voyez cette horreur là," replied the lady, meaning me, not the dog, which I was slowly emancipating from the basket-kennel. The gentleman laughed; and reassured by the presence of her husband, Madame Levasseur's anxieties concentrated themselves upon the expected Fidèle.

"Mais, mon Dieu!" she exclaimed again as I displayed the aged beauty I had brought for her inspection, "Why, that is not Fidèle!"

"Not, marm?" I answered, with quite innocent surprise. "Vy, ere is her wery tail;" and I held up the mutilated extremity for her closer inspection. The lady was not, however, to be convinced even by that evidence; and as the gentleman soon became impatient of my persistence, and hinted very intelligibly that he had a mind to hasten my passage downstairs with the toe of his boot, I, having made the best possible use of my eyes during the short interview, scrambled up the dog and basket, and departed.

"No female relative or acquaintance hasn't he?" was my exulting thought as I gained the road. "And yet if that is not M. le Breton's picture between those of the husband and wife, I am a booby, and a blind one." I no longer in the least doubted that I had struck a brilliant trail; and I could have shouted with exultation, so eager was I not only to retrieve my, as I fancied, somewhat tarnished reputation for activity and skill, but to extricate the plundered firm from their terrible difficulties; the more especially as young M. Bellebon, with the frankness of his age and nation, had hinted to me—and the suddenly tremulous light of his fine expressive eyes testified to the acuteness of his apprehensions—that his marriage with a long-loved and amiable girl depended upon his success in saving the credit of his house.

That same evening, about nine o'clock, M. Levasseur, expensively, but withal snobbishly attired, left Oak Cottage, walked to Edmonton, hailed a cab, and drove off rapidly towards town, followed by an English swell as stylishly and snobbishly dressed, wigged, whiskered, and moustached as himself: this English swell being no other than myself, as prettily metamorphosed and made up for the part I intended playing as heart could wish.

M. Levasseur descended at the end of the Quadrant, Regent Street, and took his way to Vine Street, leading out of that celebrated thoroughfare. I followed; and observing him enter a public house, unhesitatingly did the same. It was a house of call and general rendezvous for foreign servants out of place. Valets, couriers, cooks, of many varieties of shade, nation, and respectability, were assembled there, smoking, drinking, and playing at an insufferably noisy game, unknown, I believe, to Englishmen, and which must, I think, have been invented in sheer despair of cards, dice, or other implements of gambling. The sole instruments of play were the gamester's fingers, of which the two persons playing suddenly and simultaneously uplifted as many, or as few, as they pleased, each player alternately calling a number; and if he named precisely how many fingers were held up by himself and opponent, he marked a point. The hubbub of cries—"cinq," "neuf," "dix," &c.—was deafening. The players—almost everybody in the large room—were too much occupied to notice our entrance; and M. Levasseur and myself seated ourselves, and called for something to drink, without, I was glad to see, exciting the slightest observation. M. Levasseur, I soon perceived, was an intimate acquaintance of many there; and somewhat to my surprise, for he spoke French very well, I found that he was a Swiss. His name was, I therefore concluded, assumed. Nothing positive rewarded my watchfulness that evening; but I felt quite sure Levasseur had come there with the expectation of meeting someone, as he did not play, and went away about half past eleven o'clock with an obviously discontented air. The following night it was the same; but the next, who should peer into the room about half past ten, and look cautiously round, but M. Alexandre le Breton! The instant the eyes of the friends met, Levasseur rose and went out. I hesitated to follow, lest such a movement might excite suspicion; and it was well I did not, as they both presently returned, and seated themselves close by my side. The anxious, haggard countenance of Le Breton—who had, I should have before stated, been privately pointed out to me by one of the force early on the morning I visited Oak Cottage—struck me forcibly, especially in contrast with that of Levasseur, which wore only an expression of malignant and ferocious triumph, slightly dashed by temporary disappointment. Le Breton stayed but a short time; and the only whispered words I caught were—"He has, I fear, some suspicion."

The anxiety and impatience of M. Bellebon whilst this was going on became extreme, and he sent me note after note—the only mode of communication I would permit—expressive of his consternation at the near approach of the time when the engagements of his house would arrive at maturity, without anything having in the meantime been accomplished. I pitied him greatly, and after some thought and hesitation, resolved upon a new and bolder game. By affecting to drink a great deal, occasionally playing, and in other ways exhibiting a reckless, devil-may-care demeanor, I had striven to insinuate myself into the confidence and companionship of Levasseur, but hitherto without much effect; and although once I could see, startled by a casual hint I dropped to another person—one of ours—just sufficiently loud for him to hear—that I knew a sure and safe market for stopped Bank of England notes, the cautious scoundrel quickly subsided into his usual guarded reserve. He evidently doubted me, and it was imperatively necessary to remove those doubts. This was at last effectually, and, I am vain enough to think, cleverly done. One evening a rakish looking man, who ostentatiously and repeatedly declared himself to be Mr. Trelawney of Conduit Street, and who was evidently three parts intoxicated, seated himself directly in front of us, and with much braggart impudence boasted of his money, at the same time displaying a pocket-book, which seemed pretty full of Bank of England notes. There were only a few persons present in the room besides us, and they were at the other end of the room. Levasseur, I saw, noticed with considerable interest the look of greed and covetousness which I fixed on that same pocket-book. At length the stranger rose to depart. I also hurried up and slipped after him, and was quietly and slyly followed by Levasseur. After proceeding about a dozen paces I looked furtively about, but *not* behind; robbed Mr. Trelawney of his pocket-book, which he had placed in one of the tails of his coat; crossed over the street, and walked hurriedly away, still, I could hear, followed by Levasseur. I entered another public-house, strode into an empty back-room, and was just in the act of examining my prize, when in stepped Levasseur. He looked triumphant as Lucifer, as he clapped me on the shoulder, and said in a low exulting voice, "I saw that pretty trick, Williams, and can, if I like, transport you!"

My consternation was naturally extreme, and Levasseur laughed immensely at the terror he excited. "Soyez tranquille," he said at last, at the same time ringing the bell: "I shall not hurt you." He ordered some wine, and after the waiter had fulfilled the order and left the room, said, "Those notes of Mr. Trelawney's will of course be stopped in the morning, but I think I once heard you say you knew of a market for such articles?"

I hesitated, coyly unwilling to further commit myself. "Come, come," resumed Levasseur in a still low but menacing tone, "no nonsense. I have you now; you are, in fact, entirely in my power; but be candid, and you are safe. Who is your friend?"

"He is not in town now," I stammered.

"Stuff—humbug! I have myself some notes to change. There, now we understand each other. What does he give, and how does he dispose of them?"

"He gives about a third generally, and gets rid of them abroad. They reach the Bank through *bona fide* and innocent olders, and in that case the Bank is of course bound to pay."

"Is that the law also with respect to bills of exchange?"

"Yes, to be sure it is."

"And is *amount* of any consequence to your friend?"

"None, I believe, whatever."

"Well, then, you must introduce me to him."

"No, that I can't," I hurriedly answered. "He won't deal with strangers."

"You *must*, I tell you, or I will call an officer." Terrified by this threat, I muttered that his name was Levi Samuel.

"And where does Levi Samuel live?"

"That," I replied, "I *cannot* tell; but I know how to communicate with him."

Finally, it was settled by Levasseur that I should dine at Oak Cottage the next day but one, and that I should arrange with Samuel to meet us there immediately afterwards. The notes and bills he had to dispose of, I was to inform Samuel, amounted to nearly twelve thousand pounds, and I was promised £500 for effecting the bargain.

"Five hundred pounds, remember, Williams," said Levasseur as we parted; "or, if you deceive me, transportation! You can prove nothing regarding *me*, whereas, I could settle *you* off hand."

The superintendent and I had a long and rather anxious conference the next day. We agreed that, situate as Oak

Cottage was, in an open space away from any other building, it would not be advisable that any officer except myself and the pretended Samuel should approach the place. We also agreed as to the probability of such clever rogues having so placed the notes and bills that they could be consumed or otherwise destroyed on the slightest alarm, and that the open arrest of Levasseur, and a search of Oak Cottage, would in all likelihood prove fruitless. "There will be only two of them," I said in reply to a remark of the superintendent as to the somewhat dangerous game I was risking with powerful and desperate men, "even should Le Breton be there; and surely Jackson and I, aided by the surprise and our pistols, will be too many for them." Little more was said, the superintendent wished us luck, and I sought out and instructed Jackson.

I will confess that, on setting out the next day to keep my appointment, I felt considerable anxiety. Levasseur *might* have discovered my vocation, and set this trap for my destruction. Yet that was hardly possible. At all events, whatever the danger, it was necessary to face it; and having cleaned and loaded my pistols with unusual care, and bade my wife a more than usually earnest farewell, which, by the way, rather startled her, I set off, determined, as we used to say in Yorkshire, "to win the horse or lose the saddle."

I arrived in good time at Oak Cottage, and found my host in the highest possible spirits. Dinner was ready, he said, but it would be necessary to wait a few minutes for the two friends he expected.

"*Two* friends!" I exclaimed, really startled. "You told me last evening there was to be only one, a Monsieur le Breton."

"True," rejoined Levasseur carelessly; "but I had forgotten that another party as much interested as ourselves would like to be present, and invite himself, if I did not. But there will be enough for us all, never fear," he added with a coarse laugh, "especially as Madame Levasseur does not dine with us."

At this moment a loud knock was heard. "Here they are!" exclaimed Levasseur, and hastened out to meet them. I peeped through the blind, and to my great alarm saw that Le Breton was accompanied by the clerk Dubarle! My first impulse was to seize my pistols and rush out of the house; but calmer thoughts soon succeeded, and the improbability that a plan had been laid to entrap me recurred forcibly. Still, should the clerk recognize me? The situation was undoubtedly a critical one; but I was in for it, and must therefore brave the matter out in the best way I could.

Presently a conversation, carried on in a loud, menacing tone in the next room between Levasseur and the newcomers, arrested my attention, and I softly approached the door to listen. Le Breton, I soon found, was but half a villain, and was extremely anxious that the property should not be disposed of till at least another effort had been made at negotiation. The others, now that a market for the notes and securities had been obtained, were determined to avail themselves of it, and immediately leave the country. The almost agonized intreaties of Le Breton that they would not utterly ruin the house he had betrayed, were treated with scornful contempt, and he was at length silenced by their brutal menaces. Le Breton, I further learned, was a cousin of Madame Levasseur, whose husband had first pillaged him at play, and then suggested the crime which had been committed as the sole means of concealing the defalcations of which he, Levasseur, had been the occasion and promoter.

After a brief delay, all three entered the dining-room, and a slight but significant start which the clerk Dubarle gave, as Levasseur, with mock ceremony, introduced me, made my heart, as folk say, leap into my mouth. His half-formed suspicions seemed, however, to be dissipated for the moment by the humorous account Levasseur gave him of the robbery of Mr. Trelawney, and we sat down to a very handsome dinner.

A more uncomfortable one, albeit, I never assisted at. The furtive looks of Dubarle, who had been only partially reassured, grew more and more inquisitive and earnest. Fortunately Levasseur was in rollicking spirits and humor, and did not heed the unquiet glances of the young man; and as for Le Breton, he took little notice of anybody. At last this terrible dinner was over, and the wine was pushed briskly round. I drank much more freely than usual, partly with a view to calm my nerves, and partly to avoid remark. It was nearly the time for the Jew's appearance, when Dubarle, after a scrutinizing and somewhat imperious look at my face, said abruptly, "I think, Monsieur Williams, I have seen you somewhere before?"

"Very likely," I replied with as much indifference as I could assume. "Many persons have seen me before—some of them once or twice too often."

"True!" exclaimed Levasseur with a shout. "Trelawney, for instance!"

"I should like to see Monsieur with his wig off!" said the clerk with increasing insolence.

"Nonsense, Dubarle; you are a fool," exclaimed Levasseur, "and I will not have my good friend Williams insulted."

Dubarle did not persist, but it was plain enough that some dim remembrance of my features continued to haunt and perplex him.

At length, and the relief was unspeakable, a knock at the outer door announced Jackson—Levi Samuel, I mean. We all jumped up, and ran to the window. It was the Jew sure enough, and admirably he had dressed and now looked the part. Levasseur went out, and in a minute or two returned introducing him. Jackson could not suppress a start as he caught sight of the tall, moustached addition to the expected company; and although he turned it off very well, it drove the Jewish dialect in which he had been practising completely out of his thoughts and speech, as he said, "You have more company than my friend Williams led me to expect?"

"A friend—one friend extra, Mr. Samuel," said Levasseur; "that is all. Come, sit down, and let me help you to a glass of wine. You are an English Jew I perceive?"

"Yes."

A silence of a minute or two succeeded, and then Levasseur said, "You are of course prepared for business?"

"Yes—that is, if you are reasonable."

"Reasonable! the most reasonable men in the world," rejoined Levasseur with a loud laugh. "But pray where is the gold you mean to pay us with?"

"If we agree, I will fetch it in half an hour. I do not carry bags of sovereigns about with me into *all* companies," replied Jackson with much readiness.

"Well, that's right enough: and now how much discount do you charge?"

"I will tell you when I see the securities."

Levasseur rose without another word, and left the apartment. He was gone about ten minutes, and on his return, deliberately counted out the stolen Bank of England notes and bills of Exchange. Jackson got up from his chair, peered close to them, and began noting down the amounts in his pocket-book. I also rose, and pretended to be looking at a picture by the fire-place. The moment was a nervous one, as the signal had been agreed upon, and could not now be changed or deferred. The clerk Dubarle also hastily rose, and eyed Jackson with flaming but indecisive looks. The examination of the securities was at length terminated, and Jackson began counting the Bank of England notes aloud—"One—two—three—four—FIVE!" As the signal word passed his lips, he threw himself upon Le Breton, who sat next to him; and at the same moment I passed one of my feet between Dubarle's, and with a dexterous twist hurled him violently on the floor; another instant and my grasp was on the throat of Levasseur, and my pistol at his ear. "Hurrah!" we both shouted with eager excitement; and before either of the villains could recover from his surprise, or indeed perfectly comprehend what had happened, Levasseur and Le Breton were handcuffed, and resistance was out of the question. Young Dubarle was next easily secured.

Levasseur, the instant he recovered the use of his faculties, which the completeness and suddenness of the surprise and attack had paralysed, yelled like a madman with rage and anger, and but for us, would, I verily believe, have dashed his brains out against the walls of the room. The other two were calmer, and having at last thoroughly pinioned and secured them, and carefully gathered up the recovered plunder, we left Oak Cottage in triumph, letting ourselves out, for the woman-servant had gone off, doubtless to acquaint her mistress with the disastrous turn affairs had taken. No inquiry was made after either of them.

An hour afterwards the prisoners were securely locked up, and I hurried to acquaint M. Bellebon with the fortunate issue of our enterprise. His exultation, it will be readily believed, was unbounded; and I left him busy with letters to the firm, and doubtless one to "cette chère et aimable Louise," announcing the joyful news.

The prisoners, after a brief trial, which many readers of this narrative may perhaps remember, were convicted of felonious conspiracy, and were all sentenced to ten years' transportation. Le Breton's sentence, the judge told him, would have been for life, but for the contrition he had exhibited shortly before his apprehension.

As Levasseur passed me on leaving the dock, he exclaimed in French, and in a desperately savage tone, "I will repay you for this when I return, and that infernal Trelawney too." I am too much accustomed to threats of this kind to be in any way moved by them, and I therefore contented myself by smiling, and a civil "Au revoir—allons!"

VIII

THE REVENGE

Levasseur and his confederates sailed for the penal settlements on the ill-fated convict-ship, the *Amphytrion*, the total wreck of which on the coast of France, and consequent drowning of the crew and prisoners, excited so painful a sensation in England. A feeling of regret for the untimely fate of Le Breton, whom I regarded rather as a weak dupe than a purposed rascal, passed over my mind as I read the announcement in the newspapers; but newer events had almost jostled the incidents connected with his name from my remembrance, when a terrible adventure vividly recalled them, and taught me how fierce and untameable are the instincts of hate and revenge in a certain class of minds.

A robbery of plate had been committed in Portman Square with an ingenuity and boldness which left no doubt that it had been effected by clever and practised hands. The detective officers first employed having failed to discover the offenders, the threads of the imperfect and broken clue were placed in my hands, to see if my somewhat renowned dexterity, or luck, as many of my brother officers preferred calling it, would enable me to piece them out to a satisfactory conclusion. By the description obtained of a man who had been seen lurking about the house a few days previous to the burglary, it had been concluded by my predecessors in the investigation that one Martin, a fellow with half a dozen *aliases*, and a well-known traveler on the road to the hulks, was concerned in the affair; and by their advice a reward of fifty pounds had been offered for his apprehension and conviction. I prosecuted the inquiry with my usual energy and watchfulness, without alighting upon any new fact or intimation of importance. I could not discover that a single article of the missing property had been either pawned or offered for sale, and little doubt remained that the crucible had fatally diminished the chances of detection. The only hope was, that an increased reward might induce one of the gang to betray his confederates; and as the property was of large value, this was done, and one hundred guineas was promised for the required information. I had been to the printer's to order the placards announcing the increased recompense; and after indulging in a long gossip with the foreman of the establishment, whom I knew well, was passing at about a quarter-past ten o'clock through Ryder's Court, Newport Market, where a tall man met and passed me swiftly, holding a handkerchief to his face. There was nothing remarkable in that, as the weather was bitterly cold and sleety; and I walked unheedingly on. I was just in the act of passing out of the court towards Leicester Square, when swift steps sounded suddenly behind me. I instinctively turned; and as I did so, received a violent blow on the left shoulder—intended, I doubted not, for the nape of my neck—from the tall individual who had passed me a minute previously. As he still held the handkerchief to his face, I did not catch even a momentary glance at his features, and he ran off with surprising speed. The blow, sudden, jarring, and inflicted with a sharp instrument—by a strong knife or a dagger—caused a sensation of faintness; and before I recovered from it all chance of successful pursuit was at an end. The wound, which was not at all serious, I had dressed at a chemist's shop in the Haymarket; and as proclaiming the attack would do nothing towards detecting the perpetrator of it, I said little about it to anyone, and managed to conceal it entirely from my wife, to whom it would have suggested a thousand painful apprehensions whenever I happened to be unexpectedly detained from home. The brief glimpse I had of the balked assassin afforded no reasonable indication of his identity. To be sure he ran at an amazing and unusual pace, but this was a qualification possessed by so many of the light-legged as well as light-fingered gentry of my professional acquaintance, that it could not justify even a random suspicion; and I determined to forget the unpleasant incident as soon as possible.

The third evening after this occurrence I was again passing along Leicester Square at a somewhat late hour, but this time with all my eyes about me. Snow, which the wind blew sharply in one's face, was falling fast, and the cold was intense. Except myself, and a tallish snow-wreathed figure—a woman apparently—not a living being was to be seen. This figure, which was standing still at the further side of the square, appeared to be awaiting me, and as I drew near it, threw back the hood of a cloak, and to my great surprise disclosed the features of a Madame Jaubert. This lady, some years before, had carried on, not very far from the spot where she now stood, a respectable millinery business. She was a widow with one child, a daughter of about seven years of age. Marie-Louise, as she was named, was one unfortunate day sent to Coventry Street on an errand with some money in her hand, and never returned. The inquiries set on foot proved utterly without effect: not the slightest intelligence of the fate of the child was obtained—and the grief and distraction of the bereaved mother resulted in temporary insanity. She was confined in a lunatic asylum for seven or eight months, and when pronounced convalescent, found herself homeless, and almost penniless, in the world. This sad story I had heard from one of the keepers of the asylum during her sojourn there. It was a subject she herself never, I was aware, touched upon; and she had no reason to suspect that I was in the slightest degree informed of this melancholy passage in her life. She, why, I know not, changed her name from that of Duquesne to the one she now bore—Jaubert; and for the last two or three years had supported a precarious existence by plausible begging-letters addressed to persons of credulous benevolence; for which offence she had frequently visited the police-courts at the instance of the secretary of the Mendicity Society, and it was there I had consequently made her acquaintance.

"Madame Jaubert!" I exclaimed with unfeigned surprise, "Why, what on earth can you be waiting here for on such a night as this?"

"To see you!" was her curt reply.

"To see me! Depend upon it, then, you are knocking at the wrong door for not the first time in your life. The very little faith I ever had in professional widows, with twelve small children, all down in the measles, has long since vanished, and—"

"Nay," she interrupted—she spoke English, by the way, like a native—"I'm not such a fool as to be trying the whimpering dodge upon you. It is a matter of business. You want to find Jem Martin?"

"Ay, truly; but what can *you* know of him? Surely you are not *yet* fallen so low as to be the associate or accomplice of burglars?"

"Neither yet, nor likely to be so," replied the woman; "still I could tell you where to place your hand on James Martin, if I were but sure of the reward."

"There can be no doubt about that," I answered.

"Then follow me, and before ten minutes are past you will have secured your man."

I did so—cautiously, suspiciously; for my adventure three evenings before had rendered me unusually circumspect and watchful. She led the way to the most crowded quarter of St.

Giles's, and when she had reached the entrance of a dark blind alley, called Hine's Court, turned into it, and beckoned me to follow.

"Nay, nay, Madame Jaubert," I exclaimed, "that wont do. You mean fairly, I dare say; but I don't enter that respectable alley alone at this time of night."

She stopped, silent and embarrassed. Presently she said with a sneer, "You are afraid, I suppose?"

"Yes I am."

"What is to be done then?" she added after a few moments' consideration. "He is alone, I assure you."

"That is possible; still I do not enter that *cul-de-sac* tonight unaccompanied save by you."

"You suspect me of some evil design, Mr. Waters?" said the woman with an accent of reproach. "I thought you might, and yet nothing can be further from the truth. My sole object is to obtain the reward, and escape from this life of misery and degradation to my own country, and if possible begin the world respectably again. Why should you doubt me?"

"How came you acquainted with this robber's haunts?"

"The explanation is easy, but this is not the time for it. Stay; can't you get assistance?"

"Easily—in less than ten minutes; and if you are here when I return, and your information proves correct, I will ask pardon for my suspicions."

"Be it so," she said joyfully; "and be quick, for this weather is terrible."

Ten minutes had not passed when I returned with half-a-dozen officers, and found Madame Jaubert still at her post. We followed her up the court, caught Martin sure enough asleep upon a wretched pallet of straw in one of the alley hovels, and walked him off, terribly scared and surprised, to the nearest station-house, where he passed the remainder of the night.

The next day Martin proved an *alibi* of the distinctest, most undeniable kind. He had been an inmate of Clerkenwell prison for the last three months, with the exception of just six days previous to our capture of him; and he was of course at once discharged. The reward was payable only upon conviction of the offender, and the disappointment of poor Madame Jaubert was extreme. She wept bitterly at the thought of being compelled to continue her present disreputable mode of life, when a thousand francs—a sum she believed Martin's capture would have assured her—besides sufficient for her traveling expenses and decent outfit, would, she said, purchase a partnership in a small but respectable millinery shop in Paris. "Well," I remarked to her, "there is no reason for despair. You have not only proved your sincerity and good faith, but that you possess a knowledge—how acquired you best know—of the haunts and hiding-places of burglars. The reward, as you may have seen by the new placards, has been doubled; and I have a strong opinion, from something that has reached me this morning, that if you could light upon one Armstrong, *alias* Rowden, it would be as certainly yours as if already in your pocket."

"Armstrong—Rowden!" repeated the woman with anxious simplicity; "I never heard either of these names. What sort of a person is he?"

I described him minutely; but Madame Jaubert appeared to entertain little or no hope of discovering his whereabout; and ultimately went away in a very disconsolate mood, after, however, arranging to meet me the next evening.

I met her as agreed. She could obtain, she said, no intelligence of any reliable worth; and she pressed me for further particulars. Was Armstrong a drinking, a gaming, or a play-going man? I told her all I knew of his habits, and a gleam of hope glanced across her face as one or two indications were mentioned. I was to see her again on the morrow. It came; she was as far off as ever; and I advised her to waste no further time in the pursuit, but to at once endeavor to regain a position of respectability by the exercise of industry in the trade or business in which she was reputedly well-skilled. Madame Jaubert laughed scornfully; and a gleam, it seemed to me, of her never entirely subdued insanity shot out from her deep-set, flashing eyes. It was finally settled that I should meet her once more at the same place at about eight o'clock the next evening.

I arrived somewhat late at the appointed rendezvous, and found Madame Jaubert in a state of manifest excitement and impatience. She had, she was pretty sure, discovered Armstrong, and knew that he was at that moment in a house in Greek Street, Soho.

"Greek Street, Soho! Is he alone?"

"Yes; with the exception of a woman who is minding the premises, and of whom he is an acquaintance under another name. You will be able to secure him without the least risk or difficulty, but not an instant must be lost."

Madame Jaubert perceived my half-hesitation. "Surely" she exclaimed, "you are not afraid of one man! It's useless affecting to suspect *me* after what has occurred."

"True," I replied. "Lead on."

The house at which we stopped in Greek Street appeared to be an empty one, from the printed bills in the windows announcing it to be let or sold. Madame Jaubert knocked in a peculiar manner at the door, which was presently opened by a woman. "Is Mr. Brown still within?" Madame Jaubert asked in a low voice.

"Yes: what do you want with him?"

"I have brought a gentleman who will most likely be a purchaser of some of the goods he has to dispose of."

"Walk in, then, if you please," was the answer. We did so; and found ourselves, as the door closed, in pitch darkness. "This way," said the woman; "you shall have a light in half a minute."

"Let me guide you," said Madame Jaubert, as I groped onwards by the wall, and at the same time seizing my right hand. Instantly as she did so, I heard a rustle just behind me—two quick and violent blows descended on the back of my head, there was a flash before my eyes, a suppressed shout of exultation rang in my ears, and I fell insensible to the ground.

It was some time, on partially recovering my senses, before I could realize either what had occurred or the situation in which I found myself. Gradually, however, the incidents attending the artfully-prepared treachery of Madame Jaubert grew into distinctness, and I pretty well comprehended my present position. I was lying at the bottom of a cart, blindfold, gagged, handcuffed, and covered over by what, from their smell, seemed to be empty corn-sacks. The vehicle was moving at a pretty rapid rate, and judging from the roar and tumult without, through one of the busiest thoroughfares of London. It was Saturday evening; and I thought, from the character of the noises, and the tone of a clock just chiming ten, that we were in Tottenham Court Road. I endeavored to rise, but found, as I might have expected, that it was impossible to do so; my captors having secured me to the floor of the cart by strong cords. There was nothing for it, therefore, but patience and resignation; words easily pronounced, but difficult, under such circumstances, to realize in practice. My thoughts, doubtless in consequence of the blows I had received, soon became hurried and incoherent. A tumultuous throng of images swept confusedly past, of which the most constant and frequent were the faces of my wife and youngest child, whom I had kissed in his sleep just previous to leaving home. Madame Jaubert and James Martin were also there; and ever and anon the menacing countenance of Levasseur stooped over me with a hideous expression, and I felt as if clutched in the fiery grasp of a demon. I have no doubt that the voice which sounded in my ear at the moment I was felled to the ground must have suggested the idea of the Swiss—faintly and imperfectly as I caught it. This tumult of brain only gradually subsided as the discordant uproar of the streets—which no doubt added to the excitement I was suffering under by suggesting the exasperating nearness of abundant help which could not be appealed to—died gradually away into a silence only broken by the rumble of the cart-wheels, and the subdued talk of the driver and his companions, of whom there appeared to be two or three. At length the cart stopped, I heard a door unlocked and thrown open, and a few moments afterwards I was dragged from under the corn-sacks, carried up three flights of stairs, and dropped brutally upon the floor till a light could be procured. Directly one was brought, I was raised to my feet, placed upright against a wooden partition, and staples having been driven into the paneling, securely fastened in that position, with cords passed through them, and round my armpits. This effected, an authoritative voice—the now distinct recognition of which thrilled me with dismay—ordered that I should be unblinded. It was done; and when my eyes became somewhat accustomed to the suddenly-dazzling light and glare, I saw Levasseur and the clerk Dubarle standing directly in front of me, their faces kindled into flame by fiendish triumph and delight. The report that they had been drowned was then a mistake, and they had incurred the peril of returning to this country for the purpose of avenging themselves upon me; and how could it be doubted that an opportunity achieved at such fearful risk, would be effectually, remorselessly used? A pang of mortal terror shot through me, and then I strove to awaken in my heart a stern endurance, and resolute contempt of death, with, I may now confess, very indifferent success. The woman Jaubert was, I also saw, present; and a man, whom I afterwards ascertained to be Martin, was standing near the doorway, with his back towards me. These two, at a brief intimation from Levasseur, went downstairs; and then the fierce exultation of the two escaped convicts—of Levasseur especially—broke forth with wolfish rage and ferocity. "Ha—ha—ha!" shouted the Swiss, at the same time striking me over the face with his open hand, "You find, then, that others can plot as well as you can—dog, traitor, scoundrel that you are! 'Au revoir—alors!' was it, eh? Well, here we are, and I wish you joy of the meeting. Ha—ha! How dismal the rascal looks, Dubarle!"—(Again the coward struck me)—"He is hardly grateful to me, it seems, for having kept my word. I always do, my fine fellow," he added with a savage chuckle; "and never neglect to pay my debts of honor. Yours especially," he continued, drawing a pistol from his pocket, "shall be prompt payment, and with interest too, scélérat!" He held the muzzle of the pistol to within a yard of my forehead, and placed his finger on the trigger. I instinctively closed my eyes, and tasted in that fearful moment the full bitterness of death; but my hour was not yet come. Instead of the flash and report which I expected would herald me into eternity, a taunting laugh from Levasseur at the terror he excited rang through the room.

"Come—come," said Dubarle, over whose face a gleam of commiseration, almost of repentance, had once or twice passed; "you will alarm that fellow downstairs with your noise. We must, you know, wait till he is gone; and he appears to be in no hurry. In the meantime let us have a game of piquet for the first shot at the traitor's carcase."

"Excellent—capital!" shouted Levasseur with savage glee. "A game of piquet; the stake your life, Waters! A glorious game! and mind you see fair-play. In the meantime here's your health, and better luck next time if you should chance to live to see it." He swallowed a draught of wine which Dubarle, after helping himself, had poured out for him; and then approaching me, with the silver cup he had drained in his hand, said, "Look at the crest! Do you recognize it—fool, idiot that you are?"

I did so readily enough: it was a portion of the plunder carried off from Portman Square.

"Come," again interposed Dubarle, "let us have our game."

The play began, and—But I will dwell no longer upon this terrible passage in my police experience. Frequently even now the incidents of that night revisit me in dreams, and I awake with a start and cry of terror. In addition to the mental torture I endured, I was suffering under an agonizing thirst, caused by the fever of my blood, and the pressure of the absorbing gag, which still remained in my mouth. It was wonderful I did not lose my senses. At last the game was over; the Swiss won, and sprang to his feet with the roar of a wild beast.

At this moment Madame Jaubert entered the apartment somewhat hastily. "This man below," she said, "is getting insolent. He has taken it into his tipsy head that you mean to kill your prisoner, and he wont, he says, be involved in a murder, which would be sure to be found out. I told him he was talking absurdly; but he is still not satisfied, so you had better go down and speak to him yourself."

I afterwards found, it may be as well to mention here, that Madame Jaubert and Martin had been induced to assist in entrapping me, in order that I might be out of the way when a friend of Levasseur's, who had been committed to Newgate on a serious charge, came to be tried, I being the chief witness against him; and they were both assured that I had nothing more serious to apprehend than a few days' detention. In addition to a considerable money-present, Levasseur had, moreover, promised Madame Jaubert to pay her expenses to Paris, and assist in placing her in business there.

Levasseur muttered a savage imprecation on hearing the woman's message, and then said, "Come with me, Dubarle; if we cannot convince the fellow, we can at least silence him! Marie Duquesne, you will remain here."

As soon as they were gone, the woman eyed me with a compassionate expression, and approaching close to me, said in a low voice, "Do not be alarmed at their tricks and menaces. After Thursday you will be sure to be released."

I shook my head, and as distinctly as I could made a gesture with my fettered arms towards the table on which the wine was standing. She understood me. "If," said she, "you will promise not to call out, I will relieve you of the gag."

I eagerly nodded compliance. The gag was removed, and she held a cup of wine to my fevered lips. It was a draught from the waters of paradise, and hope, energy, life, were renewed within me as I drank.

"You are deceived," I said in a guarded voice, the instant my burning thirst was satisfied. "They intend to murder me, and you will be involved as an accomplice."

"Nonsense," she replied. "They have been frightening you, that's all."

"I again repeat you are deceived. Release me from these fetters and cords, give me but a chance of at least selling my life as dearly as I can, and the money you told me you stood in need of shall be yours."

"Hark!" she exclaimed. "They are coming!"

"Bring down a couple of bottles of wine," said Levasseur from the bottom of the stairs. Madame Jaubert obeyed the order, and in a few minutes returned.

I renewed my supplications to be released, and was of course extremely liberal of promises.

"It is vain talking," said the woman. "I do not believe they will harm you; but even if it were as you say, it is too late now to retrace my steps. You cannot escape. That fool below is already three-parts intoxicated: they are both armed, and would hesitate at nothing if they but suspected treachery."

It was vain to urge her. She grew sullen and menacing and was insisting that the gag should be replaced in my mouth, when a thought struck me.

"Levasseur called you Marie Duquesne just now; but surely your name is Jaubert—is it not?"

"Do not trouble yourself about my name," she replied, "that is my affair, not yours."

"Because if you *are* the Marie Duquesne who once kept a shop in Cranbourne Alley, and lost a child called Marie-Louise, I could tell you something."

A wild light broke from her dark eyes, and a suppressed scream from her lips. "I am that Marie Duquesne!" she said in a voice tremulous with emotion.

"Then I have to inform you that the child so long supposed to be lost I discovered nearly three weeks ago."

The woman fairly leapt towards me, clasped me fiercely by the arms, and peering in my face with eyes on fire with insane excitement, hissed out, "You lie—you lie, you dog! You are striving to deceive me! She is in heaven: the angels told me so long since."

I do not know, by the way, whether the falsehood I was endeavoring to palm off upon the woman was strictly justifiable or not; but I am fain to believe that there are few moralists that would not, under the circumstances, have acted pretty much as I did.

"If your child was lost when going on an errand to Coventry Street, and her name is Marie-Louise Duquesne, I tell you she is found. How should I otherwise have become acquainted with these particulars?"

"True—true," she muttered: "how else should he know? Where is she?" added the woman in tones of agonized entreaty, as she sank down and clasped my knees. "Tell me—tell me, as you hope for life or mercy, where I may find my child?"

"Release me, give me a chance of escape, and tomorrow your child shall be in your arms. Refuse, and the secret dies with me."

She sprang quickly to her feet, unclasped the handcuffs, snatched a knife from the table, and cut the cords which bound me with eager haste. "Another draught of wine," she said still in the same hurried, almost insane manner. "You have work to do! Now, whilst I secure the door, do you rub and chafe your stiffened joints." The door was soon fastened, and then she assisted in restoring the circulation to my partially-benumbed limbs. This was at last accomplished, and Marie Duquesne drew me towards a window, which she softly opened. "It is useless," she whispered, "to attempt a struggle with the men below. You must descend by this," and she placed her hand upon a lead water-pipe, which reached from the roof to within a few feet of the ground.

"And you," I said; "how are you to escape?"

"I will tell you. Do you hasten on towards Hampstead, from which we are distant in a northerly direction about a mile. There is a house at about half the distance. Procure help, and return as quickly as possible. The door-fastenings will resist some time, even should your flight be discovered. You will not fail me?"

"Be assured I will not." The descent was a difficult and somewhat perilous one, but it was safely accomplished, and I set off at the top of my speed towards Hampstead.

I had gone perhaps a quarter of a mile, when the distant sound of a horse's feet, coming at a slow trot towards me, caught my ear. I paused, to make sure I was not deceived, and as I did so, a wild scream from the direction I had left, followed by another and another, broke upon the stillness of the night. The scoundrels had no doubt discovered my escape, and were about to wreak their vengeance upon the unfortunate creature in their power. The trot of the horse which I had heard was, simultaneously with the breaking out of those wild outcries, increased to a rapid gallop. "Hallo!" exclaimed the horseman as he came swiftly up. "Do you know where these screams come from?" It was the horse-patrol who thus providentially came up! I briefly stated that the life of a woman was at the mercy of two escaped convicts. "Then for God's sake jump up behind me!" exclaimed the patrol. "We shall be there in a couple of minutes." I did so: the horse—a powerful animal, and not entirely unused to carry double—started off, as if it comprehended the necessity for speed, and in a very brief space of time we were at the door of the house from which I had so lately escaped. Marie Duquesne, with her body half out of the window, was still wildly screaming as we rushed into the room below. There was no one there, and we swiftly ascended the stairs, at the top of which we could hear Levasseur and Dubarle thundering at the door, which they had unexpectedly found fastened, and hurling a storm of imprecations at the woman within, the noise of which enabled us to approach them pretty nearly before we were heard or perceived. Martin saw us first, and his sudden exclamation alarmed the others. Dubarle and Martin made a desperate rush to pass us, by which I was momently thrown on one side against the wall; and very fortunately, as the bullet levelled at me from a pistol Levasseur held in his hand would probably have finished me. Martin escaped, which I was not very sorry for; but the patrol pinned Dubarle safely, and I griped Levasseur with a strength and ferocity against which he was powerless as an infant. Our victory was complete; and two hours afterwards, the recaptured convicts were safely lodged in a station-house.

I caused Madame Duquesne to be as gently undeceived the next morning as possible, with respect to her child; but the reaction and disappointment proved too much for her wavering intellect. She relapsed into positive insanity, and was placed in Bedlam, where she remained two years. At the end of that period she was pronounced convalescent. A sufficient sum of money was raised by myself and others, not only to send her to Paris, but to enable her to set up as a milliner in a small but respectable way. As lately as last May, when I saw her there she was in health both of mind and body, and doing comfortably.

With the concurrence of the police authorities, very little was said publicly respecting my entrapment. It might perhaps have excited a monomania amongst liberated convicts—colored and exaggerated as every incident would have been for the amusement of the public—to attempt similar exploits. I was also anxious to conceal the peril I had encountered from my wife; and it was not till I had left the police force that she was informed of it. Levasseur and Dubarle were convicted of returning from transportation before the term for which they had been sentenced had expired, and were this time sent across the seas for life. The reporters of the morning papers, or rather the reporter for the "Times," "Herald," "Chronicle," "Post," and "Advertiser," gave precisely the same account, even to the misspelling of Levasseur's name, dismissing the brief trial in the following paragraph, under the head of "Old Bailey Sessions:"—"Alphonse Dubarle (24), and Sebastian Levasson (49), were identified as unlawfully-returned convicts, and sentenced to transportation for life. The prisoners, it was understood, were connected with the late plate-robbery in Portman Square; but as conviction could not have increased their punishment, the indictment was not pressed."

Levasseur, I had almost forgotten to state, admitted that it was he who wounded me in Ryder's Court, Leicester Square.

IX

MARY KINGSFORD

Towards the close of the year 1836, I was hurriedly despatched to Liverpool for the purpose of securing the person of one Charles James Marshall, a collecting clerk, who, it was suddenly discovered, had absconded with a considerable sum of money belonging to his employers. I was too late—Charles James Marshall having sailed in one of the American liners the day before my arrival in the northern commercial capital. This fact well ascertained, I immediately set out on my return to London. Winter had come upon us unusually early; the weather was bitterly cold; and a piercing wind caused the snow, which had been falling heavily for several hours, to gyrate in fierce, blinding eddies, and heaped it up here and there into large and dangerous drifts. The obstruction offered by the rapidly-congealing snow greatly delayed our progress between Liverpool and Birmingham; and at a few miles only distant from the latter city, the leading engine ran off the line. Fortunately, the rate at which we were traveling was a very slow one, and no accident of moment occurred. Having no luggage to care for, I walked on to Birmingham, where I found the parliamentary train just on the point of starting, and with some hesitation, on account of the severity of the weather, I took my seat in one of the then very much exposed and uncomfortable carriages. We traveled steadily and safely, though slowly along, and reached Rugby Station in the afternoon, where we were to remain, the guard told us, till a fast down-train had passed. All of us hurried as quickly as we could to the large room at this station, where blazing fires and other appliances soon thawed the half-frozen bodies, and loosened the tongues of the numerous and motley passengers. After recovering the use of my benumbed limbs and faculties, I had leisure to look around and survey the miscellaneous assemblage about me.

Two persons had traveled in the same compartment with me from Birmingham, whose exterior, as disclosed by the dim light of the railway carriage, created some surprise that such a finely-attired, fashionable gentleman should stoop to journey by the plebeian penny-a-mile train. I could now observe them in a clearer light, and surprise at their apparent condescension vanished at once. To an eye less experienced than mine in the artifices and expedients familiar to a certain class of 'swells,' they might perhaps have passed muster for what they assumed to be, especially amidst the varied crowd of a 'parliamentary;' but their copper finery could not for a moment impose upon me. The watch-chains, were, I saw, mosaic; the watches, so frequently displayed, gilt; eye-glasses the same; the coats, fur-collared and cuffed, were ill-fitting and second-hand; ditto of the varnished boots and renovated velvet waistcoats; while the luxuriant moustaches and whiskers, and flowing wigs, were unmistakably mere *pièces d'occasion*—assumed and diversified at pleasure. They were both apparently about fifty years of age; one of them perhaps one or two years less than that. I watched them narrowly, the more so from their making themselves ostentatiously attentive to a young woman—girl rather she seemed—of a remarkably graceful figure, but whose face I had not yet obtained a glimpse of. They made boisterous way for her to the fire, and were profuse and noisy in their offers of refreshment—all of which, I observed, were peremptorily declined. She was dressed in deep, unexpensive mourning; and from her timid gestures and averted head, whenever either of the fellows addressed her, was, it was evident, terrified as well as annoyed by their rude and insolent notice. I quietly drew near to the side of the fire-place at which she stood, and with some difficulty obtained a sight of her features. I was struck with extreme surprise—not so much at her singular beauty, as from an instantaneous conviction that she was known to me, or at least that I had seen her frequently before, but where or when I could not at all call to mind. Again I looked, and my first impression was confirmed. At this moment the elder of the two men I have partially described placed his hand, with a rude familiarity, upon the girl's shoulder, proffering at the same time a glass of hot brandy and water for her acceptance. She turned sharply and indignantly away from the fellow; and looking round as if for protection, caught my eagerly-fixed gaze.

"Mr. Waters!" she impulsively ejaculated. "Oh, I am so glad!"

"Yes," I answered, "that is certainly my name; but I scarcely remember—. Stand back, fellow!" I angrily continued, as her tormentor, emboldened by the spirits he had drank, pressed with a jeering grin upon his face towards her, still tendering the brandy and water. "Stand back!" He replied by a curse and a threat. The next moment his flowing wig was whirling across the room, and he standing with his bullet-head bare but for a few locks of iron-gray, in an attitude of speechless rage and confusion, increased by the peals of laughter which greeted his ludicrous, unwigged aspect. He quickly put himself in a fighting attitude, and, backed by his companion, challenged me to battle. This was quite out of the question; and I was somewhat at a loss how to proceed, when the bell announcing the instant departure of the train rang out, my furious antagonist gathered up and adjusted his wig, and we all sallied forth to take our places—the young woman holding fast by my arm, and in a low, nervous voice, begging me not to leave her. I watched the two fellows take their seats, and then led her to the hindmost carriage, which we had to ourselves as far as the next station.

"Are Mrs. Waters and Emily quite well?" said the young woman coloring, and lowering her eyes beneath my earnest gaze, which she seemed for a moment to misinterpret.

"Quite, entirely so," I almost stammered. "You know us then?"

"Surely I do," she replied, reassured by my manner. "But you, it seems," she presently added with a winning smile, "have quite forgotten little Mary Kingsford."

"Mary Kingsford!" I exclaimed almost with a shout. "Why, so it is! But what a transformation a few years have effected!"

"Do you think so? Not *pretty* Mary Kingsford now then, I suppose?" she added with a light, pleasant laugh.

"You know what I mean, you vain puss you!" I rejoined quite gleefully; for I was overjoyed at meeting with the gentle, well-remembered playmate of my own eldest girl. We were old familiar friends—almost father and daughter—in an instant.

Little Mary Kingsford, I should state, was, when I left Yorkshire, one of the prettiest, most engaging children I had ever seen; and a petted favorite not only with us, but of every other family in the neighborhood. She was the only child of Philip and Mary Kingsford—a humble, worthy, and much-respected couple. The father was gardener to Sir Pyott Dalzell, and her mother eked out his wages to a respectable maintenance by keeping a cheap children's school. The change which a few years had wrought in the beautiful child was quite sufficient to account for my imperfect recognition of her; but the instant her name was mentioned, I at once recognised the rare comeliness which had charmed us all in her childhood. The soft brown eyes were the same, though now revealing profounder depths, and emitting a more pensive expression; the hair, though deepened in color, was still golden; her complexion, lit up as it now was by a sweet blush, was brilliant as ever; whilst her child-person had become matured and developed into womanly symmetry and grace. The brilliancy of color vanished from her cheek as I glanced meaningly at her mourning dress.

"Yes," she murmured in a sad quivering voice—"yes, father is gone! It will be six months come next Thursday that he died! Mother is well," she continued more cheerfully after a pause, "in health, but poorly off; and I—and I," she added with a faint effort at a smile, "am going to London to seek my fortune!"

"To seek your fortune!"

"Yes: you know my cousin, Sophy Clarke? In one of her letters, she said she often saw you."

I nodded without speaking. I knew little of Sophia Clarke, except that she was the somewhat gay, coquettish shopwoman of a highly respectable confectioner in the Strand, whom I shall call by the name of Morris.

"I am to be Sophy's fellow shop-assistant," continued Mary Kingsford; "not of course at first at such good wages as she gets. So lucky for me, is it not, since I must go to service? And so kind, too, of Sophy to interest herself for me!"

"Well, it may be so. But surely I have heard—my wife at least has—that you and Richard Westlake were engaged?—Excuse me, Mary, I was not aware the subject was a painful or unpleasant one."

"Richard's father," she replied with some spirit, "has higher views for his son. It is all off between us now," she added; "and perhaps it is for the best that it should be so."

I could have rightly interpreted these words without the aid of the partially expressed sigh which followed them. The perilous position of so attractive, so inexperienced, so guileless a young creature, amidst the temptations and vanities of London, so painfully impressed and preoccupied me, that I scarcely uttered another word till the rapidly diminishing rate of the train announced that we neared a station, after which it was probable we should have no farther opportunity for private converse.

"Those men—those fellows at Rugby—where did you meet with them?" I inquired.

"About thirty or forty miles below Birmingham, where they entered the carriage in which I was seated. At Birmingham I managed to avoid them."

Little more passed between us till we reached London. Sophia Clarke received her cousin at the Euston station, and was profuse of felicitations and compliments upon her arrival and personal appearance. After receiving a promise from Mary Kingsford to call and take tea with my wife and her old playmate on the following Sunday, I handed the two young women into a cab in waiting, and they drove off. I had not moved away from the spot when a voice a few paces behind me, which I thought I recognised, called out: "Quick, coachee, or you'll lose sight of them!" As I turned quickly round, another cab drove smartly off, which I followed at a run. I found, on reaching Lower Seymour Street, that I was not mistaken as to the owner of the voice, nor of his purpose. The fellow I had unwigged at Rugby thrust his head half out of the cab window, and pointing to the vehicle which contained the two girls, called out to the driver "to mind and make no mistake." The man nodded intelligence, and lashed his horse into a faster pace. Nothing that I might do could prevent the fellows from ascertaining Mary Kingsford's place of abode; and as that was all that, for the present at least, need be apprehended, I desisted from pursuit, and bent my steps homewards.

Mary Kingsford kept her appointment on the Sunday, and in reply to our questioning, said she liked her situation very well. Mr. and Mrs. Morris were exceedingly kind to her; so was Sophia. "Her cousin," she added in reply to a look which I could not repress, "was perhaps a little gay and free of manner, but the best-hearted creature in the world." The two fellows who had followed them had, I found, already twice visited the shop; but their attentions appeared now to be exclusively directed towards Sophia Clarke, whose vanity they not a little gratified. The names they gave were Heartly and Simpson. So entirely guileless and unsophisticated was the gentle country maiden, that I saw she scarcely comprehended the hints and warnings which I threw out. At parting, however, she made me a serious promise that she would instantly apply to me should any difficulty or perplexity overtake her.

I often called in at the confectioner's, and was gratified to find that Mary's modest propriety of behavior, in a somewhat difficult position, had gained her the goodwill of her employers, who invariably spoke of her with kindness and respect. Nevertheless, the cark and care of a London life, with its incessant employment and late hours, soon, I perceived, began to tell upon her health and spirits; and it was consequently with a strong emotion of pleasure I heard from my wife that she had seen a passage in a letter from Mary's mother, to the effect that the elder Westlake was betraying symptoms of yielding to the angry and passionate expostulations of his only son, relative to the enforced breaking off of his engagement with Mary Kingsford. The blush with which she presented the letter was, I was told, very eloquent.

One evening, on passing Morris' shop, I observed Hartley and Simpson there. They were swallowing custards and other confectionary with much gusto; and, from their new and costly habiliments, seemed to be in surprisingly good case. They were smirking and smiling at the cousins with rude confidence; and Sophia Clarke, I was grieved to see, repaid their insulting impertinence by her most elaborate smiles and graces. I passed on; and presently meeting with a brother-detective, who, it struck me, might know something of the two gentlemen, I turned back with him, and pointed them out. A glance sufficed him.

"Hartley and Simpson you say?" he remarked after we had walked away to some distance: "Those are only two of their numerous *aliases*. I cannot, however, say that I am as yet on very familiar terms with them; but as I am especially directed to cultivate their acquaintance, there is no doubt we shall be more intimate with each other before long. Gamblers, blacklegs, swindlers, I already know them to be; and I would take odds they are not unfrequently something more, especially when fortune and the bones run cross with them."

"They appear to be in high feather just now," I remarked.

"Yes: they are connected, I suspect, with the gang who cleaned out young Garslade last week in Jermyn Street. I'd lay a trifle," added my friend, as I turned to leave him, "that one or both of them will wear the queen's livery gray turned up with yellow, before many weeks are past. Goodbye."

About a fortnight after this conversation, I and my wife paid a visit to Astley's, for the gratification of our youngsters, who had long been promised a sight of the equestrian marvels exhibited at that celebrated amphitheatre. It was the latter end of February; and when we came out of the theatre, we found the weather had changed to dark and sleety, with a sharp, nipping wind. I had to call at Scotland-Yard; my wife and children consequently proceeded home in a cab without me; and after assisting to quell a slight disturbance originating in a gin-palace close by, I went on my way over Westminster Bridge. The inclement weather had cleared the streets and thoroughfares in a surprisingly short time; so that, excepting myself, no foot-passenger was visible on the bridge till I had about half-crossed it, when a female figure, closely muffled up about the head, and sobbing bitterly, passed rapidly by on the opposite side. I turned and gazed after the retreating figure: it was a youthful, symmetrical one; and after a few moments' hesitation, I determined to follow at a distance, and as unobservedly as I could. On the woman sped, without pause or hesitation, till she reached Astley's, where I observed her stop suddenly, and toss her arms in the air with a gesture of desperation. I quickened my steps, which she observing, uttered a slight scream, and darted swiftly off again, moaning and sobbing as she ran. The slight momentary glimpse I had obtained of her features beneath the gaslamp opposite Astley's, suggested a frightful apprehension, and I followed at my utmost speed. She turned at the first-cross street, and I should soon have overtaken her, but that in darting round the corner where she disappeared, I ran full butt against a stout, elderly gentleman, who was hurrying smartly along out of the weather. What with the suddenness of the shock and the slipperiness of the pavement, down we both reeled; and by the time we had regained our feet, and growled savagely at each other, the young woman, whoever she was, had disappeared, and more than half an hour's eager search after her proved fruitless. At last I bethought me of hiding at one corner of Westminster Bridge. I had watched impatiently for about twenty minutes, when I observed the object of my pursuit stealing timidly and furtively towards the bridge on the opposite side of the way. As she came nearly abreast of where I stood, I darted forward; she saw, without recognising me, and uttering an exclamation of terror, flew down towards the river, where a number of pieces of balk and other timber were fastened together, forming a kind of loose raft. I followed with desperate haste, for I saw that it was indeed Mary Kingsford, and loudly calling to her by name to stop. She did not appear to hear me, and in a few moments the unhappy girl had gained the end of the timber-raft. One instant she paused with clasped hands upon the brink, and in another had thrown herself into the dark and moaning river. On reaching the spot where she had disappeared, I could not at first see her in consequence of the dark mourning dress she had on. Presently I caught sight of her, still upborne by her spread clothes, but already carried by the swift current beyond my reach. The only chance was to crawl along a piece of round timber which projected farther into the river, and by the end of which she must pass. This I effected with some difficulty; and laying myself out at full length, vainly endeavored, with out-stretched, straining arms, to grasp her dress. There was nothing left for it but to plunge in after her. I will confess that I hesitated to do so. I was encumbered with a heavy dress, which there was no time to put off, and moreover, like most inland men, I was but an indifferent swimmer. My indecision quickly vanished. The wretched girl, though gradually sinking, had not yet uttered a cry, or appeared to struggle; but when the chilling waters reached her lips, she seemed to suddenly revive to a consciousness of the horror of her fate: she fought wildly with the engulphing tide, and shrieked piteously for help. Before one could count ten, I had grasped her by the arm, and lifted her head above the surface of the river. As I did so, I felt as if suddenly encased and weighed down by leaden garments, so quickly had my thick clothing and high boots sucked in the water. Vainly, thus burdened and impeded, did I endeavor to regain the raft; the strong tide bore us outwards, and I glared round, in inexpressible dismay, for some means of extrication from the frightful peril in which I found myself involved. Happily, right in the direction the tide was drifting us, a large barge lay moored by a chain-cable. Eagerly I seized and twined one arm firmly round it, and thus partially secure, hallooed with renewed power for assistance. It soon came: a passer-by had witnessed the flight of the girl and my pursuit, and was already hastening with others to our assistance. A wherry was unmoored: guided by my voice, they soon reached us; and but a brief interval elapsed before we were safely housed in an adjoining tavern.

A change of dress, with which the landlord kindly supplied me, a blazing fire, and a couple of glasses of hot brandy and water, soon restored warmth and vigor to my chilled and partially benumbed limbs; but more than two hours elapsed before Mary, who had swallowed a good deal of water, was in a condition to be removed. I had just sent for a cab, when two police-officers, well known to me, entered the room with official briskness. Mary screamed, staggered towards me, and clinging to my arm, besought me with frantic earnestness to save her.

"What *is* the meaning of this?" I exclaimed, addressing one of the police-officers.

"Merely," said he, "the young woman that's clinging so tight to you has been committing an audacious robbery—"

"No—no—no!" broke in the terrified girl.

"Oh! of course you'll say so," continued the officer. "All I know is, that the diamond brooch was found snugly hid away in her own box. But come, we have been after you for the last three hours; so you had better come along at once."

"Save me!—save me!" sobbed poor Mary, as she tightened her grasp upon my arm and looked with beseeching agony in my face.

"Be comforted," I whispered; "you shall go home with me. Calm yourself, Miss Kingsford," I added in a louder tone: "I no more believe you have stolen a diamond brooch than that I have."

"Bless you!—bless you!" she gasped in the intervals of her convulsive sobs.

"There is some wretched misapprehension in this business, I am quite sure." I continued; "but at all events I shall bail her—for this night at least."

"Bail her! That is hardly regular."

"No; but you will tell the superintendent that Mary Kingsford is in my custody, and that I answer for her appearance tomorrow."

The men hesitated, but I stood too well at headquarters for them to do more than hesitate; and the cab I had ordered being just then announced, I passed with Mary out of the room as quickly as I could, for I feared her senses were again leaving her. The air revived her somewhat, and I lifted her into the cab, placing myself beside her. She appeared to listen in fearful doubt whether I should be allowed to take her with me; and it was not till the wheels had made a score of revolutions that her fears vanished; then throwing herself upon my neck in an ecstacy of gratitude, she burst into a flood of tears, and continued till we reached home sobbing on my bosom like a broken-hearted child. She had, I found, been there about ten o'clock to seek me, and being told that I was gone to Astley's, had started off to find me there.

Mary still slept, or at least she had not risen, when I left home the following morning to endeavor to get at the bottom of the strange accusation preferred against her. I first saw the superintendent, who, after hearing what I had to say, quite approved of all that I had done, and intrusted the case entirely to my care. I next saw Mr. and Mrs. Morris and Sophia Clarke, and then waited upon the prosecutor, a youngish gentleman of the name of Saville, lodging in Essex Street, Strand. One or two things I heard, necessitated a visit to other officers of police, incidentally, as I found, mixed up with the affair. By the time all this was done, and an effectual watch had been placed upon Mr. Augustus Saville's movements, evening had fallen, and I wended my way homewards, both to obtain a little rest, and hear Mary Kingsford's version of the strange story.

The result of my inquiries may be thus briefly summed up. Ten days before, Sophia Clarke told her cousin that she had orders for Covent-Garden Theatre; and as it was not one of their busy nights, she thought they might obtain leave to go. Mary expressed her doubt of this, as both Mr. and Mrs. Morris, who were strict, and somewhat fanatical Dissenters, disapproved of play-going, especially for young women. Nevertheless Sophia asked, informed Mary that the required permission had been readily accorded, and off they went in high spirits; Mary especially, who had never been to a theatre in her life before. When there, they were joined by Hartley and Simpson, much to Mary's annoyance and vexation, especially as she saw that her cousin expected them. She had, in fact, accepted the orders from them. At the conclusion of the entertainments, they all four came out together, when suddenly there arose a hustling and confusion, accompanied with loud outcries, and a violent swaying to and fro of the crowd. The disturbance was, however, soon quelled; and Mary and her cousin had reached the outer door, when two police-officers seized Hartley and his friend, and insisted upon their going with them. A scuffle ensued; but other officers being at hand, the two men were secured and carried off. The cousins, terribly frightened, called a coach, and were very glad to find themselves safe at home again. And now it came out that Mr. and Mrs. Morris had been told that they were going to spend the evening at *my* house, and had no idea they were going to the play! Vexed as Mary was at the deception, she was too kindly-tempered to refuse to keep her cousin's secret; especially knowing as she did that the discovery of the deceit Sophia had practised would in all probability be followed by her immediate discharge. Hartley and his friend swaggered on the following afternoon into the shop, and whispered Sophia that their arrest by the police had arisen from a strange mistake, for which the most ample apologies had been offered and accepted. After this, matters went on as usual, except that Mary perceived a growing insolence and familiarity in Hartley's manner towards her. His language was frequently quite unintelligible, and once he asked her plainly "if she did not mean that he should go *shares* in the prize she had lately found?" Upon Mary replying that she did not comprehend him, his look became absolutely ferocious, and he exclaimed: "Oh, that's your game, is it? But don't try it on with me, my good girl, I advise you." So violent did he become, that Mr. Morris was attracted by the noise, and ultimately bundled him, neck and heels, out of the shop. She had not seen either him or his companion since.

On the evening of the previous day, a gentleman whom she never remembered to have seen before, entered the shop, took a seat, and helped himself to a tart. She observed that after a while he looked at her very earnestly, and at length approaching quite close, said, "You were at Covent Garden Theatre last Tuesday evening week?" Mary was struck, as she said, all of a heap, for both Mr. and Mrs. Morris were in the shop, and heard the question.

"Oh, no, no! you mistake," she said hurriedly, and feeling at the same time her cheeks kindle into flame.

"Nay, but you were though," rejoined the gentleman. And then lowering his voice to a whisper, he said, "And let me advise you, if you would avoid exposure and condign punishment, to restore me the diamond brooch you robbed me of on that evening."

Mary screamed with terror, and a regular scene ensued. She was obliged to confess she had told a falsehood in denying she was at the theatre on the night in question, and Mr. Morris after that seemed inclined to believe anything of her. The gentleman persisted in his charge; but at the same time vehemently iterating his assurance that all he wanted was his property; and it was ultimately decided that Mary's boxes, as well as her person, should be searched. This was done; and to her utter consternation the brooch was found concealed, they said, in a black silk reticule. Denials, asservations, were vain. Mr. Saville identified the brooch, but once more offered to be content with its restoration. This Mr. Morris, a just, stern man, would not consent to, and he went out to summon a police-officer. Before he returned, Mary, by the advice of both her cousin and Mrs. Morris, had fled the house, and hurried in a state of distraction to find me, with what result the reader already knows.

"It is a wretched business," I observed to my wife, as soon as Mary Kingsford had retired to rest, at about nine o'clock in the evening. "Like you, I have no doubt of the poor girl's perfect innocence; but how to establish it by satisfactory evidence is another matter. I must take her to Bow Street the day after tomorrow."

"Good God, how dreadful! Can nothing be done? What does the prosecutor say the brooch is worth?"

"His uncle," he says, "gave a hundred and twenty guineas for it. But that signifies little; for were its worth only a hundred and twenty farthings, compromise is, you know, out of the question."

"I did not mean that. Can you show it me? I am a pretty good judge of the value of jewels."

"Yes, you can see it." I took it out of the desk in which I had locked it up, and placed it before her. It was a splendid emerald, encircled by large brilliants.

My wife twisted and turned it about, holding it in all sorts of lights, and at last said—"I do not believe that either the emerald or the brilliants are real—that the brooch is, in fact, worth twenty shillings intrinsically."

"Do you say so?" I exclaimed as I jumped up from my chair, for my wife's words gave color and consistence to a dim and faint suspicion which had crossed my mind. "Then, this Saville is a manifest liar; and perhaps confederate with—. But give me my hat; I will ascertain this point at once."

I hurried to a jeweller's shop, and found that my wife's opinion was correct: apart from the workmanship, which was very fine, the brooch was valueless. Conjectures, suspicions, hopes, fears, chased each other with bewildering rapidity through my brain; and in order to collect and arrange my thoughts, I stepped out of the whirl of the streets into Dolly's Chop-house, and decided, over a quiet glass of negus, upon my plan of operations.

The next morning there appeared at the top of the second column of the "Times" an earnest appeal, worded with careful obscurity, so that only the person to whom it was addressed should easily understand it, to the individual who had lost or been robbed of a false stone and brilliants at the theatre, to communicate with a certain person—whose address I gave—without delay, in order to save the reputation, perhaps the life, of an innocent person.

I was at the address I had given by nine o'clock. Several hours passed without bringing any one, and I was beginning to despair, when a gentleman of the name of Bagshawe was announced: I fairly leaped for joy, for this was beyond my hopes.

A gentleman presently entered, of about thirty years of age, of a distinguished, though somewhat dissipated aspect.

"This brooch is yours?" said I, exhibiting it without delay or preface.

"It is; and I am here to know what your singular advertisement means?"

I briefly explained the situation of affairs.

"The rascals!" he broke in almost before I had finished; "I will briefly explain it all. A fellow of the name of Hartley, at least that was the name he gave, robbed me, I was pretty sure, of this brooch. I pointed him out to the police, and he was taken into custody; but nothing being found upon him, he was discharged."

"Not entirely, Mr. Bagshawe, on that account. You refused, when arrived at the station-house, to state what you had been robbed of; and you, moreover, said, in presence of the culprit, that you were to embark with your regiment for India the next day. That regiment, I have ascertained, did embark, as you said it would."

"True; but I had leave of absence, and shall take the Overland route. The truth is, that during the walk to the station-house,

I had leisure to reflect that if I made a formal charge, it would lead to awkward disclosures. This brooch is an imitation of one presented me by a valued relative. Losses at play—since, for this unfortunate young woman's sake, I *must* out with it—obliged me to part with the original; and I wore this, in order to conceal the fact from my relative's knowledge."

"This will, sir," I replied, "prove, with a little management, quite sufficient for all purposes. You have no objection to accompany me to the superintendent?"

"Not in the least: only I wish the devil had the brooch as well as the fellow that stole it."

About half-past five o'clock on the same evening, the street door was quietly opened by the landlord of the house in which Mr. Saville lodged, and I walked into the front room on the first floor, where I found the gentleman I sought languidly reclining on a sofa. He gathered himself smartly up at my appearance, and looked keenly in my face. He did not appear to like what he read there.

"I did not expect to see you today," he said at last.

"No, perhaps not: but I have news for you. Mr. Bagshawe, the owner of the hundred and twenty guinea brooch your deceased uncle gave you, did *not* sail for India, and—"

The wretched cur, before I could conclude, was on his knees begging for mercy with disgusting abjectness. I could have spurned the scoundrel where he crawled.

"Come, sir!" I cried, "Let us have no snivelling or humbug: mercy is not in my power, as you ought to know. Strive to deserve it. We want Hartley and Simpson, and cannot find them: you must aid us."

"Oh yes; to be sure I will!" eagerly rejoined the rascal "I will go for them at once," he added with a kind of hesitating assurance.

"Nonsense! *Send* for them, you mean. Do so, and I will wait their arrival."

His note was despatched by a sure hand; and meanwhile I arranged the details of the expected meeting. I, and a friend, whom I momently expected, would ensconce ourselves behind a large screen in the room, whilst Mr. Augustus Saville would run playfully over the charming plot with his two friends, so that we might be able to fully appreciate its merits. Mr. Saville agreed. I rang the bell, an officer appeared, and we took our posts in readiness. We had scarcely done so, when the street-bell rang, and Saville announced the arrival of his confederates. There was a twinkle in the fellow's green eyes which I thought I understood. "Do not try that on, Mr. Augustus Saville," I quietly remarked: "we are but two here certainly, but there are half a dozen in waiting below."

No more was said, and in another minute the friends met. It was a boisterously jolly meeting, as far as shaking hands and mutual felicitations on each other's good looks and health went. Saville was, I thought, the most obstreperously gay of all three.

"And yet now I look at you, Saville, closely," said Hartley, "you don't look quite the thing. Have you seen a ghost?"

"No; but this cursed brooch affair worries me."

"Nonsense!—humbug!—it's all right: we are all embarked in the same boat. It's a regular three-handed game. I prigged it; Simmy here whipped it into pretty Mary's reticule, which she, I suppose, never looked into till the row came; and *you* claimed it—a regular merry-go-round, ain't it, eh? Ha! ha! ha!—Ha!"

"Quite so, Mr. Hartley," said I, suddenly facing him, and at the same time stamping on the floor; "as you say, a delightful merry-go-round; and here, you perceive," I added, as the officers crowded into the room, "are more gentlemen to join in it."

I must not stain the paper with the curses, imprecations, blasphemies, which for a brief space resounded through the apartment. The rascals were safely and separately locked up a quarter of an hour afterwards; and before a month had passed away, all three were transported. It is scarcely necessary to remark, that they believed the brooch to be genuine, and of great value.

Mary Kingsford did not need to return to her employ. Westlake the elder withdrew his veto upon his son's choice, and the wedding was celebrated in the following May with great rejoicing; Mary's old playmate officiating as bride-maid, and I as bride's-father. The still young couple have now a rather numerous family, and a home blessed with affection, peace, and competence. It was some time, however, before Mary recovered from the shock of her London adventure; and I am pretty sure that the disagreeable reminiscences inseparably connected in her mind with the metropolis, will prevent at least *one* person from being present at the World's Great Fair.

X

FLINT JACKSON

Farnham hops are world-famous, or at least famous in that huge portion of the world where English ale is drunk, and whereon, I have a thousand times heard and read, the sun never sets. The name, therefore, of the pleasant Surrey village, in and about which the events I am about to relate occurred, is, I may fairly presume, known to many of my readers. I was ordered to Farnham, to investigate a case of burglary, committed in the house of a gentleman of the name of Hursley, during the temporary absence of the family, which had completely nonplussed the unpractised Dogberrys of the place, albeit it was not a riddle at all difficult to read. The premises, it was quickly plain to me, had been broken, not into, but out of; and a watch being set upon the motions of the very specious and clever person left in charge of the house and property, it was speedily discovered that the robbery had been effected by herself and a confederate, of the name of Dawkins, her brother-in-law. Some of the stolen goods were found secreted at his lodgings; but the most valuable portion, consisting of plate, and a small quantity of jewelry, had disappeared: it had questionless been converted into money, as considerable sums, in sovereigns, were found upon both Dawkins and the woman, Sarah Purday. Now, as it had been clearly ascertained that neither of the prisoners had left Farnham since the burglary, it was manifest there was a receiver near at hand who had purchased the missing articles. Dawkins and Purday were, however, dumb as stones upon the subject; and nothing occurred to point suspicion till early in the evening previous to the second examination of the prisoners before the magistrates, when Sarah Purday asked for pen, ink, and paper, for the purpose of writing to one Mr. Jackson, in whose service she had formerly lived. I happened to be at the prison, and of course took the liberty of carefully unsealing her note and reading it. It revealed nothing; and save by its extremely cautious wording, and abrupt peremptory tone, coming from a servant to her former master, suggested nothing. I had carefully reckoned the number of sheets of paper sent into the cell, and now on recounting them found that three were missing. The turnkey returned immediately, and asked for the two other letters she had written. The woman denied having written any other, and for proof pointed to the torn fragments of the missing sheets lying on the floor. These were gathered up and brought to me, but I could make nothing out of them, every word having been carefully run through with the pen, and converted into an unintelligible blot. The request contained in the actually-written letter was one simple enough in itself, merely, "that Mr. Jackson would not on any account fail to provide her, in consideration of past services, with legal assistance on the morrow." The first nine words were strongly underlined; and I made out after a good deal of trouble that the word "pretence" had been partially effaced, and "account" substituted for it.

"She need not have wasted three sheets of paper upon such a nonsensical request as that," observed the turnkey. "Old Jackson wouldn't shell out sixpence to save her or anybody else from the gallows."

"I am of a different opinion; but tell me, what sort of a person is this former master of hers?"

"All I know about him is that he's a cross-grained, old curmudgeon, living about a mile out of Farnham, who scrapes money together by lending small sums upon notes-of-hand at short dates, and at a thundering interest. Flint Jackson folk about here call him."

"At all events, forward the letter at once, and tomorrow we shall see—what we shall see. Good-evening."

It turned out as I anticipated. A few minutes after the prisoners were brought into the justice-room, a Guilford solicitor of much local celebrity arrived, and announced that he appeared for both the inculpated parties. He was allowed a private conference with them, at the close of which he stated that his clients would reserve their defence. They were at once committed for trial, and I overheard the solicitor assure the woman that the ablest counsel on the circuit would be retained in their behalf.

I had no longer a doubt that it was my duty to know something further of this suddenly-generous Flint Jackson, though how to set about it was a matter of considerable difficulty. There was no legal pretence for a search-warrant, and I doubted the prudence of proceeding upon my own responsibility with so astute an old fox as Jackson was represented to be; for, supposing him to be a confederate with the burglars, he had by this time in all probability sent the stolen property away—to London in all likelihood; and should I find nothing, the consequences of ransacking his house merely because he had provided a former servant with legal assistance would be serious. Under these circumstances I wrote to headquarters for instructions, and by return of post received orders to prosecute the inquiry thoroughly, but cautiously, and to consider time as nothing so long as there appeared a chance of fixing Jackson with the guilt of receiving the plunder. Another suspicious circumstance that I have omitted to notice in its place was that the Guilford solicitor tendered bail for the prisoners to any reasonable amount, and named Enoch Jackson as one of the securities. Bail was, however, refused.

There was no need for over-hurrying the business, as the prisoners were committed to the Surrey Spring Assizes, and it was now the season of the hop-harvest—a delightful and hilarious period about Farnham when the weather is fine and the yield abundant. I, however, lost no time in making diligent and minute inquiry as to the character and habits of Jackson, and the result was a full conviction that nothing but the fear of being denounced as an accomplice could have induced such a miserly, iron-hearted rogue to put himself to charges in defence of the imprisoned burglars.

One afternoon, whilst pondering the matter, and at the same time enjoying the prettiest and cheerfulest of rural sights, that of hop-picking, the apothecary at whose house I was lodging—we will call him Mr. Morgan; he *was* a Welshman—tapped me suddenly on the shoulder, and looking sharply round, I perceived he had something he deemed of importance to communicate.

"What is it?" I said quickly.

"The oddest thing in the world. There's Flint Jackson, his deaf old woman, and the young people lodging with him, all drinking and boozing away at yon alehouse."

"Shew them to me, if you please."

A few minutes brought us to the place of boisterous entertainment, the lower room of which was suffocatingly full of tipplers and tobacco-smoke. We nevertheless contrived to edge ourselves in; and my companion stealthily pointed out the group, who were seated together near the farther window, and then left me to myself.

The appearance of Jackson entirely answered to the popular prefix of Flint attached to his name. He was a wiry, gnarled, heavy-browed, iron-jawed fellow of about sixty, with deep-set eyes aglow with sinister and greedy instincts. His wife, older than he, and so deaf apparently as the door of a dungeon, wore a simpering, imbecile look of wonderment, it seemed to me, at the presence of such unusual and abundant cheer. The young people, who lodged with Jackson, were really a very frank, honest, good-looking couple, though not then appearing to advantage—the countenance of Henry Rogers being flushed and inflamed with drink, and that of his wife's clouded with frowns, at the situation in which she found herself, and the riotous conduct of her husband. Their brief history was this:—They had both been servants in a family living not far distant from Farnham—Sir Thomas Lethbridge's, I understood—when about three or four months previous to the present time, Flint Jackson, who had once been in an attorney's office, discovered that Henry Rogers, in consequence of the death of a distant relative in London, was entitled to property worth something like £1500. There were, however, some law-difficulties in the way, which Jackson offered, if the business was placed in his hands, to overcome for a consideration, and in the meantime to supply board and lodging and such necessary sums of money as Henry Rogers might require. With this brilliant prospect in view service became at once utterly distasteful. The fortunate legatee had for some time courted Mary Elkins, one of the ladies' maids, a pretty, bright-eyed brunette; and they were both united in the bonds of holy matrimony on the very day the "warnings" they had given expired. Since then they had lived at Jackson's house in daily expectation of their "fortune," with which they proposed to start in the public line.

Finding myself unrecognized, I called boldly for a pot and a pipe, and after some manœuvring contrived to seat myself within ear-shot of Jackson and his party. They presented a strange study. Henry Rogers was boisterously excited, and not only drinking freely himself, but treating a dozen fellows round him, the cost of which he from time to time called upon "Old Flint," as he courteously styled his ancient friend, to discharge.

"Come, fork out, Old Flint!" he cried again and again. "It'll be all right, you know, in a day or two, and a few half-pence over. Shell out, old fellow! What signifies, so you're happy?"

Jackson complied with an affectation of acquiescent gaiety ludicrous to behold. It was evident that each successive pull at his purse was like wrenching a tooth out of his head, and yet while the dismalest of smiles wrinkled his wolfish mouth, he kept exclaiming: "A fine lad—a fine lad! Generous as a prince! Good Lord, another round! He minds money no more than as if gold was as plentiful as gravel! But a fine generous lad for all that!"

Jackson, I perceived, drank considerably, as if incited thereto by compressed savageness. The pretty young wife would not taste a drop, but tears frequently filled her eyes, and bitterness pointed her words as she vainly implored her husband to leave the place and go home with her. To all her remonstrances the maudlin drunkard replied only by foolery, varied occasionally by an attempt at a line or two of the song of "The Thorn."

"But you *will* plant thorns, Henry," rejoined the provoked wife in a louder and angrier tone than she ought perhaps to have used—"not only in my bosom, but your own, if you go on in this sottish, disgraceful way."

"Always quarreling, always quarreling!" remarked Jackson, pointedly, towards the bystanders—"*Always* quarreling!"

"Who is always quarreling?" demanded the young wife sharply. "Do you mean me and Henry?"

"I was only saying, my dear, that you don't like your husband to be so generous and free-hearted—that's all," replied Jackson, with a confidential wink at the persons near him.

"Free-hearted and generous! Fool-hearted and crazy, you mean!" rejoined the wife, who was much excited. "And you ought to be ashamed of yourself to give him money for such brutish purposes."

"Always quarreling, always quarreling!" iterated Jackson, but this time unheard by Mrs. Rogers—"*Always*, perpetually quarreling!"

I could not quite comprehend all this. If so large a sum as £1500 was really coming to the young man, why should Jackson wince as he did at disbursing small amounts which he could repay himself with abundant interest? If otherwise—and it was probable he should not be repaid—what meant his eternal, "fine generous lad!" "spirited young man!" and so on? What, above all, meant that look of diabolical hate which shot out from his cavernous eyes towards Henry Rogers when he thought himself unobserved, just after satisfying a fresh claim on his purse? Much practice in reading the faces and deportment of such men made it pretty clear to me that Jackson's course of action respecting the young man and his money was not yet decided upon in his own mind; that he was still perplexed and irresolute; and hence the apparent contradiction in his words and acts.

Henry Rogers at length dropped asleep with his head upon one of the settle-tables; Jackson sank into sullen silence; the noisy room grew quiet; and I came away.

I was impressed with a belief that Jackson entertained some sinister design against his youthful and inexperienced lodgers and I determined to acquaint them with my suspicions. For this purpose Mr. Morgan, who had a patient living near Jackson's house, undertook to invite them to tea on some early evening, on the pretence that he had heard of a tavern that might suit them when they should receive their fortune. Let me confess, too, that I had another design besides putting the young people on their guard against Jackson. I thought it very probable that it would not be difficult to glean from them some interesting and suggestive particulars concerning the ways, means, practices, outgoings and incomings, of their worthy landlord's household.

Four more days passed unprofitably away, and I was becoming weary of the business, when about five o'clock in the afternoon the apothecary galloped up to his door on a borrowed horse, jumped off with surprising celerity, and with a face as white as his own magnesia, burst out as he hurried into the room where I was sitting: "Here's a pretty kettle of fish! Henry Rogers has been poisoned, and by his wife!"

"Poisoned!"

"Yes, poisoned; although, thanks to my being on the spot I think he will recover. But I must instantly to Dr. Edwards: I will tell you all when I return."

The promised "all" was this: Morgan was passing slowly by Jackson's house, in the hope of seeing either Mr. or Mrs. Rogers, when the servant-woman, Jane Riddet, ran out and begged him to come in, as their lodger had been taken suddenly ill. Ill indeed! The surface of his body was cold as death, and the apothecary quickly discovered that he had been poisoned with sulphuric acid (oil of vitriol), a quantity of which he, Morgan, had sold a few days previously to Mrs. Rogers, who, when purchasing it, said Mr. Jackson wanted it to apply to some warts that annoyed him. Morgan fortunately knew the proper remedy, and desired Jackson, who was in the room, and seemingly very anxious and flurried, to bring some soap instantly, a solution of which he proposed to give immediately to the seemingly dying man. The woman-servant was gone to find Mrs. Rogers, who had left about ten minutes before, having first made the tea in which the poison had been taken. Jackson hurried out of the apartment, but was gone so long that Morgan, becoming impatient, scraped a quantity of plaster off the wall, and administered it with the best effect. At last Jackson came back, and said there was unfortunately not a particle of soap in the house. A few minutes afterwards the young wife, alarmed at the woman-servant's tidings, flew into the room in an agony of alarm and grief. Simulated alarm, crocodile grief,

Mr. Morgan said; for there could, in his opinion, be no doubt that she had attempted to destroy her husband. Mr. Jackson, on being questioned, peremptorily denied that he had ever desired Mrs. Rogers to procure sulphuric acid for him, or had received any from her—a statement which so confounded the young woman that she instantly fainted. The upshot was that Mrs. Rogers was taken into custody and lodged in prison.

This terrible news flew through Farnham like wildfire. In a few minutes it was upon everybody's tongue: the hints of the quarrelsome life the young couple led, artfully spread by Jackson, were recalled, and no doubt appeared to be entertained of the truth of the dreadful charge. I had no doubt either, but my conviction was not that of the Farnham folk. This, then, was the solution of the struggle I had seen going on in Jackson's mind; this the realization of the dark thought which I had imperfectly read in the sinister glances of his restless eyes. He had intended to destroy both the husband and wife—the one by poison, and the other by the law! Doubtless, then, the £1500 had been obtained, and this was the wretched man's infernal device for retaining it! I went over with Morgan early the next morning to see the patient, and found that, thanks to the prompt antidote administered, and Dr. Edwards' subsequent active treatment, he was rapidly recovering. The still-suffering young man, I was glad to find, would not believe for a moment in his wife's guilt. I watched the looks and movements of Jackson attentively—a scrutiny which he, now aware of my vocation, by no means appeared to relish.

"Pray," said I, suddenly addressing Riddet, the woman-servant—"pray, how did it happen that you had no soap in such a house as this yesterday evening?"

"No soap!" echoed the woman, with a stare of surprise. "Why—"

"No—no soap," hastily broke in her master with loud and menacing emphasis. "There was not a morsel in the house. I bought some afterwards in Farnham."

The cowed and bewildered woman slunk away. I was more than satisfied; and judging by Jackson's countenance, which changed beneath my look to the color of the lime-washed wall against which he stood, he surmised that I was.

My conviction, however, was not evidence, and I felt that I should need even more than my wonted good-fortune to bring the black crime home to the real perpetrator. For the present, at all events, I must keep silence—a resolve I found hard to persist in at the examination of the accused wife, an hour or two afterwards, before the county magistrates. Jackson had hardened himself to iron, and gave his lying evidence with ruthless self-possession. He had *not* desired Mrs. Rogers to purchase sulphuric acid; had *not* received any from her. In addition also to his testimony that she and her husband were always quarreling, it was proved by a respectable person that high words had passed between them on the evening previous to the day the criminal offence was committed, and that foolish, passionate expressions had escaped her about wishing to be rid of such a drunken wretch. This evidence, combined with the medical testimony, appeared so conclusive to the magistrates, that spite of the unfortunate woman's wild protestations of innocence, and the rending agony which convulsed her frame, and almost choked her utterance, she was remanded to prison till that day-week, when, the magistrates informed her, she would be again brought up for the merely formal completion of the depositions, and be then fully committed on the capital charge.

I was greatly disturbed, and walked for two or three hours about the quiet neighborhood of Farnham, revolving a hundred fragments of schemes for bringing the truth to light, without arriving at any feasible conclusion. One only mode of procedure seemed to offer, and that but dimly, a hope of success. It was, however, the best I could hit upon, and I directed my steps towards the Farnham prison. Sarah Purday had not yet, I remembered, been removed to the county jail at Guilford.

"Is Sarah Purday," I asked the turnkey, "more reconciled to her position than she was?"

"She's just the same—bitter as gall, and venomous as a viper."

This woman, I should state, was a person of fierce will and strong passions, and in early life had been respectably situated.

"Just step into her cell," I continued, "upon some excuse or other, and carelessly drop a hint that if she could prevail upon Jackson to get her brought by *habeas* before a judge in London, there could be no doubt of her being bailed."

The man stared, but after a few words of pretended explanation, went off to do as I requested. He was not long gone. "She's all in a twitteration at the thoughts of it," he said; "and must have pen, ink, and paper, without a moment's delay, bless her consequence!"

These were supplied; and I was soon in possession of her letter, couched cautiously, but more peremptorily than the former one. I need hardly say it did not reach its destination. She passed the next day in a state of feverish impatience; and no answer returning, wrote again, her words this time conveying an evident though indistinct threat. I refrained from visiting her till two days had thus passed, and found her, as I expected, eaten up with fury. She glared at me as I entered the cell like a chained tigress.

"You appear vexed," I said, "no doubt because Jackson declines to get you bailed. He ought not to refuse you such a trifling service, considering all things."

"All what things?" replied the woman, eyeing me fiercely.

"That you know best, though I have a shrewd guess."

"What do you guess? And what are you driving at?"

"I will deal frankly with you, Sarah Purday. In the first place, you must plainly perceive that your *friend* Jackson has cast you off—abandoned you to your fate; and that fate will, there can be no doubt, be transportation."

"Well," she impatiently snarled, "suppose so; what then?"

"This—that you can help yourself in this difficulty by helping me."

"As how?"

"In the first place, give me the means of convicting Jackson of having received the stolen property."

"Ha! How do you know that?"

"Oh, I know it very well—as well almost as you do. But this is not my chief object; there is another far more important one," and I ran over the incidents relative to the attempt at poisoning. "Now," I resumed, "tell me, if you will, your opinion on this matter."

"That it was Jackson administered the poison, and certainly not the young woman," she replied with vengeful promptness.

"My own conviction! This, then, is my proposition:—you are sharp-witted, and know this fellow's ways, habits, and propensities thoroughly—I, too, have heard something of them—and it strikes me that you could suggest some plan, some device grounded on that knowledge, whereby the truth might come to light."

The woman looked fixedly at me for some time without speaking. As I meant fairly and honestly by her I could bear her gaze without shrinking.

"Supposing I could assist you," she at last said, "how would that help me?"

"It would help you greatly. You would no doubt be still convicted of the burglary, for the evidence is irresistible; but if in the meantime you should have been instrumental in saving the life of an innocent person, and of bringing a great criminal to justice, there cannot be a question that the Queen's mercy would be extended to you, and the punishment be merely a nominal one."

"If I were sure of that!" she murmured with a burning scrutiny in her eyes, which were still fixed upon my countenance—"If I were sure of that! But you are misleading me."

"Believe me, I am not. I speak in perfect sincerity. Take time to consider the matter. I will look in again in about an hour; and pray, do not forget that it is your sole and last chance."

I left her, and did not return till more than three hours had passed away. Sarah Purday was pacing the cell in a frenzy of inquietude.

"I thought you had forgotten me. Now," she continued with rapid vehemence, "tell me, on your word and honor as a man, do you truly believe that if I can effectually assist you it will avail me with Her Majesty?"

"I am as positive it will as I am of my own life."

"Well, then, I *will* assist you. First, then, Jackson was a confederate with Dawkins and myself, and received the plate and jewelry, for which he paid us less than one-third of the value."

"Rogers and his wife were not, I hope, cognizant of this?"

"Certainly not; but Jackson's wife, and the woman-servant, Riddet, were. I have been turning the other business over in my mind," she continued, speaking with increasing emotion and rapidity; "and oh, believe me, Mr. Waters, if you can, that it is not solely a selfish motive which induces me to aid in saving Mary Rogers from destruction. I was once myself—Ah God!"

Tears welled up to the fierce eyes, but they were quickly brushed away, and she continued somewhat more calmly:—"You have heard, I dare say, that Jackson has a strange habit of talking in his sleep?"

"I have, and that he once consulted Morgan as to whether there was any cure for it. It was that which partly suggested—"

"It is, I believe, a mere fancy of his," she interrupted; "or at any rate the habit is not so frequent, nor what he says so intelligible, as he thoroughly believes and fears it, from some former circumstances, to be. His deaf wife cannot undeceive him, and he takes care never even to doze except in her presence only."

"This is not, then, so promising as I hoped."

"Have patience. It is full of promise, as we will manage. Every evening Jackson frequents a low gambling-house, where he almost invariably wins small sums at cards—by craft, no doubt, as he never drinks there. When he returns home at about ten o'clock, his constant habit is to go into the front-parlor, where his wife is sure to be sitting at that hour. He carefully locks the door, helps himself to brandy and water—plentifully of late—and falls asleep in his arm-chair; and there they both doze away, sometimes till one o'clock—always till past twelve."

"Well; but I do not see how"—

"Hear me out, if you please. Jackson never wastes a candle to drink or sleep by, and at this time of the year there will be no fire. If he speaks to his wife he does not expect her, from her wooden deafness, to answer him. Do you begin to perceive my drift?"

"Upon my word, I do not."

"What; if upon awaking, Jackson finds that his wife is Mr. Waters, and that Mr. Waters relates to him all that he has disclosed in his sleep: that Mr. Hursley's plate is buried in the garden near the lilac-tree; that he, Jackson, received a thousand pounds six weeks ago of Henry Roger's fortune, and that the money is now in the recess on the top-landing, the key of which is in his breast-pocket; that he was the receiver of the plate stolen from a house in the close at Salisbury a twelvemonth ago, and sold in London for four hundred and fifty pounds. All this hurled at him," continued the woman with wild energy and flashing eyes, "what else might not a bold, quick-witted man make him believe he had confessed, revealed in his brief sleep?"

I had been sitting on a bench; but as these rapid disclosures burst from her lips, and I saw the use to which they might be turned, I rose slowly and in some sort involuntarily to my feet, lifted up, as it were, by the energy of her fiery words.

"God reward you!" I exclaimed, shaking both her hands in mine. "You have, unless I blunder, rescued an innocent woman from the scaffold. I see it all. Farewell!"

"Mr. Waters," she exclaimed, in a changed, palpitating voice, as I was passing forth; "when all is done, you will not forget me?"

"That I will not, by my own hope of mercy in the hereafter. Adieu!"

At a quarter past nine that evening I, accompanied by two Farnham constables, knocked at the door of Jackson's house. Henry Rogers, I should state, had been removed to the village. The door was opened by the woman-servant, and we went in. "I have a warrant for your arrest, Jane Riddet," I said, "as an accomplice in the plate stealing the other day. There, don't scream, but listen to me." I then intimated the terms upon which alone she could expect favor. She tremblingly promised compliance; and after placing the constables outside, in concealment, but within hearing, I proceeded to the parlor, secured the terrified old woman, and confined her safely in a distant out-house.

"Now, Riddet," I said, "quick with one of the old lady's gowns, a shawl, cap, *etcetera*." These were brought, and I returned to the parlor. It was a roomy apartment, with small, diamond-paned windows, and just then but very faintly illumined by the star-light. There were two large high-backed easy-chairs, and I prepared to take possession of the one recently vacated by Jackson's wife. "You must perfectly understand," were my parting words to the trembling servant, "that we intend standing no nonsense with either you or your master. You cannot escape; but if you let Mr. Jackson in as usual, and he enters this room as usual, no harm will befall you: if otherwise, you will be unquestionably transported. Now, go."

My toilet was not so easily accomplished as I thought it would be. The gown did not meet at the back by about a foot; that, however, was of little consequence, as the high-chair concealed the deficiency; neither did the shortness of the sleeves matter much, as the ample shawl could be made to hide my too great length of arm; but the skirt was scarcely lower than a Highlander's, and how the deuce I was to crook my booted legs up out of view, even in that gloomy starlight, I could hardly imagine. The cap also was far too small; still, with an ample kerchief in my hand, my whiskers might, I thought, be concealed. I was still fidgeting with these arrangements when Jackson knocked at his door. The servant admitted him without remark, and he presently entered the room, carefully locked the door, and jolted down, so to speak, in the fellow easy-chair to mine.

He was silent for a few moments, and then he bawled out: "She'll swing for it, they say—swing for it, d'ye hear, dame? But no, of course she don't—deafer and deafer, deafer and deafer every day. It'll be a precious good job when the parson says his last prayers over her as well as others."

He then got up, and went to a cupboard. I could hear—for I dared not look up—by the jingling of glasses and the outpouring of liquids that he was helping himself to his spirituous sleeping-draughts. He reseated himself, and drank in moody silence, except now and then mumbling drowsily to himself, but in so low a tone that I could make nothing out of it save an occasional curse or blasphemy. It was nearly eleven o'clock before the muttered self-communing ceased, and his heavy head sank upon the back of the easy-chair. He was very restless, and it was evident that even his sleeping brain labored with affrighting and oppressive images; but the mutterings, as before he slept, were confused and indistinct. At length—half an hour had perhaps thus passed—the troubled meanings became for a few moments clearly audible. "Ha—ha—ha!" he burst out, "how are you off for soap? Ho—ho! done there, my boy; ha—ha! But no—no. Wall-plaster! Who could have thought it?

But for that I—I—What do you stare at me so for, you infernal blue-bottle? You—you"—Again the dream-utterance sank into indistinctness, and I comprehended nothing more.

About half-past twelve o'clock he awoke, rose, stretched himself, and said:—"Come, dame, let's to bed; it's getting chilly here."

"Dame" did not answer, and he again went towards the cupboard. "Here's a candle-end will do for us," he muttered. A lucifer-match was drawn across the wall, he lit the candle, and stumbled towards me, for he was scarcely yet awake. "Come, dame, come! Why, thee beest sleeping like a dead un! Wake up, will thee—Ah! murder! thieves! mur— "

My grasp was on the wretch's throat; but there was no occasion to use force: he recognized me, and nerveless, paralyzed, sank on the floor incapable of motion much less of resistance, and could only gaze in my face in dumb affright and horror.

"Give me the key of the recess upstairs, which you carry in your breast-pocket. In your sleep, unhappy man, you have revealed everything."

An inarticulate shriek of terror replied to me. I was silent; and presently he gasped: "Wha—at, what have I said?"

"That Mr. Hursley's plate is buried in the garden by the lilac-tree; that you have received a thousand pounds belonging to the man you tried to poison; that you netted four hundred and fifty pounds by the plate stolen at Salisbury; that you dexterously contrived to slip the sulphuric acid into the tea unseen by Henry Roger's wife."

The shriek or scream was repeated, and he was for several moments speechless with consternation. A ray of hope gleamed suddenly in his flaming eyes. "It is true—it is true!" he hurriedly ejaculated; "Useless—useless—useless to deny it. But you are alone, and poor, poor, no doubt. A thousand pounds!—more, more than that: *two* thousand pounds in gold—gold, all in gold—I will give you to spare me, to let me escape!"

"Where did you hide the soap on the day when you confess you tried to poison Henry Rogers?"

"In the recess you spoke of. But think! Two thousand pounds in gold—all in gold"—

As he spoke, I suddenly grasped the villain's hands, pressed them together, and in another instant the snapping of a handcuff pronounced my answer. A yell of anguish burst from the miserable man, so loud and piercing, that the constables outside hurried to the outer-door, and knocked hastily for admittance. They were let in by the servant-woman; and in half an hour afterwards the three prisoners—Jackson, his wife, and Jane Riddet—were safe in Farnham prison.

A few sentences will conclude this narrative. Mary Rogers was brought up on the following day, and, on my evidence, discharged. Her husband, I have heard, has since proved a better and a wiser man. Jackson was convicted at the Guilford assize of guiltily receiving the Hursley plate, and sentenced to transportation for life. This being so, the graver charge of attempting to poison was not pressed. There was no moral doubt of his guilt; but the legal proof of it rested solely on his own hurried confession, which counsel would no doubt have contended ought not to be received. His wife and the servant were leniently dealt with.

Sarah Purday was convicted, and sentenced to transportation. I did not forget my promise; and a statement of the previously-narrated circumstances having been drawn up and forwarded to the Queen and the Home Secretary, a pardon, after some delay, was issued. There were painful circumstances in her history which, after strict inquiry, told favorably for her. Several benevolent persons interested themselves in her behalf, and she was sent out to Canada, where she had some relatives, and has, I believe, prospered there.

This affair caused considerable hubbub at the time, and much admiration was expressed by the country people at the boldness and dexterity of the London "runner;" whereas, in fact, the successful result was entirely attributable to the opportune revelations of Sarah Purday.

XI

THE MODERN SCIENCE OF THIEF-TAKING

If thieving be an Art (and who denies that its more subtle and delicate branches deserve to be ranked as one of the Fine Arts?), thief-taking is a Science. All the thief's ingenuity, all his knowledge of human nature; all his courage; all his coolness; all his imperturbable powers of face; all his nice discrimination in reading the countenances of other people; all his manual and digital dexterity; all his fertility in expedients, and promptitude in acting upon them; all his Protean cleverness of disguise and capability of counterfeiting every sort and condition of distress; together with a great deal more patience, and the additional qualification, integrity, are demanded for the higher branches of thief-taking.

If an urchin picks your pocket, or a bungling "artist" steals your watch so that you find it out in an instant, it is easy enough for any private in any of the seventeen divisions of London Police to obey your panting demand to "Stop thief!" But the tricks and contrivances of those who wheedle money out of your pocket rather than steal it; who cheat you with your eyes open; who clear every vestige of plate out of your pantry while your servant is on the stairs; who set up imposing warehouses, and ease respectable firms of large parcels of goods; who steal the acceptances of needy or dissipated young men;—for the detection and punishment of such impostors a superior order of police is requisite.

To each division of the Force is attached two officers, who are denominated "detectives." The staff, or headquarters, consists of six sergeants and two inspectors. Thus the Detective Police, of which we hear so much, consists of only forty-two individuals, whose duty it is to wear no uniform, and to perform the most difficult operations of their craft. They have not only to counteract the machinations of every sort of rascal whose only means of existence is avowed rascality, but to clear up family mysteries, the investigation of which demands the utmost delicacy and tact.

One instance will show the difference between a regular and a detective policeman. Your wife discovers on retiring for the night, that her toilette has been plundered; her drawers are void; except the ornaments she now wears, her beauty is as unadorned as that of a quakeress: not a thing is left; all the fond tokens you gave her when her pre-nuptial lover, are gone; your own miniature, with its setting of gold and brilliants; her late mother's diamonds; the bracelets "dear papa" presented on her last birthday; the top of every bottle in the dressing-case brought from Paris by Uncle John, at the risk of his life, in February 1848, are off—but the glasses remain. Every valuable is swept away with the most discriminating villainy; for no other thing in the chamber has been touched; not a chair has been moved; the costly pendule on the chimney-piece still ticks; the entire apartment is as neat and trim as when it had received the last finishing sweep of the housemaid's duster. The entire establishment runs frantically upstairs and downstairs; and finally congregates in my Lady's Chamber. Nobody knows anything whatever about it; yet everybody offers a suggestion, although they have not an idea "who ever did it." The housemaid bursts into tears; the cook declares she thinks she is going into hysterics; and at last you suggest sending for the Police; which is taken as a suspicion of, and insult on the whole assembled household, and they descend into the lower regions of the house in the sulks.

X 49 arrives. His face betrays sheepishness, combined with mystery. He turns his bull's-eye into every corner, and upon every countenance (including that of the cat), on the premises. He examines all the locks, bolts, and bars, bestowing extra diligence on those which enclosed the stolen treasures. These he declares have been "Violated;" by which he means that there has been more than one "Rape of the Lock." He then mentions about the non-disturbance of other valuables; takes you solemnly aside, darkens his lantern, and asks if you suspect any of your servants, in a mysterious whisper, which implies that *he* does. He then examines the upper bedrooms, and in that of the female servants he discovers the least valuable of the rings, and a cast-off silver toothpick between the mattresses. You have every confidence in your maids; but what *can* you think? You suggest their safe custody; but your wife intercedes, and the policeman would prefer speaking to his inspector before he locks anybody up.

Had the whole matter remained in the hands of X 49, it is possible that your troubles would have lasted you till now. A train of legal proceedings—actions for defamation of character and suits for damages—would have followed, which would have cost more than the value of the jewels, find the entire execration of all your neighbors and every private friend of your domestics. But, happily, the Inspector promptly sends a plain, earnest-looking man, who announces himself as one of the two Detectives of the X division. He settles the whole matter in ten minutes. His examination is ended in five. As a connoisseur can determine the painter of a picture at the first glance, or a wine-taster the precise vintage of a sherry by the merest sip; so the Detective at once pounces upon the authors of the work of art under consideration, by the style of performance; if not upon the precise executant, upon the "school" to which he belongs. Having finished the toilette branch of the inquiry, he takes a short view of the parapet of your house, and makes an equally cursory investigation of the attic-window fastenings. His mind is made up, and most likely he will address you in these words:—

"All right, Sir. This is done by one of 'The Dancing School!' "

"Good Heavens!" exclaims your plundered partner. "Impossible, why *our* children go to Monsieur Pettitoes, of No. 81, and I assure you he is a highly respectable professor. As to his pupils, I—"

The Detective smiles and interrupts. "Dancers," he tells her, "is a name given to the sort of burglar by whom she had been robbed; and every branch of the thieving profession is divided into gangs, which are termed 'Schools.' From No. 82 to the end of the street the houses are unfinished. The thief made his way to the top of one of these, and crawled to your garrett—"

"But we are forty houses distant, and why did he not favor one of my neighbors with his visit?" you ask.

"Either their uppermost storeys are not so practicable, or the ladies have not such valuable jewels."

"But how do they know that?"

"By watching and inquiry. This affair may have been in action for more than a month. Your house has been watched; your habits ascertained; they have found out when you dine—how long you remain in the dining-room. A day is selected; while you are busy dining, and your servants busy waiting on you, the thing is done. Previously, many journeys have been made over the roofs, to find out the best means of entering your house. The attic is chosen; the robber gets in, and creeps noiselessly, or 'dances' into the place to be robbed."

"Is there *any* chance of recovering our property?" you ask anxiously, seeing the whole matter at a glance.

"I hope so. I have sent some brother officers to watch the Fences' houses."

"Fences?"

"Fences," explains the Detective, in reply to your innocent wife's inquiry, "are purchasers of stolen goods. Your jewels will be forced out of their settings, and the gold melted."

The lady tries, ineffectually, to suppress a slight scream.

"We shall see, if, at this unusual hour of the night, there is any bustle in or near any of these places; if any smoke is coming out of any one of their furnaces, where the melting takes place. *I* shall go and seek out the precise 'garretter'—that's another name these plunderers give themselves—whom I suspect. By his trying to 'sell' your domestics by placing the ring and toothpick in their bed, I think I know the man. It is just in his style."

The next morning, you find all these suppositions verified. The Detective calls, and obliges you at breakfast—after a sleepless night—with a complete list of the stolen articles, and produces some of them for identification. In three months, your wife gets nearly every article back; her damsels' innocence is fully established; and the thief is taken from his "school" to spend a long holiday in a penal colony.

This is a mere common-place transaction, compared with the achievements of the staff of the little army of Detective policemen at headquarters. Sometimes they are called upon to investigate robberies; so executed, that no human ingenuity appears to ordinary observers capable of finding the thief. He leaves not a trail or a trace. Every clue seems cut off; but the experience of a Detective guides him into tracks quite invisible to other eyes. Not long since, a trunk was rifled at a fashionable hotel. The theft was so managed, that no suspicion could rest on anyone. The Detective sergeant who had been sent for, fairly owned, after making a minute examination of the case, that he could afford no hope of elucidating the mystery. As he was leaving the bedroom, however, in which the plundered portmanteau stood, he picked up an ordinary shirt-button from the carpet. He silently compared it with those on the shirts in the trunk. It did not match them. He said nothing, but hung about the hotel for the rest of the day. Had he been narrowly watched, he would have been set down for an eccentric critic of linen. He was looking out for a shirt-front or wristband without a button. His search was long and patient; but at length it was rewarded. One of the inmates of the house showed a deficiency in his dress, which no one but a Detective would have noticed. He looked as narrowly as he dared at the pattern of the remaining fasteners. It corresponded with that of the little tell-tale he had picked up. He went deeper into the subject, got a trace of some of the stolen property, ascertained a connexion between it and the suspected person, confronted him with the owner of the trunk, and finally succeeded in convicting him of the theft.—At another hotel-robbery, the blade of a knife, broken in the lock of a portmanteau, formed the clue. The Detective employed in that case was for some time indefatigable in seeking out knives with broken blades. At length he found one belonging to an under-waiter, who proved to have been the thief.

The swell-mob—the London branch of which is said to consist of from one hundred and fifty to two hundred members—demand the greatest amount of vigilance to detect. They hold the first place in the "profession."

Their cleverness consists in evading the law; the most expert are seldom taken. One "swell," named Mo. Clark, had an iniquitous career of a quarter of a century, and never was captured during that time. He died a "prosperous gentleman" at Boulogne, whither he had retired to live on his "savings," which he had invested in house property. An old hand named White lived unharmed to the age of eighty; but he had not been prudent, and existed on the contributions of the "mob," till his old acquaintances were taken away, either by transportation or death, and the new race did not recognize his claims to their bounty. Hence he died in a workhouse. The average run of liberty which one of this class counts upon is four years.

The gains of some of the swell mob are great. They can always command capital to execute any especial scheme. Their traveling expenses are large; for their harvests are great public occasions, whether in town or country. As an example of their profits, the exploits of four of them at the Liverpool Cattle Show some seven years ago, may be mentioned. The London Detective Police did not attend, but one of them waylaid the rogues at the Euston Station. After an attendance of four days, the gentleman he was looking for appeared, handsomely attired, the occupants of first-class carriages. The Detective, in the quietest manner possible, stopped their luggage; they entreated him to treat them like "gentlemen." He did so, and took them into a private room, where, they were so good as to offer him fifty pounds to let them go. He declined, and overhauled their booty; it consisted of several gold pins, watches, (some of great value,) chains and rings, silver snuff-boxes, and bank-notes of the value of one hundred pounds! Eventually, however, as owners could not be found for some of the property, and some others would not prosecute, they escaped with a light punishment.

In order to counteract the plans of the swell mob, two of the sergeants of the Detective Police make it their business to know every one of them personally. The consequence is, that the appearance of either of these officers upon any scene of operations is a bar to anything or anybody being "done". This is an excellent characteristic of the Detectives, for they thus become as well a Preventive Police. We will give an illustration:—

You are at the Oxford commemoration. As you descend the broad stairs of the Roebuck to dine, you overtake on the landing a gentleman of foreign aspect and elegant attire. The variegated pattern of his vest, the jetty gloss of his boots, and the exceeding whiteness of his gloves—one of which he crushes in his somewhat delicate hand—convince you that he is going to the grand ball, to be given that evening at Merton. The glance he gives you while passing, is sharp, but comprehensive; and if his eye does rest upon any one part of your person and its accessories more than another, it is upon the gold watch which you have just taken out to see if dinner be "due." As you step aside to make room for him, he acknowledges the courtesy with "Par-r-r-don," in the richest Parisian *gros parle*, and a smile so full of intelligence and courtesy, that you hope he speaks English, for you set him down as an agreeable fellow, and mentally determine that if he dines in the Coffee-room, you will make his acquaintance.

On the mat at the stair-foot there stands a man. A plain, honest-looking fellow, with nothing formidable in his appearance, or dreadful in his countenance; but the effect his apparition takes on your friend in perspective, is remarkable. The poor little fellow raises himself on his toes, as if he had been suddenly overbalanced by a bullet; his cheek pales, and his lip quivers, as he endeavors ineffectually to suppress the word "*coquin!*" He knows it is too late to turn back (he evidently would, if he could), for the man's eye is upon him. There is no help for it, and he speaks first; but in a whisper. He takes the newcomer aside, and all you can overhear is spoken by the latter, who says he insists on Monsieur withdrawing his "School" by the seven o'clock train.

You imagine him to be some poor wretch of a school-master in difficulties; captured, alas, by a bailiff. They leave the inn together, perhaps for a sponging house. So acute is your pity, that you think of rushing after them, and offering bail. You are, however, very hungry, and, at this moment, the waiter announces that dinner is on table.

In the opposite box there are covers for four, but only three convives. They seem quiet men—not gentleman, decidedly, but well enough behaved.

"What has become of Monsieur?" asks one. None of them can divine.

"Shall we wait any longer for him?"

"Oh, no—Waiter—Dinner!"

By their manner, you imagine that the style of the Roebuck is a "cut above them." They have not been much used to plate. The silver forks are so curiously heavy, that one of the guests, in a dallying sort of way, balances a prong across his fingers, while the chasing of the castors engages the attention of a second. This is all done while they talk. When the fish is brought, the third casts a careless glance or two at the dish cover, and when the waiter has gone for the sauce, he taps it with his nails, and says enquiringly to his friend across the table "Silver?"

The other shakes his head, and intimates a hint that it is *only* plated. The waiter brings the cold punch, and the party begin to enjoy themselves. They do not drink much, but they mix their drinks rather injudiciously. They take sherry upon cold punch, and champagne upon that, dashing in a little port and bottled stout between. They are getting merry, not to say jolly, but not at all inebriated. The amateur of silver dish-covers has told a capital story, and his friends are revelling in the heartiest of laughs, when an apparition appears at the end of the table. You never saw such a change as his presence causes, when he places his knuckles on the edge of the table and looks at the diners *seriatim*; the courtiers of the sleeping beauty suddenly struck somniferous were nothing to this change. As if by magic, the loud laugh is turned to silent consternation. You now, most impressively, understand the meaning of the term "dumbfoundered." The mysterious stranger makes some enquiry about "any cash?"

The answer is "Plenty."

"All square with the landlord, then?" asks the same inflexible voice as—to my astonishment—that which put the French man to the torture.

"To a penny," the reply.

"*Quite* square?" continues the querist, taking with his busy eye a rapid inventory of the plate.

"S' help me—"

"Hush!" interrupts the dinner spoiler, holding up his hand in a cautionary manner. "Have you done anything today?"

"Not a thing."

Then there is some more in a low tone; but you again distinguish the word "school," and "seven o'clock train." They are too old to be the Frenchman's pupils; perhaps they are his assistants. Surely they are not all the victims of the same *capias* and the same officer!

By this time the landlord, looking very nervous, arrives with his bill: then comes the head waiter, who clears the table; carefully counting the forks. The reckoning is paid, and the trio steal out of the room with the man of mystery behind them,—like sheep driven to the shambles.

You follow to the Railway station, and there you see the Frenchman, who complains bitterly of being "sold for noting" by his enemy. The other three utter a confirmative groan. In spite of the evident omnipotence of their persevering follower, your curiosity impels you to address him. You take a turn on the platform together, and he explains the whole mystery. "The fact is," he begins, "I am Sergeant Witchem, of the Detective police."

"And your four victims are?—"

"Members of a crack school of swell-mobsmen."

"What do you mean by 'school?' "

"Gang. There is a variety of gangs—that is to say, of men who 'work' together, who play into one another's hands. These gentlemen hold the first rank, both for skill and enterprise, and had they been allowed to remain would have brought back a considerable booty. Their chief is the Frenchman."

"Why do they obey your orders so passively?"

"Because they are sure that if I were to take them into custody, which I could do, knowing what they are, and present them before a magistrate, they would all be committed to prison for a month, as rogues and vagabonds."

"They prefer then to have lost no inconsiderable capital in dress and dinner, to being laid up in jail."

"Exactly so."

The bell rings, and all five go off into the same carriage to London.

This is a circumstance that actually occurred; and a similar one happened when the Queen went to Dublin. The mere appearance of one the Detective officers before a "school" which had transported itself in the Royal train, spoilt their speculation; for they all found it more advantageous to return to England in the same steamer with the officer, than to remain with the certainty of being put in prison for fourteen or twenty-eight days as rogues and vagabonds.

So thoroughly well acquainted with these men are the Detective officers we speak of, that they frequently tell what they have been about by the expression of their eyes and their general manner. This process is aptly termed "reckoning them up." Some days ago, two skillful officers, whose personal acquaintance with the swell mob is complete, were walking along the Strand on other business, when they saw two of the best dressed and best mannered of the gang enter a jeweller's shop. They waited till they came out, and, on scrutinising them, were convinced, by a certain conscious look which they betrayed, that they had stolen something. They followed them, and in a few minutes something was passed from one to the other. The officers were convinced, challenged them with the theft, and succeeded in eventually convicting them of stealing two gold eye-glasses, and several jeweled rings. "The eye," said our informant, "is the great detector. We can tell in a crowd what a swell-mobsman is about by the expression of his eye."

It is supposed that the number of persons who make a trade of thieving in London is not more than six thousand; of these, nearly two hundred are first-class thieves or swell-mobsmen, six hundred "macemen," and trade swindlers, bill-swindlers, dog-stealers, &c.; About forty burglars, "dancers," "garretteers," and other adepts with the skeleton-keys. The rest are pickpockets, "gonophs—" mostly young thieves who sneak into areas, and rob tills—and other pilferers.

To detect and circumvent this fraternity, is the science of thief-taking. Here, it is, however, impossible to give even an imperfect notion of the high amount of skill, intelligence, and knowledge, concentrated in the character of a clever Detective Policeman. We shall therefore finish the sketch in another part.

XII

A DETECTIVE POLICE PARTY

In pursuance of the intention mentioned at the close of a former paper on "The Modern Science of Thief-taking," we now proceed to endeavor to convey to our readers some faint idea of the extraordinary dexterity, patience, and ingenuity, exercised by the Detective Police. That our description may be as graphic as we can render it, and may be perfectly reliable, we will make it, so far as in us lies, a piece of plain truth. And first, we have to inform the reader how the anecdotes we are about to communicate, came to our knowledge.

We are not by any means devout believers in the Old Bow-Street Police. To say the truth, we think there was a vast amount of humbug about those worthies. Apart from many of them being men of very indifferent character, and far too much in the habit of consorting with thieves and the like, they never lost a public occasion of jobbing and trading in mystery and making the most of themselves. Continually puffed besides by incompetent magistrates anxious to conceal their own deficiencies, and hand-in-glove with the penny-a-liners of that time, they became a sort of superstition. Although as a Preventive Police they were utterly ineffective, and as a Detective Police were very loose and uncertain in their operations, they remain with some people, a superstition to the present day.

On the other hand, the Detective Force organized since the establishment of the existing Police, is so well chosen and trained, proceeds so systematically and quietly, does its business in such a workman-like manner, and is always so calmly and steadily engaged in the service of the public, that the public really do not know enough of it, to know a tithe of its usefulness. Impressed with this conviction, and interested in the men themselves, we represented to the authorities at Scotland Yard, that we should be glad, if there were no official objection, to have some talk with the Detectives. A most obliging and ready permission being given, a certain evening was appointed with a certain Inspector for a social conference between ourselves and the Detectives, at our Office in Wellington Street, Strand, London. In consequence of which appointment the party "came off," which we are about to describe. And we beg to repeat that, avoiding such topics as it might for obvious reasons be injurious to the public, or disagreeable to respectable individuals to touch upon in print, our description is as exact as we can make it.

Just at dusk, Inspectors Wield and Stalker are announced; but we do not undertake to warrant the orthography of any of the names here mentioned. Inspector Wield presents Inspector Stalker. Inspector Wield is a middle-aged man of a portly presence, with a large, moist, knowing eye, a husky voice, and a habit of emphasising his conversation by the aid of a corpulent forefinger, which is constantly in juxtaposition with his eyes or nose. Inspector Stalker is a shrewd, hard-headed Scotchman—in appearance not at all unlike a very acute, thoroughly-trained school-master, from the Normal Establishment at Glasgow. Inspector Wield one might have known, perhaps, for what he is—Inspector Stalker, never.

The ceremonies of reception over, Inspectors Wield and Stalker observe that they have brought some sergeants with them. The sergeants are presented—five in number, Sergeant

Dornton, Sergeant Witchem, Sergeant Mith, Sergeant Fendall, and Sergeant Straw. We have the whole Detective Force from Scotland Yard with one exception. They sit down in a semicircle (the two Inspectors at the two ends) at a little distance from the round table, facing the editorial sofa. Every man of them, in a glance, immediately takes an inventory of the furniture and an accurate sketch of the editorial presence. The Editor feels that any gentleman in company could take him up, if need should be, without the smallest hesitation, twenty years hence.

The whole party are in plain clothes. Sergeant Dornton, about fifty years of age, with a ruddy face and a high sunburnt forehead, has the air of one who has been a Sergeant in the army—he might have sat to Wilkie for the Soldier in the Reading of the Will. He is famous for steadily pursuing the inductive process, and, from small beginnings, working on from clue to clue until he bags his man. Sergeant Witchem, shorter and thicker-set, and marked with the small-pox, has something of a reserved and thoughtful air, as if he were engaged in deep arithmetical calculations. He is renowned for his acquaintance with the swell mob. Sergeant Mith, a smooth-faced man with a fresh bright complexion, and a strange air of simplicity, is a dab at housebreakers. Sergeant Fendall, a light-haired, well-spoken, polite person, is a prodigious hand at pursuing private inquiries of a delicate nature. Straw, a little wiry Sergeant of meek demeanor and strong sense, would knock at a door and ask a series of questions in any mild character you chose to prescribe to him, from a charity-boy upwards, and seem as innocent as an infant. They are, one and all, respectable-looking men; of perfectly good deportment and unusual intelligence; with nothing lounging or slinking in their manners; with an air of keen observation, and quick perception when addressed; and generally presenting in their faces, traces more or less marked of habitually leading lives of strong mental excitement. They have all good eyes; and they all can, and they all do, look full at whomsoever they speak to.

We light the cigars, and hand round the glasses (which are very temperately used indeed), and the conversation begins by a modest amateur reference on the Editorial part to the swell mob. Inspector Wield immediately removes his cigar from his lips, waves his right hand, and says, "Regarding the Swell Mob, Sir, I can't do better than call upon Sergeant Witchem. Because the reason why? I'll tell you. Sergeant Witchem is better acquainted with the Swell Mob than any officer in London."

Our heart leaping up when we beheld this rainbow in the sky, we turn to Sergeant Witchem, who very concisely, and in well-chosen language, goes into the subject forthwith. Meantime, the whole of his brother officers are closely interested in attending to what he says, and observing its effect. Presently they begin to strike in, one or two together, when an opportunity offers, and the conversation becomes general. But these brother officers only come in to the assistance of each other—not to the contradiction—and a more amicable brotherhood there could not be. From the swell mob, we diverge to the kindred topics of cracksmen, fences, public-house dancers, area-sneaks, designing young people who go out "gonophing," and other "schools," to which our readers have already been introduced. It is observable throughout these revelations, that Inspector Stalker, the Scotchman, is always exact and statistical, and that when any question of figures arises, everybody as by one consent pauses, and looks to him.

When we have exhausted the various schools of Art—during which discussion the whole body have remained profoundly attentive, except when some unusual noise at the Theatre over the way, has induced some gentleman to glance inquiringly towards the window in that direction, behind his next neighbor's back—we burrow for information on such points as the following. Whether there really are any highway robberies in London, or whether some circumstances not convenient to be mentioned by the aggrieved party, usually precede the robberies complained of, under that head, which quite change their character? Certainly the latter, almost always. Whether in the case of robberies in houses, where servants are necessarily exposed to doubt, innocence under suspicion ever becomes so like guilt in appearance, that a good officer need be cautious how he judges it? Undoubtedly. Nothing is so common or deceptive as such appearances at first. Whether in a place of public amusement, a thief knows an officer, and an officer knows a thief,—supposing them, beforehand, strangers to each other—because each recognizes in the other, under all disguise, an inattention to what is going on, and a purpose that is not the purpose of being entertained? Yes. That's the way exactly. Whether it is reasonable or ridiculous to trust to the alleged experiences of thieves as narrated by themselves, in prisons, or penitentiaries, or anywhere? In general, nothing more absurd. Lying is their habit and their trade; and they would rather lie—even if they hadn't an interest in it, and didn't want to make themselves agreeable—than tell the truth.

From these topics, we glide into a review of the most celebrated and horrible of the great crimes that have been committed within the last fifteen or twenty years. The men engaged in the discovery of almost all of them, and in the pursuit or apprehension of the murderers, are here, down to the very last instance. One of our guests gave chase to and boarded the Emigrant Ship, in which the murderess last hanged in London was supposed to have embarked. We learn from him that his errand was not announced to the passengers, who may have no idea of it to this hour. That he went below, with the captain, lamp in hand—it being dark, and the whole steerage abed and sea-sick—and engaged the Mrs. Manning who *was* on board, in a conversation about her luggage, until she was, with no small pains, induced to raise her head, and turn her face towards the light. Satisfied that she was not the object of his search, he quietly re-embarked in the Government steamer alongside, and steamed home again with the intelligence.

When we have exhausted these subjects, too, which occupy a considerable time in the discussion, two or three leave their chairs, whisper Sergeant Witchem, and resume their seats. Sergeant Witchem, leaning forward a little, and placing a hand on each of his legs, then modestly speaks as follows:

"My brother-officers wish me to relate a little account of my taking Tally-ho Thompson. A man oughtn't to tell what he has done himself; but still, as nobody was with me, and, consequently, as nobody but myself can tell it, I'll do it in the best way I can, if it should meet your approval."

We assure Sergeant Witchem that he will oblige us very much, and we all compose ourselves to listen with great interest and attention.

"Tally-ho Thompson," says Sergeant Witchem, after merely wetting his lips with his brandy and water, "Tally-ho Thompson was a famous horse-stealer, couper, and magsman. Thompson, in conjunction with a pal that occasionally worked with him, gammoned a countryman out of a good round sum of money, under pretence of getting him a situation—the regular old dodge—and was afterwards in the 'Hue and Cry' for a horse—a horse that he stole, down in Hertfordshire. I had to look after Thompson, and I applied myself, of course, in the first instance, to discovering where he was. Now, Thompson's wife lived, along with a little daughter, at Chelsea. Knowing that Thompson was somewhere in the country, I watched the house—especially at post-time in the morning—thinking Thompson was pretty likely to write to her. Sure enough, one morning the postman comes up, and delivers a letter at Mrs. Thompson's door. Little girl opens the door, and takes it in. We're not always sure of postmen, though the people at the post-offices are always very obliging. A postman may help us, or he may not,—just as it happens. However, I go across the road, and I say to the postman, after he has left the letter, 'Good morning! How are you?' 'How are you?' says he. 'You've just delivered a letter for Mrs. Thompson.' 'Yes, I have.' 'You didn't happen to remark what the post-mark was, perhaps?' 'No,' says he, 'I didn't.' 'Come,' says I, 'I'll be plain with you. I'm in a small way of business, and I have given Thompson credit, and I can't afford to lose what he owes me. I know he's got money, and I know he's in the country, and if you could tell me what the post-mark was, I should be very much obliged to you, and you'd do a service to a tradesman in a small way of business that can't afford a loss.' 'Well,' he said, 'I do assure you that I did not observe what the post-mark was; all I know is, that there was money in the letter—I should say a sovereign.' This was enough for me, because of course I knew that Thompson having sent his wife money, it was probable she'd write to Thompson, by return of post, to acknowledge the receipt. So I said 'Thankee' to the postman, and I kept on the watch. In the afternoon I saw the little girl come out. Of course I followed her. She went into a stationer's shop, and I needn't say to you that I looked in at the window. She bought some writing-paper and envelopes, and a pen. I think to myself, 'That'll do!'—watch her home again—and don't go away, you may be sure, knowing that Mrs. Thompson was writing her letter to Tally-ho, and that the letter would be posted presently. In about an hour or so, out came the little girl again, with the letter in her hand. I went up, and said something to the child, whatever it might have been; but I couldn't see the direction of the letter, because she held it with the seal upwards. However, I observed that on the back of the letter there was what we call a kiss—a drop of wax by the side of the seal—and again, you understand, that was enough for me. I saw her post the letter, waited till she was gone, then went into the shop, and asked to see the Master. When he came out, I told him, 'Now, I'm an Officer in the Detective Force; there's a letter with a kiss been posted here just now, for a man that I'm in search of; and what I have to ask of you is, that you will let me look at the direction of that letter.' He was very civil—took a lot of letters from the box in the window—shook 'em out on the counter with the faces downwards—and there among 'em was the identical letter with the kiss. It was directed, Mr. Thomas Pigeon, Post-Office, B—, to be left 'till called for. Down I went to B—(a hundred and twenty miles or so) that night. Early next morning I went to the Post-Office; saw the gentleman in charge of that department; told him who I was; and that my object was to see, and track, the party that should come for the letter for Mr. Thomas Pigeon. He was very polite, and said, 'You shall have every assistance we can give you; you can wait inside the office; and we'll take care to let you know when anybody comes for the letter.' Well, I waited there three days, and began to think that nobody ever *would* come. At last the clerk whispered to me, 'Here! Detective! Somebody's come for the letter!' 'Keep him a minute,' said I, and I ran round to the outside of the office. There I saw a young chap with the appearance of an Ostler, holding a horse by the bridle—stretching the bridle across the pavement, while he waited at the Post-Office Window for the letter. I began to pat the horse, and that; and I said to the boy, 'Why, this is Mr. Jones's Mare!' 'No. It an't.' 'No?' said I. 'She's very like Mr. Jones's Mare.' 'She an't Mr. Jones's Mare, anyhow,' says he. 'It's Mr. So-and-So's, of the Warwick Arms.' And up he jumped, and off he went—letter and all. I got a cab, followed on the box, and was so quick after him that I came into the stableyard of the Warwick Arms, by one gate, just as he came in by another. I went into the bar, where there was a young woman serving, and called for a glass of brandy and water. He came in directly, and handed her the letter. She casually looked at it, without saying anything, and stuck it up behind the glass over the chimney-piece. What was to be done next?

"I turned it over in my mind while I drank my brandy and water (looking pretty sharp at the letter the while), but I couldn't see my way out of it at all. I tried to get lodgings in the house, but there had been a horse-fair, or something of that sort, and it was full. I was obliged to put up somewhere else, but I came backwards and forwards to the bar for a couple of days, and there was the letter, always behind the glass. At last I thought I'd write a letter to Mr. Pigeon myself, and see what that would do. So I wrote one, and posted it, but I purposely addressed it, Mr. John Pigeon, instead of Mr. Thomas Pigeon, to see what *that* would do. In the morning (a very wet morning it was) I watched the postman down the street, and cut into the bar, just before he reached the Warwick Arms. In he came presently with my letter. 'Is there a Mr. John Pigeon staying here?' 'No!—stop a bit though,' says the barmaid; and she took down the letter behind the glass. 'No,' says she, 'it's Thomas, and *he* is not staying here. Would you do me a favor, and post this for me, as it is so wet?' The postman said Yes; she folded it in another envelop, directed it, and gave it him. He put it in his hat, and away he went.

"I had no difficulty in finding out the direction of that letter. It was addressed, Mr. Thomas Pigeon, Post-Office, R—, Northamptonshire, to be left till called for. Off I started directly for R—; I said the same at the Post-Office there, as I had said at B—; and again I waited three days before anybody came. At last another chap on horseback came. 'Any letters for Mr. Thomas Pigeon?' 'Where do you come from?' 'New Inn, near R—.' He got the letter, and away *he* went—at a canter.

"I made my enquiries about the New Inn, near R—, and hearing it was a solitary sort of house, a little in the horse line, about a couple of miles from the station, I thought I'd go and have a look at it. I found it what it had been described, and sauntered in, to look about me. The landlady was in the bar, and I was trying to get into conversation with her; asked her how business was, and spoke about the wet weather, and so on; when I saw, through an open door, three men sitting by the fire in a sort of parlor, or kitchen; and one of those men, according to the description I had of him, was Tally-ho Thompson!

"I went and sat down among 'em, and tried to make things agreeable; but they were very shy—wouldn't talk at all—looked at me, and at one another, in a way quite the reverse of sociable. I reckoned 'em up, and finding that they were all three bigger men than me, and considering that their looks were ugly—that it was a lonely place—railroad station two miles off—and night coming on—thought I couldn't do better than have a drop of brandy and water to keep my courage up. So I called for my brandy and water; and as I was sitting drinking it by the fire, Thompson got up and went out.

"Now the difficulty of it was, that I wasn't sure it *was* Thompson, because I had never set eyes on him before; and what I had wanted was to be quite certain of him. However, there was nothing for it now, but to follow, and put a bold face upon it. I found him talking, outside in the yard, with the landlady. It turned out afterwards, that he was wanted by a Northampton officer for something else, and that, knowing that officer to be pock-marked (as I am myself), he mistook me for him. As I have observed, I found him talking to the landlady, outside. I put my hand upon his shoulder—this way—and said, 'Tally-ho Thompson, it's no use. I know you. I'm an officer from London, and I take you into custody for felony!' 'That be d—d!' says Tally-ho Thompson.

"We went back into the house, and the two friends began to cut up rough, and their looks didn't please me at all, I assure you. 'Let the man go. What are you going to do with him?' 'I'll tell you what I'm going to do with him. I'm going to take him to London tonight, as sure as I'm alive. I'm not alone here, whatever you may think. You mind your own business, and keep yourselves to yourselves. It'll be better for you, for

I know you both very well.' *I*'d never seen or heard of 'em in all my life, but my bouncing cowed 'em a bit, and they kept off, while Thompson was making ready to go. I thought to myself, however, that they might be coming after me on the dark road, to rescue Thompson; so I said to the landlady, 'What men have you got in the house, Missis?' 'We haven't got no men here,' she says, sulkily. 'You have got an ostler, I suppose?' 'Yes, we've got an ostler.' 'Let me see him.' Presently he came, and a shaggy-headed young fellow he was. 'Now attend to me, young man,' says I; 'I'm a Detective Officer from London. This man's name is Thompson. I have taken him into custody for felony. I'm going to take him to the railroad station. I call upon you in the Queen's name to assist me; and mind you, my friend, you'll get yourself into more trouble than you know of, if you don't!' You never saw a person open his eyes so wide. 'Now, Thompson, come along!' says I. But when I took out the handcuffs, Thompson cries, 'No! None of that! I won't stand *them*! I'll go along with you quiet, but I won't bear none of that!' 'Tally-ho Thompson,' I said, 'I'm willing to behave as a man to you, if you are willing to behave as a man to me. Give me your word that you'll come peaceably along, and I don't want to handcuff you.' 'I will,' says Thompson, 'but I'll have a glass of brandy first.' 'I don't care if I've another,' said I. 'We'll have two more, Missis,' said the friends, 'and confound you, Constable, you'll give your man a drop, won't you?' I was agreeable to that, so we had it all round, and then my man and I took Tally-ho Thompson safe to the railroad, and I carried him to London that night. He was afterwards acquitted, on account of a defect in the evidence; and I understand he always praises me up to the skies, and says I'm one of the best of men."

This story coming to a termination amidst general applause, Inspector Wield, after a little grave smoking, fixes his eye on his host, and thus delivers himself:

"It wasn't a bad plant that of mine, on Fikey, the man accused of forging the Sou' Western Railway debentures—it was only t'other day—because the reason why? I'll tell you.

"I had information that Fikey and his brother kept a factory over yonder there," indicating any region on the Surrey side of the river, "where he bought second-hand carriages; so after I'd tried in vain to get hold of him by other means, I wrote him a letter in an assumed name, saying that I'd got a horse and shay to dispose of, and would drive down next day, that he might view the lot, and make an offer—very reasonable it was, I said—a reg'lar bargain. Straw and me then went off to a friend of mine that's in the livery and job business, and hired a turn-out for the day, a precious smart turn-out, it was—quite a slap-up thing! Down we drove, accordingly, with a friend (who's not in the Force himself); and leaving my friend in the shay near a public-house, to take care of the horse, we went to the factory, which was some little way off. In the factory, there was a number of strong fellows at work, and after reckoning 'em up, it was clear to me that it wouldn't do to try it on there. They were too many for us. We must get our man out of doors. 'Mr. Fikey at home?' 'No, he ain't.' 'Expected home soon?' 'Why, no, not soon.' 'Ah! is his brother here?' '*I*'m his brother.' 'Oh! well, this us an ill-conwenience, this is. I wrote him a letter yesterday, saying I'd got a little turn-out to dispose of, and I've took the trouble to bring the turn-out down, a' purpose, and now he ain't in the way.' 'No, he an't in the way. You couldn't make it convenient to call again, could you?' 'Why, no, I couldn't. I want to sell; that's the fact; and I can't put it off. Could you find him anywheres?' At first he said no, he couldn't, and then he wasn't sure about it, and then he'd go and try. So, at last he went upstairs, where there was a sort of loft, and presently down comes my man himself, in his shirt-sleeves.

" 'Well,' he says, 'this seems to be rayther a pressing matter of yours.' 'Yes,' I says, 'it *is* rayther a pressing matter, and you'll find it a bargain—dirt-cheap.' 'I ain't in partickler want of a bargain just now,' he says, 'but where is it?' 'Why,' I says, 'the turn-out's just outside. Come and look at it.' He hasn't any suspicions, and away we go. And the first thing that happens is, that the horse runs away with my friend (who knows no more of driving than a child) when he takes a little trot along the road to show his paces. You never saw such a game in your life!

"When the bolt is over, and the turn-out has come to a stand-still again, Fikey walks round and round it, as grave as a judge—me too. 'There, Sir!' I says. 'There's a neat thing!' 'It an't a bad style of thing,' he says. 'I believe you,' says I. 'And there's a horse!'—for I saw him looking at it. 'Rising eight!' I says, rubbing his fore-legs. (Bless you, there an't a man in the world knows less of horses than I do, but I'd heard my friend at the Livery Stables say he was eight years old, so I says, as knowing as possible, 'Rising Eight.') 'Rising eight, is he?' says he. 'Rising eight,' says I. 'Well,' he says, 'what do you want for it?' 'Why, the first and last figure for the whole concern is five-and-twenty pound!' 'That's very cheap!' he says, looking at me. 'An't it?' I says. 'I told you it was a bargain! Now, without any higgling and haggling about it, what I want is to sell, and that's my price. Further, I'll make it easy to you, and take half the money down, and you can do a bit of stiff for the balance.' 'Well,' he says again, 'that's very cheap.' 'I believe you,' says I; 'get in and try it, and you'll buy it. Come! take a trial!'

"Ecod, he gets in, and we get in, and we drive along the road, to show him to one of the railway clerks that was hid in the public-house window to identify him. But the clerk was bothered, and didn't know whether it was him, or wasn't—because the reason why? I'll tell you,—on account of his having shaved his whiskers. 'It's a clever little horse,' he says, 'and trots well; and the shay runs light.' 'Not a doubt about it,' I says. 'And now, Mr. Fikey, I may as well make it all right, without wasting any more of your time. The fact is, I'm Inspector Wield, and you're my prisoner.' 'You don't mean that?' he says. 'I do, indeed.' 'Then burn my body,' says Fikey, 'if this ain't *too* bad!'

"Perhaps you never saw a man so knocked over with surprise. 'I hope you'll let me have my coat?' he says. 'By all means.' 'Well, then, let's drive to the factory.' 'Why, not exactly that, I think,' said I; 'I've been there, once before, today. Suppose we send for it.' He saw it was no go so he sent for it, and put it on, and we drove him up to London, comfortable."

This reminiscence is in the height of its success, when a general proposal is made to the fresh-complexioned, smooth-faced officer, with the strange air of simplicity, to tell the "Butcher's story."

BUTCHER'S STORY

The fresh-complexioned, smooth-faced officer, with the strange air of simplicity, began, with a rustic smile, and in a soft, wheedling tone of voice, to relate the Butcher's Story, thus:

"It's just about six years ago, now, since information was given at Scotland Yard of there being extensive robberies of lawns and silks going on, at some wholesale houses in the City. Directions were given for the business being looked into; and Straw, and Fendall, and me, we were all in it."

"When you received your instructions," said we, "you went away, and held a sort of Cabinet Council together?"

The smooth-faced officer coaxingly replied, "Ye-es. Just so. We turned it over among ourselves a good deal. It appeared, when we went into it, that the goods were sold by the receivers extraordinarily cheap—much cheaper than they could have been if they had been honestly come by. The receivers were in the trade, and kept capital shops—establishments of the first respectability—one of 'em at the West End, one down in Westminster. After a lot of watching and inquiry, and this and that among ourselves, we found that the job was managed, and the purchases of the stolen goods made, at a little public-house near Smithfield, down by Saint Bartholomew's; where the Warehouse Porters, who were the thieves, took 'em for that purpose, don't you see? and made appointments to meet the people that went between themselves and the receivers. This public-house was principally used by journeymen butchers from the country, out of place, and in want of situations; so, what did we do, but—ha, ha, ha!—we agreed that I should be dressed up like a butcher myself, and go and live there!"

Never, surely, was a faculty of observation better brought to bear upon a purpose, than that which picked out this officer for the part. Nothing in all creation, could have suited him better. Even while he spoke, he became a greasy, sleepy, shy, good-natured, chuckle-headed, unsuspicious, and confiding young butcher. His very hair seemed to have suet in it, as he made it smooth upon his head, and his fresh complexion to be lubricated by large quantities of animal food.

—"So I—ha, ha, ha!" (always with the confiding snigger of the foolish young butcher) "so I dressed myself in the regular way, made up a little bundle of clothes, and went to the public-house, and asked if I could have a lodging there? They says, 'Yes, you can have a lodging here,' and I got a bedroom, and settled myself down in the tap. There was a number of people about the place, and coming backwards and forwards to the house; and first one says, and then another says, 'Are you from the country, young man?' 'Yes,' I says, 'I am. I'm come out of Northamptonshire, and I'm quite lonely here, for I don't know London at all, and it's such a mighty big town?' 'It is a big town,' they says. 'Oh, it's a *very* big town!' I says. 'Really and truly I never was in such a town. It quite confuses of me!'—and all that, you know.

"When some of the Journeyman Butchers that used the house, found that I wanted a place, they says, 'Oh, we'll get you a place!' And they actually took me to a sight of places, in Newgate Market, Newport Market, Clare, Carnaby—I don't know where all. But the wages was—ha, ha, ha!—was not sufficient, and I never could suit myself, don't you see? Some of the queer frequenters of the house, were a little suspicious of me at first, and I was obliged to be very cautious indeed, how I communicated with Straw or Fendall. Sometimes, when I went out, pretending to stop and look into the shop-windows, and just casting my eye round, I used to see some of 'em following me; but, being perhaps better accustomed than they thought for, to that sort of thing, I used to lead 'em on as far as I thought necessary or convenient—sometimes a long way—and then turn sharp round, and meet 'em, and say, 'Oh, dear, how glad I am to come upon you so fortunate! This London's such a place, I'm blowed if I an't lost again!' And then we'd go back all together, to the public-house, and—ha, ha, ha! and smoke our pipes, don't you see?

"They were very attentive to me, I am sure. It was a common thing, while I was living there, for some of 'em to take me out, and show me London. They showed me the Prisons—showed me Newgate—and when they showed me Newgate, I stops at the place where the Porters pitch their loads, and says, 'Oh dear,' is this where they hang the men! Oh Lor!' 'That!' they says, 'What a simple cove he is! *That* an't it!' And then they pointed out which *was* it, and I says, 'Lor!' and they says, 'Now you'll know it agen, won't you?' And I said I thought I should if I tried hard—and I assure you I kept a sharp look out for the City Police when we were out in this way, for if any of 'em had happened to know me, and had spoke to me, it would have been all up in a minute. However, by good luck such a thing never happened, and all went on quiet: though the difficulties I had in communicating with my brother officers were quite extraordinary.

"The stolen goods that were brought to the public-house, by the Warehouse Porters, were always disposed of in a back parlor. For a long time, I never could get into this parlor, or see what was done there. As I sat smoking my pipe, like an innocent young chap, by the tap-room fire, I'd hear some of the parties to the robbery, as they came in and out, say softly to the landlord, 'Who's that? What does *he* do here?' 'Bless your soul,' says the landlord, 'He's only a'—ha, ha, ha!—'he's only a green young fellow from the country, as is looking for a butcher's sitiwation. Don't mind *him*!' So, in course of time, they were so convinced of my being green, and got to be so accustomed to me, that I was as free of the parlor as any of 'em, and I have seen as much as Seventy Pounds worth of fine lawn sold there, in one night, that was stolen from a warehouse in Friday Street. After the sale, the buyers always stood treat—hot supper, or dinner, or what not—and they'd say on those occasions 'Come on, Butcher! Put your best leg foremost, young 'un, and walk into it!' Which I used to do—and hear, at table, all manner of particulars that it was very important for us Detectives to know.

"This went on for ten weeks. I lived in the public-house all the time, and never was out of the Butcher's dress—except in bed. At last, when I had followed seven of the thieves, and set 'em to rights—that's an expression of ours, don't you see, by which I mean to say that I traced 'em, and found out where the robberies were done, and all about 'em—Straw, and Fendall, and I, gave one another the office, and at a time agreed upon, a descent was made upon the public-house, and the apprehensions effected. One of the first things the officers did, was to collar me—for the parties to the robbery weren't to suppose yet, that I was anything but a Butcher—on which the landlord cries out, 'Don't take *him*,' he says, 'whatever you do! He's only a poor young chap from the country, and butter wouldn't melt in his mouth!' However, they—ha, ha, ha!—they took me, and pretended to search my bedroom, where nothing was found but an old fiddle belonging to the landlord, that had got there somehow or another. But, it entirely changed the landlord's opinion, for when it was produced, he says, 'My fiddle! The Butcher's a purloiner! I give him into custody for the robbery of a musical instrument!'

"The man that had stolen the goods in Friday Street was not taken yet. He had told me, in confidence, that he had his suspicions there was something wrong (on account of the City Police having captured one of the party), and that he was going to make himself scarce. I asked him, 'Where do you mean to go, Mr. Shepherdson?' 'Why, Butcher,' says he, 'the Setting Moon, in the Commercial Road, is a snug house, and I shall hang out there for a time. I shall call myself Simpson, which appears to me to be a modest sort of a name. Perhaps you'll give us a look in, Butcher?' 'Well,' says I, 'I think I *will* give you a call'—which I fully intended, don't you see, because, of course, he was to be taken! I went over to the Setting Moon next day, with a brother officer, and asked at the bar for Simpson. They pointed out his room upstairs. As we were going up, he looks down over the banisters, and calls out, 'Halloa, Butcher! is that you?' 'Yes, it's me.' 'How do you find yourself?' 'Bobbish,' he says; 'but who's that with you?' 'It's only a young man, that's a friend of mine,' I says. 'Come along, then,' says he; 'any friend of the Butcher's is as welcome as the Butcher!' So, I made my friend acquainted with him, and we took him into custody.

"You have no idea, Sir, what a sight it was, in Court, when they first knew that I wasn't a Butcher, after all! I wasn't produced at the first examination, when there was a remand; but I was at the second. And when I stepped into the box, in full police uniform, and the whole party saw how they had been done, actually a groan of horror and dismay proceeded from 'em in the dock!

"At the Old Bailey, when their trials came on, Mr. Clarkson was engaged for the defence, and he *couldn't* make out how it was, about the Butcher. He thought, all along, it was a real Butcher. When the counsel for the prosecution said, 'I will now call before you, gentlemen, the Police-officer,' meaning myself, Mr. Clarkson says, 'Why Police-officer? Why more Police-officers? I don't want Police. We have had a great deal too much of the Police. I want the Butcher!' However, Sir, he had the Butcher and the Police-officer, both in one. Out of seven prisoners committed for trial, five were found guilty, and some of 'em were transported. The respectable firm, at the West End got a term of imprisonment; and that's the Butcher's Story!"

The story done, the chuckle-headed Butcher again resolved himself into the smooth-faced Detective. But, he was so extremely tickled by their having taken him about, when he was that Dragon in disguise, to show him London, that he could not help reverting to that point in his narrative; and gently repeating, with the Butcher's snigger, " 'Oh, dear!' I says, 'is that where they hang the men? Oh, Lor!' *'That!'* says they. 'What a simple cove he is!' "

It being now late, and the party very modest in their fear of being too diffuse, there were some tokens of separation; when Serjeant Dornton, the soldierly-looking man, said, looking round him with a smile:

"Before we break up, Sir, perhaps you might have some amusement in hearing of the Adventures of a Carpet Bag. They are very short; and, I think, curious."

We welcomed the Carpet Bag, as cordially as Mr. Shepherdson welcomed the false Butcher at the Setting Moon. Serjeant Dornton proceeded:

"In 1847, I was dispatched to Chatham, in search of one Mesheck, a Jew. He had been carrying on, pretty heavily, in the bill-stealing way, getting acceptances from young men of good connexions (in the army chiefly), on pretence of discount, and bolting with the same.

"Mesheck was off, before I got to Chatham. All I could learn about him was, that he had gone, probably to London, and had with him—a Carpet Bag.

"I came back to town, by the last train from Blackwall, and made inquiries concerning a Jew passenger with—a Carpet Bag.

"The office was shut up, it being the last train. There were only two or three porters left. Looking after a Jew with a Carpet Bag, on the Blackwall Railway, which was then the high road to a great Military Depôt, was worse than looking after a needle in a hay-rick. But it happened that one of these porters had carried, for a certain Jew, to a certain public-house, a certain—Carpet Bag.

"I went to the public-house, but the Jew had only left his luggage there for a few hours, and had called for it in a cab, and taken it away. I put such questions there, and to the porter, as I thought prudent, and got at this description of—the Carpet Bag.

"It was a bag which had, on one side of it, worked in worsted, a green parrot on a stand. A green parrot on a stand was the means by which to identify that—Carpet Bag.

"I traced Mesheck, by means of this green parrot on a stand to Cheltenham, to Birmingham, to Liverpool, to the Atlantic Ocean. At Liverpool he was too many for me. He had gone to the United States, and I gave up all thoughts of Mesheck, and likewise of his—Carpet Bag.

"Many months afterwards—near a year afterwards—there was a Bank in Ireland robbed of seven thousand pounds, by a person of the name of Doctor Dundey, who escaped to America; from which country some of the stolen notes came home. He was supposed to have bought a farm in New Jersey. Under proper management, that estate could be seized and sold, for the benefit of the parties he had defrauded. I was sent off to America for this purpose.

"I landed at Boston. I went on to New York. I found that he had lately changed New York paper-money for New Jersey paper-money, and had banked cash in New Brunswick. To take this Doctor Dundey, it was necessary to entrap him into the State of New York, which required a deal of artifice and trouble. At one time, he couldn't be drawn into an appointment. At another time, he appointed to come to meet me, and a New York officer, on a pretext I made; and then his children had the measles. At last, he came, per steamboat, and I took him, and lodged him in a New York Prison called the Tombs; which I dare say you know, Sir?"

Editorial acknowledgment to that effect.

"I went to the Tombs, on the morning after his capture, to attend the examination before the magistrate. I was passing through the magistrate's private room, when, happening to look round me to take notice of the place, as we generally have a habit of doing, I clapped my eyes, in one corner, on a—Carpet Bag.

"What did I see upon that Carpet Bag, if you'll believe me, but a green parrot on a stand, as large as life!

" 'That Carpet Bag, with the representation of a green parrot on a stand,' said I, 'belongs to an English Jew, named Aaron Mesheck, and to no other man alive or dead!'

"I give you my word the New York Police officers were doubled up with surprise.

" 'How do you ever come to know that?' said they.

" 'I think I ought to know that green parrot by this time,' said I, 'for I have had as pretty a dance after that bird, at home, as ever I had, in all my life!' "

"And *was* it Mesheck's?" we submissively inquired.

"Was it, Sir? Of course it was! He was in custody for another offence, in that very identical Tombs, at that very identical time. And, more than that! Some memoranda, relating to the fraud for which I had vainly endeavored to take him, were found to be, at that moment, lying in that very same individual—Carpet Bag!"

Such are the curious coincidences and such is the peculiar ability, always sharpening and being improved by practice, and always adapting itself to every variety of circumstances, and opposing itself to every new device that perverted ingenuity can invent, for which this important social branch of the public service is remarkable! Forever on the watch, with their wits stretched to the utmost, these officers have, from day to day and year to year, to set themselves against every novelty of trickery and dexterity that the combined imaginations of all the lawless rascals in England can devise, and to keep pace with every such invention that comes out. In the Courts of Justice, the materials of thousands of such stories as we have narrated—often elevated into the marvelous and romantic, by the circumstances of the case—are dryly compressed into the set phrase, "in consequence of information I received, I did so and so." Suspicion was to be directed, by careful inference and deduction, upon the right person; the right person was to be taken, wherever he had gone, or whatever he was doing to avoid detection: he is taken; there he is at the bar; that is enough. From information I, the officer, received, I did it; and, according to the custom in these cases, I say no more.

These games of chess, played with live pieces, are played before small audiences, and are chronicled nowhere. The interest of the game supports the player. Its results are enough for Justice. To compare great things with small, suppose LEVERRIER or ADAMS informing the public that from information he had received he had discovered a new planet; or COLUMBUS informing the public of his day that from information he had received, he had discovered a new continent; so the Detectives inform it that they have discovered a new fraud or an old offender, and the process is unknown.

Thus, at midnight, closed the proceedings of our curious and interesting party. But one other circumstance finally wound up the evening, after our Detective guests had left us. One of the sharpest among them, and the officer best acquainted with the Swell Mob, had his pocket picked, going home!

XIII

THREE "DETECTIVE" ANECDOTES

THE PAIR OF GLOVES

"It's a singular story, Sir," said Inspector Wield, of the Detective Police, who, in company with Sergeants Dornton and Mith, paid us another twilight visit, one July evening; "and I've been thinking you might like to know it.

"It's concerning the murder of the young woman, Eliza Grimwood, some years ago, over in the Waterloo Road. She was commonly called The Countess, because of her handsome appearance, and her proud way of carrying of herself; and when I saw the poor Countess (I had known her well to speak to), lying dead, with her throat cut, on the floor of her bedroom, you'll believe me that a variety of reflections calculated to make a man rather low in his spirits, came into my head.

"That's neither here nor there. I went to the house the morning after the murder, and examined the body, and made a general observation of the bedroom where it was. Turning down the pillow of the bed with my hand, I found, underneath it, a pair of gloves. A pair of gentleman's dress gloves, very dirty; and inside the lining, the letters TR, and a cross.

"Well, Sir, I took them gloves away, and I showed 'em to the magistrate, over at Union Hall, before whom the case was. He says, 'Wield,' he says, 'there's no doubt this is a discovery that may lead to something very important; and what you have got to do, Wield, is, to find out the owner of these gloves.'

"I was of the same opinion, of course, and I went at it immediately. I looked at the gloves pretty narrowly, and it was my opinion that they had been cleaned. There was a smell of sulphur and rosin about 'em, you know, which cleaned gloves usually have, more or less. I took 'em over to a friend of mine at Kennington, who was in that line, and I put it to him. 'What do you say now? Have these gloves been cleaned?' 'These gloves have been cleaned,' says he. 'Have you any idea who cleaned them?' says I. 'Not at all,' says he; 'I've a very distinct idea who *didn't* clean 'em, and that's myself. But I'll tell you what, Wield, there ain't above eight or nine reg'lar glove cleaners in London,'—there were not, at that time, it seems—'and I think I can give you their addresses, and you may find out, by that means, who did clean 'em.' Accordingly, he gave me the directions, and I went here, and I went there, and I looked up this man, and I looked up that man; but, though they all agreed that the gloves had been cleaned, I couldn't find the man, woman, or child, that had cleaned that aforesaid pair of gloves.

"What with this person not being at home, and that person being expected home in the afternoon, and so forth, the inquiry took me three days. On the evening of the third day, coming over Waterloo Bridge from the Surrey side of the river, quite beat, and very much vexed and disappointed, I thought I'd have a shilling's worth of entertainment at the Lyceum Theatre to freshen myself up. So I went into the Pit, at half-price, and I sat myself down next to a very quiet, modest sort of young man. Seeing I was a stranger (which I thought it just as well to appear to be) he told me the names of the actors on the stage, and we got into conversation. When the play was over, we came out together, and I said, 'We've been very companionable and agreeable, and perhaps you wouldn't object to a drain?' 'Well, you're very good,' says he; 'I *shouldn't* object to a drain.' Accordingly, we went to a public house, near the Theatre, sat ourselves down in a quiet room upstairs on the first floor, and called for a pint of half-and-half, a-piece, and a pipe.

"Well, Sir, we put our pipes aboard, and we drank our half-and-half, and sat a talking, very sociably, when the young man says, 'You must excuse me stopping very long,' he says, 'because I'm forced to go home in good time. I must be at work all night.' 'At work all night?' says I. 'You ain't a Baker?' 'No,' he says, laughing, 'I ain't a baker.' 'I thought not,' says I, 'you haven't the looks of a baker.' 'No,' says he, 'I'm a glove cleaner.'

"I never was more astonished in my life, than when I heard them words come out of his lips. 'You're a glove cleaner, are you?' says I. 'Yes,' he says, 'I am.' 'Then, perhaps,' says I, taking the gloves out of my pocket, 'you can tell me who cleaned this pair of gloves? It's a rum story,' I says. 'I was dining over at Lambeth, the other day, at a free-and-easy—quite promiscuous—with a public company—when some gentleman, he left these gloves behind him! Another gentleman and me, you see, we laid a wager of a sovereign, that I wouldn't find out who they belonged to. I've spent as much as seven shillings already, in trying to discover; but, if you could help me, I'd stand another seven and welcome. You see there's TR and a cross, inside.' 'I see,' he says. 'Bless you, *I* know these gloves very well! I've seen dozens of pairs belonging to the same party.' 'No?' says I. 'Yes,' says he. 'Then you know who cleaned 'em?' says I. 'Rather so,' says he. 'My father cleaned 'em.'

" 'Where does your father live?' says I. 'Just round the corner,' says the young man, 'near Exeter Street, here. He'll tell you who they belong to, directly.' 'Would you come round with me now?' says I. 'Certainly,' says he, 'but you needn't tell my father that you found me at the play, you know, because he mightn't like it.' 'All right!' We went round to the place, and there we found an old man in a white apron, with two or three daughters, all rubbing and cleaning away at lots of gloves, in a front parlor. 'Oh, Father!' says the young man, 'here's a person been and made a bet about the ownership of a pair of gloves, and I've told him you can settle it.' 'Good evening, Sir,' says I to the old gentleman. 'Here's the gloves your son speaks of. Letters TR, you see, and a cross.' 'Oh yes,' he says, 'I know these gloves very well; I've cleaned dozens of pairs of 'em. They belong to Mr. Trinkle, the great upholsterer in Cheapside.' 'Did you get 'em from Mr. Trinkle, direct,' says I, 'if you'll excuse my asking the question?' 'No,' says he; 'Mr. Trinkle always sends 'em to Mr. Phibbs's, the haberdasher's opposite his shop, and the haberdasher sends 'em to me.' 'Perhaps *you* wouldn't object to a drain?' says I. 'Not in the least!' says he. So I took the old gentleman out, and had a little more talk with him and his son, over a glass, and we parted excellent friends.

"This was late on a Saturday night. First thing on the Monday morning, I went to the haberdasher's shop, opposite Mr. Trinkle's, the great upholsterer's in Cheapside. 'Mr. Phibbs in the way?' 'My name is Phibbs.' 'Oh! I believe you sent this pair of gloves to be cleaned?' 'Yes, I did, for young Mr. Trinkle over the way. There he is, in the shop!' 'Oh! that's him in the shop, is it? Him in the green coat?' 'The same individual.' 'Well, Mr. Phibbs, this is an unpleasant affair; but the fact is, I am Inspector Wield of the Detective Police, and I found these gloves under the pillow of the young woman that was murdered the other day, over in the Waterloo Road?' 'Good Heaven!' says he. 'He's a most respectable young man, and if his father was to hear of it, it would be the ruin of him!' 'I'm very sorry for it,' says I, 'but I must take him into custody.' 'Good Heaven!' says Mr. Phibbs, again; 'Can nothing be done?' 'Nothing,' says I. 'Will you allow me to call him over here,' says he, 'that his father may not see it done?' 'I don't object to that,' says I; 'but unfortunately, Mr. Phibbs, I can't allow of any communication between you. If any was attempted, I should have to interfere directly. Perhaps you'll beckon him over here?' Mr. Phibbs went to the door and beckoned, and the young fellow came across the street directly; a smart, brisk young fellow.

" 'Good morning, Sir' says I. 'Good morning, Sir,' says he 'Would you allow me to inquire, Sir,' says I, 'if you ever had any acquaintance with a party of the name of Grimwood?' 'Grimwood! Grimwood!' says he, 'No!' 'You know the Waterloo Road?' 'Oh! of course I know the Waterloo Road!' 'Happen to have heard of a young woman being murdered there?' 'Yes, I read it in the paper, and very sorry I was to read it.' 'Here's a pair of gloves belonging to you, that I found under her pillow the morning afterwards!'

" 'He was in a dreadful state, Sir; a dreadful state!' 'Mr. Wield,' he says, 'upon my solemn oath I never was there I never so much as saw her, to my knowledge, in my life!' 'I am very sorry,' says I. 'To tell you the truth; I don't think you *are* the murderer, but I must take you to Union Hall in a cab. However, I think it's a case of that sort, that, at present, at all events, the magistrate will hear it in private.'

A private examination took place, and then it came out that this young man was acquainted with a cousin of the unfortunate Eliza Grimwoods, and that, calling to see this cousin a day or two before the murder, he left these gloves upon the table. Who should come in, shortly afterwards, but Eliza Grimwood! 'Whose gloves are these?' she says, taking 'em up. 'Those are Mr. Trinkle's gloves,' says her cousin. 'Oh!' says she, 'they are very dirty, and of no use to him, I am sure, I shall take 'em away for my girl to clean the stoves with.' And she put 'em in her pocket. The girl had used 'em to clean the stoves, and, I have no doubt, had left 'em lying on the bedroom mantelpiece, or on the drawers, or somewhere; and her mistress, looking round to see that the room was tidy, had caught 'em up and put 'em under the pillow where I found 'em.

"That's the story, Sir."

THE ARTFUL TOUCH

"One of the most *beautiful* things that ever was done, perhaps," said Inspector Wield, emphasising the adjective, as preparing us to expect dexterity or ingenuity rather than strong interest, "was a move of Serjeant Witchem's. It was a lovely idea!

"Witchem and me were down at Epsom one Derby Day, waiting at the station for the Swell Mob. As I mentioned, when we were talking about these things before, we are ready at the station when there's races, or an Agricultural Show, or a Chancellor sworn in for an university, or Jenny Lind, or any thing of that sort; and as the Swell Mob come down, we send 'em back again by the next train. But some of the Swell Mob, on the occasion of this Derby that I refer to, so far kiddied us as to hire a horse and shay; start away from London by Whitechapel, and miles round; come into Epsom from the opposite direction; and go to work, right and left, on the course, while we were waiting for 'em at the Rail. That, however, ain't the point of what I'm going to tell you.

"While Witchem and me were waiting at the station, there comes up one Mr. Tatt; a gentleman formerly in the public line, quite an amateur Detective in his way, and very much respected. 'Halloa, Charley Wield,' he says. 'What are you doing here? On the look out for some of your old friends?' 'Yes, the old move, Mr. Tatt.' 'Come along,' he says, 'you and Witchem, and have a glass of sherry.' 'We can't stir from the place,' says I, 'till the next train comes in; but after that, we will with pleasure.' Mr. Tatt waits, and the train comes in, and then Witchem and me go off with him to the Hotel. Mr. Tatt he's got up quite regardless of expense, for the occasion; and in his shirt-front there's a beautiful diamond prop, cost him fifteen or twenty pound—a very handsome pin indeed. We drink our sherry at the bar, and have had our three or four glasses, when Witchem cries, suddenly, 'Look out, Mr. Wield! Stand fast!' and a dash is made into the place by the swell mob—four of 'em—that have come down as I tell you, and in a moment Mr. Tatt's prop is gone! Witchem, he cuts 'em off at the door, I lay about me as hard as I can, Mr. Tatt shows fight like a good 'un, and there we are, all down together, heads and heels, knocking about on the floor of the bar—perhaps you never see such a scene of confusion! However, we stick to our men (Mr. Tatt being as good as any officer), and we take 'em all, and carry 'em off to the station. The station's full of people, who have been took on the course; and it's a precious piece of work to get 'em secured. However, we do it at last, and we search 'em; but nothing's found upon 'em, and they're locked up; and a pretty state of heat we are in by that time, I assure you!

"I was very blank over it, myself, to think that the prop had been passed away; and I said to Witchem, when we had set 'em to rights, and were cooling ourselves along with Mr. Tatt, 'We don't take much by *this* move, any way, for nothing's found upon 'em, and it's only the braggadocia after all.' 'What do you mean, Mr. Wield?' says Witchem. 'Here's the diamond pin!' and in the palm of his hand there it was, safe and sound! 'Why, in the name of wonder,' says me and Mr. Tatt, in astonishment, 'how did you come by that?' 'I'll tell you how I come by it,' says he. 'I saw which of 'em took it; and when we were all down on the floor together, knocking about, I just gave him a little touch on the back of his hand, as I knew his pal would; and he thought it WAS his pal; and gave it me!' It was beautiful, beau-ti-ful!

"Even that was hardly the best of the case, for that chap was tried at the Quarter Sessions at Gruildford. You know what Quarter Sessions are, Sir. Well, if you'll believe me, while them slow justices were looking over the Acts of Parliament, to see what they could do to him, I'm blowed if he didn't cut out of the dock before their faces! He cut out of the dock, Sir, then and there; swam across a river; and got up into a tree to dry himself. In the tree he was took—an old woman having seen him climb up—and Witchem's artful touch transported him!"

THE SOFA

"What young men will do, sometimes, to ruin themselves and break their friends' hearts," said Serjeant Dornton, "it's surprising! I had a case at Saint Blank's Hospital which was of this sort. A bad case, indeed, with a bad end!

"The Secretary, and the House-Surgeon, and the Treasurer, of Saint Blank's Hospital, came to Scotland Yard to give information of numerous robberies having been committed on the students. The students could leave nothing in the pockets of their great-coats, while the great-coats were hanging at the Hospital, but it was almost certain to be stolen. Property of various descriptions was constantly being lost; and the gentlemen were naturally uneasy about it, and anxious, for the credit of the Institution, that the thief or thieves should be discovered. The case was entrusted to me, and I went to the Hospital.

" 'Now, gentlemen,' said I, after we had talked it over, 'I understand this property is usually lost from one room.'

"Yes, they said. It was.

" 'I should wish, if you please,' said I, 'to see that room.'

"It was a good-sized bare-room downstairs, with a few tables and forms in it, and a row of pegs, all round, for hats and coats.

" 'Next, gentlemen,' said I, 'do you suspect anybody?'

"Yes, they said. They did suspect somebody. They were sorry to say, they suspected one of the porters.

" 'I should like,' said I, 'to have that man pointed out to me, and to have a little time to look after him.'

"He was pointed out, and I looked after him, and then I went back to the Hospital, and said, 'Now, gentlemen, it's not the porter. He's, unfortunately for himself, a little too fond of drink, but he's nothing worse. My suspicion is, that these robberies are committed by one of the students; and if you'll put me a sofa into that room where the pegs are—as there's no closet—I think I shall be able to detect the thief. I wish the sofa, if you please, to be covered with chintz, or something of that sort, so that I may lie on my chest, underneath it, without being seen.'

"The sofa was provided, and next day at eleven o'clock, before any of the students came, I went there, with those gentlemen, to get underneath it. It turned out to be one of those old-fashioned sofas with a great cross beam at the bottom, that would have broken my back in no time if I could ever have got below it. We had quite a job to break all this away in the time: however, I fell to work, and they fell to work, and we broke it out, and made a clear place for me. I got under the sofa, lay down on my chest, took out my knife, and made a convenient hole in the chintz to look through. It was then settled between me and the gentlemen that when the students were all up in the wards, one of the gentlemen should come in, and hang up a great-coat on one of the pegs. And that that great-coat should have, in one of the pockets, a pocket-book containing marked money.

"After I had been there some time, the students began to drop into the room, by ones, and twos, and threes, and to talk about all sorts of things, little thinking there was anybody under the sofa—and then to go upstairs. At last there came in one who remained until he was alone in the room by himself. A tallish, good-looking young man of one or two and twenty, with a light whisker. He went to a particular hat-peg, took off a good hat that was hanging there, tried it on, hung his own hat in its place, and hung that hat on another peg, nearly opposite to me. I then felt quite certain that he was the thief, and would come back by-and-bye.

"When they were all upstairs, the gentleman came in with the great-coat. I showed him where to hang it, so that I might have a good view of it; and he went away; and I lay under the sofa on my chest, for a couple of hours or so, waiting.

"At last, the same young man came down. He walked across the room, whistling—stopped and listened—took another walk and whistled—stopped again, and listened—then began to go regularly round the pegs, feeling in the pockets of all the coats. When he came to THE great-coat, and felt the pocket-book, he was so eager and so hurried that he broke the strap in tearing it open. As he began to put the money in his pocket, I crawled out from under the sofa, and his eyes met mine.

"My face, as you may perceive, is brown now, but it was pale at that time, my health not being good; and looked as long as a horse's. Besides which, there was a great draught of air from the door, underneath the sofa, and I had tied a handkerchief round my head; so what I looked like, altogether, I don't know. He turned blue—literally blue—when he saw me crawling out, and I couldn't feel surprised at it.

" 'I am an officer of the Detective Police,' said I, 'and have been lying here, since you first came in this morning. I regret, for the sake of yourself and your friends, that you should have done what you have; but this case is complete. You have the pocket-book in your hand and the money upon you; and I must take you into custody!'

"It was impossible to make out any case in his behalf, and on his trial he pleaded guilty. How or when he got the means I don't know; but while he was awaiting his sentence, he poisoned himself in Newgate."

We inquired of this officer, on the conclusion of the foregoing anecdote, whether the time appeared long, or short, when he lay in that constrained position under the sofa?

"Why, you see, Sir," he replied, "if he hadn't come in, the first time, and I had not been quite sure he was the thief, and would return, the time would have seemed long. But, as it was, I being dead-certain of my man, the time seemed pretty short."

XIV

THE MARTYRS OF CHANCERY

In Lambeth Marsh stands a building better known than honored. The wealthy merchant knows it as the place where an unfortunate friend, who made that ruinous speculation during the recent sugar-panic, is now a denizen; the man-about-town knows it as a spot to which several of his friends have been driven, at full gallop, by fleet race-horses and dear dog-carts; the lawyer knows it as the "last scene of all," the catastrophe of a large proportion of law-suits; the father knows it as a bugbear wherewith to warn his scapegrace spendthrift son; but the uncle knows it better as the place whence nephews date protestations of reform and piteous appeals, "this once," for bail. Few, indeed, are there who has not heard of the Queen's Prison, or, as it is more briefly and emphatically termed, "The Bench!"

Awful sound! What visions of folly and roguery, of sloth and seediness, of ruin and recklessness, are conjured up to the imagination in these two words! It is the "Hades" of commerce—the "Inferno" of fortune. Within its grim walls—surmounted by a chevaux de frise, classically termed "Lord Ellenborough's teeth"—dwell at this moment members of almost every class of society. Debt—the grim incubus riding on the shoulders of his victim, like the hideous old man in the

Eastern fable—has here his captives safely under lock and key, and within fifty-feet walls. The church, the army, the navy, the bar, the press, the turf, the trade of England, have each and all their representatives in this "house." Every grade, from the ruined man of fortune, to the petty tradesman who has been undone by giving credit to others still poorer than himself, sends its members to this Bankrupts' Parliament.

Nineteen-twentieths in this Royal House of Detention owe their misfortunes directly or indirectly to themselves; and, for them, every free and prosperous man has his cut-and-dry moral, or scrap of pity, or screed of advice; but there is a proportion of prisoners—happily a small one—within those huge brick boundaries, who have committed no crime, broken no law, infringed no commandment. They are the victims of a system which has been bequeathed to us from the dark days of the "Star Chambers" and "Courts of High Commission"—we mean the Martyrs of Chancery.

These unhappy persons were formerly confined in the Fleet Prison, but on the demolition of that edifice, were transferred to the Queen's Bench. Unlike prisoners of any other denomination, they are frequently ignorant of the cause of their imprisonment, and more frequently still, are unable to obtain their liberation by any acts or concessions of their own. There is no act of which they are permitted to take the benefit—no door left open for them in the Court of Bankruptcy. A Chancery prisoner is, in fact, a far more hopeless mortal than a convict sentenced to transportation; for the latter knows that at the expiration of a certain period, he will, in any event, be a free man. The Chancery prisoner has no such certainty; he may, and he frequently does, waste a lifetime in the walls of a jail, whither he was sent in innocence—because, perchance, he had the ill-luck to be one of the next of kin of some testator who made a will which no one could comprehend, or the heir of some intestate who made none. Any other party interested in the estate commences a Chancery suit, which he must defend or be committed to prison for "contempt." A prison is his portion, whatever he does; for, if he answers the bill filed against him, and cannot pay the costs, he is also clapped in jail for "contempt." Thus, what in ordinary life is but an irrepressible expression of opinion or a small discourtesy, is, "in Equity," a high crime, punishable with imprisonment—sometimes perpetual. Whoever is pronounced guilty of contempt in a Chancery sense, is taken from his family, his profession, or his trade, (perhaps his sole means of livelihood,) and consigned to a jail where he must starve, or live on a miserable pittance of three shillings and sixpence a week, charitably doled out to him from the county rate.

Disobedience of an order of the Court of Chancery—though that order may command you to pay more money than you ever had, or to hand over property which is not yours and was never in your possession—is contempt of court. No matter how great soever your natural reverence for the time-honored institutions of your native land—no matter, though you regard the Lord High Chancellor of Great Britain as the most wonderful man upon earth, and his court as the purest fount of Justice, where she sits weighing out justice with a pair of Oertling's balances, you may yet be pronounced to have been guilty of "contempt." For this there is no pardon. You are in the catalogue of the doomed, and are doomed accordingly.

A popular fallacy spreads a notion that no one need "go into Chancery," unless he pleases. Nothing but an utter and happy innocence of the bitter irony of "Equity" proceedings keeps such an idea current. Men have been imprisoned for many years, some for a lifetime, on account of Chancery proceedings, of the very existence of which they were almost in ignorance before they "somehow or other were found in contempt."

See yonder slatternly old man in threadbare garments, with pinched features telling of long years of anxiety and privation, and want. He has a weak, starved voice, that sounds as though years of privation have shrunk it as much as his cheeks. He always looks cold, and (God help him) feels so too; for Liebig tells us that no quantity of clothing will repel cold without the aid of plenty of food—and little of that passes his lips. His eye has an unquiet, timid, half-frightened look, as if he could not look you straight in the face for lack of energy. His step is a hurried shuffle, though he seldom leaves his room; and when he does, he stares at the racket-players as if they were beings of a different race from himself. No one ever sees his hands—they are plunged desperately into his pockets, which never contain anything else. He is like a dried fruit, exhausted, shrunken, and flung aside by the whole world. He is a man without hope—a Chancery prisoner! He has lived in a jail for twenty-eight weary years! His history has many parallels. It is this:—

It was his misfortune to have an uncle, who died leaving him his residuary legatee. The uncle, like most men who make their own wills, forgot an essential part of it—he named no executor. Our poor friend administered, and all parties interested received their dues—he, last of all, taking but a small sum. It was his only fortune, and having received it he looked about for an investment. There were no railways in those days, or he might have speculated in the Diddlesex Junction. But there were Brazilian Mining Companies, and South Sea Fishing Companies, and various other companies, comprehensively termed "Bubble." Our friend thought these companies were not safe, and he was quite right in his supposition. So he determined to intrust his money to no bubble speculation; but to invest it in Spanish Bonds. After all, our poor friend had better have tried the Brazilian Mines; for the Bonds proved worth very little more than the paper on which they were written. His most Catholic Majesty did not repudiate, (like certain transatlantic States,) but buttoned up his pockets and told his creditors he had "no money."

Some five years after our friend was startled by being requested to come up to Doctors' Commons, and tell the worthy Civilians there all about his uncle's will—which one of the legatees, after receiving all he was entitled to under it, and probably spending the money—suddenly took it into his head to dispute the validity of. Meanwhile the Court of Chancery also stepped in, and ordered him (pending the ecclesiastical suit) to pay over into court "that little trifle" he had received. What could the poor man do? His Catholic Majesty had got the money—he, the legatee, had not a farthing of it, nor of any other money whatsoever. He was in contempt! An officer tapped him on the shoulder, displayed a little piece of parchment, and he found that he was the victim of an unfortunate "attachment." He was walked to the Fleet Prison, where, and in the Queen's Prison, he has remained ever since—a period of twenty-eight years! Yet no less a personage than a Lord Chancellor has pronounced his opinion that the will, after all, was a good and valid will—though the little family party of Doctors' Commons thought otherwise.

There is another miserable-looking object yonder—greasy, dirty, and slovenly. He, too, is a Chancery prisoner. He has been so for twenty years. Why, he has not the slightest idea. He can only tell you that he was found out to be one of the relations of some one who had left "a good bit of money." The lawyers "put the will into Chancery; and at last I was ordered to do something or other, I can't recollect what, which I was also told I couldn't do nohow if I would. So they said I was in contempt, and they took and put me into the Fleet. It's a matter of twenty years I have been in prison; of course I'd like to get out, but I'm told there's no way of doing it anyhow." He is an artisan, and works at his trade in the prison, by which he gains just enough to keep him without coming upon the county-rate.

In that room over the chapel is the infirmary. There was a death lately. The deceased was an old man of sixty-eight, and nearly blind; he had not been many years in prison, but the confinement, and the anxiety, and the separation from his family, had preyed upon his mind and body. He was half-starved, too; for after being used to all the comforts of life, he had to live in jail on sixpence a-day. Yet there was one thousand pounds in the hands of the Accountant-General of the Court of Chancery, which was justly due to him. He was in contempt for not paying some three hundred pounds. But Death purged his contempt, and a decree was afterwards made for paying over the one thousand pounds to his personal representatives; yet himself had died, for want of a twentieth part of it, of slow starvation!

It must not, however, be supposed that Chancery never releases its victims. We must be just to the laws of "Equity." There is actually a man now in London whom they have positively let out of prison! They had, however, prolonged his agonies during seventeen years. He was committed for contempt in not paying certain costs, as he had been ordered. He appealed from the order; but until his appeal was heard, he had to remain in durance vile. The Court of Chancery, like all dignified bodies, is never in a hurry; and, therefore, from having no great influence, and a very small stock of money to forward his interest, the poor man could only get his cause finally heard and decided on in December, 1849—seventeen years from the date of his imprisonment. And, after all, the Court decided that the original order was wrong; so that he had been committed for seventeen years *by mistake*!

How familiar to him must have been the face of that poor, tottering man, creeping along to rest on the bench under the wall yonder. He is very old, but not so old as he looks. He is a poor prisoner, and another victim to Chancery. He has long ago forgotten, if he ever knew, the particulars of his own case, or the order which sent him to a jail. He can tell you more of the history of this gloomy place and its defunct brother, the Fleet, than any other man. He will relate you stories of the "palmy days" of the Fleet, when great and renowned men were frequently its denizens; when soldiers and sailors, authors and actors, whose names even then filled England with their renown, were prisoners within its walls; when whistling shops flourished and turnkeys were smugglers; when lodgings in the prison were dearer than rooms at the west-end of the town; and when a young man was not considered to have finished his education until he had spent a month or two in the Bench or the Fleet. He knows nothing of the world outside—it is dead to him. Relations and friends have long ceased to think of him, or perhaps even to know of his existence. His thoughts range not beyond the high walls which surround him, and probably if he had but a little better supply of food and clothing, he might almost be considered a happy man. But it is the happiness of apathy, not of the intelligence and the affections—the painless condition of a trance, rather than the joyous feeling which has hope for its bright-eyed minister. What has *he* to do with hope? He has been thirty-eight years a Chancery prisoner. He is another out of twenty-four, still prisoners here, more than half of whom have been prisoners for above ten years, and not one of whom has any hope of release! A few have done something fraudulent in "contempt" of all law and equity; but is not even *their* punishment greater than their crime?

Let us turn away. Surely we have seen enough, though many other sad tales may be told, rivaling the horrors of Speilberg and French Lettres-de-cachet.

XV

LAW AT A LOW PRICE

Low, narrow, dark, and frowning are the thresholds of our Inns of Court. If there is one of these entrances of which I have more dread than another, it is that leading out of Holborn to Gray's Inn. I never remember to have met a cheerful face at it, until the other morning, when I encountered Mr. Ficker, attorney-at-law. In a few minutes we found ourselves arm in arm, and straining our voices to the utmost amid the noise of passing vehicles. Mr. Ficker stretched himself on tiptoe in a frantic effort to inform me that he was going to a County Court. "But perhaps you have not heard of these places?"

I assured Mr. Ficker that the parliamentary discussions concerning them had made me very anxious to see how justice was administered in these establishments for low-priced Law. "I am going to one now;" but he impressively added, "you must understand, that professionally I do not approve of their working. There can be no doubt that they seriously prejudice the regular course of law. Comparing the three quarters preceding with three quarters subsequent to the establishment of these Courts, there was a decrease of nearly 10,000 writs issued by the Court of Queen's Bench alone, or of nearly 12,500 on the year."

We soon arrived at the County Court. It is a plain, substantial looking building, wholly without pretension, but at the same time not devoid of some little architectural elegance of exterior. We entered, by a gateway far less austere than that of Gray's Inn, a long, well-lighted passage, on either side of which were offices connected with the Court. One of these was the Summons Office, and I observed on the wall a "Table of Fees," and as I saw Mr. Ficker consulting it with a view to his own business, I asked him his opinion of the charges.

"Why," said he, "the scale of fees is too large for the client and too small for the lawyer. But suitors object less to the amount than to the intricacies and perplexities of the Table. In some districts the expense of recovering a sum of money is one-third more than it is in others; though in both the same scale of fees is in operation. This arises from the variety of interpretations which different judges and officers put upon the charges."

Passing out of the Summons Office, we entered a large hall, placarded with lists of trials for the ensuing week. There were more than one hundred of them set down for trial on nearly every day.

"I am glad," I said, "to think that this is not all additional litigation. I presume these are the thousands of causes a-year withdrawn from the superior Courts?"

"The skeletons of them," said Mr. Ficker, with a sigh. "There were some pickings out of the old processes; but I am afraid there is nothing but the bone here."

"I see here," said I, pointing to one of the lists, "a single plaintiff entered, as proceeding against six-and-twenty defendants in succession."

"Ah," said Mr. Ficker, rubbing his hands, "a knowing fellow that—quite awake to the business of these Courts. A cheap and easy way, sir, of recovering old debts. I don't know who the fellow is—a tailor, very likely—but no doubt you will find his name in the list in this way once every half-year. If his Midsummer and Christmas bills are not punctually paid, it is far cheaper to come here and get a summons served, than to send all over London to collect the accounts, with the chance of not finding the customer at home. And this is one way, you see, in which we solicitors are defrauded. No doubt, this fellow formerly employed an attorney to write letters for him, requesting payment of the amount of his bill, and 6*s*. 8*d*. for the cost of the application. Now, instead of going to an attorney, he comes here and gets the summons served for 2*s*. A knowing hand that—a knowing hand."

"But," I said, "surely no respectable tradesman—"

"*Respectable*," said Mr. Ficker, "I said nothing about respectability. This sort of thing is very common among a certain class of trades-people, especially puffing tailors and boot-makers. Such people rely less on regular than on chance-custom, and therefore they care less about proceeding against those who deal with them."

"But," said I, "this is a decided abuse of the power of the Court. Such fellows ought to be exposed."

"Phoo, phoo," said Mr. Ficker; "they are, probably, soon known here, and then if the judge does his duty, they get bare justice, and nothing more. I am not sure, indeed, that sometimes their appearance here may not injure rather than be of advantage to them; for the barrister may fix a distant date for payment of a debt which the tradesman, by a little civility, might have obtained from his customer a good deal sooner."

"The Court" I found to be a lofty room, somewhat larger and handsomer than the apartment in which the Hogarths are hung up in the National Gallery. One-half was separated from the other by a low partition, on the outer side of which stood a miscellaneous crowd of persons who appeared to be waiting their turn to be called forward. Though the appearance of the Court was new and handsome, everything was plain and simple.

I was much struck by the appearance and manner of the Judge. He was comparatively a young man; but I fancied that he displayed the characteristics of experience. His attention to the proceedings was unwearied; his discrimination appeared admirable; and there was a calm self-possession about him that bordered upon dignity.

The suitors who attended were of every class and character. There were professional men, tradesmen, costermongers, and a peer. Among the plaintiffs, there were specimens of the considerate plaintiff, the angry plaintiff, the cautious plaintiff, the bold-swearing plaintiff, the energetic plaintiff, the practiced plaintiff, the shrewish (female) plaintiff, the nervous plaintiff, and the revengeful plaintiff. Each plaintiff was allowed to state his or her case in his or her own way, and to call witnesses, if there were any. When the debt appeared to be *primâ facie* proved, the Barrister turned to the defendant, and perhaps asked him if he disputed it?

The characteristics of the defendants were quite as different as the characteristics of the plaintiffs. There was the factious defendant, and the defendant upon principle—the stormy defendant, and the defendant who was timid—the impertinent defendant, and the defendant who left his case entirely to the Court—the defendant who would never pay, and the defendant who would if he could. The causes of action I found to be as multifarious as the parties were diverse. Besides suits by trades-people for every description of goods supplied, there were claims for every sort and kind of service that can belong to humanity, from the claim of a monthly nurse, to the claim of the undertaker's assistant.

In proving these claims the Judge was strict in insisting that a proper account should have been delivered, and that the best evidence should be produced as to the correctness of the items. No one could come to the court and receive a sum of money merely by swearing that "Mr. So-and-so owes me so much."

With regard to defendants, the worst thing they could do, was to remain away when summoned to attend. It has often been observed that those persons about whose dignity there is any doubt, are the most rigorous in enforcing its observance. It is with Courts as it is with men; and as Small Debt Courts are sometimes apt to be held in some contempt, I found the Judge here very prompt in his decision, whenever a defendant did not appear by self or agent. Take a case in point:

Barrister (to the Clerk of the Court). Make an order in favor of the plaintiff.

Plaintiff's Attorney. Your honor will give us speedy recovery?

Barrister. Will a month do, Mr. Docket?

Plaintiff's Attorney. The defendant is not here to assign any reason for delay, your honor.

Barrister. Very well; then let him pay in a fortnight.

I was much struck, in some of the cases, by a friendly sort of confidence which characterized some of the proceedings. Here again the effect in a great measure was attributable to the Barrister. He seemed to act—as indeed he is—rather as an authorized arbitrator than as a judge. He advised rather than ordered; "I really think, he said, to one defendant, "I really think, sir, you have made yourself liable." "Do you, sir?" said the man, pulling out his purse, without more ado, "Then, sir, I am sure I will pay."

It struck me, too, as remarkable, that though some of the cases were hotly contested, none of the defeated parties complained of the decision. In several instances, the parties even appeared to acquiesce in the propriety of the verdict.

A Scotch shoeing-smith summoned a man who, from his appearance, I judged to be a hard, keen-dealing Yorkshire horse-jobber; he claimed a sum of money for putting shoes upon six-and-thirty horses. His claim was just, but there was an error in his particulars of demand which vitiated it. The Barrister took some trouble to point out that in consequence of this error even if he gave a decision in his favor, he should be doing him an injury. The case was a hard one, and I could not help regretting that the poor plaintiff should be non-suited. Did *he* complain? Neither by word or action. Folding up his papers, he said, sorrowfully, "Well, sir, I assure you I would not have come here, if it had not been a just claim." The Barrister evidently believed him, for he advised a compromise, and adjourned the case that the parties might try to come to terms. But the defendant would not arrange, and the plaintiff was driven to elect a non-suit.

The mode of dealing with documentary evidence afforded me considerable satisfaction. Private letters—such as the tender effusions of faithless love—are not, as in the higher Courts, thrust one after the other, into the dirty face of a grubby-looking witness who was called to prove the handwriting, sent the round of the twelve jurymen in the box, and finally passed to the reporters that they might copy certain flowery sentences and a few stanzas from "Childe Harold," which the short-hand writers "could not catch," but are handed up, seriatim, to the Judge who looks through them carefully and then passes them over without observation for the re-perusal of the defendant. Not a word transpires except such extracts as require comment.

There was a claim against a gentleman for a butcher's bill. He had the best of all defences, for he had paid ready money for every item as it was delivered. The plaintiff was the younger partner of a butchering firm which had broken up, leaving him in possession of the books and his partner in possession of the credit. The proprietor of the book-debts proved the order and delivery of certain joints prior to a certain date, and swore they had not been paid for. To show his title to recover the value of them, he somewhat unnecessarily thrust before the Barrister, the deed which constituted him a partner. The Judge instantly compared the deed with the bill. "Why," he said, turning to the butcher, "all the items you have sworn to were purchased anterior to the date of your entering into partnership. If anyone is entitled to recover, it is your partner, whom the defendant alleges he has paid." In one, as they are called, of the "Superior Courts," I very much doubt whether either Judge or Jury would have discovered for themselves this important discrepancy.

The documentary evidence was not confined to deeds and writings, stamped or unstamped. Even during the short time I was present, I saw some curious records produced before the Barrister—records as primitive in their way as those the Chancellor of the Exchequer used to keep in the Tally-Office, before the comparatively recent introduction of book-keeping into the department of our national accountant.

Among other things received in evidence, were a milkwoman's score and a baker's notches. Mr. Ficker appeared inclined to think that no weight ought to be attached to such evidence as this. But, when I recollect that there have occasionally been such things as tombstones produced in evidence before Lord Volatile in his own particular Court, the House of Lords, ("the highest jurisdiction," as they call it, "in the realm,") I see no good reason why Mrs. Chalk, the milkwoman, should not be permitted to produce her tallies in a County Court. For every practical purpose the score upon the one seems just as good a document as the epitaph upon the other.

I was vastly pleased by the great consideration which appeared to be displayed towards misfortune and adversity. These Courts are emphatically Courts for the *recovery* of debts; and inasmuch as they afford great facilities to plaintiffs, it is therefore the more incumbent that defendants should be protected against hardship and oppression. A man was summoned to show why he had not paid a debt pursuant to a previous order of the Court. The plaintiff attended to press the case against him, and displayed some rancor.

"Why have you not paid, sir?" demanded the Judge sternly.

"Your honor," said the man, "I have been out of employment six months, and within the last fortnight everything I have in the world has been seized in execution."

In the Superior Courts this would have been no excuse. The man would probably have gone to prison, leaving his wife and family upon the parish. But here that novel sentiment in law proceedings—sympathy—peeped forth.

"I believe this man would pay," said the Barrister, "if possible. But he has lost everything in the world. At present I shall make no order."

It did not appear to me that the plaintiffs generally in this Court were anxious to press very hardly upon defendants. Indeed it would be bad policy to do so. Give a man time, and he can often meet demands that it would be impossible for him to defray if pressed at once.

"Immediate execution" in this Court, seemed to be payment within a fortnight. An order to pay in weekly installments is a common mode of arranging a case, and as it is usually made by agreement between the parties, both of them are satisfied. In fact, the rule of the Court seemed not dissimilar from that of trades-people who want to do a quick business, and who proceed upon the principle that "No reasonable offer is refused."

I had been in the Court sufficiently long to make these and other observations, when Mr. Ficker introduced me to the clerk. On leaving the Court by a side-door, we repaired to Mr. Nottit's room, where we found that gentleman (an old attorney) prepared to do the honors of "a glass of sherry and a biscuit." Of course the conversation turned upon "the County Court."

"Doing a pretty good business here?" said Mr. Ficker.

"Business—we're at it all day," replied Mr. Nottit. "I'll show you. This is an account of the business of the County Courts in England and Wales in the year 1848—the account for 1849 is not yet made up."

"Take six months, I suppose, to make it," said Mr. Ficker, rather ill-naturedly.

"Total 'Number of Plaints or Causes entered,' " read the clerk, "427,611."

"Total amount of money sought to be recovered by the plaintiffs," continued Mr. Nottit, "£1,346,802."

"Good gracious!" exclaimed Ficker, his face expressing envy and indignation; "What a benefit would have been conferred upon society, if all this property had been got into the legitimate Law Courts! What a benefit to the possessors of all this wealth! I have no doubt whatever that during the past year the suitors, who have recovered this million and a quarter, have spent the whole of it, squandered it upon what they called "necessaries of life." Look at the difference if it had only been locked up for them—say in Chancery. It would have been preserved with the greatest possible safety; accounted for—every fraction of it—in the books of the Accountant-General; and we, sir, we—the respectable practitioners in the profession—should have gone down three or four times every year to the Master's offices to see that it was all right, and to have had a little consultation as to the best means of holding it safely for our client, until his suit was properly and equitably disposed of."

"But, perhaps, Ficker," I suggested, "these poor clients make better use of their own money after all than the Courts of Law and Equity could make it for them."

"Then the costs," said Mr. Ficker, with an attorney's ready eye to business, "let us hear about them."

"The total amount of costs adjudged to be paid by defendants on the amount (£752,500) for which judgment was obtained, was £199,980," was the answer—"being an addition of 26.5 per cent, on the amount ordered to be paid."

"Well," said Mr. Ficker, "that's not so very bad. Twenty five per cent," turning to me, "is a small amount undoubtedly for the costs of an action duly brought to trial; but, as the greater part of these costs are costs of Court, twenty-five per cent, cannot be considered inadequate."

"It seems to me a great deal too much," said I. "Justice ought to be much cheaper."

"All the fees to counsel and attorneys are included in the amount," remarked the clerk, "and so are allowances to witnesses. The fees on causes amounted to very nearly £300,000. Of this sum, the Officers' fees were, in 1848, £234,274, and the General Fund fees £51,784."

"Not so bad!" said Mr. Ficker, smiling.

"The Judges' fees amounted to nearly £90,000. This would have given them all £1500 each; but the Treasury has fixed their salaries at a uniform sum of £1000, so that the sixty Judges only draw £60,000 of the £90,000."

"Where does the remainder go?" I inquired.

The County Court Clerk shook his head.

"But you don't mean," said I, "that the suiters are made to pay £90,000 a year for what only costs £60,000?"

"I am afraid it is so," said Mr. Nottit.

"Dear me!" said Mr. Ficker; "I never heard of such a thing in all my professional experience. I am sure the Lord Chancellor would never sanction that in his Court. You ought to apply to the Courts above, Mr. Nottit—you ought, indeed."

"And yet," said I, "I think I have heard something about a Suitors' Fee Fund in those Courts above—eh, Ficker?"

"Ah—hem—yes," said Mr. Ficker. "Certainly—but the cases are not at all analogous. By the way, how are the other fees distributed?"

"The Clerks," said Mr. Nottit, "received £87,283, nearly as much as the Judges. As there are 491 clerks, the average would be £180 a-year to each. But as the Clerks' fees accumulate in each Court according to the business transacted, of course the division is very unequal. In one Court in Wales the Clerk only got £8 10*s.* in fees; in another Court, in Yorkshire, his receipts only amounted to £9 4*s.* 3*d.* But some of my colleagues made a good thing of it. The Clerks' fees in some of the principal Courts' are very 'Comfortable.'

"The Clerk of Westminster netted	£2731
The Clerk of Clerkenwell	2227
The Clerk of Southwark	1710

Bristol, Sheffield, Bloomsbury, Birmingham, Shoreditch, Leeds. Marylebone, received £1000 a-year and upwards."

"But," continued our friend, "three-fourths of the Clerks get less than £100 a-year."

"Now," said Mr. Ficker, "tell us what you all do for this money?"

"Altogether," said the clerk, "the Courts sat in 1848, 8,386 days, or an average for each Judge of 140 days. The greatest number of sittings was in Westminster, where the Judge sat 246 days. At Liverpool, there were sittings on 225 days. The number of trials, as I have before mentioned, was 259,118, or an average of about 4,320 to each Judge, and 528 to each Court. In some of the Courts, however, as many as 20,000 cases are tried in a year."

"Why," said Mr. Ficker, "they can't give five minutes to each case! Is this 'administration of justice?' "

"When," said the clerk, "a case is undefended, a plaintiff appears, swears to his debt, and obtains an order for its payment, which takes scarcely two minutes."

"How long does a defended case take?"

"On the average, I should say, a quarter of an hour; that is, provided counsel are not employed."

"Jury cases occupy much longer?"

"Undoubtedly."

"Are the jury cases frequent?" I inquired—some feeling of respect for 'our time-honored institution' coming across me as I spoke.

"Nothing," said our friend, "is more remarkable in the history of the County Courts than the very limited resort which suitors have to juries. It is within the power of either party to cause the jury to be summoned in any case where the plaint is upwards of £5. The total number of cases tried in 1848 was 259,118. Of these, upwards of 50,000 were cases in which juries might have been summoned. But there were only 884 jury cases in all the Courts, or one jury for about every 270 trials! The party requiring the jury obtained a verdict in 446 out of the 884 cases, or exactly one-half.

"At any rate, then, there is no imputation on the juries," said Mr. Ficker.

"The power of resorting to them is very valuable," said our friend. "There is a strong disposition among the public to rely upon the decision of the Barrister, and that reliance is not without good foundation, for certainly justice in these Courts have been well administered. But there may be occasions when it would be very desirable that a jury should be interposed between a party to a cause and the presiding Judge; and certainly if the jurisdiction of these Courts is extended, it will be most desirable that suitors should be able to satisfy themselves that every opportunity is open to them of obtaining justice."

"For my own part," said I, "I would as soon have the decision of one honest man as of twelve honest men, and perhaps I would prefer it. If the Judge is a liberal-minded and enlightened man, I would rather take his judgment than submit my case to a dozen selected by chance, and among whom there would most probably be at least a couple of dolts. By the way, why should not the same option be given to suitors in Westminster Hall as is given in the County Courts?"

"What!" exclaimed Mr. Ficker, "Abolish trial by Jury! The palladium of British liberty! Have you *no* respect for antiquity?"

"We must adapt ourselves to the altered state of society, Ficker. Observe the great proportion of cases *tried* in these

Courts—more than sixty per cent. of the entire number of plaints entered. This is vastly greater than the number in the Superior Courts, where there is said to be scarcely one cause tried for fifty writs issued. Why is this? Simply because the cost deters parties from continuing the actions. They settle rather than go to a jury."

"And a great advantage, too," said Mr. Ficker.

"Under the new bill," said our friend, the Clerk, "Ficker's clients will all be coming to us. They will be able to recover £50 in these Courts, without paying Ficker a single 6s. 8*d.* unless they have a peculiar taste for law expenses."

"And a hideous amount of rascality and perjury will be the consequence," said Mr. Ficker. "You will make these Courts mere Plaintiffs' Courts, sir—Courts to which every rogue will be dragging the first man who he thinks can pay him £50, if he only swears hard enough that it is due to him. I foresee the greatest danger from this extension of litigation, under the pretence of providing cheap law.

"Fifty pounds," said I, "is, to a large proportion of the people, a sum of money of very considerable importance. I must say, I think it would be quite right that inferior courts should not have the right of dealing with so much of a man's property, without giving him a power of appeal, at least under restrictions. But, at the same time, looking at the satisfactory way in which this great experiment has worked—seeing how many righteous claims have been established and just defences maintained, which would have been denied under any other system—I cannot but hope to see the day when, attended by proper safeguards for the due administration of justice, these Courts will be open to even a more numerous class of suitors than at present. It is proposed that small Charitable Trust cases shall be submitted to the Judges of these Courts; why not also refer to them cases in which local magistrates cannot now act without suspicion of partisanship?—cases, for example, under the Game Laws, or the Turnpike Laws, and, more than all, offences against the Truck Act, which essentially embody matters of account. Why not," said I, preparing for a burst of eloquence—"why not—"

"Overthrow at once the Seat of Justice, the Letter of the Law, and our glorious constitution in Church and State!"

It was Mr. Ficker who spoke, and he had rushed frantically from the room ere I could reply.

Having no one to argue the point further with, I made my bow to Mr. Nottit and retired also.

XVI

THE LAW

The most litigious fellow I ever knew, was a Welshman, named Bones. He had got possession, by some means, of a bit of waste ground behind a public-house in Hogwash Street. Adjoining this land was a yard belonging to the parish of St. Jeremiah, which the Parish Trustees were fencing in with a wall. Bones alleged that one corner of their wall was advanced about ten inches on his ground, and as they declined to remove it back, he kicked down the brick-work before the mortar was dry. The Trustees having satisfied themselves that they were not only within their boundary, but that they had left Bones some feet of the parish land to boot, built up the wall again. Bones kicked it down again.

The Trustees put it up a third time, under the protection of a policeman. The inexorable Bones, in spite of the awful presence of this functionary, not only kicked down the wall again, but kicked the brick-layers into the bargain. This was too much, and Bones was marched off to Guildhall for assaulting the brick-layers. The magistrate rather pooh-poohed the complaint, but bound over Bones to keep the peace. The *causa belli*, the wall, was re-edified a fourth time; but when the Trustees revisited the place next morning, it was again in ruins! While they were in consultation upon this last insult, they were politely waited on by an attorney's clerk, who served them all with "writs" in an action of trespass, at the suit of Bones, for encroaching on his land.

Thus war was declared about a piece of dirty land literally not so big as a door-step, and the whole fee-simple of which would not sell for a shilling. The Trustees, however, thought they ought not to give up the rights of the parish to the obstinacy of a perverse fellow, like Bones, and resolved to indict Bones for assaulting the workmen. Accordingly, the action and the indictment went on together.

The action was tried first, and as the evidence clearly showed the Trustees had kept within their own boundary, they got the verdict. Bones moved for a new trial; that failed. The Trustees now thought they would let the matter rest, as it had cost the parish about one hundred and fifty pounds, and they supposed Bones had had enough of it. But they had mistaken their man. He brought a writ of error in the action, which carried the cause into the Exchequer Court, and tied it up nearly two years, and in the meantime he forced them *nolens volens* to try the indictment. When the trial came on, the judge said, that as the whole question had been decided in the action, there was no occasion for any further proceedings, and therefore the Defendant had better be acquitted, and so make an end of it.

Accordingly, Bones was acquitted; and the very next thing Bones did was to sue the Trustees in a new action, for maliciously instituting the indictment against him without reasonable cause! The new action went on to trial; and it being proved that one of the Trustees had been overheard to say that they would punish him; this was taken as evidence of malice, and Bones got a verdict for forty shillings damages besides all the costs. Elated with this victory, Bones pushed on his old action in the Exchequer Chamber to a hearing, but the Court affirmed the judgment against him, without hearing the Trustees' counsel.

The Trustees were now sick of the very name of Bones, which had become a sort of bugbear, so that if a Trustee met a friend in the street he would be greeted with an inquiry after the health of his friend, Mr. Bones. They would have gladly let the whole matter drop into oblivion, but Jupiter and Bones had determined otherwise; for the indomitable Briton brought a Writ of Error in the House of Lords, on the judgment of the Exchequer Chamber. The unhappy Trustees had caught a Tartar, and follow him into the Lords they must. Accordingly, after another year or two's delay, the case came on in the Lords. Their Lordships pronounced it the most trumpery Writ of Error they had ever seen, and again affirmed the judgment, with costs, against Bones. The Trustees now taxed their costs, and found that they had spent not less than five hundred pounds in defending their claims to a bit of ground that was not of the value of an old shoe. But, then, Bones was condemned to pay the costs. True—so they issued execution against Bones; caught him, after some trouble, and locked him up in jail. The next week, Bones petitioned the Insolvent Court, got out of prison, and, on examination of his schedule, his effects appeared to be £0 0*s*. 0*d*.! Bones had, in fact, been fighting the Trustees on credit for the last three years; for his own attorney was put down as a creditor to a large amount, which was the only satisfaction the Trustees obtained from perusing his schedule.

They were now obliged to have recourse to the Parish funds to pay their own law expenses, and were consoling themselves with the reflection that these did not come out of *their own pockets*—when they received the usual notification that a Bill in Chancery had been filed against them, at Mr. Bones's suit, to overhaul their accounts with the parish, and *prevent the misapplication of the Parish money* to the payment of their law costs! This was the climax. And being myself a disciple of Coke, I have heard nothing further of it; being unwilling, as well perhaps as unqualified, to follow the case into the labyrinthic vaults of the Court of Chancery. The catastrophe, if this were a tale, could hardly be mended—so the true story may end here.

XVII

THE DUTIES OF WITNESSES AND JURYMEN

I am not a young man, and have passed much of my life in our Criminal Courts. I am, and have been, in active practice at the Bar, and I believe myself capable of offering some hints toward an improved administration of justice.

I do not allude to any reform in the law, though I believe much to be needed. I mean to confine myself to amendments which it is in the power of the people to make for themselves, and indeed, which no legislature, however enlightened, can make for them.

In no country can the laws be well administered, where the popular mind stands at a low point in the scale of intelligence, or where the moral tone is lax. The latter defect is of course the most important, but it is so intimately connected with the former, that they commonly prevail together, and the causes which remove the one, have, almost without exception, a salutary effect upon the other.

That the general diffusion of morals and intelligence is essential to the healthy working of jurisprudence in all countries, will be admitted, when it is recollected that no tribunal, however skillful, can arrive at the truth by any other way than by the testimony of witnesses, and that consequently on their trustworthiness the enjoyment of property, character, and life, must of necessity depend.

Again, wherever trial by jury is established, a further demand arises for morals and intelligence among the people. It follows then, as a consequence almost too obvious to justify the remark, that whatever in any country enlarges and strengthens these great attributes of civilization, raises its capacity for performing that noblest duty of social man, the administration of justice.

Let me first speak of witnesses and their testimony. It is sometimes supposed that the desire to be veracious is the only quality essential to form a trustworthy witness—and an essential quality it is beyond all doubt—but it is possessed by many who are nevertheless very unsafe guides to truth. In the first place, this general desire for truth in a mind not carefully regulated, is apt to give way, oftentimes unconsciously, to impressions which overpower habitual veracity. It may be laid down as a general rule that witnesses are partisans, and that, often without knowing it, their evidence takes a color from the feeling of partisanship, which gives it all the injurious effects of willful falsehood—nay, it is frequently more pernicious. The witness who knowingly perverts the truth, often betrays his mendicity by his voice, his countenance, or his choice of words; while the unconscious perverter gives his testimony with all the force of sincerity. Let the witness who intends to give evidence worthy of confidence, be on his guard against the temptations to become a partisan. Witnesses ought to avoid consorting together on the eve of a trial; still more, discussing the matters in dispute, and comparing their intended statements. Musicians have observed that if two instruments, not in exact accordance, are played together, they have a tendency to run into harmony. Witnesses are precisely such instruments, and act on each other in like manner.

So much with regard to the moral tone of the witness; but the difficulties which I have pointed out may be surmounted, and yet leave his evidence a very distorted narrative of the real facts. Consideration must be given to the intellectual requirements of a witness. It was the just remark of Dr. Johnson that complaints of the memory were often very unjust toward that faculty which was reproached with not retaining what had never been confided to its care. The defect is not a failure of memory, but a lack of observation; the ideas have not run out of the mind—they never went into it.

This is a deficiency, which cannot be dealt with in any special relation to the subject in hand; it can only be corrected by cultivating a general habit of observation, which, considering that the dearest interests of others may be imperiled by errors arising out of the neglect to observe accurately, must be looked upon in the light of a duty.

A still greater defect is the absence of the power of distinguishing fact and inference. Nothing but a long experience in Courts of Justice, can give a notion of the extent to which testimony is adulterated by this defect. It is often exemplified in the depositions of witnesses, or rather in the comparison between the depositions which, as your readers know, are taken in writing before the committing magistrate, and the evidence given on the trial.

Circumstances on which the witness had been silent when examined before the magistrate shortly after the event, make their appearance in his evidence on the day of trial; so that his memory purports to augment inaccuracy in proportion to their time which has elapsed since the transaction of which he speaks!

I have observed this effect produced in a marvelous degree in cases of new trial, which in civil suits are often awarded, and which frequently take place years after the event to which they relate. The comparison of the evidence of the same witness as it stands upon the shorthand writer's notes of the two trials, would lead an unpracticed reader to the conclusion that nothing but perjury could account for the diversities; and this impression would be confirmed, if he should find, as in all probability he would, that the points on which the latter memory was better supplied than the earlier, were just those on which the greatest doubt had prevailed on the former occasion, and which were made in favor of the party on whose side the witness had been called. But the critic would be mistaken. The witness was not dishonest, but had failed to keep watch over the operations of his own mind. He had perhaps often adverted to the subject, and often discoursed upon it, until at length he confounded the facts which had occurred, with the inference which he had drawn from such facts, in establishment of the existence of others, which had in reality no place except in his own cogitation, but which after a time took rank in his memory with its original impressions.

The best safeguard a witness could employ to preserve the unalloyed memory of transactions, is to commit his narrative to writing, as soon after the event as he shall have learned that his evidence respecting them is likely to be required; and yet I can hardly recommend such a course, because so little is the world, and even that portion of the world which passes its life in Courts of Justice, acquainted with what may be called the Philosophy of Evidence, that a conscientious endeavor of this kind to preserve his testimony in its purity, might draw upon him the imputation of having fabricated his narrative; and this is the more probable, because false witnesses have not unfrequently taken similar means for abiding by their fictions.

It is worthy of note how much these disturbing causes, both moral and intellectual, fasten upon these portions of evidence which are most liable to distortion. Words, as contra-distinguished from facts, exemplify the truth of this position. Every witness ought to feel great distrust of himself in giving evidence of a conversation. Language, if it runs to any length, is very liable to be misunderstood, at least in passages.

But supposing it to be well understood at the moment, the exact wording of it can rarely be recalled, unless the witness's memory were tantamount in minuteness and accuracy to the record of a shorthand writer. He is consequently permitted to give an abstract, or, as it is usually called, the substance of what occurred. But here a new difficulty arises; to abstract correctly is an intellectual effort of no mean order, and is rarely accomplished with a decent approach to perfection. Let the juryman bear this in mind. He will be often tempted to rely on alleged confessions of prisoners sworn to by witnesses who certainly desire to speak the truth. These confessions often go so straight to the point, that they offer to the juryman a species of relief from that state of doubt, which, to minds unpracticed in weighing probabilities, is irksome, almost beyond description. Speaking from the experience of thirty years, I should pronounce the evidence of words to be so dangerous in its nature as to demand the utmost vigilance, in all cases, before it is allowed to influence the verdict to any important extent.

While I am on the subject of evidence, infirm in its nature, I must not pass over that of identity of person. The number of persons who resemble each other is not inconsiderable in itself; but the number is very large of persons, who, though very distinguishable when standing side by side, are yet sufficiently alike to deceive those who are without the means of immediate comparison.

Early in life an occurrence impressed me with the danger of relying on the most confidential belief of identity. I was at Vauxhall Gardens where I thought I saw, at a short distance, an old country gentleman whom I highly respected, and whose favor I should have been sorry to lose. I bowed to him, but obtained no recognition. In those days the company amused themselves by walking round in a circle, some in one direction, some in the opposite, by which everyone saw and was seen—I say, in those days, because I have not been at Vauxhall for a quarter of a century. In performing these rounds I often met the gentleman, and tried to attract his attention, until I became convinced that either his eyesight was so weakened that he did not know me, or that he chose to disown my acquaintance. Some time afterward, going into the county in which he resided, I received, as usual, an invitation to dinner; this led to an explanation, when my friend assured me he had not been in London for twenty years. I afterwards met the person whom I had mistaken for my old friend, and wondered how I could have fallen into the error. I can only explain it by supposing that, if the mind feels satisfied of identity, which it often does at the first glance, it ceases to investigate that question, and occupies itself with other matter; as in my case, where my thoughts ran upon the motives my friend might have, for not recognizing me, instead of employing themselves on the question of whether or no the individual before my eyes was indeed the person I took him for.

If I had had to give evidence on this matter my mistake would have been the more dangerous, as I had full means of knowledge. The place was well lighted, the interviews were repeated, and my mind was undisturbed. How often have I known evidence of identity acted upon by juries, where the witness was in a much less favorable position (for correct observation) than mine.

Sometimes, a mistaken verdict is avoided by independent evidence. Rarely, however, is this rock escaped, by cross-examination, even when conducted with adequate skill and experience. The belief of the witness is belief in a matter of opinion resulting from a combination of facts so slight and unimportant, separately considered, that they furnish no handle to the cross-examiner. A striking case of this kind occurs to my recollection, with which I will conclude.

A prisoner was indicted for shooting at the prosecutor, with intent to kill him. The prosecutor swore that the prisoner had demanded his money, and that upon refusal, or delay, to comply with his requisition, he fired a pistol, by the flash of which his countenance became perfectly visible; the shot did not take effect, and the prisoner made off. Here the recognition was momentary, and the prosecutor could hardly have been in an undisturbed state of mind, yet the confidence of his belief made a strong impression on all who heard the evidence, and probably would have sealed the fate of the prisoner without the aid of an additional fact of very slight importance, which was, however, put in evidence by way of corroboration, that the prisoner, who was a stranger to the neighborhood, had been seen passing near the spot in which the attack was made about noon of the same day. The judge belonged to a class, now, thank God! obsolete, who always acted on the reverse of the constitutional maxim, and considered every man guilty, until he was proved to be innocent.

If the case had closed without witnesses on behalf of the prisoner, his life would have been gone; fortunately, he possessed the means of employing an able and zealous attorney, and, more fortunately, it so happened that several hours before the attack the prisoner had mounted upon a coach, and was many miles from the scene of the crime at the hour of its commission.

With great labor, and at considerable expense, all the passengers were sought out, and with the coachman and guard, were brought into court, and testified to the presence among them of the prisoner. An *alibi* is always a suspected defence, and by no man was ever more suspiciously watched than by this judge. But then witness after witness appeared, their names corresponding exactly with the way-bill produced by the clerk of a respectable coach-office, the most determined scepticism gave way, and the prisoner was acquitted by acclamation. He was not, however, saved by his innocence, but by his good fortune. How frequently does it happen to us all to be many hours at a time without having witnesses to prove our absence from one spot by our presence at another! And how many of us are too prone to avail ourselves of such proof in the instances where it may exist!

A remarkable instance of mistake in identity, which put the life of a prisoner in extreme peril, I heard from the lips of his counsel. It occurred at the Special Commission held at Nottingham after the riots consequent on the rejection of the Reform Bill by the House of Lords, in 1831.

The prisoner was a young man of prepossessing appearance, belonging to what may be called the lower section of the middle rank of life, being a framework knitter, in the employment of his father, a master manufacturer in a small way. He was tried on an indictment charging him with the offence of arson. A mob, of which he was alleged to be one, had burnt Colwick Hall, near Nottingham, the residence of Mr. Musters, the husband of Mary Chaworth, whose name is so closely linked with that of Byron. This ill-fated lady was approaching the last stage of consumption, when, on a cold and wet evening in autumn, she was driven from her mansion, and compelled to take refuge among the trees of her shrubbery—an outrage which probably hastened her death.

The crime with its attendant circumstances, created, as was natural, a strong sympathy against the criminals. Unhappily, this feeling, so praiseworthy in itself, is liable to produce a strong tendency in the public mind to believe in the guilt of the party accused. People sometimes seem to hunger and thirst after a criminal, and are disappointed when it turns out that they are mistaken in their man, and are, consequently, slow to believe that such an error has been made. Doubtless, the impression is received into the mind unconsciously; but although on that ground pardonable, it is all the more dangerous. In this case, the prisoner was identified by several witnesses as having taken an active part in setting fire to the house.

He had been under their notice for some considerable space of time. They gave their evidence against him without hesitation, and probably the slightest doubt of its accuracy. His defence was an *alibi*. The frame at which he worked had its place near the entrance to the warehouse, the room frequented by the customers and all who had business to transact at the manufactory. He acted, therefore, as doorkeeper, and in that capacity had been seen and spoken with by many persons, who in their evidence more than covered the whole time which elapsed between the arrival of the mob at Colwick Hall and its departure. The *alibi* was believed, and the prisoner, after a trial which lasted a whole day, was acquitted.

The next morning he was to be tried again on another indictment, charging him with having set fire to the Castle of Nottingham. The counsel for the prosecution, influenced by motives of humanity, and fully impressed with the prisoner's guilt on both charges, urged the counsel for the prisoner to advise his client to plead guilty, undertaking that his life should be spared, but observing at the same time that his social position, which was superior to that of the other prisoners, would make it impossible to extend the mercy of the Crown to him unless he manifested a due sense of his offences by foregoing the chance of escape. "You know," said they, "how rarely an *alibi* obtains credit with a jury. You can have no other defence today than that of yesterday. The Castle is much nearer than Colwick Hall to the manufactory, and a very short absence from his work on the part of the prisoner might reconcile the evidence of all the witnesses, both for him and against him; moreover, who ever heard of a successful *alibi* twice running?"

The counsel for the prisoner had his client taken into a room adjoining the court, and having explained to him the extreme danger in which he stood, informed him of the offer made by the prosecutors. The young man evinced some emotion, and asked his counsel to advise what step he should take. "The advice," he was answered, "must depend upon a fact known to himself alone—his guilt or innocence. If guilty, his chance of escape was so small that it would be the last degree of rashness to refuse the offer; if, on the other hand, he were innocent, his counsel, putting himself in the place of the prisoner, would say, that no peril, however imminent, would induce him to plead guilty." The prisoner was further told, that in the course of a trial circumstances often arose at the moment, unforeseen by all parties, which disclosed the truth; that this consideration was in his favor if he were innocent but showed at the same time that there were now chances of danger, if he were guilty, the extent of which could not be calculated, nor even surmised. The youth, with perfect self-possession, and unshaken firmness, replied, "I am innocent, and will take my trial." He did so. Many painful hours wore away, every moment diminishing the prisoner's chance of acquittal, until it seemed utterly extinguished, when some trifling matter which had escaped the memory of the narrator, occurred, leading him to think it was possible that another person, who must much resemble the prisoner, had been mistaken for him. Inquiry was instantly made of the family, whether they knew of any such resemblance; when it appeared that the prisoner had a cousin so much like himself that the two were frequently accosted in the street, the one for the other. The cousin had absconded.

It is hardly credible, though doubtless true, that a family of respectable station could have been unaware of the importance of such a fact, or that the prisoner, who appeared not deficient in intelligence, and who was assuredly in full possession of his faculties, could be insensible to its value. That either he or they could have placed such reliance on his defence as to induce them to screen his guilty relative, is to the last degree improbable, especially as the cousin had escaped. Witnesses, however, were quickly produced, who verified the resemblance between the two, and the counsel for the prosecution abandoned their case, expressing their belief that their witnesses had given their evidence under a mistake of identity.

The narrator added that an *alibi* stood a less chance of favorable reception at Nottingham than elsewhere, although in every place received with great jealousy. In one of the trials arising out of the outrages committed by the Luddites, who broke into manufactories and destroyed all lace frames of a construction which they thought oppressive to working-men, an *alibi*, he said had been concocted, which was successful in saving the life of a man notoriously guilty, and which had therefore added to the disrepute of this species of defence. The hypothesis was, that the prisoner, at the time when the crime was committed, at Loughborough, sixteen miles from Nottingham, was engaged at a supper party at the latter place; and the prisoner having the sympathy of a large class in his favor, whose battle he had been fighting, no difficulty was experienced by his friends in finding witnesses willing to support this hypothesis on their oaths; but it would have been a rash measure to have called them into the box unprepared. And when it is considered how readily a preconcerted story might have been destroyed by cross-examination, the task of preparing the witnesses so as to elude this test, was one requiring no ordinary care and skill. The danger would arise thus:—Every witness would be kept out of court, except the one in the box. He would be asked where he sat at the supper? Where the prisoner sat, and each of the other guests? What were the dishes, what was the course of conversation, and so forth—the questions being capable of multiplication *ad infinitum*; so that however well tutored, the witnesses would inevitably contradict each other upon some matters, on which the tutor had not foreseen that the witness would be cross-examined, or to which he had forgotten the answer prescribed. The difficulty was, however, surmounted. After the prisoner's apprehension, the selected witnesses were invited to a mackerel supper, which took place at an hour corresponding to that at which the crime was committed; and so careful was the ingenious agent who devised this conspiracy against the truth that, guided by a sure instinct, he fixed upon the same day of the week as that on which the crime had been committed, though without knowing how fortunate it would be for the prisoner that he took this precaution. When, on cross-examination, it was found that the witnesses agreed as to the order in which the guests were seated, the contents of the dishes, the conversation which had taken place, and so forth—the counsel for the Crown suspected the plot; but not imagining that it had been so perfectly elaborated, they inquired of their attorneys as to whether there was any occurrence peculiar to the day of the week in question, and were told that, upon the evening of such day, a public bell was always rung, which must have been heard at the supper, if it had taken place at the time pretended. The witnesses were separately called back and questioned separately as to the bell. They had all heard it; and thus not only were the cross-examiners utterly baffled, but the cross-examination gave ten-fold support to the examination in chief, that is, to the evidence as given by the witnesses in answer to the questions put by the prisoner's counsel in his behalf. The triumph of falsehood was complete. The prisoner was acquitted.

When, however, the attention of prosecutors is called to the possibility of such fabrications they become less easy of management. The friends of a prisoner are often known to the police, and may be watched—the actors may be surprised at the rehearsal; a false ally may be inserted among them; in short, there are many chances of the plot failing. This, however, is an age of improvement, and the thirty years which have elapsed since the days of Luddism have not been a barren period in any art or science. The mystery of cookery in dishes, accounts, and *alibis*, has profited by this general advancement.

The latest device which my acquaintance with courts has brought to my knowledge is an *alibi* of a very refined and subtle nature. The hypothesis is, that the prisoner was walking from point A to point Z, along a distant road, at the hour when the crime was committed. The witnesses are supposed each to see him, and some to converse with him, at points which may be indicated by many or all the letters of the alphabet. Each witness must be alone when he sees him, so that no two may speak to what occurred at the same spot or moment of time; but, with this reservation, each may safely indulge his imagination with any account of the interview which he has wit to make consistent with itself, and firmness to abide by, under the storm of a cross-examination. "The force of *falsehood* can no farther go." No rehearsal is necessary. Neither of the witnesses needs know of the existence of the others. The agent gives to each witness the name of the spot at which he is to place the prisoner. The witness makes himself acquainted with that spot, so as to stand a cross-examination as to the surrounding objects, and his education is complete. But as panaceas have only a fabulous existence, so this exquisite *alibi* is not applicable to all cases; the witness must have a reason for being on the spot, plausible enough to foil the skill of the cross-examiner; and, as false witnesses cannot be found at every turn, the difficulty of making it accord with the probability that the witness was where he pretends to have been on the day and at the hour in question is often insuperable, to say nothing of the possibility and probability of its being clearly established, on the part of the prosecution, that the prisoner could not have been there. I should add, that, except in towns of the first magnitude, it must be difficult to find mendacious witnesses who have in other respects the proper qualifications to prove a concocted *alibi*, save always where the prisoner is the champion of a class; and then, according to my experience—sad as the avowal is—the difficulty is greatly reduced.

These incidents illustrate the soundness of the well-known proposition, that mixture of truth with falsehood, augments to the highest degree the noxious power of the venomous ingredient. That man was no mean proficient in the art of deceiving, who first discovered the importance of the liar being parsimonious in mendacity. The mind has a stomach as well as an eye, and if the bolus be neat falsehood, it will be rejected like an overdose of arsenic which does not kill.

Let the juryman ponder these things, and beware how he lets his mind lapse into a conclusion either for or against the prisoner. To perform the duties of his office, so that the days which he spends in the jury-box will bear retrospection, his eye, his ears, and his intellect, must be ever on the watch. A witness in the box, and the same man in common life, are different creatures. Coming to give evidence, "he doth suffer a law change." Sometimes he becomes more truthful, as he ought to do, if any change is necessary; but unhappily this is not always so, and least of all in the case of those whose testimony is often required.

I remember a person, whom I frequently heard to give evidence quite out of harmony with the facts; but I shall state neither his name nor his profession. A gentleman who knew perfectly well the unpalatable designation which his evidence deserved, told me of his death. I ventured to think it was a loss which might be borne, and touched upon his infirmity, to which my friend replied in perfect sincerity of heart, "Well! after all, I do not think he ever told a falsehood in his life—*out of the witness' box*!"

XVIII

BANK-NOTE FORGERIES

I

Viotti's division of violin-playing into two great classes—good playing and bad playing—is applicable to Bank-note making. We shall now cover a few pages with a faint outline of the various arts, stratagems, and contrivances employed in concocting bad Bank-notes. The picture cannot be drawn with very distinct or strong markings. The tableaux from which it is copied, are so intertwisted and complicated with clever, slippery, ingenious scoundrelism, that a finished chart of it would be worse than morally displeasing—it would be tedious.

All arts require time and experience for their development. When anything great is to be done, first attempts are nearly always failures. The first Bank-note forgery was no exception to this rule, and its story has a spice of romance in it. The affair has never been circumstantially told; but some research enables us to detail it:

In the month of August, 1757, a gentleman living in the neighborhood of Lincoln's Inn Fields, named Bliss, advertised for a clerk. There were, as was usual at that time, many applicants; but the successful one was a young man of twenty-six, named Richard William Vaughan. His manners were so winning and his demeanor so much that of a gentleman, (he belonged indeed to a good county family in Staffordshire, and had been a student at Pembroke Hall, Oxford,) that Mr. Bliss at once engaged him. Nor had he occasion, during the time the new clerk served him, to repent the step. Vaughan was so diligent, intelligent, and steady, that not even when it transpired that he was, commercially speaking, "under a cloud," did his master lessen confidence in him. Some inquiry into his antecedents showed that he had, while at College, been extravagant—that his friends had removed him thence—set him up in Stafford as a wholesale linen-draper, with a branch establishment in Aldersgate Street, London—that he had failed, and that there was some difficulty about his certificate. But so well did he excuse his early failings and account for his misfortunes, that his employer did not check the regard he felt growing towards him. Their intercourse was not merely that of master and servant. Vaughan was a frequent guest at Bliss's table; by-and-by a daily visitor to his wife, and—to his ward.

Miss Bliss was a young lady of some attractions, not the smallest of which was a hansome fortune. Young Vaughan made the most of his opportunities. He was well-looking, well-informed, dressed well, and evidently made love well, for he won the young lady's heart. The guardian was not flinty-hearted, and acted like a sensible man of the world. "It was not," he said, on a subsequent and painful occasion, "till I learned from the servants and observed by the girl's behavior, that she greatly approved Richard Vaughan, that I consented; but on condition that he should make it appear that he could maintain her. I had no doubt of his character as a servant, and I knew his family were respectable. His brother is an eminent attorney." Vaughan boasted that his mother (his father was dead) was willing to re-instate him in business with a thousand pounds—five hundred of which was to be settled upon Miss Bliss for her separate use.

So far all went on prosperously. Providing Richard Vaughan could attain a position satisfactory to the Blisses, the marriage was to take place on the Easter Monday following, which, the Calendar tells us, happened early in April, 1758. With this understanding, he left Mr. Bliss's service, to push his fortune.

Months passed on, and Vaughan appears to have made no way in the world. He had not even obtained his bankrupt's certificate. His visits to his affianced were frequent, and his protestations passionate; but he had effected nothing substantial towards a happy union. Miss Bliss's guardian grew impatient; and, although there is no evidence to prove that the young lady's affection for Vaughan was otherwise than deep and sincere, yet even she began to lose confidence in him. His excuses were evidently evasive, and not always true. The time fixed for the wedding was fast approaching, and Vaughan saw that something must be done to restore the young lady's confidence.

About three weeks before the appointed Easter Tuesday, Vaughan went to his mistress in high spirits. All was right—his certificate was to be granted in a day or two—his family had come forward with the money, and he was to continue the Aldersgate business he had previously carried on as a branch of the Stafford trade. The capital he had waited so long for, was at length forthcoming. In fact, here were two hundred and forty pounds of the five hundred he was to settle on his beloved. Vaughan then produced twelve twenty-pound notes; Miss Bliss could scarcely believe her eyes. She examined them. The paper, she remarked, seemed thicker than usual. "Oh," said Bliss, "all Bank bills are not alike." The girl was naturally much pleased. She would hasten to apprise Mistress Bliss of the good news.

Not for the world! So far from letting any living soul know he had placed so much money in her hands, Vaughan exacted an oath of secresy from her, and sealed the notes up in a parcel with his own seal—making her swear that she would on no account open it till after their marriage.

Some days after, that is, "on the twenty-second of March," (1758) we are describing the scene in Mr. Bliss's own words—"I was sitting with my wife by the fireside. The prisoner and the girl were sitting in the same room—which was a small one—and although they whispered, I could distinguish that Vaughan was very urgent to have something returned which he had previously given to her. She refused, and Vaughan went away in an angry mood. I then studied the girl's face, and saw that it expressed much dissatisfaction. Presently a tear broke out. I then spoke, and insisted on knowing the dispute. She refused to tell, and I told her that until she did, I would not see her. The next day I asked the same question of Vaughan—he hesitated. 'Oh,' I said, 'I dare say it is some ten or twelve pound matter—something to buy a wedding bauble with.' He answered that it was much more than that—it was near three hundred pounds! 'But why all this secrecy?' I said; and he answered that it was not proper for people to know that he had so much money till his certificate was signed. I then asked him to what intent he had left the notes with the young lady? He said, as I had of late suspected him, he designed to give her a proof of his affection and truth. I said, 'You have demanded them in such a way that it must be construed as an abatement of your affection towards her.' " Vaughan was again exceedingly urgent in asking back the packet; but Bliss remembering his many evasions, and supposing that this was a trick, declined advising his niece to restore the parcel without proper consideration. The very next day it was discovered that the notes were counterfeits.

This occasioned stricter inquiries into Vaughan's previous career. It turned out that he bore the character in his native place of a dissipated and not very scrupulous person. The intention of his mother to assist him was an entire fabrication, and he had given Miss Bliss the forged notes solely for the purpose of deceiving her on that matter. Meanwhile the forgeries became known to the authorities, and he was arrested. By what means, does not clearly appear. The "Annual Register" says, that one of the engravers gave information; but we find nothing in the newspapers of the time to support that statement; neither was it corroborated at Vaughan's trial.

When Vaughan was arrested, he thrust a piece of paper into his mouth, and began to chew it violently. It was, however, rescued, and proved to be one of the forged notes; fourteen of them were found on his person, and when his lodgings were searched twenty more were discovered.

Vaughan was tried at the Old Bailey on the seventh of April, before Lord Mansfield. The manner of the forgery was detailed minutely at the trial:—On the first of March, (about a week before he gave the twelve notes to the young lady,) Vaughan called on Mr. John Corbould, an engraver, and gave an order for a promissory note to be engraved with these words:

"No.—.

"I promise to pay to—, or Bearer,—London—."

There was to be a Britannia in the corner. When it was done, Mr. Sneed (for that was the *alias* Vaughan adopted) came again, but objected to the execution of the work. The Britannia was not good, and the words "I promise" were too near the edge of the plate. Another was in consequence engraved, and on the fourth of March, Vaughan took it away. He immediately repaired to a printer, and had forty-eight impressions taken on thin paper, provided by himself. Meanwhile, he had ordered, on the same morning, of Mr. Charles Fourdrinier, another engraver, a second plate, with what he called "a direction," in the words, "For the Governor and Company of the Bank of England." This was done, and about a week later he brought some paper, each sheet "folded up," said the witness, "very curiously, so that I could not see what was in them. I was going to take the papers from him, but he said he must go upstairs with me, and see them worked off himself. I took him upstairs; he would not let me have them out of his hands. I took a sponge and wetted them, and put them one by one on the plate in order for printing them. After my boy had done two or three of them, I went downstairs, and my boy worked the rest off, and the prisoner came down and paid me."

Here the Court pertinently asked, "What imagination had you when a man thus came to you to print on secret paper, 'the Governor and Company of the Bank of England?' "

The engraver's reply was:—"I then did not suspect anything; but I shall take care for the future." As this was the first Bank-of-England-note forgery that was ever perpetrated, the engraver was held excused.

It may be mentioned, as an evidence of the delicacy of the reporters, that in their account of the trial, Miss Bliss's name is not mentioned. Her designation is "a young lady." We subjoin the notes of her evidence:

"A young lady (sworn). The prisoner delivered me some bills; these are the same (producing twelve counterfeit Bank notes sealed up in a cover, for twenty pounds each;) said they were Bank bills. I said they were thicker paper—he said all bills are not alike. I was to keep them till after we were married. He put them into my hands to show he put confidence in me, and desired me not to show them to anybody; sealed them up with his own seal, and obliged me by an oath not to discover them to anybody, and I did not till he discovered them himself; he was to settle so much in Stock on me."

Vaughan urged in his defence that his sole object was to deceive his affianced, and that he intended to destroy all the notes after his marriage. But it had been proved that the prisoner had asked one John Ballingar to change first one, and then twenty of the notes; but which that person was unable to do. Besides, had his sole object been to dazzle Miss Bliss with his fictitious wealth, he would most probably have intrusted more, if not all the notes, to her keeping.

He was found guilty, and passed the day that had been fixed for his wedding, as a condemned criminal.

On the 11th May, 1758, Richard William Vaughan was executed at Tyburn. By his side, on the same gallows, there was another forger—William Boodgere, a military officer, who had forged a draught on an army-agent named Calcroft, and expiated the offence with the first forger of Bank-of-England notes.

The gallows may seem hard measure to have meted out to Vaughan, when it is considered that none of his notes were negotiated and no person suffered by his fraud. Not one of the forty-eight notes, except the twelve delivered to Miss Bliss, had been out of his possession; indeed the imitation must have been very clumsily executed, and detection would have instantly followed any attempt to pass the counterfeits. There was no endeavor to copy the style of engraving on a real Bank-note. That was left to the engraver; and as each sheet passed through the press twice, the words added at the second printing, "For the Governor and Company of the Bank of England," could have fallen into their proper place on any one of the sheets, only by a miracle. But what would have made the forgery clear to even a superficial observer, was the singular omission of the second "n" in the word England.

The criticism on Vaughan's note of a Bank clerk examined on the trial was—"There is some resemblance to be sure; but this note" (that upon which the prisoner was tried) "is numbered thirteen thousand eight hundred and forty, and we never reach so high a number." Besides, there was no water-mark in the paper. The note, of which a facsimile appeared in our eighteenth number, and dated so early as 1699, has a regular design in the texture of the paper, showing that the water-mark is as old as the Bank-notes themselves.

Vaughan was greatly commiserated. But despite the unskillfulness of the forgery, and the insignificant consequences which followed it, the crime was considered of too dangerous a character not to be marked, from its very novelty, with exemplary punishment. Hanging created at that time no remorse in the public mind, and it was thought necessary to set up Vaughan as a warning to all future Bank-note forgers. The crime was too dangerous not to be marked with the severest penalties. Forgery differs from other crimes not less in the magnitude of the spoil it may obtain and of the injury it inflicts, than in the facilities attending its accomplishment. The common thief finds a limit to his depredations in the bulkiness of his booty, which is generally confined to such property as he can carry about his person; the swindler raises insuperable and defeating obstacles to his frauds if the amount he seeks to obtain is so considerable as to awaken close vigilance or inquiry. To carry their projects to any very profitable extent, these criminals are reduced to the hazardous necessity of acting in concert, and thus infinitely increasing the risks of detection. But the forger need have no accomplice—he is burdened with no bulky and suspicious property—he needs no receiver to assist his contrivances. The skill of his own individual right-hand can command thousands—often with the certainty of not being detected, and oftener with such rapidity as to enable him to baffle the pursuit of justice.

It was a long time before Vaughan's rude attempt was improved upon; but in the same year, (1758,) another department of the crime was commenced with perfect success, namely, an ingenious alteration, for fraudulent purposes, of real Bank-notes. A few months after Vaughan's execution, one of the northern mails was stopped and robbed by a highwayman; several Bank-notes were comprised in the spoil, and the robber, setting up with these as a gentleman, went boldly to the Hatfield Post-office, ordered a chaise-and-four, rattled away down the road, and changed a note at every change of horses. The robbery was of course soon made known, and the numbers and dates of the stolen notes were advertised as having been stopped at the Bank. To the genius of a highwayman this offered but a small obstacle, and the gentleman-thief changed all the figures "1" he could find, into "4's." These notes passed currently enough; but on reaching the Bank, the alteration was detected, and the last holder was refused payment. As that person had given a valuable consideration for the note, he brought an action for the recovery of the amount; and at the trial it was ruled by the Lord Chief Justice, that "any person paying a valuable consideration for a Bank-note, payable to bearer, in a fair course of business, has an understood-right to receive the money of the Bank."

It took a quarter of a century to bring the art of forging Bank notes to perfection. In 1779, this was nearly attained by an ingenious gentleman named Mathison, a watch-maker, from the matrimonial village of Gretna Green. Having learnt the arts of engraving and of simulating signatures, he tried his hand at the notes of the Darlington Bank; but, with the confidence of skill, was not cautious in passing them, was suspected and absconded to Edinburgh. Scorning to let his talent be wasted, he favored the Scottish public with many spurious Royal Bank-of-Scotland notes, and regularly forged his way by their aid to London. At the end of February he took handsome lodgings in the Strand, opposite Arundel Street. His industry was remarkable; for, by the 12th of March, he had planned and polished rough pieces of copper, engraved them, forged the water-mark, printed, and negotiated several impressions. His plan was to travel and to purchase articles in shops. He bought a pair of shoe-buckles at Coventry with a forged note, which was eventually detected at the Bank of England. He had got so bold that he paid such frequent visits in Threadneedle Street that the Bank clerks became familiar with his person. He was continually changing notes of one for another denomination. These were his originals, which he procured to make spurious copies of. One day seven thousand pounds came in from the Stamp Office. There was a dispute about one of the notes. Mathison, who was present, though at some distance, declared, oracularly, that the note was a good one. How could he know so well? A dawn of suspicion arose in the minds of the clerks; one trail led into another, and Mathison was finally apprehended. So well were his notes forged, that, on the trial, an experienced Bank clerk declared he could not tell whether the note handed him to examine, was forged or not. Mathison offered to reveal his secret of forging the water-mark, if mercy were shown to him; this was refused, and he suffered the penalty of his crime.

Mathison was a genius in his criminal way, but a greater than he appeared in 1786. In that year perfection seemed to have been reached. So considerable was the circulation of spurious paper-money that it appeared as if some unknown power had set up a bank of its own. Notes were issued from it, and readily passed current, in hundreds and thousands. They were not to be distinguished from the genuine paper of Threadneedle Street. Indeed, when one was presented there, in due course, so complete were all its parts, so masterly the engraving, so correct the signatures, so skillful the water-mark, that it was promptly paid, and only discovered to be a forgery when it reached a particular department. From that period forged paper continued to be presented, especially at the time of lottery-drawing. Consultations were held with the police. Plans were laid to help detection. Every effort was made to trace the forger. Clarke, the best detective of his day, went like a sluth-hound, on the track; for in those days the expressive word "blood-money" was known. Up to a certain point there was little difficulty; but beyond that, consummate art defied the ingenuity of the officer. In whatever way the notes came, the train of discovery always paused at the lottery-offices.

Advertisements offering large rewards were circulated; but the unknown forger baffled detection.

While this base paper was in full currency, there appeared an advertisement in the Daily Advertiser for a servant. The successful applicant was a young man, in the employment of a musical-instrument maker, who, sometime after, was called upon by a coachman, and informed that the advertiser was waiting in a coach to see him. The young man was desired to enter the conveyance, where he beheld a person with something of the appearance of a foreigner, sixty or seventy years old, apparently troubled with the gout. A camlet surtout was buttoned round his mouth, a large patch was placed over his left eye, and nearly every part of his face was concealed. He affected much infirmity. He had a faint hectic cough; and invariably presented the patched side to the view of the servant. After some conversation—in the course of which he represented himself as guardian to a young nobleman of great fortune—the interview concluded with the engagement of the applicant, and the new servant was directed to call on Mr Brank, at 29 Titchfield Street, Oxford Street. At this interview Brank inveighed against his whimsical ward for his love of speculating in lottery tickets, and told the servant that his principal duty would be to purchase them. After one or two meetings, at each of which Brank kept his face muffled, he handed a forty and twenty pound Bank-note; told the servant to be very careful not to lose them, and directed him to buy lottery-tickets at separate offices. The young man fulfilled his instructions, and at the moment he was returning, was suddenly called by his employer from the other side of the street, congratulated on his rapidity, and then told to go to various other offices in the neighborhood of the Royal Exchange, and to purchase more shares. Four hundred pounds in Bank-of-England notes were handed him, and the wishes of the mysterious Mr. Brank were satisfactorily effected. These scenes were continually enacted.

Notes to a large amount were thus circulated, lottery tickets purchased, and Mr. Brank—always in a coach, with his face studiously concealed—was ever ready on the spot to receive them. The surprise of the servant was somewhat excited; but had he known that from the period he left his master to purchase the tickets, one female figure accompanied all his movements, that, when he entered the offices, it waited at the door, peered cautiously in at the window, hovered round him like a second shadow, watched him carefully, and never left him until once more he was in the company of his employer—that surprise would have been greatly increased. Again and again were these extraordinary scenes rehearsed. At last the Bank obtained a clue, and the servant was taken into custody. The directors imagined that they had secured the actor of so many parts, that the flood of forged notes which had inundated that establishment would at length be dammed up at his source. Their hopes proved fallacious, and it was found that "Old Patch" (as the mysterious forger was, from the servant's description, nicknamed) had been sufficiently clever to baffle the Bank directors. The house in Titchfield street was searched; but Mr. Brank had deserted it, and not a trace of a single implement of forgery was to be seen.

All that could be obtained was some little knowledge of "Old Patch's" proceedings. It appeared that he carried on his paper-coining entirely by himself. His only confidant was his mistress. He was his own engraver. He even made his own ink. He manufactured his own paper. With a private press he worked his own notes, and counterfeited the signatures of the cashiers, completely. But these discoveries had no effect, for it became evident that Mr. Patch had set up a press elsewhere. Although his secret continued as impenetrable, his notes became as plentiful as ever. Five years of unbounded prosperity ought to have satisfied him—but it did not. Success seemed to pall him. His genius was of that insatiable order which demands new excitements, and a constant succession of new flights. The following paragraph from a newspaper of 1786, relates to the same individual:—

"On the 17th of December, ten pounds was paid into the Bank, for which the clerk, as usual, gave a ticket to receive a Bank-note of equal value. This ticket ought to have been carried immediately to the cashier, instead of which the bearer took it home, and curiously added an 0 to the original sum, and returning, presented it so altered to the cashier, for which he received a note of one hundred pounds. In the evening, the clerks found a deficiency in the accounts, and on examining the tickets of the day, not only that but two others were discovered to have been obtained in the same manner. In one, the figure 1 was altered to 4, and in another to 5, by which the artist received, upon the whole, nearly one thousand pounds."

To that princely felony, Old Patch, as will be seen in the sequel, added smaller misdemeanors which one would think were far beneath his notice, except to convince himself and his mistress of the unbounded facility of his genius for fraud.

At that period the affluent public were saddled with a tax on plate, and many experiments were made to evade it. Among others one was invented by a Mr. Charles Price, a stock-jobber and lottery-office keeper, which, for a time, puzzled the tax-gatherer. Mr. Charles Price lived in great style, gave splendid dinners, and did everything on the grandest scale. Yet Mr. Charles Price had no plate! The authorities could not find so much as a silver tooth-pick on his magnificent premises. In truth, what he was too cunning to possess, he borrowed. For one of his sumptuous entertainments, he hired the plate of a silversmith in Cornhill, and left the value in Bank-notes as security for its safe return. One of these notes having proved a forgery, was traced to Mr. Charles Price; and Mr. Charles Price was not to be found at that particular juncture Although this excited no surprise—for he was often an absentee from his office for short periods—yet, in due course and as a formal matter of business, an officer was sent to find him, and to ask his explanation regarding the false notes. After tracing a man whom he had a strong notion was Mr. Charles Price, through countless lodgings and innumerable disguises, the officer (to use his own expression) "nabbed" Mr. Charles Price. But, as Mr. Clark observed, his prisoner and his prisoner's lady were even then "too many" for him; for although he lost not a moment in trying to secure the forging implements, after he had discovered that Mr. Charles Price, and Mr. Brank, and Old Patch, were all concentrated in the person of his prisoner, he found the lady had destroyed every trace of evidence. Not a vestige of the forging factory was left; not the point of a graver, nor a single spot of ink, nor a shred of silver paper, nor a scrap of anybody's handwriting, was to be met with. Despite, however, this paucity of evidence to convict him, Mr. Charles Price had not the courage to face a jury, and eventually he saved the judicature and the Tyburn executive much trouble and expense, by hanging himself in Bridewell.

The success of Mr. Charles Price has never been surpassed, and even after the darkest era in the history of Bank forgeries—which dates from the suspension of cash payments, in February, 1797, and which will be treated of in the succeeding chapter—"Old Patch" was still remembered as the Cæsar of Forgers.

II

In the history of crime, as in all other histories, there is one great epoch by which minor dates are arranged and defined. In a list of remarkable events, one remarkable event more remarkable than the last, is the standard around which all smaller circumstances are grouped. Whatever happens in Mohammedan annals, is set down as having occurred so many years after the flight of the Prophet; in the records of London commerce a great fraud or a great failure is mentioned as having come to light so many months after the flight of Rowland Stephenson. Sporting men date from remarkable struggles for the Derby prize, and refer to 1840, as "Bloomsbury's year." The highwayman of old dated from Dick Turpin's last appearance on the fatal stage at Tyburn turnpike. In like manner, the standard epoch in the annals of Bank-Note Forgery, is the year 1797, when (on the 25th of February) one-pound notes were put into circulation instead of golden guineas; or, to use the City idiom, 'cash payments were suspended.'

At that time the Bank-of-England note was no better in appearance—had not improved as a work of art—since the days of Vaughan, Mathison, and Old Patch; it was just as easily imitated, and the chances of the successful circulation of counterfeits were increased a thousand-fold.

Up to 1793 no notes had been issued even for sums so small as five pounds. Consequently all the Bank paper then in use, passed through the hands and under the eyes of the affluent and educated, who could more readily distinguish the false from the true. Hence, during the fourteen years which preceded the non-golden and small-note era, there were only three capital convictions for the crime. When, however, the Bank-of-England notes became "common and popular," a prodigious quantity—to complete the quotation—was also made "base," and many persons were hanged for concocting them.

To a vast number of the humbler orders, Bank-notes were a rarity and a "sight." Many had never seen such a thing before they were called upon to take one or two-pound notes in exchange for small merchandise, or their own labor. How were they to judge? How were they to tell a good from a spurious note?—especially when it happened that the officers of the Bank themselves, were occasionally mistaken, so complete and perfect were the imitations then afloat. There cannot be much doubt that where one graphic rascal was found out, ten escaped. They snapped their fingers at the executioner, and went on enjoying their beef-steaks and porter—their winter treats to the play—their summer excursions to the suburban tea-gardens—their fashionable lounges at Tunbridge Wells, Bath, Margate, and Ramsgate—doing business with wonderful unconcern, and "face" all along their journeys. These usually expensive, but to them profitable enjoyments, were continually coming to light at the trials of the lesser rogues who undertook the issue department; for, from the ease with which close imitation was effected, the manufacture was more readily completed than the uttering. The fraternity and sisterhood of utterers played many parts, and were banded in strict compact with the forgers. Some were turned loose into fairs and markets, in all sorts of appropriate disguises. Farmers, who could hardly distinguish a field of standing wheat from a field of barley—butchers, who never wielded more deadly weapons than two-prong forks—country boys, with cockney accents, bought gingerbread, and treated their so-called sweethearts with ribbons and muslins, all by the interchange of false "flimseys." The better-mannered disguised themselves as ladies and gentlemen, paid their losings at cards or hazard, or their tavern bills, their milliners, and coachmakers, in motley money, composed of part real and part base bank paper. Some went about in the cloak of the Samaritan, and generously subscribed to charities wherever they saw a chance of changing a bad "five" for three or four good "ones." Ladies of sweet disposition went about doing good among the poor—personally inquired into distress, relieved it by sending out a daughter or a son to a neighboring shop for change, and left five shillings for present necessities, walking off with fifteen. So openly—in spite of the gallows—was forgery carried on, that whoever chose to turn utterer found no difficulty in getting a stock-in-trade to commence with. Indeed, in the days of highwaymen, no traveling-gentleman's pocket or valise was considered properly furnished without a few forged notes wherewith to satisfy the demands of the members of the "High Toby." This offence against the laws of the road, however, soon became too common, and wayfarers who were stopped and rifled, had to pledge their sacred words of honor that their notes were the genuine promises of Abraham Newland, and that their watches were not of the factory of Mr. Pinchbeck.

With temptations so strong, it is no wonder that the forgers' trade flourished, with only an occasional check from the strong arm of the law. It followed, therefore, that from the issue of small notes in February, 1797, to the end of 1817—twenty years—there were no fewer than eight hundred and seventy prosecutions connected with Bank-Note Forgery, in which there were only one hundred and sixty acquittals, and upwards of three hundred executions! 1818 was the culminating point of the crime. In the first three months there were no fewer than one hundred and twenty-eight prosecutions by the Bank; and by the end of that year, two-and-thirty individuals had been hanged for Note Forgery. So far from this appalling series of examples having any effect in checking the progress of the crime, it is proved that at, and after that very time, base notes were poured into the Bank at the rate of *a hundred a day*!

The enormous number of undetected forgeries afloat, may be estimated by the fact, that from the 1st of January, 1812, to the 10th April, 1818, one hundred and thirty-one thousand three hundred and thirty-one pieces of paper were ornamented by the Bank officers with the word "Forged"—upwards of one hundred and seven thousand of them were one-pound counterfeits.

Intrinsically, it would appear from an Hibernian view of the case, then, that bad notes were nearly as good, (except not merely having been manufactured at the Bank,) as good ones. So thoroughly and completely did some of them resemble the authorized engraving of the Bank, that it was next to impossible to distinguish the false from the true. Countless instances, showing rather the skill of the forger than the want of vigilance in Bank officials, could be brought forward. Respectable persons were constantly taken into custody on a charge of uttering forgeries, imprisoned for days and then liberated. A close scrutiny proving that the accusations were made upon genuine paper. In September, 1818 Mr. A. Burnett, of Portsmouth, had the satisfaction of having a note which had passed through his hands, returned to him from the Bank of England, with the base mark upon it. Satisfied of its genuineness, he re-inclosed it to the cashier, and demanded its payment. By return of post he received the following letter:—

"*Bank of England, 16 Sept., 1818.*

"Sir,—I have to acknowledge your letter to Mr. Hase, of the 13th inst., inclosing a one-pound note, and, in answer thereto, I beg leave to acquaint you, that on inspection it appears to be a genuine Note of the Bank of England; I therefore, agreeably to your request, inclose you one of the like value, No. 26, 276, dated 22nd August, 1818.

"I am exceedingly sorry, sir, that such an unusual oversight should have occurred to give you so much trouble, which I trust your candor will induce you to excuse when I assure you that the unfortunate mistake has arisen entirely out of the hurry and multiplicity of business.

"I am, sir,

"Your most obedient servant,

"J. RIPPON.

"A. Burnett, Esq. "7 Belle Vue Terrace. "Southsea, near Portsmouth."

A more extraordinary case is on record:—A note was traced to the possession of a tradesman, which had been pronounced by the Bank Inspectors to have been forged. The man would not give it up, and was taken before a magistrate, charged with "having a note in his possession, well knowing it to be forged." He was committed to prison on evidence of the Bank Inspector, but was afterwards released on bail to appear when called on. He was *not* called on; and, at the expiration of twelve months, (having kept the note all that time,) he brought an action against the Bank for false imprisonment. On the trial the note was proved to be genuine! And the plaintiff was awarded damages of one hundred pounds.

It is a fact sufficiently dreadful that three hundred and thirty human lives should have been sacrificed in twenty-one years; but when we relate a circumstance which admits the merest probability that some—even one—of those lives may have been sacrificed in innocence of the offence for which they suffered, the consideration becomes appalling.

Sometime after the frequency of the crime had in other respects subsided, there was a sort of bloody assize at Haverfordwest, in Wales; several prisoners were tried for forging and uttering, and thirteen were convicted—chiefly on the evidence of Mr. Christmas, a Bank Inspector, who swore positively, in one case, that the document named in the indictment, "was not an impression from a Bank-of-England plate—was not printed on the paper with the ink or water-mark of the Bank—neither was it in the handwriting of the signing clerk." Upon this testimony the prisoner, together with twelve participators in similar crimes, were condemned to be hanged!

The morning after the trial, Mr. Christmas was leaving his lodging, when an acquaintance stepped up and asked him, as a friend, to give his opinion on a note he had that morning received. It was a bright day; Mr. Christmas put on his spectacles, and carefully scrutinized the document in a business-like and leisurely manner. He pronounced it to be forged. The gentleman, a little chagrined, brought it away with him to town. It is not a little singular that he happened to know Mr. Burnett, of Portsmouth, whom he accidentally met, and to whom he showed the note. Mr. Burnett was evidently a capital judge of bank paper. He said nothing, but slipping his hand into one pocket, handed to the astonished gentleman full change, and put the note into another. "It cannot be a good note," exclaimed the latter, "for my friend Christmas told me at Haverfordwest that it is a forgery!" But as Mr. Burnett had backed his opinion to the amount of twenty shillings, he declined to retract it; and lost no time in writing to Mr. Henry Hase (Abraham Newland's successor) to test its accuracy.

It was lucky that he did so; for this little circumstance saved thirteen lives!

Mr. Christmas's co-inspectors at the Bank of England actually reversed his non-official judgment that the note was a forgery. It was officially pronounced to be a good note; yet upon the evidence of Mr. Christmas as regards other notes, the thirteen human beings at Haverford west were trembling at the foot of the gallows. It was promptly and cogently argued that as Mr. Christmas's judgment had failed him in the deliberate examination of one note, it might also err as to others, and the convicts were respited.

The converse of this sort of mistake often happened. Bad notes were pronounced to be genuine by the Bank. Early in January, 1818, a well-dressed woman entered the shop of Mr. James Hammond, of 40 Bishopsgate Street Without, and having purchased three pounds worth of goods, tendered in payment a ten-pound note. There was something hesitating and odd in her manner; and, although Mr. Hammond could see nothing the matter with the note, yet he was ungallant enough to suspect—from the uncomfortable demeanor of his customer—that all was not right. He hoped she was not in a hurry, for he had no change; he must send to a neighbor for it. He immediately dispatched his shopman to the most affluent of all his neighbors—to her of Threadneedle Street. The delay occasioned the lady to remark, "I suppose he is gone to the Bank!" Mr. Hammond having answered in the affirmative, engaged his customer in conversation, and they freely discussed the current topics of the day; till the young man returned with ten one pound Bank-of-England Notes. Mr. Hammond felt a little remorse at having suspected his patroness, who departed with the purchases with the utmost dispatch. She had not been gone half an hour before two gentlemen rushed into the shop in a state of grievous chagrin; one was the Bank clerk who had changed the note. He begged Mr. Hammond would be good enough to give him another for it. "Why?" asked the puzzled shopkeeper. "Why, sir," replied the distressed clerk, "it is forged!" Of course his request was not complied with The clerk declared that his dismissal was highly probable; but Mr. Hammond was inexorable.

The arguments in favor of death-punishments never fail so signally as when brought to the test of the scaffold and its effect on Bank forgeries. When these were most numerous, although from twenty to thirty persons were put to death in one year, the gallows was never deprived of an equal share of prey during the next. As long as simulated notes could be passed with ease, and detected with difficulty, the Old Bailey had no terrors for clever engravers and dexterous imitators of the hieroglyphic autographs of the Bank-of-England signers.

At length public alarm at the prevalence of forgeries, and the difficulty of knowing them as such, arose to the height of demanding some sort of relief. In 1819 a committee was appointed by the Government to inquire into the best means of prevention. One hundred and eighty projects were submitted. They mostly consisted of intricate designs such as rendered great expense necessary to imitate. But none were adopted for the obvious reason that ever so indifferent and easily executed imitation of an elaborate note is quite sufficient to deceive an uneducated eye, as had been abundantly proved in the instance of the Irish "black note." The Bank had not been indifferent or idle on the subject, for it had spent some hundred thousand pounds in projects for inimitable notes. At last—not long before the Commission was appointed—they were on the eve of adopting an ingenious and costly mechanism for printing a note so precisely alike on both sides as to appear as one impression, when one of the Bank printers imitated it exactly by the simple contrivance of two plates and a hinge. This may serve as a sample of the other one hundred and seventy-nine projects.

Neither the gallows nor expensive and elaborate works of art having been found effectual in preventing forgery, the true expedient for at least lessening the crime was adopted in 1821:—the issue of small notes was wholly discontinued, and sovereigns were brought into circulation. The forger's trade was nearly annihilated. Criminal returns inform us that during the nine years after the resumption of gold currency the number of convictions for offences having reference to the Bank-of-England notes were less than one hundred, and the executions only eight. This clinches the argument against the efficacy of the gallows. In 1830 death-punishments were repealed for all minor offences, and, although the cases of Bank-Note Forgeries slightly increased for a time, yet there is no reason to suppose that they are greater now than they were between 1821 and 1830.

At present, Bank-paper forgeries are not numerous. One of the latest was that of the twenty-pound note, of which about sixty specimens found their way into the Bank. It was well executed in Belgium by foreigners, and the impressions were passed among the Change-agents in various towns in France and the Netherlands. The speculation did not succeed; for the notes got into, and were detected at the Bank, a little too soon to profit the schemers much.

The most considerable frauds now perpetrated are not forgeries; but are done upon the plan of the highwayman mentioned in our first chapter. In order to give currency to stolen or lost notes which have been stopped at the Bank, (lists of which are supplied to every banker in the country,) the numbers and dates are fraudulently altered. Some years since, a gentleman, who had been receiving a large sum of money at the Bank, was robbed of it in an omnibus. The notes gradually came in, but all were altered. The last was one for five hundred pounds, dated the 12th March, 1846, and numbered 32109. On the Monday (3rd June) after the last "Derby Day," amid the *twenty-five thousand pieces* of paper that were examined by the Bank Inspectors, there was one note for five hundred pounds, dated 12th March, 1848, and numbered 32409. At that note an inspector suddenly arrested his rapid examination of the pile of which it was one. He scrutinized it for a minute, and pronounced it "altered." On the next day, that same note, with a perfect one for five hundred pounds, is shown to us with an intimation of the fact. We look at every letter—we trace every line—follow every flourish; we hold both up to the light—we undulate our visuals with the waves of the water-mark. We confess that we cannot pronounce decisively, but we have an opinion derived from a slight "goutiness" in the fine stroke of the figure 4 that No. 32409 is the forgery! So indeed it was. Yet the Bank Inspector had picked it out from the hundred genuine notes as instantaneously—pounced upon it as rapidly as if it had been printed with green ink upon cardboard.

This, then, O gentlemen forgers and sporting-note alterers, is the kind of odds which is against you. A minute investigation of the note assured us of your exceeding skill and ingenuity; but it also convinced us of the superiority of the detective ordeal which you have to blind and to pass. In this instance you had followed the highwayman's plan, and had put with great cunning, the additional marks to the 1 in 32109 to make it into a 4. To hide the scraping out of the top or serif of the figure 1—to make the angle from which to draw the fine line of the 4—you had artfully inserted with a pen the figures "£16 16," as if that sum had been received from a person bearing a name that you had written above. You had with extraordinary neatness cut out the "6" from 1846, and filled up the hole with an 8, abstracted from some note of lesser value. You had fitted it with remarkable precision—only you had not got the 8 quite upright enough to pass the shrewd glance of the Bank Inspector.

We have seen a one-pound note made up of refuse pieces of a hundred other Bank-notes, and pasted on a piece of paper, (like a note that had been accidentally torn,) so as to present an entire and *passable* whole.

To alter with a pen a 1 into a 4 is an easy task—to cut out the numeral from the *date* in one note and insert it into another needs only a tyro in paper-cutting; but to change the special *number* by which each note is distinguished, is a feat only second in impossibility to trumping every court-card of every suit six times running in a rubber of whist. Yet we have seen a note so cleverly altered by this expedient, that it was actually paid by the Bank cashiers. If the reader will take a Bank-note out of his purse, and examine its "number," he will at once appreciate the combination of chances required to find, on any other note, any other figure that shall displace any one of the numerals so as to avoid detections. The "number" of every Bank-note is printed twice on one line—first, on the words "I promise," secondly, on the words, "or bearer." Sometimes the figures cover the whole of those words—sometimes they only partly obscure them. No. 99066 now lies before us. Suppose we wished to substitute the "0" of another note for the first "9" of the one now under our eye; we see that the "9" covers a little bit of the "P," and intersects in three places the "r," in "Promise." Now, to give this alteration the smallest chance, we must look through hundreds of other notes till we find an "0" which not only covers a part of the "P" and intersects the "r" in three places, but in precisely *the same* places as the "9" on our note does; else the strokes of those letters would not meet when the "0" was let in, and instant detection would ensue. But even then the job would only be half done. The second initial "9" stands upon the "or" in "or bearer," and we should have to investigate several hundred more notes, to find an "0" that intersected that little word exactly in the same manner, and then let it in with such mathematical nicety, that not the hundredth part of a hair's breath of the transferred paper should fail to range with the rest of the letters and figures on the altered note; to say nothing of hiding the joins in the paper. This is the triumph of ambidexterity; it is a species of patchwork far beyond the most sublime achievements of "Old Patch" himself."

Time has proved that the steady perseverance of the Bank—despite the most furious clamor—in gradually improving their original note and thus preserving those most essential qualities, simplicity and uniformity—has been a better preventive to forgery than any one of the hundreds of plans, pictures, complications, chemicals, and colors, which have been forced upon the Directors' notice. Whole-note forgery is nearly extinct. The lives of Eminent Forgers need only wait for a single addendum; for only one man is left who can claim superiority over Mathison, and he was, unfortunately for the Bank of England, born a little too late, to trip up his heels, or those of the late Mr. Charles Price. He can do everything with a note that the patchers, and alterers, and simulators can do, and a great deal more. Flimsy as a Bank-note is to a proverb, he can split it into three perfect continuous, flat, and even leaves. He has forged more than one design sent into the Bank as an infallible preventive to forgery. You may, if you like, lend him a hundred-pound note; he will undertake to discharge every trace of ink from it, and return it to you perfectly uninjured and a perfect blank. We are not quite sure that if you were to burn a Bank-note and hand him the black cinders, that he would not bleach it, and join it, and conjure it back again into a very good-looking, payable piece of currency. But we *are* sure of the truth of the following story, which we have from our friend the transcendent forger referred to, and who is no other than the chief of the Engraving and Engineering department of the Bank of England:

Some years ago—in the days of the thirty-shilling notes—a certain Irishman saved up the sum of eighty-seven pounds ten, in notes of the Bank of Ireland. As a sure means of securing this valuable property, he put it in the foot of an old stocking, and buried it in his garden, where Bank-note paper couldn't fail to keep dry, and to come out, when wanted, in the best preservation.

After leaving his treasure in this excellent place of deposit for some months, it occurred to the depositor to take a look at it, and see how it was getting on. He found the stocking-foot apparently full of the fragments of mildewed and broken mushrooms. No other shadow of a shade of eighty-seven pounds ten.

In the midst of his despair, the man had the sense not to disturb the ashes of his property. He took the stocking-foot in his hand, posted off to the Bank in Dublin, entered it one morning as soon as it was opened, and, staring at the clerk with a most extraordinary absence of all expression in his face, said,

"Ah, look at that, sir! Can ye do anything for me?"

"What do you call this?" said the clerk.

"Eighty-siven pound ten, praise the Lord, as I'm a sinner! Ohone! There was a twenty as was paid to me by Mr. Phalim O'Dowd, sir, and a ten as was changed by Pat Rielly, and a five as was owen by Tim; and, Ted Connor, ses he to ould Phillips—"

"Well!—never mind old Phillips. You have done it, my friend!"

"Oh, Lord, sir, and it's done it I have, most complate! Oh, good luck to you, sir; can you do nothing for me?"

"I don't know what's to be done with such a mess as this. Tell me, first of all, what you put in the stocking, you unfortunate blunderer?"

"Oh yes, sir, and tell you true as if it was the last word I had to spake entirely, and the Lord be good to you, and Ted Conner ses he to ould Phillips, regarden the five as was owen by Tim, and not includen of the ten which was changed by Pat Rielly—"

"You didn't put Pat Rielly or ould Phillips into the stocking did you?"

"Is it Pat or ould Phillips as was ever the valy of eighty-sivin pound ten, lost and gone, and includen the five as was owen by Tim, and Ted Connor—"

"Then tell me what you *did* put in the stocking, and let me take it down. And then hold your tongue, if you can, and go your way, and come back tomorrow."

The particulars of the notes were taken, without any reference to ould Phillips, who could not, however, by any means be kept out of the story; and the man departed.

When he was gone, the stocking-foot was shown to the then Chief Engraver of the notes, who said, that if anybody could settle the business, his son could. And he proposed that the particulars of the notes should not be communicated to his son, who was then employed in his department of the Bank, but should be put away under lock and key; and that if his son's ingenuity should enable him to discover from these ashes what notes had really been put in the stocking, and the two lists should tally, the man should be paid the lost amount. To this prudent proposal the Bank of Ireland readily assented, being extremely anxious that the man should not be a loser, but, of course, deeming it essential to be protected from imposition.

The son readily undertook the delicate commission proposed to him. He detached the fragments from the stocking with the utmost care, on the fine point of a pen-knife—laid the whole gently in a basin of warm water, and presently saw them, to his delight, begin to unfold and expand like flowers. By and by, he began to "tease them" with very light touches of the ends of a camel's-hair pencil, and so, by little and little, and by the most delicate use of the warm water, the camel's-hair pencil, and the pen-knife, got the various morsels separate before him, and began to piece them together. The first piece laid down was faintly recognizable by a practiced eye as a bit of the left-hand bottom corner of a twenty-pound note; then came a bit of a five—then of a ten—then more bits of a twenty—then more bits of a five and ten—then, another left-hand bottom corner of a twenty—so there were two twenties!—and so on, until, to the admiration and astonishment of the whole Bank, he noted down the exact amount deposited in the stocking, and the exact notes of which it had been composed. Upon this—as he wished to see and divert himself with the man on his return—he provided himself with a bundle of corresponding new, clean, rustling notes, and awaited his arrival.

He came exactly as before, with the same blank staring face, and the same inquiry, "Can you do anything for me, sir!"

"Well," said our friend, "I don't know. Maybe I *can* do something. But I have taken a great deal of pains, and lost a great deal of time, and I want to know what you mean to give me!"

"Is it give, sir? Thin, is there anything I wouldn't give for my eighty-sivin pound tin, sir; and it's murdered I am by ould Phillips."

"Never mind him; there were two twenties, were there not?"

"Oh, holy mother, sir, there was! Two most illigant twenties! and Ted Conner—and Phalim—which Rielly—"

He faltered, and stopped as our friend, with much ostentatious rustling of the crisp paper, produced a new twenty, and then the other twenty, and then a ten, and then a five, and so forth. Meanwhile, the man occasionally murmuring an exclamation of surprise or a protestation of gratitude, but gradually becoming vague and remote in the latter as the notes reappeared, looked on, staring, evidently inclined to believe that they were the real lost notes, reproduced in that state by some chemical process. At last they were all told out, and in his pocket, and he still stood staring and muttering, "Oh, holy mother, only to think of it! Sir, it's bound to you forever, that I am!"—but more vaguely and remotely now than ever.

"Well," said our friend, "what do you propose to give me for this?"

After staring and rubbing his chin for some time longer, he replied with the unexpected question—

"Do you like bacon?"

"Very much," said our friend.

"Then it's a side as I'll bring your honor tomorrow morning, and a bucket of new milk—and ould Phillips—"

"Come," said our friend, glancing at a notable shillelah the man had under his arm, "let me undeceive you. I don't want anything of you, and I am very glad you have got your money back. But I suppose you'd stand by me, now, if I wanted a boy to help me in a little skirmish?"

They were standing by a window on the top storey of the Bank, commanding a courtyard, where a sentry was on duty. To our friend's amazement, the man dashed out of the room without speaking one word, suddenly appeared in the courtyard, performed a war-dance round this astonished soldier—who was a modest young recruit—made the shillelah flutter, like a wooden butterly, round his musket, round his bayonet, round his head, round his body, round his arms, inside and outside his legs, advanced and retired, rattled it all around him like a firework, looked up at the window, cried out with a high leap in the air, "Whooroo! Thry me!"—vanished—and never was beheld at the Bank again from that time forth.

XIX

THE DOOM OF ENGLISH WILLS

CATHEDRAL NUMBER ONE

There are few things in this beautiful country of England, more picturesque to the eye, and agreeable to the fancy, than an old Cathedral town. Seen in the distance, rising from among cornfields, pastures, orchards, gardens, woods, the river, the bridge, the roofs of ancient houses, and haply the ruins of a castle or abbey, the venerable Cathedral spires, opposed for many hundred years to the winter wind and summer sun, tower, like a solemn historical presence, above the city, conveying to the rudest mind associations of interest with the dusky Past. On a nearer approach, this interest is heightened. Within the building, by the long perspectives of pillars and arches; by the earthy smell, preaching more eloquently than deans and chapters, of the common doom; by the praying figures of knights and ladies on the tombs, with little headless generations of sons and daughters kneeling around them; by the stained glass windows, softening and mellowing the light; by the oaken carvings of the stalls, where the shorn monks told their beads; by the battered effigies of archbishops and bishops, found built up in the walls, when all the world had been unconscious, for centuries, of their blunt stone noses; by the mouldering chapter-room; the crypt, with its barred loopholes, letting in long gleams of slanting light from the Cloisters where the dead lie, and where the ivy, bred among the broken arches, twines about their graves; by the sound of the bells, high up in the massive tower; by the universal gravity, mystery, decay, and silence. Without, by the old environing Cathedral-close, with its red-brick houses and staid gardens; by the same stained glass, so dark on that side though so bright within; by the pavement of half-obliterated tombstones; by the long echoes of the visitors' footsteps; by the wicket-gate, that seems to shut the moving world out of that retirement; by the grave rooks and jackdaws that have built their nests in steeple crevices, where the after-hum of the chimes reminds them, perhaps, of the wind among the boughs of lofty trees; by the ancient scraps of palace and gateway; by the ivy again, that has grown to be so thick and strong; by the oak, famous in all that part, which has struck its mighty root through the Bishop's wall; by the Cathedral organ, whose sound fills all that space, and all the space it opens in the charmed imagination.

There may be flaws in this whole, if it be examined, too closely. It may not be improved by the contemplation of the shivering choristers on a winter morning, huddling on their gowns as they drowsily go to scamper through their work; by the drawling voice, without a heart, that drearily pursues the dull routine; by the avaricious functionary who lays aside the silver mace to take the silver pieces, and who races through the Show as if he were the hero of a sporting wager. Some uncomfortable doubts may, under special circumstances, obtrude themselves, of the practical Christianity of the head of some particular Foundation. He may be a brawler, or a proud man, or a sleek, or an artful. He may be usually silent, in the House of Lords when a Christian minister should speak, and may make a point of speaking when he should be silent. He may even be oblivious of the truth; a stickler by the letter, not the spirit, for his own purposes; a pettifogger in the supreme court of God's high law, as there are pettifoggers in the lower courts administering the laws of mortal man. Disturbing recollections may arise, of a few isolated cases here and there, where country curates with small incomes and large families, poor gentlemen and scholars, are condemned to work, like blind horses in a mill, while others who do not work get their rightful pay; or of the inconsistency and indecorum of the Church being made a Robe and Candlestick question, while so many shining lights are hidden under bushels, and so many black-cloth coats are threadbare. The question may present itself, by remote chance, whether some shovel-hats be not made too much on the model of the banker's shovel with which the gold is gathered on the counter, and too little in remembrance of that other kind of shovel that renders ashes unto ashes, and dust to dust. But, on the whole, the visitor will probably be content to say, "the time was, and this old Cathedral saw it, when these things were infinitely worse; they will be better; I will do all honor to the good that is in them, (which is much), and I will do what in me lies for the speedier amendment of the bad."

In this conclusion, we think the visitor of the old Cathedral would be right. But, it is important to bring to the knowledge of all visitors of old Cathedrals in England, and of all who stay at home too, the most gigantic and least known abuse, attaching to those establishments. It is one which affects, not only the history and learning of the country, and that powerfully, but the legal rights and titles of all classes—of every man, woman, and child, rich and poor, great and small, born into this English portion of this breathing world.

For the purpose of the object on which we now enter, we have consulted a great mass of documents, and have had recourse to the personal experience of a gentleman who has made this kind of research his business. In every statement we make, we shall speak by the card, that equivocation may not undo us. The proof of every assertion, is ready to our hand.

The public have lately heard some trifling facts relative to Doctors' Commons, through the medium of a young gentleman who was articled, by his aunt, to a proctor there. Our readers may possibly be prepared to hear that the Registry of the Diocese of Canterbury, in which are deposited all the wills proved in that large, rich, and populous district, is a job so enormous as to be almost incredible. That the Registrars, with deputies, and deputies' deputies, are sinecurists of from sixteen to seventeen thousand pounds, to seven or eight thousand pounds, a-year; that the wills are not even kept secure from fire; that the real working men are miserably paid out of the rich plunder of the public; that the whole system is one of greed, corruption, and absurdity, from beginning to end. It is not, however, with the Registry of Canterbury that our business lies at present, but with the Registries and Peculiars of other dioceses, which are attached to the old Cathedrals throughout Great Britain, and of which our readers may be by no means prepared to hear what we shall have to tell.

Let us begin by setting forth from London on a little suppositious excursion—say with Mr. William Wallace, of the Middle Temple and the Royal Society of Antiquaries.

Mr. William Wallace, for the purpose of a literary pursuit in which he is engaged, involving the gratification of a taste he has for the history of old manners and old families, is desirous, at his own proper cost and charge, to search the registers in some Cathedral towns, for wills and records. Having heard whispers of corruption in these departments, and difficulty of search, Mr. Wallace arms himself with letters from the Bishops of those places. Putting money in his purse besides, he goes down, pretty confidently.

Mr. William Wallace arrives at Cathedral number one; and, after being extremely affected, despite a heavy shower of rain, by the contemplation of the building, inquires for the Registrar. He is shown a very handsome house in the Cathedral-close—a house very superior to the Bishop's—wherein the Registrar resides. For, the Registrar keeps a first rate roof over his own head, though he keeps his deeds in a dilapidated Gate-house; at which he takes toll to the amount of seven thousand a-year; and where, as at other toll-houses, "no trust" is the rule; for he exacts his fees beforehand.

Mr. William Wallace now learns that, locally, the Registrar is a person of almost inordinate power; besides his seven thousand-pound-per-annum place, he is Chapter Clerk, Town Clerk, Clerk to the Magistrates—a Proctor, moreover, in boundless practice. He lives in great state; he keeps horses, carriages, dogs, and a yacht; he is—could he be anything else?—a staunch Tory; he generally proposes the Tory members for the county, and has been known to pay the entire electioneering expenses of a favorite Tory candidate. Mr. Wallace, although fortified with a letter bearing the mitred seal of the Bishop of the diocese, feels that he is about to come in contact with a great power; an awful something that is not to be trifled with; one of the noblest institutions of our land, who is a very Miller of Dee, and accountable to nobody.

With a due sense of the importance of this outside buttress of the Church, Mr. Wallace presents himself with the Bishop's letter. The Registrar storms, and takes it extremely ill. He appears to confound Mr. Wallace with his own foot-boy. He says the Bishop has no power to interfere with *him*, and he won't endure it. He says the Bishop don't know what harm may come of showing wills. He can't make out, what people want to see wills for. He grudgingly concedes some obstructed search, on the usual terms; namely, two guineas per day for all the days a clerk—not fond of any sort of fatigue—may choose to take in making any particular search. "But perhaps you will allow me to look at the indexes?" asks Mr. Wallace.

"*That's* of no use," is the reply, "for a great many of the years are missing; and in those we have got, a great many wills are not entered. We often have to spend two months in finding a will." Our friend then performs a little mental arithmetic:—two months—or, even say fifty days—means one hundred guineas, to ferret out one will. Complete indexes would only occasion ten minutes' search, equal to one day, or, according to the Registrar's tariff, two guineas. Mr. Wallace then draws the inevitable conclusion, that bad indexes partly occasion the inordinate income of the Registrar, whose manifest interest it is to keep them as imperfect as possible. One little trait of the very early volumes (the earliest wills are dated A. D. 1180) is as quaint, as it is productive to the Registrar: the names of the testators are arranged—alphabetically, it is true—but under the Christian instead of the Surnames. Imagine the number of days, or couples of guineas, that would drop into the Registrar's coffers, for picking out one particular John Smith from the thousands of "Johns," under the letter "J!" Since the year 1800, the index is better: indeed it is almost as available as the old catalogues of the British Museum, though not quite so perfect.

All this was despair to Mr. William Wallace, who modestly hinted that his archæological necessities pressed him to ask admission to the actual depository of the wills. The Registrar was petrified with astonishment. His figure expanded with a burst of indignation, which presently exploded in the interrogative interjection, "What?" that went off, like the sharp crack of a rifle.

What? Exhibit, to any living soul, the dilapidative neglect, the hideous disorder, the wilful destruction of documents, involving the transfer of the property, personal and landed, of seven counties; and which he, the Registrar, obtains seven thousand pounds per annum for preserving carefully, and arranging diligently! Why, only last year the Archæological Institute of Great Britain, itself, was peremptorily refused admission; and was it likely that the Registrar would allow Mr. William Wallace—the friend of a mere Bishop—to be turned loose, to browse at will upon the waste the Registrar and his predecessors had committed and permitted?

But what will not an enthusiastic antiquary dare, in his loved pursuit? Mr. Wallace was bold enough to hint that a Bishop had perhaps some power in his diocese—even over a Registrar. This appeared in a degree to lull the tempest; and after all storms there is a calm. The Registrar reflected. There was nothing very formidable in the applicant's appearance; he had not the hungry look of a legacy or pedigree hunter—a foolish young fellow, perhaps, with a twist about old manners and customs: and, in short, he *may* take a look at the repositories.

Up a narrow stair, under the guidance of a grumpy clerk, our persevering Middle Templar wends. In a long room, over the arches of the gateway, he sees parallel rows of shelves laden with wills: not tied up in bundles, not docketed, not protected in any way from dust or spiders by the flimsiest covering. Only the modern wills are bound up; but—not to encroach upon the Registrar's hard earnings—the backings of the bindings are composed of such original wills as were written on parchment. These are regularly cut up—that is, wilfully destroyed—for bookbinding purposes!

Mr. Wallace sees, at a glance, that he may as well try to find a lost shell on a sea-shore, or a needle in a haystack, as attempt to discover what he is desirous of picking out of this documentary chaos. He looks round in mute grief; his archaic heart is heavy; he understands, exactly, how Rienzi felt amidst the Ruins of Rome, or the daughters of Jerusalem when they wept. Wherever he turns his eyes, he sees black, barbarous Ruin. In one corner, he observes decayed boxes filled with rotten wills; in another, stands a basket, containing several lumps of mediæval mortar, and a few brick-bats of the early pointed style—the edges, possibly, of some hole in the wall too large for even poor seven thousand a-year to shirk the stopping of. Despite the hints of the clerk that his time is valuable, Mr. Wallace is contemplating these relics with the eager gaze of an F.S.A., when he descries, hanging over the edge of the basket, something like an ancient seal. He scrutinizes it intensely—there is a document attached to it. He rescues it from the rubbish.

"What can this be?" asks Mr. Wallace with glistening eye.

"Oh!" answers the clerk, with listless indifference, "Nothing of any consequence, *I'm* sure."

By this time, Mr. Wallace has found out that this "nothing of any consequence," is a Charter of King William the Conqueror; *the identical instrument by which the See of Dorchester was transferred to Lincoln*—that's all! The broken seal is not of "much consequence" either. Oh, no!

Now it happens that there is only one impression of the great seal of the Great Norman extant, and that is in the British Museum, broken in half; this, being a counterpart, supplies the entire seal! Such is the priceless historical relic found in the year 1850, by chance, in a lime-basket, in the very place where it ought to have been as zealously preserved as if it had been the jewel of a diadem!

But, other treasures—equally of "no consequence," and about to be carried off by bricklayers' laborers, to where rubbish may be shot—are dug out by Mr. William Wallace:—Item, a bundle of pardons from King John to certain barons and bishops: Item, a Confession of the Protestant Faith made on his death-bed by Archbishop Toby Matthew, hitherto supposed by his biographers to have died a Catholic: Item, a contemporary poem on the Battle of Bosworth. The Registrar's clerk is of opinion, when these are shown to him, that "they an't worth much," but growlingly saves them, on remonstrance, and bundles them into his desk; where we trust they still remain; and whence we hope they may be rescued by the proper authorities.

As Mr. Wallace follows his surly guide up the stairs of the Gate-house, the rain patters sharply against the casements, and a fusty, damp odor emerges from the upper storey. Under a broken roof, and a ceiling being unplastered in huge patches by time and rain, in the top room, lie—or, more correctly, rot—the wills of the Archdeaconry of Blowe; a "Peculiar" of the diocese. The papers below stairs are merely worm-eaten, spider-woven, dusty, ill-arranged; but, compared with those which Mr. Wallace now sees—and smells—are in fastidious glass-case order. After dodging the rain-drops which filter through the ceiling, down among the solemn injunctions of the dead, Mr. Wallace is able to examine one or two bundles. Mildew and rot are so omnipotent in this damp depository, that the shelves have, in some places, broken and crumbled away. A moment's comparison between the relative powers of wood and paper, in resisting water, will give a vivid idea of the condition of the wills in this Archdiaconal shower-bath. The corners of most of the piles are as thoroughly rounded off, as if a populous colony of water rats (the ordinary species could not have existed there) had been dining off them since the days of King Stephen. Others are testamentary agglomerations, soddened into pulp,—totally illegible and inseparable; having been converted by age, much rain, and inordinate neglect, into *post-mortem* papier maché.

All these, are original wills: no such copies of them—which Registrars are enjoined to provide—having been made by the predecessors of the present pluralist. In order that the durability of parchment should be of no avail in arresting the most complete destruction within the scope of possibility, it is the sheepskin testaments of this collection that are regularly shredded to bind up the modern wills ranged in books below.

The very sight of this place, shows the futility of anything like research. Mr. Wallace examines a few of the documents, only to see their extreme historical as well as local importance; turns away; and descends the stairs.

"Thus, then," says Mr. William Wallace solemnly, as he takes a parting look at the ancient Gate-house, "are documents, involving the personal and real property of Seven English Counties, allowed to crumble to destruction; thus, is ruin brought on families by needless litigation; thus, do Registrars roll in carriages, and Proctors grow rich; thus, are the historical records of the great English nation doomed—by an officer whom the nation pays the income of a prince to be their conservator—to rottenness, mildew, and dust."

Mr. Wallace having added nothing to the object of his pursuits and inquiries, in the Registry of this Cathedral number one, departed at once for Cathedral number two. How he fared there, the reader shall soon learn.

CATHEDRAL NUMBER TWO

Mr. William Wallace, having taken some repose in the bosom of his family, and having recruited his nervous system, impaired for the moment by the formidable demonstrations made in unimpeachable Ecclesiastical Registry number one, resolved on making a visit to unimpeachable Ecclesiastical Registry number two; upheld by the consideration that, although an Ecclesiastical Registry is a fine Institution, for which any Englishman would willingly die; and without which he could, in no patriotic acceptation worth mentioning, be an Englishman at all; still, that the last wills and testaments of Englishmen are not exactly waste-paper, and that their depositaries ought, perhaps to be kept as dry—say as skittle grounds, which are a cheaper luxury than Registries, with the further advantage that no man need frequent them unless he likes: whereas, to Registries he *must* go.

The literary object which Mr. Wallace had in view, in this second expedition, beckoned him to the North of England. "Indeed," said Mr. Wallace, pausing. "Possibly, to the second city of England; an Archbishopric; giving one of the princes of the blood his title; enjoying the dignity of a Lord Mayor of its own; an ancient and notable place; renowned for its antiquities; famous for its Cathedral; possessing walls, four gates, six posterns, a castle, an assembly-room, and a Mansion House; this is surely the place for an unimpeachable Registry!"

He arrived at the venerable city of his purpose, at ten minutes past three P.M., according to Greenwich, or at three-ten, according to Bradshaw.

Our traveler's first proceeding, was, to take a walk round the walls, and gratify his fancy with a bird's-eye-view of the unimpeachable registry. He could hardly hit upon the roof of that important building. There was a building in a severe style of architecture—but it was the jail. There was another that looked commodious—but it was the mansion house. There were others that looked comfortable—but they were private residences. There appeared to be nothing in the way of Registry, answering to the famous monkish legend in a certain Chapter-House:

> As shines the rose above all common flowers,
> So above common piles this building towers.

Yet such a building must be somewhere! Mr. Wallace went into the town and bought a Guide-book, to find out where.

He walked through the quiet narrow streets, with their gabled houses, craning their necks across the road to pry into one another's affairs; and he saw the churches where the people were married; and the habitations where the doctors lived, who were knocked up when the people were born; and he accidentally passed the residence of Mrs. Pitcher, who likewise officiated on those occasions; and he remarked an infinity of shops where every commodity of life was sold. He saw the offices of the lawyers who made the people's wills, the banks where the people kept their money, the shops of the undertakers who made the people's coffins, the churchyards where the people were buried, but *not* the Registry where the people's wills were taken care of. "Very extraordinary!" said Mr. Wallace. "In the great city of a great Ecclesiastical See, where all kinds of moving reverses and disasters have been occurring for many centuries, where all manner of old foundation and usage, piety, and superstition, were, and a great deal of modern wealth is, a very interesting and an unimpeachable Registry there must be, somewhere!"

In search of this great public edifice, the indefatigable Mr. Wallace prowled through the city. He discovered many mansions; but he *could not* satisfy himself about the Registry.

The uneasiness of Mr. Wallace's mind increasing with the growth of his suspicion that there must surely be a flaw in the old adage, and that where there was a will (and a great many wills) there was no way at all, he betook himself to the Cathedral-close. Passing down an uncommonly pure, clean, tidy little street, where the houses looked like a tasteful sort of missionary-subscription-boxes, into which subscribers of a larger growth were expected to drop their money down the chimneys, he came by a turnstile, into that haven of rest, and looked about him.

"Do you know where the Registry is?" he asked a farmer-looking man.

"The wa'at!" said he.

"The Registry; where they keep the wills?"

"A'dinnot know for shower," said the farmer, looking round. "Ding! If I shouldn't wondther if *thot* wur it!"

Mr. Wallace concealed his disparaging appreciation of the farmer's judgment, when he pointed with his ash-stick to a kind of shed—such as is usually called a lean-to—squeezing itself, as if it were (with very good reason) ashamed, into the south-west corner of the cross, which the ground-plan of the cathedral forms, and sticking to it like a dirty little pimple. But, what was his dismay, on going thither to inquire, to discover that this actually WAS the unimpeachable Registry; and that a confined den within, which would have made an indifferent chandler's shop, with a pestilent little chimney in it, filling it with smoke like a Lapland hut, was the "Searching Office."

Mr. Wallace was soon taught that seven thousand pounds per annum is, after all, but a poor pittance for the Registrar of a simple bishopric, when calculated by the ecclesiastical rule of three; for the registry of Cathedral number two, produces to its fortunate patentees twenty thousand per annum; about ten thousand a year for the Registrar who does nothing, and the like amount for his Deputy who helps him.

The portentous personage to whom Mr. Wallace was accredited, received him in state in the small office surrounded by a Surrogate (apparently retained on purpose to cross-examine Mr. Wallace) and the clerks. Mr. Wallace mentioned that he believed the Archbishop had written to the Deputy-Registrar to afford him every facility in consulting the documents under his charge. The Deputy Registrar owned that the Archbishop had done so, but declared that the Archbishop had no jurisdiction whatever over him; and, claiming as he did, complete immunity from, and irresponsibility to, all human control, he begged to say that his Grace the Archbishop, in presuming to write to the high-authorities of that unimpeachable Registry on such a subject, had taken a very great liberty. Mr. William Wallace inquired if that was to be the answer he was expected to convey to the Archbishop? bowed, and was about to retire, when the awful Deputy recalled him. What did he want to search for? Mr. Wallace repeated that his object was wholly literary and archæological. The chief clerk who here came in as a reinforcement, was so good as to intimate that he "didn't believe a word of it." Whereupon a strong opinion was added that Mr. Wallace wanted surreptitiously to obtain pedigrees, and to consult wills. A powerful battery of cross-questionings was then opened by the heavier authorities, aided by a few shots from the light-bob, or skirmishing party—the clerk. But had Mr. William Wallace been his great ancestor, he could not have held his position against such odds more firmly. At length the preliminaries of a treaty were proposed by the enemy, the terms of which were that Mr. Wallace should be allowed to consult any records dated before the year one thousand four hundred! This was demurred to as utterly useless. Negotiations were then resumed, and the authorities liberally threw in another century, out of the fullness of a respect for the Archbishop, which they had refrained from condescending to express;—Mr. Wallace might consult documents up to the year fifteen hundred.

With this munificent concession, Mr. Wallace was obliged to be satisfied, and proceeded to venture on another stipulation:—

The researches which he had proposed to himself at this Cathedral number two, were elaborate and complicated; they would require such facilities as had been asked on his behalf by the Archbishop. Could he have access to the documents themselves?

The effect which this simple request produced in the office, was prodigious! A small schoolboy who should, at dinner, ask for a piece of the master's apple-pie; or a drummer on parade, who should solicit from his captain a loan of five shillings, could not produce a more sublime degree of astonishment, than that which glared through the smoke from the faces of the deputy-registrar, the surrogate, the chief clerk, and all the junior clerks, then and there assembled. The effect produced amounted to temporary petrefaction; the principals neither spoke nor moved; the subordinates left off writing and poking the fire. So superlative was the audacity of the request, that it paralyzed the pendulum of that small, rusty, dusty, smoky old ecclesiastical clock, and stopped the works!

Refusal in words was not vouchsafed to Mr. William Wallace; neither did he need that condescension. The silent but expressive pantomine was enough. As the Eastern culprit receives his doom by the speechless gesture of the judge's hand across his own neck; so Mr. William Wallace fully understood that, access to the record depositories of the province appertaining to Cathedral number two, was nearly equivalent to getting into a freemason's lodge after it has been "tiled," or to obtaining admission to St. Paul's cathedral without two-pence.

He therefore waved as perfectly impossible that item of the treaty. For the public, however, the evidence of that gentleman is hardly necessary to bring them acquainted with the manner in which the trust imposed on the Registrar and his Deputy is performed; for while the Deputy Registrar and Mr. William Wallace are settling their differences over the next clause of their treaty, we shall dip into the reports of the Ecclesiastical Commission issued in 1832, to show what the state of things was at that time; and to anyone who can prove that those venerable documents have been by any means rescued from decay since that year, the public will doubtless be much obliged. At page one hundred and seventy of the report, Mr. Edward Protheroe, M.P., states, on oath, that in the instance of every Court he had visited the records suffered more or less from damp and the accumulation of dust and dirt. Then, speaking of the Registry of this same Cathedral number two, he declares its documents to have been in a scandalous state. "I found them," he continues, "perfectly to accord with the description I had received from various literary and antiquarian characters who had occasion to make searches in the office; and I beg leave to remark that the place must have been always totally inadequate as a place of deposit for the records, both as to space and security." Some of the writings he found in two small cells, "in a state of the most disgraceful filth;" others in "two apertures in the thick walls, scarcely to be called windows; and the only accommodation for these records are loose wooden shelves, upon which the wills are arranged in bundles, tied up with common strings, and without any covering to them; exposed to the effect of the damp of the weather and the necessary accumulation of dirt." To these unprotected wills the Deputy Registrar was perhaps wise in his generation to deny access; for Mr. Protheroe says in addition that, "if it was the object of any person to purloin a will, such a thing might be accomplished." Perfectly and safely accessible copies might be made, at "an expense quite trifling." What? Mr. Protheroe, would you rob these poor Registrars of a shilling of their hard earnings, just to save landed and other property, of some millions value, from litigation and fraud? Would you discount their twenty thousand a year by even a fraction per cent?

The clause of the treaty, offensive and defensive, which was being negotiated all this while, between the Deputy Registrar and his visitor, was drawn up by the former in these concise words, "How long do you want to be here?"

That, Mr. Wallace replied, would depend upon the facilities afforded him, the condition of the calendars and indexes, and the assistance he might be allowed to call in. After much battling, the conference ended by Mr. William Wallace, and a friend who accompanied him, being allowed to set to work upon the calendars of such wills as had been deposited before the year 1500.

The two antiquaries would have commenced their researches immediately; only, on examining their dress, they found it in such a state of filth from the smoke with which the office had been filled during the arrangement of this important compact, that they were obliged to return to the hotel to change their linen. The prospect of spending a week in such a place was not altogether agreeable. Mr. Wallace did not enjoy the notion of being smoke-dried; and of returning to the Middle Temple a sort of animated ham. A sojourn in the place was not to be thought of without terror; yet the poor clerks endured their smoking fate with fortitude. Use was to them a second nature; and every man connected with these Registries must be completely inured to dust. But the man of the Middle Temple was a kind of knight-errant in the matter of rescuing ancient documents from their tombs of filth; and not to be daunted. He and his friend opened the campaign directly in the face of the enemy's fire—which, so great was their ardor, they only wished would become a little more brisk and less smoky.

That day and the next day they bored on with patience and perseverance through every obstacle. When they found in the calendar a reference to what they wanted, every possible obstacle was thrown in their way. The required document was either lost, or had been stolen, or had strayed. Nor was there the slightest reason to doubt that this was true. It was well known to the searchers that one class of documents at least had been actually made away with by a former Deputy Registrar. Dr. Thelwall, of Newcastle, wrote in the Gentleman's Magazine for 1819, page four hundred and ninety:—"It is a fact well known that, by a Canon of James the First, the clergyman of every parish was required to send a copy of the Register annually to the Bishop of the Diocese. The most shameful negligence is attributable to the person (the Deputy Registrar) in whose keeping they have been placed. Indeed I have some reason to suppose this, as I lately saw in the possession of a friend, a great number of extracts from the Register of a certain parish in this neighborhood, and, on questioning him as to the way in which he became possessed of them, I was informed they were given to him by his cheesemonger, and that they were copies forwarded by the clergyman of the parish to the proper officer in a bordering diocese, and had been allowed through the negligence of their keeper to obtain the distinguished honor of wrapping up cheese and bacon."

The sale of Records, for waste paper, was the mode adopted to revenge the meanness of the legislature, in not providing the underpaid Registrars with remuneration for this addition to their duties. Was it possible to keep life and soul together upon the ten or fifteen thousand sterling per annum which these two poor fellows were then obliged to starve upon? Certainly not! Therefore, to eke out a wretched existence, they found themselves driven to sell the property of the public, if not for the necessaries, for the luxuries, of life. They had, perhaps, managed to keep their families, by a rigid, pinching economy in bread—dry bread; but to butter it; to indulge themselves with the proper diet of even Church mice, they were obliged to dispose of paper—worth, perhaps, thousands and thousands of pounds to the parties whose names were inscribed on it—at a few pence per pound, to the cheesemonger.

From this doom of some of the parochial records of the province, Mr. William Wallace inferred the degree of care and exactitude with which the wills were kept. Previous knowledge had prepared him for it; but he was not prepared to find that *the whole* of another and most important class of records, up to a comparatively late date, had been abstracted, in the lump, from the Registry of this Cathedral number two. The case was this:—

In the course of his investigations, it was necessary for him to refer to a "marriage allegation,"—that is, a copy of the statement made by a bridegroom previous to converting himself, by the help of the Bishop's license, into a husband. He then learnt that most of such documents are the "private property" of one of the clerks, who kept them in his own private house; that he had bought them of a deceased member of the Herald's College, and that for each search into them he charged according to a sliding scale, arranged according to the station of the applicant, the maximum of which was five pounds for the simple search, and five pounds more if what the party wanted were found. The English of this is, that the present custodier of these papers purchased of a dead Herald what did not belong to him; and what there could have been no difficulty whatever in restoring to the true owner; (because no one could have known better than the purchaser that they were public property); and that their proper place was not his private house, but the provincial Registry. The produce of this abstraction is an illegal income better possibly than the legal gains of an Admiral or a Government Commissioner; double that of a physician in good practice, or of a philanthropist in easy circumstances,—and treble that of our best dramatist, or our best poet.

Besides these hindrances, which could not be helped, a certain number of wilful obstructions were thrown in the way of our inquiring friends, because they had been desired by the Archbishop to be placed on the fee free-list. They were watched by the entire office; for it became Argus for the occasion. Remarks of a satirical character were discharged point-blank from behind the desks, whenever a good opening occurred. The non-paying searchers were "in the way"—(this was true, so unfit is the apartment for public accommodation); "what people got they ought to pay for, as other people did." Spies slid silently out from behind the ramparts, or desks, to look over their shoulders, and to see that they did not purloin any information posterior to the fifteenth century.

Mr. William Wallace stood all this manfully; but his ally was obliged to retire at the expiration of the second day. Mr. William Wallace at length found he could not advance the objects of his inquiries any more efficiently at this Cathedral number two, than he had advanced them at Cathedral number one; so, at the end of a week, he beat a dignified retreat with all the honors of war. He then turned his face towards the unimpeachable Registry of Cathedral number three, hoping for better success.

CATHEDRAL NUMBER THREE

The core of the inquiry which Mr. William Wallace had a heart, lay imbedded in the depositories of unimpeachable Ecclesiastical Registry number three. To the city of that See he therefore repaired, warmed by that flaming zeal which only burns in the breast of an earnest antiquary, and which no amount of disappointment can quench. Though sanguine, even for an antiquity-hunter, the hopes which rebounded from his previous failures, sunk within him, when he remembered that whereas he was in former instances fortified with letters of recommendation—almost of command—from the Bishops of each Diocese; on this occasion, he had to fight single-handed, (like another St. George,) the dragons that "guarded" the treasures he sought. He had no better introduction to the third Deputy-Registrar than an honest purpose; and, his former experience taught him that that was about as unpromising an usher into such a Presence as could be imagined. Mr. Wallace therefore commenced this new attack with no strong presentiment of success.

Strengthened with an ally, in the person of a friendly attorney, Mr. William Wallace marched boldly to the great functionary's house, a splendid edifice in the Cathedral-close, with thirty-three windows in front, extensive grounds behind, detached stables and a tasteful boat-house at the edge of what is here called the "Minster Pool."

Into this great house of a great man, Mr. William Wallace was ushered by his friend. Nothing could exceed the obsequiousness of the man of law, and great was the civility of the man of wills. The interview was going on pleasantly and the antiquary was beginning to believe that at last he had found a pattern Deputy-Registrar, when the lawyer happened to mention that Mr. William Wallace was a literary man. Mr. Wallace felt that this would be fatal—and it was so. He knew the condign contempt Ecclesiastical Registrars entertained for the literary world, from the little circumstance of hearing only the week before in another Registry, the most eminent historian of the present day, and our best archaic topographer, designated as "contemptible penny-a-liners." Mr. Wallace was therefore not at all astonished when the Deputy-Registrar folded up his smiling countenance into a frown. He evidently knew what was coming. Literary men never pay, and Mr. William Wallace wanted to consult "his" registers gratis.

When this shrewd surmise was, by a word from the attorney, realized, the Registrar struggled hard to smoothe his face again to a condition of bland composure; but in vain. The wound which had pierced through his pocket, rankled within. The depravity of literary people in endeavoring to dig and delve for historical information without paying for the privilege of benefitting the public by their researches, was *too* abominable! The Registrar was so good as to say that he would grant Mr. Wallace the privilege of consulting any wills he pleased—on the usual terms: namely, two shillings and sixpence for every document.

With this condescending permission (which placed Mr. Wallace on exactly the same footing as the great body of the public which had not done itself the honor of visiting the Deputy-Registrar) he repaired to the Searching Office. The point he had set himself to ascertain at this Cathedral Registry number three, hinged upon an authentic attestation of the decease of the father of a distinguished general under Charles the First. The name was a very common one in the diocese, and of course continually occurred in the index. Will after will was produced by the clerks; half-crown after half-crown fell glibly out of Mr. Wallace's pocket. Still no success. This proved an expensive day. Mr. Wallace had had to pay, in the course of it, twenty-five pounds; although he was not allowed, as at the other places, to make a single extract.

The income of the office even of Deputy Registrar sometimes admits of the maintenance of from six to a dozen race-horses, but the expense of compiling paper calendars could never be tolerated. To make indexes of wills that have never been catalogued would be quite out of the question; for the Registrar charges his clients for the *time* of his clerks in making searches, and it was owned to Mr. Wallace that it would take a year (at from one to two guineas per day) to find any will dated before the year 1526.

The searching office of this Registry was, like the others, inconvenient, small, and often crowded. The policy of the clerks was, therefore, to despatch the inquirers as fast as possible, so as to ensure a rapid change of visitors and a streaming influx of half-crowns. On the second day of Mr. Wallace's search the trouble he had given on the previous day for his money was intelligibly hinted to him. He was broadly told that he was "very much in the way;" for room was so much required that some applicants were plainly told that they must "come again tomorrow." To others who had not their inquiries ready cut and dried, in a business form, and who threatened long explanations respecting testators, a deaf ear was turned, or a pretended search was made, and they were told "there was no such will in the place." A pleasant case occurred on the second morning. An illiterate laborer tried to make the officials understand that an uncle of his wife had, he had heard, left him a legacy, and "he wanted to know the rights o' it." He gave the name and the exact date of the death, and a clerk retired under pretence of searching for the document. In a very short time he returned with—

"No such will in the place—half-a-crown, please."

"Half-a-croone?" said the countryman, "Wat vor?"

"Half-a-crown!" repeated the clerk.

"Wat, vor telling me nought?"

"Half-a-crown!" was again let off with a loud explosion, over the stiff embrasure of white cravat.

"But darn me if oi pay't," persisted the expectant legatee.

"Half-a-crown!"

The countryman went on raising a storm in the office, in midst of which the "Half-a-crown!" minute guns were discharged with severe regularity. At length, however, the agriculturist was obliged to succumb, and after a mighty effort to disinter the coin from under a smock-frock, and out of the depths of a huge pocket and a leather purse, the poor man was obliged to produce and pay over what was probably a fifth of his week's earnings.

This circumstance having attracted Mr. Wallace's attention and pity, he took a note of the name of the testator; and, after the inquirer had left, found it in the Calendar, and by-and-by, by dint of a little manœuvring, got a sight of the will. In it he actually found that the poor man *had* been left a small legacy.

Meanwhile Mr. William Wallace had been actively employed in calling for wills and paying out half-crowns. It was quite evident from the calendars that no greater care was taken of paper and parchment here than in the other Registries. Several wills entered in it, as having been once in the depository—wherever that was—had against them the words "wanting" and "lost." That ancient records should in the course of centuries fall aside, cannot be wondered at, even in a Registry, which produces at present to its officers from seven to ten thousand per annum; but what excuse can there be for the loss of comparatively modern ones? Certain wills were not to be found of the years 1746; 1750; 1753; and 1757.

Mr. Wallace soon found that in a place where dropping half-crowns into the till and doing as little as possible in return for them, is considered the only legitimate business, he was looked upon even at twenty-five pounds per day as a sort of bad bargain, who required a great deal too much for his money. They could not coin fast enough by Mr. William Wallace, and the Deputy-Registrar indulged the office with his august presence to inform him, that as he gave so much trouble for the searches he was making, he must pay, besides two-and-six-pence for every future search, two guineas per diem for the use of the office!

It happened that the Bishop of Cathedral number three was then in the city, officiating at an ordination, and to him Mr. William Wallace determined to apply for relief from this extortion. He enclosed to his Lordship his letters from other prelates and stated his case. The answer he received was the Bishop's *unqualified authority* to search wherever and for whatever he wanted in the Registers of his Lordship's diocese.

Although this letter was addressed by the Bishop to the servant or deputy of *his* servant, the Registrar, yet Mr. Wallace's dear-bought sagacity had taught him to place very little faith in a Bishop's power over his inferiors. As it turned out, he found himself one of those who are blessed, because, expecting nothing, they are not disappointed. The Deputy-Registrar received his superior's mandate with supercilious *sangfroid*. The old story—"The Bishop had no jurisdiction whatever over him," but this once, &c. &c.

Mr. William Wallace had met in Cathedrals numbers one and two, repulses and rudeness. But each Cerberus who pretended to guard the documentary treasures of those dioceses, honestly showed his teeth. *They* had not been guilty of deceit. Deputy-Registrar number three was wiser in his generation. He gave a cold assent to the Bishop's mandate in Mr. Wallace's behalf; but with it such wily instructions to his clerks, as rendered it as nugatory as if he had put it in his waste basket or had lighted his cigar. During the two days that half-crowns rained in silver showers from the Antiquary's purse, nearly every Will he asked for was produced; but now, on the third day, when the Bishop's letter had closed his purse-strings, Mr. Wallace demanded document after document, and was told by the "Conservators" of this important kind of public property, that they had "been lost," "could not be found," "mislaid." But the most frequent return was, "destroyed at the siege of the City, in the year 1643"—stolen away with the Tomb of Marmion when

"Fanatic Brooke
The fair Cathedral storm'd and took."

The result of the three days' investigations stood thus: "During the two paying days, out of a hundred Wills asked for, eighty were produced. Throughout the non-paying day, out of ninety Wills asked for, only *one* was produced!"

When half-crowns were rife, not one word was said about "the siege of the City, in the year 1643," although nearly all the Wills Mr. Wallace was obliged with a sight of, were dated anterior to that destructive event.

For some explanation Mr. Wallace repaired to the Deputy-Registrar's abode. It was too late. The clever sub. knew what was coming—and retreated from the field. The servant's answer to Mr. Wallace was,

"Out of town, sir!"

But Mr. William Wallace was foiled even more completely in another point: he had a great desire to see where and how the Wills were kept. He knew their condition in 1832, from what Ulster King-at-Arms said before the Ecclesiastical Commission, "I consider the records very dirty; they have not, apparently, been dusted for many years." The remarkable result of Mr. Wallace's urgent inquiries was that not a soul he asked could, or would, tell in what place the ecclesiastical records of Cathedral number three were deposited.

Mr. Wallace gave up this investigation in despair and left the city. The *locus* of the documents was to him a mystery and a wonder!

The habits of the antiquary do not, however, dispose him to indulge in listless despair. To find out the secret masses of the records of Cathedral number three was a task Mr. William Wallace had so earnestly set himself, that next to his domestic relations and his literary labors, it grew into one of the duties of his existence; therefore, on his way to Cathedral number four, he paid another visit to the city of Cathedral number three, fortified with letters to some of its clergy. To be sure *they* could clear up the mystery.

His first application was to one of the Canons. Did he know where the ecclesiastical records were kept? Well, it was odd, but it never entered his head to inquire. He really did *not* know. Perhaps some of the Chapter officials could tell.

To one of these, hies Mr. Wallace. Even that functionary—whose courteousness, together with that of his colleague, was pleasant to the applicant by the force of mere contrast—was equally unable to reveal the secret. "But surely," he added, "such a place cannot, when one sets about it, be so impenetrable a mystery. I have an idea that the *Miller* could enlighten you."

"The Miller?"

"Yes. He knows everything about the town. Try him."

Mr. Wallace had business at the searching office, and having transacted it, determined to make another effort in this legitimate quarter. The following short dialogue occurred between him and the clerk:—"Pray," said Mr. Wallace, "where are the Wills kept?"

"That's not your business!" was the answer. Mr. Wallace returned to the charge but the clerk became deaf, and went on with some writing, precisely as if Mr. William Wallace were invisible and inaudible.

The Miller was the only resource. He was from home, and his wife gave the same answer as everybody else had done. "But," she said, pointing to an individual who was sauntering into the Close, "there's one as can tell 'ee. He's a *rachetty* man—he is." Without waiting to inquire the meaning of this strange expression, off starts the record-hunter upon the new secret. He runs down his game in no time. It consists of a burly biped, bearing a cage of fine ferrets. Round his person is displayed the broad insignia of office,—he is a rat-catcher.

Here Mr. William Wallace's perseverance triumphs. The Rat-catcher knows all about it. "Why you see, Sir," he said, "I contracts for the Registrar."

"What for?"

"What for? Why, I catches the rats for him at so much a-year."

"And where do you catch them?"

"Where do I catch them? Why, where the old wills is."

"And where is that?"

"Where is that? Why, *there*."

The Rat-catcher points to a sort of barn that rises from the edge of the Minster Pool. It has no windows on the ground-floor. On the first-floor are six—two in the front of the building and four at the end,—twenty-seven windows less than are displayed in the front of the Registrar's beautifully glazed house; but much of the little glass afforded to the registry is broken. To mend it upon seven thousand a-year would never do, especially when old parchment is lying about in heaps. Why pay glaziers' charges when ancient wills and other ecclesiastical records keep out wind and weather as well as glass?—for light is a thing rather to be shunned than admitted into such places. Accordingly, as the Rat-catcher points to the shed, Mr. Wallace observes numberless ends of record rolls and bundles of engrossed testaments poked into the broken windows: in some places variegated with old rags.

Judging from the exterior, and from the contract for rat-catching, the interior of this depository of the titles of hundreds of thousands of pounds worth of property, must be an archæological Golgotha, a dark mouldy sepulchre of parchment and dust.

Lawyers say that there is not an estate in this country with an impregnable title; in other words, it is on the cards in the game of ecclesiastical and common law, for any family to be deprived of their possessions in consequence of being unable to establish a perfect title to them. How can it be otherwise when the very deeds by which they have and hold what they enjoy, are left to be eaten by rats, or to be stuffed into broken windows?

CATHEDRAL NUMBER FOUR

An antiquary cannot approach the city of Chester from London, even in an express railway train, without emotions more lively than that class of observers generally have credit for. Despite a sensation akin to that of being fired off in a rocket, and a pardonable fancy that the hedges are endless bands of green ribbon in eternal motion, that the houses, and cottages, and churches, and trees, and villages, as they dart past the confines of the carriage window, are huge missiles shot across fields which are subjected to a rapid dispensation of distorted perspective; yet these mighty evidences of the Present do not dull his mind to the Past. He remembers, with wonder, that two thousand years ago, it was over this identical line of country that the legions of Suetonius lagged along after they had blunted the scythes of Boadicea, routed her hordes, and driven her to suicide.

We will not say that our own fellow of the Society of Antiquaries, Mr. William Wallace, retrojected his imagination so far into the past while crossing the Chester platform with his carpet-bag, because we are led to believe, from his report to us, that his views were immediately directed to the more modern times of St. Werburgh, who founded the Abbey of Chester (once the most splendid in England); seeing that it is in the still-standing gateway of that obsolete establishment, that the objects of Mr. Wallace's especial solicitude are now, and always have been deposited, since Henry the Eighth erected Chester into a diocese.

His hopes of success in seeking out certain facts from the testamentary records of this See, were more slender than they had been while entering upon his errand at the other three cathedrals. He had written to the bishop for that permission to search which had been by other prelates so readily granted, but which had been rendered by the respective Registrars so utterly nugatory, and had received no answer. Awkward reminiscences of the state of this Registry, as disclosed before the last Parliamentary Committee on the Ecclesiastical Courts, fell like a dark shadow over his hopes. Up to the year 1832, the gateway where the wills are kept was, upon the Deputy Registrar's own showing, neither "fire-proof, sufficiently large, nor absolutely free from plunder." The searching-office was a part of the gateway; and was as inadequate as other searching offices. The Chief Registrar in 1837 was a sinecurist in the *seventieth* year of office, and was verging towards the hundredth of his age; having received, in his time, not less than three hundred and fifty thousand pounds of the public money for doing nothing. The fees for searches and extracts were heavy, and nobody was allowed, as in most other Registries, to see how the wills were kept.

Such were the gloomy prepossessions of Mr. William Wallace, as he approached the archway which held the testamentary treasures of Diocese Number Four. He sought the searching office in vain, and at length was fain to address himself to the first passenger—a burly blacksmith—who, at once, in answer to his inquiry, pointed to a handsome new stone building, that stood within the Abbey Square.

Mr. William Wallace ascended the steps doubtingly; and when he found himself in the wide passage of an evidently well-planned public office—so contrary was the whole aspect of the place to his preconceptions of it, and to his previous experience of other ecclesiastical Registries—that he would have retired, had not the words, "Searching Office," as plain as paint and capitals could make them, stared him full in the face from a door on his right. This he boldly opened, and beheld a handsome apartment, so mounted with desks, counters, and every appurtenance for public convenience, as to put him in mind of the interior of a flourishing assurance office. "The room," says Mr. William Wallace, in his report to us, "is furnished with a counter of ample size, extending round it, on which you examine the indexes. On calling for one or two modern wills, the clerks brought me a substantial, well-bound book, in which he informed me all modern wills have been, since the appointment of the present Registrar, enrolled at length, in a round text, so distinct and plain, that illiterate persons might read them; and not engrossed, so as to become a source of revenue, as at Doctor's Commons, where the unlearned, in what is called 'court-hand,' are obliged to call in the aid of a clerk, and disburse a fee for the wills to be read to them. I was informed that I could see the originals on giving a satisfactory reason to the Registrar, or, in his absence, to a principal clerk. So promptly is business done here, that I found the wills which had been received from Manchester and other places that day, had been already indexed—very different to York, where wills are sometimes not indexed for six or eight months, and, consequently, often not at all. I next inquired for some earlier wills, and stated that I might probably want to have two or three days' research, for a literary purpose. On hearing this, the clerk informed me that the Registrar made no charge under such circumstances, except for the clerks' time. I then called for about six early wills, and only one of the six could not be found. Afterwards I asked for the returns of several Parish Registers; each set of which are well and substantially bound in a separate volume; for this a fee of three shillings and eight-pence is demanded; at York, for the production of a similar quantity of records, fifteen pounds is the price, without clerks' fees; and at Lincoln it would be impossible to collect them at all, many having been used to bind up modern wills, and for other such purposes."

Mr. William Wallace, pleasingly surprised at the contrast this Registry number four presented to others he had visited, and where he had been so egregiously snubbed, determined to learn and see as much respecting it as possible. With this view, he applied, without any other introduction than his card, to the Registrar; whose excellent custom it was, he understood, to be in attendance daily for several hours. At that time he was examining witnesses in a case for the Ecclesiastical Court, and handed the card to the bishop's secretary, who was also in official attendance. "That gentleman," says Mr. Wallace, "immediately came down, and informed me that the Bishop had written to me, in answer to my application, two days before, giving me permission to search, at reasonable hours, and that the Registrar, as was his usual custom, had not the slightest objection. I then asked to be shown the various parts of the building, the modes of preserving the records, which request was granted without the smallest hesitation."

Our informant then goes on to say that he found the building—which was raised solely at the expense of the present Registrar, since his appointment in 1837—conveniently divided into different departments like the best of the Government offices,—each department legibly indicated for the benefit of the inquirer, on the different doors.

The manner in which the records are preserved at this Cathedral number four, is spoken of by our friend with satisfaction. His report to us is silent on rats, wet, mildew, smoke, broken windows, torn testaments, and illegible calendars. "Modern wills," he repeats, "are copied at length into volumes, by the present Registrar, a practice which I regret is not adopted at York, Lincoln, Lichfield, Winchester, and other places I have visited. If wills of an earlier date than that of the enrolment books are required to be taken out of the office for production in any Court of Law, &c., an examined copy made for the purpose, is deposited in its place during its temporary removal from the Registry. The principal portion of the wills are deposited in a dry, but not a fire-proof building, in good repair, called the Abbey Gateway; where, during the office hours, two clerks are constantly kept at work in copying wills that come in. These are kept in boxes, arranged upon shelves with just sufficient space to admit them, like drawers; and upon the top of the wills is a sheet of pasteboard fitting the box, as a further protection from dust. The wills are alphabetically arranged in the boxes, which are of uniform size, and contain more or less letters; the first box for 1835, for instance, contains the wills of testators whose names commence with A. or B. The wills of each letter are placed separately, and are divided into packets of one month each, so that the exact date of Probate being known, the will is found immediately."

Before the period of its renovation, the Registry of Chester was as inefficient and exacting as the other three we have described. To whom the merit of the change and the contrast is really due, is not easily to be ascertained, although the present incumbent of the office must necessarily have the largest share of credit for it. We suspect, however, that the proximate impetus of the reform can be traced to the geographical position of the See. It includes the busiest of the manufacturing towns, and the most business-like, practical, and hard-handed examples of the English character. The thorough-going Manchester or Liverpool legatee would not endure, beyond a certain point and a certain time, the impositions, delays, destructions, and muddling confusion of the will offices in the more easy-going districts. Time with him is cash. What he wants he must have at once, especially if he pays for it. He may be put off once or twice with a rotten, illegible index, or a "Come again tomorrow;" but when he once sees that these may be obviated, he takes care to let there be no delay on his part, and agitates immediately. To engage a Free Trade Hall, and get up a public meeting, is with him a matter of no more consideration than scolding his clerk, or bringing a creditor to book. He has discredited the maxim that "talking is not doing;" and a constant iteration of pertinent speeches, ending with stinging "resolutions," has been found to *do* greater feats, to perform much greater wonders than setting ecclesiastical registries in order. It is possible, therefore, that the lay authorities of the Chester Registry, having the dread of an uncompromising community before their eyes, saw their safety in renovation; and, like sensible men, made it, without that whining sophistication, that grim tenacity, with which abuses are excused and clung to, in exact proportion to their absurdity, profitableness, and injustice.

XX

DISAPPEARANCES

Now, my dear cousin, Mr. B., charming as he is in many points, has the little peculiarity of liking to change his lodgings once every three months on an average, which occasions some bewilderment to his country friends, who have no sooner learnt the 19 Belle Vue Road, Hampstead, than they have to take pains to forget that address, and to remember the 27½, Upper Brown Street, Camberwell; and so on, till I would rather learn a page of "Walker's Pronouncing Dictionary," than try to remember the variety of directions which I have had to put on my letters to Mr. B. during the last three years. Last summer it pleased him to remove to a beautiful village not ten miles out of London, where there is a railway station. Thither his friend sought him. (I do not now speak of the following scent there had been through three or four different lodgings, where Mr. B. had been residing, before his country friend ascertained that he was now lodging at R—.) He spent the morning in making inquiries as to Mr. B.'s whereabouts in the village; but many gentlemen were lodging there for the summer, and neither butcher nor baker could inform him where Mr. B. was staying; his letters were unknown at the post-office, which was accounted for by the circumstance of their always being directed to his office in town. At last the country friend sauntered back to the railway office, and while he waited for the train he made inquiry, as a last resource, of the book-keeper at the station. "No, sir, I cannot tell you where Mr. B. lodges—so many gentlemen go by the trains; but I have no doubt but that the person standing by that pillar can inform you." The individual to whom he directed the inquirer's attention had the appearance of a tradesman—respectable enough, yet with no pretensions to "gentility," and had, apparently, no more urgent employment than lazily watching the passengers who came dropping in to the station. However, when he was spoken to, he answered civilly and promptly. "Mr. B.? Tall gentleman, with light hair? Yes, sir, I know Mr. B. He lodges at No. 8 Morton Villas—has done these three weeks or more; but you'll not find him there, sir, now. He went to town by the eleven o'clock train, and does not usually return until the half-past four train."

The country friend had no time to lose in returning to the village, to ascertain the truth of this statement. He thanked his informant, and said he would call on Mr. B. at his office in town; but before he left R—station, he asked the book-keeper who the person was to whom he had referred him for information as to his friend's place of residence. "One of the detective police, sir," was the answer. I need hardly say, that Mr. B., not without a little surprise, confirmed the accuracy of the policeman's report in every particular.

When I heard this anecdote of my cousin and his friend, I thought that there could be no more romances written on the same kind of plot as Caleb Williams; the principal interest of which, to the superficial reader, consists in the alternation of hope and fear, that the hero may, or may not, escape his pursuer. It is long since I have read the story, and I forget the name of the offended and injured gentleman, whose privacy Caleb has invaded; but I know that his pursuit of Caleb—his detection of the various hiding-places of the latter—his following up of slight clews—all, in fact, depended upon his own energy, sagacity, and perseverance. The interest was caused by the struggle of man against man; and the uncertainty as to which would ultimately be successful in his object; the unrelenting pursuer, or the ingenious Caleb, who seeks by every device to conceal himself. Now, in 1851, the offended master would set the detective police to work; there would be no doubt as to their success; the only question would be as to the time that would elapse before the hiding-place could be detected, and that could not be a question long. It is no longer a struggle between man and man, but between a vast organised machinery, and a weak, solitary individual; we have no hopes, no fears—only certainty. But if the materials of pursuit and evasion, as long as the chase is confined to England, are taken away from the storehouse of the romancer, at any rate we can no more be haunted by the idea of the possibility of mysterious disappearances; and anyone who has associated much with those who were alive at the end of the last century, can testify that there was some reason for such fears.

When I was a child I was sometimes permitted to accompany a relation to drink tea with a very clever old lady, of one hundred and twenty—or, so I thought then; I now think she, perhaps, was only about seventy. She was lively and intelligent, and had seen and known much that was worth narrating. She was a cousin of the Sneyds, the family whence Mr. Edgeworth took two of his wives; had known Major Andre; had mixed in the old Whig Society that the beautiful Duchess of Devonshire and "Buff and Blue Mrs. Crewe" gathered round them; her father had been one of the early patrons of the lovely Miss Linley. I name these facts to show that she was too intelligent and cultivated by association, as well as by natural powers, to lend an over easy credence to the marvelous; and yet I have heard her relate stories of disappearances which haunted my imagination longer than any tale of wonder. One of her stories was this:—Her father's estate lay in Shropshire, and his park gates opened right on to a scattered village, of which he was landlord. The houses formed a straggling, irregular street—here a garden, next a gable end of a farm, there a row of cottages, and so on. Now, at the end of the house or cottage lived a very respectable man and his wife. They were well known in the village, and were esteemed for the patient attention which they paid to the husband's father, a paralytic old man. In winter his chair was near the fire; in summer they carried him out into the open space in front of the house to bask in the sunshine, and to receive what placid amusement he could from watching the little passings to and fro of the villagers. He could not move from his bed to his chair without help. One hot and sultry June day all the village turned out to the hay fields. Only the very old and the very young remained.

The old father of whom I have spoken was carried out to bask in the sunshine that afternoon, as usual, and his son and daughter-in-law went to the hay making. But when they came home, in the early evening, their paralyzed father had disappeared—was gone! and from that day forwards nothing more was ever heard of him. The old lady, who told this story, said, with the quietness that always marked the simplicity of her narrations, that every inquiry which her father could make was made, and that it could never be accounted for. No one had observed any stranger in the village; no small household robbery, to which the old man might have been supposed an obstacle, had been committed in his son's dwelling that afternoon. The son and daughter-in-law (noted, too, for their attention to the helpless father) had been afield among all the neighbors the whole of the time. In short, it never was accounted for, and left a painful impression on many minds.

I will answer for it, the detective police would have ascertained every fact relating to it in a week.

This story from its mystery was painful, but had no consequences to make it tragical. The next which I shall tell, (and although traditionary, these anecdotes of disappearances which I relate in this paper are correctly repeated, and were believed by my informants to be strictly true,) had consequences, and melancholy ones, too. The scene of it is in a little country town, surrounded by the estates of several gentlemen of large property. About a hundred years ago there lived in this small town an attorney, with his mother and sisters. He was agent for one of the 'squires near, and received rents for him on stated days, which, of course, were well known. He went at these times to a small public house, perhaps five miles from—, where the tenants met him, paid their rents, and were entertained at dinner afterwards. One night he did not return from this festivity. He never returned. The gentleman whose agent he was employed the Dogberrys of the time to find him and the missing cash; the mother, whose support and comfort he was, sought him with all the perseverance of faithful love. But he never returned, and by and by the rumor spread that he must have gone abroad with the money; his mother heard the whispers all around her, and could not disprove it; and so her heart broke, and she died. Years after, I think as many as fifty, the well-to-do butcher and grazier of—died; but, before his death, he confessed that he had waylaid Mr.—on the heath close to the town, almost within call of his own house, intending only to rob him; but meeting with more resistance than he anticipated, had been provoked to stab him, and had buried him that very night deep under the loose sand of the heath. There his skeleton was found; but too late for his poor mother to know that his fame was cleared. His sister, too, was dead, unmarried, for no one liked the possibilities which might arise from being connected with the family. None cared if he was guilty or innocent now.

If our detective police had only been in existence!

This last is hardly a story of unaccounted for disappearance. It is only unaccounted for in one generation. But disappearances never to be accounted for on any supposition are not uncommon, among the traditions of the last century. I have heard (and I think I have heard it in one of the earlier numbers of "Chambers's Journal") of a marriage which took place in Lincolnshire about the year 1750. It was not then *de riguer* that the happy couple should set out on a wedding journey; but instead, they and their friends had a merry, jovial dinner at the house of either bride or groom; and in this instance the whole party adjourned to the bridegroom's residence, and dispersed; some to ramble in the garden, some to rest in the house until the dinner hour. The bridegroom, it is to be supposed, was with his bride, when he was suddenly summoned away by a domestic, who said that a stranger wished to speak to him; and henceforward he was never seen more. The same tradition hangs about an old deserted Welsh hall, standing in a wood near Festiniog; there, too, the bridegroom was sent for to give audience to a stranger on his wedding day, and disappeared from the face of the earth from that time; but there they tell in addition, that the bride lived long,—that she passed her threescore years and ten, but that daily, during all those years, while there was light of sun or moon, to lighten the earth, she sat watching,—watching at one particular window, which commanded a view of the approach to the house. Her whole faculties, her whole mental powers, became absorbed in that weary watching; long before she died she was childish, and only conscious of one wish—to sit in that long, high window, and watch the road along which he might come. She was as faithful as Evangeline, if pensive and inglorious.

That these two similar stories of disappearance on a wedding-day "obtained," as the French say, shows us that anything which adds to our facility of communication, and organization of means, adds to our security of life. Only let a bridegroom try to disappear from an untamed *Katherine* of a bride, and he will soon be brought home like a recreant coward, overtaken by the electric telegraph, and clutched back to his fate by a detective policeman.

Two more stories of disappearance, and I have done. I will give you the last in date first, because it is the most melancholy; and we will wind up cheerfully (after a fashion).

Sometime between 1820 and 1830, there lived in North Shields a respectable old woman and her son, who was trying to struggle into sufficient knowledge of medicine to go out as ship surgeon in a Baltic vessel, and perhaps in this manner to earn money enough to spend a session in Edinburgh. He was furthered in all his plans by the late benevolent Dr. G—, of that town. I believe the usual premium was not required in his case; the young man did many useful errands and offices which a finer young gentleman would have considered beneath him; and he resided with his mother in one of the alleys (or "chares") which lead down from the main street of North Shields to the river. Dr. G—had been with a patient all night, and left her very early on a winter's morning to return home to bed; but first he stepped down to his apprentice's home, and bade him get up, and follow him to his own house, where some medicine was to be mixed, and then taken to the lady. Accordingly the poor lad came, prepared the dose, and set off with it sometime between five and six on a winter's morning. He was never seen again. Dr. G—waited, thinking he was at his mother's house; she waited, considering that he had gone to his day's work. And meanwhile, as people remembered afterwards, the small vessel bound to Edinburgh sailed out of port. The mother expected him back her whole life long; but some years afterwards occurred the discoveries of the Hare and Burke horrors, and people seemed to gain a dark glimpse at his fate; but I never heard that it was fully ascertained, or indeed, more than surmised. I ought to add, that all who knew him spoke emphatically as to his steadiness of purpose and conduct, so as to render it improbable in the highest degree that he had run off to sea, or suddenly changed his plan of life in any way.

My last story is one of a disappearance which was accounted for after many years. There is a considerable street in Manchester, leading from the centre of the town to some of the suburbs. This street is called at one part Garratt, and afterwards, where it emerges into gentility and comparatively country, Brook Street. It derives its former name from an old black-and-white hall of the time of Richard the Third, or thereabouts, to judge from the style of building; they have closed in what is left of the old hall now; but a few years since this old house was visible from the main road; it stood low, on some vacant ground, and appeared to be half in ruins. I believe it was occupied by several poor families, who rented tenements in the tumble-down dwelling. But formerly it was Gerard Hall, (what a difference between Gerard and Garratt!) and was surrounded by a park, with a clear brook running through it, with pleasant fish ponds (the name of these was preserved, until very lately, on a street near), orchards, dove-cotes, and similar appurtenances to the manor-houses of former days. I am almost sure that the family to whom it belonged were Mosleys; probably a branch of the tree of the lord of the Manor of Manchester. Any topographical work of the last century relating to their district would give the name of the last proprietor of the old stock, and it is to him that my story refers.

Many years ago there lived in Manchester two old maiden ladies, of high respectability. All their lives had been spent in the town, and they were fond of relating the changes which had taken place within their recollection; which extended back to seventy or eighty years from the present time. They knew much of its traditionary history from their father, as well; who, with his father before him, had been respectable attorneys in Manchester, during the greater part of the last century; they were, also, agents for several of the county families, who, driven from their old possessions by the enlargement of the town, found some compensation in the increased value of any land which they might choose to sell. Consequently the Messrs. S—, father and son, were conveyancers in good repute, and acquainted with several secret pieces of family history; one of which related to Garratt Hall.

The owner of this estate, sometime in the first half of the last century, married young; he and his wife had several children, and lived together in a quiet state of happiness for many years. At last, business of some kind took the husband up to London; a week's journey those days. He wrote, and announced his arrival; I do not think he ever wrote again. He seemed to be swallowed up in the abyss of the metropolis, for no friend (and the lady had many and powerful friends) could ever ascertain for her what had become of him; the prevalent idea was that he had been attacked by some of the street robbers who prowled about in those days, that he had resisted, and had been murdered. His wife gradually gave up all hopes of seeing him again, and devoted herself to the care of her children; and so they went on, tranquilly enough, until the heir became of age, when certain deeds were necessary before he could legally take possession of the property. These deeds Mr. S—(the family lawyer) stated had been given up by him into the missing gentleman's keeping just before the last mysterious journey to London, with which I think they were in some way concerned. It was possible that they were still in existence, someone in London might have them in possession, and be either conscious or unconscious of their importance. At any rate, Mr. S—'s advice to his client was that he should put an advertisement in the London papers, worded so skillfully that anyone who might hold the important documents should understand to what it referred, and no one else. This was accordingly done; and although repeated, at intervals, for some time, it met with no success. But, at last, a mysterious answer was sent, to the effect that the deeds were in existence, and should be given up; but only on certain conditions, and to the heir himself. The young man, in consequence, went up to London; and adjourned, according to directions, to an old house in Barbacan; where he was told by a man, apparently awaiting him, that he must submit to be blindfolded, and must follow his guidance. He was taken through several long passages before he left the house; at the termination of one of these he was put into a sedan chair, and carried about for an hour or more; he always reported that there were many turnings, and that he imagined he was set down finally not very far from his starting-point.

When his eyes were unbandaged, he was in a decent sitting-room, with tokens of family occupation lying about. A middle-aged gentleman entered, and told him that, until a certain time had elapsed (which should be indicated to him in a particular way, but of which the length was not then named), he must swear to secrecy as to the means by which he obtained possession of the deeds. This oath was taken, and then the gentleman, not without some emotion, acknowledged himself to be the missing father of the heir. It seems that he had fallen in love with a damsel, a friend of the person with whom he lodged. To this young woman he had represented himself as unmarried; she listened willingly to his wooing, and her father, who was a shopkeeper in the city, was not averse to the match, as the Lancashire 'squire had a goodly presence, and many similar qualities, which the shopkeeper thought might be acceptable to his customers. The bargain was struck; the descendant of a knightly race married the only daughter of the city shopkeeper, and became a junior partner in the business. He told his son that he had never repented the step he had taken; that his lowly-born wife was sweet, docile and affectionate; that his family by her was large; and that he and they were thriving and happy. He inquired after his first (or rather, I should say, his true) wife with friendly affection; approved of what she had done with regard to his estate, and the education of his children; but said that he considered he was dead to her, as she was to him. When he really died he promised that a particular message, the nature of which he specified, should be sent to his son at Garratt; until then they would not hear more of each other; for it was of no use attempting to trace him under his incognito, even if the oath did not render such an attempt forbidden. I dare say the youth had no great desire to trace out the father, who had been one in name only. He returned to Lancashire; took possession of the property at Manchester; and many years elapsed before he received the mysterious intimation of his father's real death. After that he named the particulars connected with the recovery of the title-deeds to Mr. S—, and one or two intimate friends. When the family became extinct, or removed from Garratt, it became no longer any very closely kept secret, and I was told the tale of the disappearance by Miss S—, the aged daughter of the family agent.

Once more, let me say, I am thankful I live in the days of the detective police; if I am murdered, or commit a bigamy, at any rate my friends will have the comfort of knowing all about it.

XXI

LOADED DICE

Several years ago I made a tour through some of the southern counties of England with a friend. We travelled in an open carriage, stopping for a few hours a day, or a week, as it might be, wherever there was anything to be seen; and we generally got through one stage before breakfast, because it gave our horses rest, and ourselves the chance of enjoying the brown bread, new milk, and fresh eggs of those country roadside inns, which are fast becoming subjects for archæological investigation.

One evening my friend said, "Tomorrow, we will breakfast at T—. I want to inquire about a family named Lovell, who used to live there. I met the husband and wife and two lovely children, one summer, at Exmouth. We became very intimate, and I thought them particularly interesting people, but I have never seen them since."

The next morning's sun shone as brightly as heart could desire, and after a delightful drive, we reached the outskirts of the town about nine o'clock.

"O, what a pretty inn!" said I, as we approached a small white house, with a sign swinging in front of it, and a flower garden on one side.

"Stop, John," cried my friend; "we shall get a much cleaner breakfast here than in the town, I dare say; and if there is anything to be seen there, we can walk to it;" so we alighted, and were shown into a neat little parlor, with white curtains, where an unexceptionable rural breakfast was soon placed before us.

"Pray do you happen to know anything of a family called Lovell?" inquired my friend, whose name, by the way, was Markham. "Mr. Lovell was a clergyman."

"Yes, ma'am," answered the girl who attended us, apparently the landlord's daughter, "Mr. Lovell is the vicar of our parish."

"Indeed! And does he live near here?"

"Yes, ma'am, he lives at the vicarage. It is just down that lane opposite, about a quarter of a mile from here; or you can go across the fields, if you please, to where you see that tower, it's close by there."

"And which is the pleasantest road?" inquired Mrs. Markham.

"Well, ma'am, I think by the fields is the pleasantest, if you don't mind a stile or two; and, besides, you get the best view of the abbey by going that way."

"Is that tower we see part of the abbey?"

"Yes, ma'am," answered the girl; "and the vicarage is just the other side of it."

Armed with these instructions, as soon as we had finished our breakfast we started across the fields, and after a pleasant walk of twenty minutes we found ourselves in an old churchyard, amongst a cluster of the most picturesque ruins we had ever seen. With the exception of the gray tower, which we had espied from the inn, and which had doubtless been the belfry, the remains were not considerable. There was the outer wall of the chancel, and the broken step that had led to the high altar, and there were sections of aisles, and part of a cloister, all gracefully festooned with mosses and ivy; whilst mingled with the grass-grown graves of the prosaic dead, there were the massive tombs of the Dame Margerys and the Sir Hildebrands of more romantic periods. All was ruin and decay; but such poetic ruins! Such picturesque decay! And just beyond the tall great tower, there was the loveliest, smiling little garden, and the prettiest cottage, that imagination could picture. The day was so bright, the grass so green, the flowers so gay, the air so balmy with their sweet perfumes, the birds sang so cheerily in the apple and cherry trees, that all nature seemed rejoicing.

"Well," said my friend, as she seated herself on the fragment of a pillar, and looked around her, "now that I see this place, I understand the sort of people the Lovells were."

"What sort of people were they?" said I.

"Why, as I said before, interesting people. In the first place, they were both extremely handsome."

"But the locality had nothing to do with their good looks, I presume," said I.

"I am not sure of that," she answered; "when there is the least foundation of taste or intellect to set out with, the beauty of external nature, and the picturesque accidents that harmonise with it, do, I am persuaded, by their gentle and elevating influences on the mind, make the handsome handsomer, and the ugly less ugly. But it was not alone the good looks of the Lovells that struck me, but their air of refinement and high breeding, and I should say high birth—though I know nothing about their extraction—combined with their undisguised poverty and as evident contentment. Now, I can understand such people finding here an appropriate home, and being satisfied with their small share of this world's goods; because here the dreams of romance writers about love in a cottage might be somewhat realized; poverty might be graceful and poetical here; and then, you know, they have no rent to pay."

"Very true," said I; "but suppose they had sixteen daughters, like a half-pay officer I once met on board a steam packet?"

"That would spoil it, certainly," said Mrs. Markham; "but let us hope they have not. When I knew them they had only two children, a boy and a girl, called Charles and Emily; two of the prettiest creatures I ever beheld."

As my friend thought it yet rather early for a visit, we had remained chattering in this way for more than an hour, sometimes seated on a tombstone, or a fallen column; sometimes peering amongst the carved fragments that were scattered about the ground, and sometimes looking over the hedge into the little garden, the wicket of which was immediately behind the tower. The weather being warm, most of the windows of the vicarage were open, and the blinds were all down; we had not yet seen a soul stirring, and were just wondering whether we might venture to present ourselves at the door, when a strain of distant music struck upon our ears. "Hark!" I said; "How exquisite! It was the only thing wanting to complete the charm."

"It is a military band, I think," said Mrs. Markham; "you know we passed some barracks before we reached the inn."

Nearer and nearer drew the sounds, solemn and slow; the band was evidently approaching by the green lane that skirted the fields we had come by. "Hush!" said I, laying my hand on my friend's arm, with a strange sinking of the heart; "they are playing the Dead March in Saul! Don't you hear the muffled drums? It's a funeral, but where's the grave?"

"There!" said she, pointing to a spot close under the hedge where some earth had been thrown up; but the aperture was covered with a plank, probably to prevent accidents.

There are few ceremonies in life at once so touching, so impressive, so sad, and yet so beautiful as a soldier's funeral! Ordinary funerals, with their unwieldy hearses and feathers, and the absurd looking mutes, and the "inky cloaks" and weepers of hired mourners, always seem to me like a mockery of the dead; the appointments border so closely on the grotesque; they are so little in keeping with the true, the only view of death that can render life endurable!

There is such a tone of exaggerated—forced, heavy, overacted gravity about the whole thing, that one had need to have a deep personal interest involved in the scene, to be able to shut one's eyes to the burlesque side of it. But a military funeral, how different! There you see death in life and life in death! There is nothing overstrained, nothing overdone. At once simple and solemn, decent and decorous, consoling, yet sad. The chief mourners, at best, are generally true mourners, for they have lost a brother with whom "they sat but yesterday at meat," and whilst they are comparing memories, recalling how merry they had many a day been together, and the solemn tones of that sublime music float upon the air, we can imagine the freed and satisfied soul wafted on those harmonious breathings to its heavenly home; and our hearts are melted, our imaginations exalted, our faith invigorated, and we come away the better for what we have seen.

I believe some such reflections as these were passing through our minds, for we both remained silent and listening, till the swinging to of the little wicket, which communicated with the garden, aroused us; but nobody appeared, and the tower being at the moment betwixt us and it, we could not see who had entered. Almost at the same moment a man came in from a gate on the opposite side, and advancing to where the earth was thrown up, lifted the plank and discovered the newly-made grave. He was soon followed by some boys, and several respectable-looking persons came into the enclosure, whilst nearer and nearer drew the sound of the muffled drums; and now we descried the firing party and their officer, who led the procession with their arms reversed, each man wearing above the elbow a piece of black crape and a small bow of white satin ribbon; the band still playing that solemn strain. Then came the coffin, borne by six soldiers. Six officers bore up the pall, all quite young men; and on the coffin lay the shako, sword, side-belt, and white gloves of the deceased. A long train of mourners marched two and two, in open file, the privates first, the officers last. Sorrow was imprinted on every face; there was no unseemly chattering, no wandering eyes; if a word was exchanged, it was in a whisper, and the sad shake of the head showed of whom they were discoursing. All this we observed as they marched through the lane that skirted one side of the churchyard. As they neared the gate the band ceased to play.

"See there!" said Mrs. Markham, directing my attention to the cottage; "There comes Mr. Lovell. O, how he has changed!" and whilst she spoke, the clergyman, entering by the wicket, advanced to meet the procession at the gate, where he commenced reading the funeral service as he moved backwards towards the grave, round which the firing party, leaning on their firelocks, now formed. Then came those awful words, "Ashes to ashes, dust to dust," the hollow sound of the earth upon the coffin, and three volleys fired over the grave finished the solemn ceremony.

When the procession entered the churchyard, we had retired behind the broken wall of the chancel, whence, without being observed, we had watched the whole scene with intense interest. Just as the words "Ashes to ashes! Dust to dust!" were pronounced, I happened to raise my eyes towards the gray tower, and then, peering through one of the narrow slits, I saw the face of a man—such a face! Never to my latest day can I forget the expression of those features! If ever there was despair and anguish written on a human countenance, it was there! And yet so young! So beautiful! A cold chill ran through my veins as I pressed Mrs. Markham's arm. "Look up at the tower!" I whispered.

"My God! What can it be?" she answered, turning quite pale. "And Mr. Lovell, did you observe how his voice shook? At first I thought it was illness; but he seems bowed down with grief. Every face looks awestruck! There must be some tragedy here—something more than the death of an individual!"

and fearing, under this impression, that our visit might prove untimely, we resolved to return to the inn, and endeavor to discover if anything unusual had really occurred. Before we moved I looked up at the narrow slit—the face was no longer there; but as we passed round to the other side of the tower, we saw a tall, slender figure, attired in a loose coat, pass slowly through the wicket, cross the garden, and enter the house. We only caught a glimpse of the profile; the head hung down upon the breast; the eyes were bent upon the ground; but we knew it was the same face we had seen above.

We went back to the inn, where our inquiries elicited some information which made us wish to know more; but it was not till we went into the town that we obtained the following details of this mournful drama, of which we had thus accidentally witnessed one impressive scene.

Mr. Lovell, as Mrs. Markham had conjectured, was a man of good family, but no fortune; he might have had a large one, could he have made up his mind to marry Lady Elizabeth Wentworth, a bride selected for him by a wealthy uncle who proposed to make him his heir; but preferring poverty with Emily Dering, he was disinherited. He never repented his choice, although he remained vicar of a small parish, and a poor man all his life. The two children whom Mrs. Markham had seen were the only ones they had, and through the excellent management of Mrs. Lovell, and the moderation of her husband's desires, they had enjoyed an unusual degree of happiness in this sort of graceful poverty, till the young Charles and Emily were grown up, and it was time to think what was to be done with them. The son had been prepared for Oxford by the father, and the daughter, under the tuition of her mother, was remarkably well educated and accomplished; but it became necessary to consider the future: Charles must be sent to college, since the only chance of finding a provision for him was in the church, although the expense of maintaining him there could be ill afforded; so, in order in some degree to balance the outlay, it was, after much deliberation, agreed that Emily should accept a situation as governess in London. The proposal was made by herself, and the rather consented to, that, in case of the death of her parents, she would almost inevitably have had to seek some such means of subsistence. These partings were the first sorrows that had reached the Lovells.

At first all went well. Charles was not wanting in ability nor in a moderate degree of application: and Emily wrote cheerily of her new life. She was kindly received, well treated, and associated with the family on the footing of a friend. Neither did further experience seem to diminish her satisfaction. She saw a great many gay people, some of whom she named; and, amongst the rest, there not unfrequently appeared the name of Herbert. Mr. Herbert was in the army, and being a distant connection of the family with whom she resided, was a frequent visitor at their house. "She was sure papa and mamma would like him." Once the mother smiled, and said she hoped Emily was not falling in love; but no more was thought of it. In the mean time Charles had found out that there was time for many things at Oxford, besides study. He was naturally fond of society, and had a remarkable capacity for excelling in all kinds of games. He was agreeable, lively, exceedingly handsome, and sang charmingly, having been trained in part singing by his mother. No young man at Oxford was more *fêté*; but alas! he was very poor, and poverty poisoned all his enjoyments. For some time he resisted temptation; but after a terrible struggle—for he adored his family—he gave way, and ran in debt, and although his imprudence only augmented his misery, he had not resolution to retrace his steps, but advanced further and further on this broad road to ruin, so that he had come home for the vacation shortly before our visit to T—, threatened with all manner of annoyances if he did not carry back a sufficient sum to satisfy his most clamorous creditors. He had assured them he would do so, but where was he to get the money? Certainly not from his parents; he well knew they had it not; nor had he a friend in the world from whom he could hope assistance in such an emergency. In his despair he often thought of running away—going to Australia, America, New Zealand, anywhere; but he had not even the means to do this. He suffered indescribable tortures, and saw no hope of relief.

It was just at this period that Herbert's regiment happened to be quartered at T—. Charles had occasionally seen his name in his sister's letters, and heard that there was a Herbert now in the barracks, but he was ignorant whether or not it was the same person; and when he accidentally fell into the society of some of the junior officers, and was invited by Herbert himself to dine at the mess, pride prevented his ascertaining the fact. He did not wish to betray that his sister was a governess. Herbert, however, knew full well that their visitor was the brother of Emily Lovell, but partly for reasons of his own, and partly because he penetrated the weakness of the other, he abstained from mentioning her name.

Now, this town of T—was, and probably is, about the dullest quarter in all England. The officers hated it; there was no flirting, no dancing, no hunting, no anything. Not a man of them knew what to do with himself. The old ones wandered about and played at whist, the young ones took to hazard and three-card loo, playing at first for moderate stakes, but soon getting on to high ones. Two or three civilians of the neighborhood joined the party, Charles Lovell among the rest. Had they begun with playing high, he would have been excluded for want of funds; but whilst they played low, he won, so that when they increased the stakes, trusting to a continuance of his good fortune, he was eager to go on with them. Neither did his luck altogether desert him; on the whole he rather won than lost: but he foresaw that one bad night would break him, and he should be obliged to retire, forfeiting his amusement and mortifying his pride. It was just at this crisis, that one night, an accident, which caused him to win a considerable sum, set him upon the notion of turning chance into certainty. Whilst shuffling the cards he dropped the ace of spades into his lap, caught it up, replaced it in the pack, and dealt it to himself. No one else had seen the card, no observation was made, and a terrible thought came into his head!

Whether loo or hazard was played, Charles Lovell had, night after night, a most extraordinary run of luck. He won large sums, and saw before him the early prospect of paying his debts and clearing all his difficulties.

Amongst the young men who played at the table, some had plenty of money and cared little for their losses; but others were not so well off, and one of these was Edward Herbert. He, too, was the son of poor parents who had straightened themselves to put him in the army, and it was with infinite difficulty and privation that his widowed mother had amassed the needful sum to purchase for him a company, which was now becoming vacant. The retiring officer's papers were already sent in, and Herbert's money was lodged at Cox and Greenwood's; but before the answer from the Horse Guards arrived, he had lost every sixpence. Nearly the whole sum had become the property of Charles Lovell.

Herbert was a fine young man, honorable, generous, impetuous, and endowed with an acute sense of shame. He determined instantly to pay his debts, but he knew that his own prospects were ruined for life; he wrote to the agents to send him the money and withdraw his name from the list of purchasers. But how was he to support his mother's grief? How meet the eye of the girl he loved? She, who he knew adored him, and whose hand, it was agreed between them, he should ask of her parents as soon as he was gazetted a captain! The anguish of mind he suffered threw him into a fever, and he lay for several days betwixt life and death, and happily unconscious of its misery.

Meantime, another scene was being enacted elsewhere. The officers, who night after night found themselves losers, had not for some time entertained the least idea of foul play, but at length, one of them observing something suspicious, began to watch, and satisfied himself, by a peculiar method adopted by Lovell in "throwing his mains," that he was the culprit. His suspicions were whispered from one to another, till they nearly all entertained them, with the exception of Herbert, who, being looked upon as Lovell's most especial friend, was not told. So unwilling were these young men to blast forever the character of the visitor whom they had so much liked, and to strike a fatal blow at the happiness and respectability of his family, that they were hesitating how to proceed, whether to openly accuse him or privately reprove and expel him, when Herbert's heavy loss decided the question.

Herbert himself, overwhelmed with despair, had quitted the room, the rest were still seated around the table, when having given each other a signal, one of them, called Frank Houston, arose and said: "Gentlemen, it gives me great pain to have to call your attention to a very strange, a very distressing circumstance. For some time past there has been an extraordinary run of luck in one direction—we have all observed it—all remarked on it. Mr. Herbert has at this moment retired a heavy loser. There is, indeed, as far as I know, but one winner amongst us; but one, and he a winner to a considerable amount; the rest are all losers. God forbid that I should rashly accuse any man! Lightly blast any man's character! But I am bound to say, that I fear the money we have lost has not been fairly won. There has been foul play! I forbear to name the party—the facts sufficiently indicate him."

Who would not have pitied Lovell, when, livid with horror and conscious guilt, he vainly tried to say something?

"Indeed—I assure you—I never"—but words would not come; he faultered and rushed out of the room in a transport of agony. They did pity him; and when he was gone, agreed amongst themselves to hush up the affair; but unfortunately, the civilians of the party, who had not been let into the secret, took up his defence. They not only believed the accusation unfounded, but felt it as an affront offered to their townsman; they blustered about it a good deal, and there was nothing left for it but to appoint a committee of investigation. Alas! the evidence was overwhelming! It turned out that the dice and cards had been supplied by Lovell. The former, still on the table, were found on examination to be loaded. In fact, he had had a pair as a curiosity long in his possession, and had obtained others from a disreputable character at Oxford. No doubt remained of his guilt.

All this while Herbert had been too ill to be addressed on the subject; but symptoms of recovery were now beginning to appear; and as nobody was aware that he had any particular interest in the Lovell family, the affair was communicated to him. At first he refused to believe in his friend's guilt, and became violently irritated. His informants assured him they would be too happy to find they were mistaken, but that since the inquiry no hope of such an issue remained, and he sank into a gloomy silence.

On the following morning, when his servant came to his room door, he found it locked. When, at the desire of the surgeon, it was broken open, Herbert was found a corpse, and a discharged pistol lying beside him. An inquest sat upon the body, and the verdict brought in was *Temporary Insanity*. There never was one more just.

Preparations were now made for the funeral—that funeral which we had witnessed; but before the day appointed for it arrived, another chapter of this sad story was unfolded.

When Charles left the barracks on that fatal night, instead of going home, he passed the dark hours in wandering wildly about the country; but when morning dawned, fearing the eye of man, he returned to the vicarage, and slunk unobserved to his chamber. When he did not appear at breakfast, his mother sought him in his room, where she found him in bed. He said he was very ill—and so indeed he was—and begged to be left alone; but as he was no better on the following day, she insisted on sending for medical advice. The doctor found him with all those physical symptoms that are apt to supervene from great anxiety of mind; and saying he could get no sleep, Charles requested to have some laudanum; but the physician was on his guard, for although the parties concerned wished to keep the thing private, some rumors had got abroad that awakened his caution.

The parents, meanwhile, had not the slightest anticipation of the thunderbolt that was about to fall upon them. They lived a very retired life, were acquainted with none of the officers, and they were even ignorant of the amount of their son's intimacy with the regiment. Thus, when news of Herbert's lamentable death reached them, the mother said to her son, "Charles, did you know a young man in the barracks called Herbert; a lieutenant, I believe? By the bye, I hope it's not Emily's Mr. Herbert."

"Did I know him?" said Charles, turning suddenly towards her, for, under pretence that the light annoyed him, he always lay with his face to the wall. "Why do you ask, mother?"

"Because he's dead. He had a fever and—"

"Herbert dead!" cried Charles, suddenly sitting up in the bed.

"Yes, he had a fever, and it is supposed he was delirious, for he blew out his brains; there is a report that he had been playing high, and lost a great deal of money. What's the matter dear? O, Charles, I shouldn't have told you! I was not aware that you knew him?"

"Fetch my father here, and mother, you come back with him!" said Charles, speaking with a strange sternness of tone, and wildly motioning her out of the room.

When the parents came, he bade them sit down beside him; and then, with a degree of remorse and anguish that no words could portray, he told them all; whilst they, with blanched cheeks and fainting hearts, listened to the dire confession.

"And here I am," he exclaimed, as he ended, "a cowardly scoundrel, that has not dared to die! O Herbert! happy, happy Herbert! Would I were with you!"

At that moment the door opened, and a beautiful, bright, smiling, joyous face peeped in. It was Emily Lovell, the beloved daughter, the adored sister, arrived from London in compliance with a letter received a few days previously from Herbert, wherein he had told her that by the time she received it, he would be a captain. She had come to introduce him to her parents as her affianced husband. She feared no refusal; well she knew how rejoiced they would be to see her the wife of so kind and honorable a man. But they were ignorant of all this, and in the fulness of their agony, the cup of woe ran over, and she drank of the draught. They told her all before she had been five minutes in the room. How else could they account for their tears, their confusion, their bewilderment, their despair?

Before Herbert's funeral took place, Emily Lovell was lying betwixt life and death in a brain fever. Under the influence of a feeling easily to be comprehended, thirsting for a self-imposed torture, that by its very poignancy should relieve the dead weight of wretchedness that lay upon his breast, Charles crept from his bed, and slipping on a loose coat that hung in his room, he stole across the garden to the tower, whence, through the arrow slit, he witnessed the burial of his sister's lover, whom he had hastened to the grave.

Here terminates our sad story. We left T—on the following morning, and it was two or three years before any farther intelligence of the Lovell family reached us. All we then heard was, that Charles had gone, a self-condemned exile, to Australia; and that Emily had insisted on accompanying him thither.

Yellowback range available...

1. The Old Man in the Corner by Orczy, Baroness Emma
2. The Complete Max Carrados Vol 1 by Bramah, Ernest
3. The Complete Max Carrados Vol 2 by Bramah, Ernest

THE ARSÈNE LUPIN SERIES BY LEBLANC, MAURICE:

4. Arsène Lupin 1: The Extraordinary Adventures of Arsène Lupin - Gentleman Burglar
5. Arsène Lupin 2: Arsène Lupin vs. Herlock Sholmes
6. Arsène Lupin 3. The Hollow Needle
7. Arsène Lupin 4: 813
8. Arsène Lupin 5: The Crystal Stopper
9. Arsène Lupin 6: The Confessions of Arsène Lupin
10. Arsène Lupin 7: The Teeth of the Tiger
11. Arsène Lupin 8: The Shell Shard (aka The Woman of Mystery)
12. Arsène Lupin 9: The Return of Arsène Lupin (aka The Golden Triangle)
13. Arsène Lupin 10: The secret of Sarek (aka Island of Thirty Coffins)
14. Arsène Lupin 11: The Eight Strokes of the Clock
15. Arsène Lupin 12: The Secret Tomb
16. Arsène Lupin 13: The Countess of Cagliostro (aka Memoirs of Arsène Lupin)
17. Arsène Lupin (bonus book): Arsène Lupin (novelised by Edgar Jepson from LeBlanc's original play)

18. The Complete Raffles by Hornung, E. W.
19. The Mysterious Mickey Finn by Paul, Eliott
20. You Play the Black and the Red Comes Up by Hallas, Richard
21. The Mr. Moto Omnibus Vol 1 by Marquand, John P.
22. The Mr. Moto Omnibus Vol 2 by Marquand, John P.
23. The Complete Father Brown Vol 1 (with original illustrations) by Chesterton, G. K.
24. The Complete Father Brown Vol 2 (with original illustrations) by Chesterton, G. K.
25. A Peter Wimsey omnibus: Murder Must Advertise & The Nine Tailors by Sayers, Dorothy L.
26. Was it Murder? by Hilton, James
27. The Complete Just Men Volume 1 by Wallace, Edgar
28. The Complete Just Men Volume 2 by Wallace, Edgar
29. Carnacki by Hodgson, William Hope
30. Grey Mask by Wentworth, Patricia
31. The Case With Nine Solutions by Connington, J. J.
32. Murder by Matchlight by Lorac, E. C. R.
33. The Crossword Mystery by Punshon, E. R.
34. The Cask by Crofts, Freeman Wills
35. The Bells of Old Bailey by Bowers, Dorothy
36. Crime Unlimited by Hume, David
37. The A. A. Milne Mystery Omnibus (contains: The Red house and Four days' wonder) by Milne, A. A.
38. She Faded into Air by White, Ethel Lina
39. The Wheel Spins by White, Ethel Lina
40. The Spiral Staircase by White, Ethel Lina
41. Murder of a Lady by Wynne, Anthony
42. Thirteen Guests by Farjeon, J. Jefferson
43. The Daughter of Time by Tey, Josephine
44. The Man in the Queue by Tey, Josephine
45. A Shilling for Candles by Tey, Josephine
46. The Franchise Affair by Tey, Josephine
47. Tragedy at Law by Hare, Cyril
48. The Moonstone by Collins, Wilkie
49. The Woman in White by Collins, Wilkie
50. The Circular Staircase by Rinehart, Mary Roberts
51. The Benson Murder Case by Van Dine, S. S.
52. The Philip Marlowe Omnibus by Chandler, Raymond
53. Monsieur Lecoq by Gaboriau, Emile
54. Aurora Floyd by Braddon, Mary Elizabeth
55. The Big Bow Mystery by Zangwill, Israel
56. Dossier 113 (aka The Blackmailers) by Gaboriau, Emile
57. The Mystery of a Hansom Cab by Hume, Fergus
58. The W Plan by Seton, Graham
59. Inspector French's Greatest Case by Crofts, Freeman Wills

60. Mr Bowling Buys a Newspaper by Henderson, Donald
61. A Voice Like Velvet by Henderson, Donald
62. The Deductions of Colonel Gore by Brock, Lynn
63. The Rogue's Syndicate by Froest, Frank
64. The Middle Temple Murder by Fletcher, J. S.
65. The Millionaire Mystery by Hume, Fergus
66. Below the Clock by Turner, J. V.
67. The Rouletabille Omnibus: The Mystery of the Yellow Room and The Perfume of the Lady in Black by Leroux, Gaston
68. The Complete Dupin by Poe, Edgar Allan
69. The Complete Thinking Machine Vol 1 by Futrelle, Jacques
70. The Complete Thinking Machine Vol 2 by Futrelle, Jacques
71. The Complete Thinking Machine Vol 3 by Futrelle, Jacques
72. The Complete Montague Egg by Sayers, Dorothy L.
73. The Complete J. G. Reeder by Wallace, Edgar
74. The Complete Charlie Chan Vol 1 by Biggers, Earl der
75. The Complete Charlie Chan Vol 2 by Biggers, Earl der
76. The Dr Nikola Omnibus Vol 1 by Boothby, Guy
77. The Dr Nikola Omnibus Vol 2 by Boothby, Guy
78. A Prince of Swindlers: The Simon Carne collection by Boothby, Guy
79. The Slim Callaghan Omnibus by Cheyney, Peter
80. The Fu Manchu Omnibus by Rohmer, Sax
81. The Bulldog Drummond Omnibus: The Complete Peterson Rounds by Sapper
82. The Avenging Ray by Seamark
83. The Richard Chandos Omnibus by Yates, Dornford
84. The Alan Quatermain Omnibus: King Solomon's Mines & Allan Quatermain by Haggard, H. Rider
85. The 39 steps by Buchan, John
86. At The Villa Rose by Mason, A.E.W.
87. The Eye of Osiris by Freeman, R. Austin
88. The Weapons of Mystery by Hocking, Joseph
89. The House of Dr. Edwardes by Beeding, Francis
90. The Seven Secrets by Le Queux, William
91. Call Mr Fortune by Bailey, H. C.
92. The Three Taps by Knox, Ronald
93. The Girl at Central by Bonner, Geraldine
94. The Experiences of Loveday Brooke, Lady Detective by Pirkis, Catherine Louisa
95. Mary Louise by Baum, L. Frank
96. That Affair Next Door by Green, Anna Katherine
97. Dead Letter by Regester, Seeley
98. The Tragedy of Pudd'nhead Wilson by Twain, Mark
99. The Big Clock by Fearing, Kenneth
100. The Woman in the Window by Wallis, J. H.
101. The Sexton Blake Collection Vol 1 by Hal Meredeth (or many?)
102. The Complete Simon Iff Stories by Crowley, Aleister
103. The Castle of Otranto by Walpole, Horace
104. The Adventures of the Infallible Godahl by Anderson, Frederick Irving

THE COMPLETE SHERLOCK HOLMES

105. A Study In Scarlet
106. The Sign Of Four
107. The Adventures Of Sherlock Holmes
108. The Memoirs Of Sherlock Holmes
109. The Hound Of The Baskervilles
110. The Return Of Sherlock Holmes
111. His Last Bow
112. The Valley Of Fear
113. The Case-Book Of Sherlock Holmes

114. Graustark: The Story of a Love Behind a Throne by George Barr McCutcheon
115. Beverly of Graustark by George Barr McCutcheon
116. Truxton King: A Story of Graustark by George Barr McCutcheon
117. The Prince of Graustark by George Barr McCutcheon
118. The Complete Zenda Omnibus by Anthony Hope
119. The Mad king by Burroughs, Edgar Rice
120. The Fantomas Omnibus by Souvestre, Pierre

121. The Problemist by Clinton H. Stagg
122. The Dorrington Deed-Box by Morrison, Arthur
123. The Lone Wolf by Vance, L. J.
124. The Complete Martin Hewitt Collection Vol 1: Martin Hewitt, Investigator & Chronicles of Martin Hewitt by Morrison, Arthur
125. The Complete Martin Hewitt Collection Vol 2: Adventures of Martin Hewitt & The Red Triangle: Further Chronicles of Martin Hewitt by Morrison, Arthur
126. Seven Keys to Baldpate by Earl Derr Biggers
127. No Pockets in a Shroud by McCoy, Horace
128. The John Silence Collection by Blackwood, Algernon
129. Lady Molly Of Scotland Yard by Orczy, Baroness Emma
130. Skin O' My Tooth by Orczy, Baroness Emma
131. The Wrong Box by Stevenson, R. L. and Lloyd Osbourne
132. Tutt and Mr Tutt by Train, Arthur C.
133. The Clue by Wells, Carolyn
134. The Complete Trent Case Book by Bentley, E. C.
135. The Luck of the Vails by Benson, E. F.
136. The Rome Express by Griffiths, Arthur
137. The Complete Curious Mr Tarrant by C. Daly King
138. Rope and Gaslight (2-in-1 text) by Hamilton, Patrick
139. Prince Zaleski and Cumming's King Monk by Shiel, M. P.
140. The Assassination Bureau Ltd. by London, Jack
141. Introducing Clubfoot by Williams, Valentine
142. Master of Mysteries: The complete Uncle Abner collection by Post, Melville Davisson
143. The Red Redmaynes by Phillpotts, Eden
144. Thrilling Stories of the Railway by Whitechurch, Victor L.
145. The Grey Wig: Stories and Novelettes by Zangwill, Israel
146. The Lodger by Lowndes, Marie Belloc
147. The Man from Manchester by Donovan, Dick (Joyce Emerson Preston Muddock)
148. Mr. Meeson's Will by H. Rider Haggard by Haggard, H. Rider
149. Devlin the Barber by Farjeon, B. L.
150. Checkmate by Joseph Sheridan Le Fanu
151. Recollections of a Detective Police-Officer by Waters
152. The Widow Lerouge by Gaboriau, Emile
153. The Expressman and the Detective by Pinkerton, Allan
154. Zadig and Vathek by Voltaire
155. The Stillwater Tragedy by Aldrich, Thomas Bailey
156. The Memoirs of Constantine Dix by Pain, Barry
157. Ashes to Ashes by Ostrander, Isabel
158. The Jewel of Seven Stars by Stoker, Bram
159. The Thomas Love Peacock Collection by Peacock, Thomas Love

THE COMPLETE DERLETH SOLAR PONS

160. In Re: Sherlock Holmes - The Adventures of Solar Pons
161. The Memoirs of Solar Pons
162. The Return of Solar Pons
163. The Reminiscences of Solar Pons
164. The Casebook of Solar Pons
165. The Novels of Solar Pons: Terror over London and Mr. Fairlie's Final Journey
166. The Chronicles of Solar Pons
167. The Apocrypha of Solar Pons

168. The Triumphs of Eugene Valmont
169. The Female Detective by Forrester, Andrew
170. Cain's Jawbone by Torquemada
171. The Great Impersonation by Oppenheim, E. Phillips

THE DASHIELL HAMMETT COLLECTION

172. The Complete Sam Spade
173. The Complete Thin Man
174. The Complete Continental Op Vol 1
175. The Complete Continental Op Vol 2